THE WRONG MAN

MJ ELLIOTT

copyright

The Solopreneur Publishing Company Ltd focuses on the needs of each individual author. This book has been published through their 'Solopreneur Self-Publishing (SSP)' brand that enables authors to have complete control over their finished book whilst utilising the expert advice and services usually reserved for traditionally published print, in order to produce an attractive, engaging, quality product. Please note, however, that final editorial decisions and approval to print reside solely with the author.

disclaimer

This is a work of fiction. Names, characters, places, and incidents either are the product of the author's imagination or are used fictitiously. Any resemblance to actual persons, living or dead, events, or locales is entirely coincidental.

Printed in the U.K.

dedication

I'd like to dedicate this book, my debut novel to the three most important people in my life. My wife Debbie and my two beautiful daughters, Heather and Georgina. I love you all.

chapter one

Venice 26th May 2012

Tristano was sat in a plush hotel in Venice, just off St. Mark's Square, thinking back twenty years to the day he became a *made man.* The enormous sense of pride and respect he had experienced that came with the honour. But today wasn't about him. It was about his godson Luca. Tristano hoped he would be feeling the same.

Tristano wanted to please his godson, who very soon was to become a *made man.* A *made man* is a fully initiated member of the Mafia. To become *made,* an associate first has to be sponsored by another *made man.* An inductee is required to take the oath of Omertà, the Mafia code of silence. After the induction ceremony, the associate would become a *made man* and hold the rank of soldier in the Mafia hierarchy. Tristano was Luca's sponsor. Luca had proved himself as an associate for long enough now. He was ready.

Tristano was waiting for Luca with his wife Martina, his brother Filippo, and his wife, Anna. Tristano was a little over six feet tall. He was of medium build with dark olive skin, shiny black hair, which he parted on the left and swept over very neatly. He looked like a 1950's film star. Tristano kept himself fit despite being in his early fifties. In his line of work, you had to be fit. Strength was all well and good, but you also needed the fitness, and he'd always preferred cardio to chucking weights around.

Filippo, on the other hand, was different in looks and stature. He was shorter in height, and had last been for a run over twenty years ago and only because he was chasing after a local thug who owed him money. After Filippo caught him, the guy had to be fed through a straw for six months and never fully recovered. Since then, he'd had no reason to run after anyone as people soon paid up before they even thought of running. Filippo was two years older than Tristano, and whereas Tristano preferred to use violence only if necessary, Filippo saw it as a necessity.

The hotel was busy. Busy with tourists mainly. In and out, they came through the doors looking like they'd just fallen asleep for a few hours in the baking sun. Lots of nationalities came in and out of the door, but only the Chinese seemed to have the sense to use a sun brolly. The Chinese had pale skin and appeared to want to keep it that way. The Europeans attitude was different as they seemed to want to get as much sun on their skin as possible, which only resulted in them looking perpetually hot and bothered. Everyone was always in a rush, though. As Tristano sipped on his Black Russian, he watched the traffic of people in and out of the hotel and tutted to himself as one guy knocked two blokes to the ground as he ran out of the hotel lobby and through the front door, never stopping to check if they were okay.

What a wanker he thought as he watched the two guys get up and shout the very same thing to the guy in the suit who'd knocked them over. The guy wouldn't have heard them, as he was already out of the lobby and running down over the two little bridges towards St. Mark's Square.

'He'll be fucking sweltering in that suit, running like that. Must be a tourist,' said Filippo, laughing as he took a swig of his beer.

'Probably,' Tristano replied with a smile. 'Otherwise, he'd have apologised.'

Mind you; he may not have been, as he had a briefcase with him and a gym bag or something. Have you ever seen a tourist in Venice with a briefcase? A gym bag, maybe, but not a briefcase.'

They both laughed out loud.

Fair point,' replied Filippo. 'Anyway, where the hell is that godson of yours?' he said, looking at Anna. 'We want to get going, don't we? We have the table booked for eight o'clock.'

Anna replied in the soft, calming voice she always used whenever she wanted to keep Filippo calm. 'Chill out, Filippo, we have plenty of time; it's only six-thirty. We didn't tell Luca to be down until close to seven anyway. Plus, his new girlfriend is meeting us here too, in the bar anytime now, remember.'

'Oh yeah, I forgot. Where is it she works again... some bar, isn't it?'

Anna rolled her eyes as she looked at Martina, who just smiled, a reassuring smile. 'Yes, she does, some bar in San Polo. She reckons they do a cracking Black Russian, Tristano.'

'Excellent, maybe we'll get a discount. Let's have another one here whilst we wait.'

Tristano looked over his shoulder for the waiter, caught his eye, and nodded. As he did so, he surveyed the bar. After all he'd initially said about the hotel, as he took in the surroundings, he actually quite liked it. It wasn't too over the top, quite elegant but casual. The six cream leather chairs at the corner bar were all taken. Three couples, he guessed, all out for a good time, just like they all were. He often wondered if people knew he was Mafia. He caught the eye of one of the guys at the bar on the bar stools and couldn't help but fix his gaze. It was just instinctive. Never look away. It was a sign of weakness. Even though he was sure the guy was just out with his wife or girlfriend and posed no threat to Tristano, he could not look away until the other guy had. The guy held it for a couple of seconds and then looked back to his girlfriend, still aware that the guy staring at him had kept the gaze for a few seconds afterwards. Tristano smiled to himself. The guy was lucky he hadn't caught Filippo's eye. If he had, he'd now be staring at the ceiling.

Tristano felt relaxed. He was looking forward to tonight.

'Elisa, you look absolutely gorgeous. No wonder Luca spends so much time in Venice,' said Martina.

Luca's girlfriend had just walked into the bar, and Martina had clocked her straight away. Elisa was grateful for the compliment. She liked Martina. Even though Martina was fifty-three and would still be able to grace the catwalks of Milan, everyone saw her beauty except Martina herself. She was just naturally beautiful with a bust that just defied gravity. No work, nothing but her breasts just sat there as though they belonged to a twenty-year-old.

After the customary greetings, Elisa made her way up to Luca's bedroom for two reasons. One was to hurry him up as Filippo had indicated to Elisa that time was ticking. The other was because she always felt uneasy in the company of the Mafia without Luca by her side. She knew the score. The Mafia was big business in Italy. Elisa had only ever seen them in movies and read about them in books, or at least she thought she had. I mean, who, in their right mind, would think that the two guys in the bar having a civilised drink with their wives were the Mafia? Maybe she'd met more Mafia than she realised. Anyway, all that was on her mind right now was getting to Luca, giving him a huge kiss on the lips, and reminding him of what she had on offer for him later that night!

The whole hotel must have heard Elisa's scream; it was piercing. Tristano knew what he saw that day would stay with him forever, and as he looked at the body of Luca lying on the bed, with blood gushing from his head, all he could think of was revenge. Someone must pay. No one yet knew of the other body lying in the room next door. That one wasn't found until the following morning by the cleaner. Her scream was just as piercing.

chapter two

Mansfield, Nottinghamshire, March 1990

Richie stood on Ratcliffe Gate, a street just outside of Mansfield's town centre, trying to decide which tattoo to get for the World cup in Italy in three months. Mansfield was a mining town, some fourteen miles from Nottingham. A town where nothing really happened, but it had a tight-knit community where people were proud of their working-class roots. Mansfield also had one of the best nights out for miles around.

A good night out was one thing, but Richie wondered why people drank all day too. He wondered as he watched the group of knobheads over the road sup can after can of White Lightning and smoke roll-up after roll-up. Mansfield only had about 70,000 residents, and he was sure at least half of them must be in the park opposite supping cider. Most of them would have at some point worked in the pits in and around Mansfield, but since old Maggie got her way, a lot of them had closed. Mansfield pit closed in 1988, along with Blidworth and Sutton pits in 1989. Most people that did work in the pits that still existed around the area had to travel to Shirebrook or Ollerton. Looking at the shower over the road, they weren't travelling anywhere. The only place they were going was oblivion.

Richie was lucky. He didn't have to consider working down a pit. In fact, he didn't have to work at all. His dad and grandad had seen to that. His grandad had moved down from Newcastle in the fifties to work in the Nottinghamshire pits as the pay and conditions were better apparently. His dad Frank had seen what the mines had done to his grandad and thought *fuck that* and decided to make something of himself. Frank didn't want to end up like his dad, where he could spit on the fire and keep it going for another couple of hours with the coal dust in his phlegm. Frank wanted better, and boy did he get it. Frank was the guy who ran Nottinghamshire and Derby. Nothing happened here without Frank knowing about it and getting his cut. If you wanted to make money, dirty money in the Nottingham and Derby areas, you'd better give Frank his cut, or else Frank would give you yours. If you were lucky, he'd cut your body. If you were unlucky, it'd be the face, or worse.

At nineteen years old Richie was, along with his twin brother Daniel, just starting to get into the "business". Frank was beginning to trust them with the odd little job, collecting money, and going on "a visit" with some of the older hands. "A visit" was the term used locally where someone needed "a little visit" that usually involved some form of violence, a bit of blood, and a lot of squirming from the recipient. It always amused Richie how the so-called "hard men" of the area squirmed and begged for mercy when the big boys came knocking. "Wannabes" was what his dad Frank called them. People who wanted to be hard men, but when it mattered fucking shat themselves.

"Not worth a wank", his brother Daniel would say. Daniel was Richie's twin, older by fifteen minutes, but given the accolades he'd received over the years, you'd

think Daniel was fucking royalty. They both had a
solid frame, weighed roughly thirteen stone with dark
brown hair and blue eyes. Both had a centre-parting
and quite long hair, but Daniel had recently had a soft
perm, which had given it a slight curl. Richie thought
it looked shit. He was one inch taller than Richie at
five feet, eleven inches, and had a slightly deeper
voice, but apart from that, their own mother would
have been hard-pressed to tell them apart. That's if
their mother had lived, that is. She died giving birth to
Richie. Fifteen minutes earlier, when king Daniel had
arrived, their mother Renee had been fine, but after
Richie was born, they couldn't stop the bleeding from
a tear inside the uterus. Richie knew Frank blamed
him for this. It had been apparent all his life. He was
never good enough, never up to Daniel's standard, and
many times his dad had told him that if it "wasn't for
you, your mother would still be here". Frank always
said that the fifteen minutes it took Richie to "decide to
make an appearance" was too long, which resulted in
the tear. The doctors couldn't confirm this, of course,
but it never stopped Frank saying it. Whenever Richie
had been late for anything as a kid, even by a minute
or so, Frank would say, "You're always fucking late
you are. That's why your mother died, cos you were
late".

Over the years, Richie had grown to have a real issue
with punctuality and was now known for always being
on time. No one ever mentioned it, though, as they
knew Frank would disapprove of Richie being praised
for his timekeeping. Frank could no longer remind
Richie of why his mother died. Richie was now never
late, and it frustrated him whenever other people were
late, just as it did now as he waited outside the tattoo

shop for his best mate Paul White to meet him. Eleven o'clock, they'd said, and it was now seven minutes past. Richie could feel the anger boil away inside him as time ticked on. At nine minutes past, Whitey came bouncing around the corner without a care in the world, in his baggy jeans and Adidas top flicking his dark hair out of his eyes. He always looked like he should have a drawstring at the side of his head to open the curtains, such was the middle parting and length of his hair on each side. He was an ugly fucker, though. Big nose and a pockmarked face. Whitey had bad acne a few years ago, and the scars were still visible.

'For fuck's sake Whitey, eleven o'clock, we said. I ain't got all fucking day.'

Whitey just threw his arms out to his side as if to say, what's up its only nine minutes, but he knew better than to reiterate that he was late. He reckoned he could take Richie if it came to it, but Richie was the top lad in their little football firm, and Whitey knew he had to bite his lip even if it was only really because of who Richie's dad was. Richie could handle himself, that was for sure, and in a fight, he was a game lad who was respected in his own right, but everyone knew that even at nineteen, he called the shots because of Frank Pearson.

'Yeah, sorry mate, remember that lass in Limos last night, well I ended up stopping at hers, and when we woke up this morning, she still wanted some more. I'm red raw.' Whitey chuckled as he took out a Benson's and lit it. 'So, what you going for Richie, Bulldog on ya bicep?'

No chance, that's what everyone will have. You know me Whitey, gotta be different. Trouble is, I can't see anything else to go for, and believe me, I've had time to look. Nine minutes, in fact, tosser!' They both laughed together as the fact Whitey was late now seemed to be a thing of the past.

It was a football match day, which meant only one thing to Richie and Paul... showing the rival firm who ran this town.

'Hurry up! Shrewsbury will be here soon. You know they always turn up early. Word is they're coming through Pleasley, so I reckon they'll camp up in the Rufford on Chesterfield Road.' Whitey told Richie.

'I know that. I am aware of what's happening, you know. I've already arranged for a couple of the lads to be in the New England to try and spot them coming out of Pleasley. Plus, they might pop into the England for a pint first. It's sorted. Don't worry. They always come into town, do Shrewsbury. Good lads, those EBF lads. We'll get a bit, you'll see.'

With that, Richie had made a decision on his tattoo. You know what Whitey lad, I'm just gonna have "Italia 90" tattooed on my neck. No good hiding it on your arm, is it. Nice and simple. None of this British Bulldog bollocks—just "Italia 90" on my neck. Left-hand side, though... that's my best side. I think it's cos I sleep on my right-hand side. My hair never goes right on that side. Must be the way I sleep. Anyway, left-hand side it is. It'll only take a few minutes, I bet. We'll be in town to welcome the EBF for twelve.'

'You gonna have it done in that italic writing then, or whatever it is. You know, the one that slants to the side. Seems fitting for Italia 90. Italic writing and all that.'

'You know what, Mr. White, I think I will. *Italia 90...* nice one Whitey.'

Richie walked into the tattoo shop, and as expected, people made way for him. He jumped the queue, ordered a coffee, and sat down thinking about the EBF. Shrewsbury turned up, came into town, looked the part but did fuck all.

chapter three

March 1990, Berry Hill, Mansfield

Frank looked at Jez Carrington, his right-hand man, Number Two, second in command. However, you wanted to define Jez Carrington; the bottom line was he was always at Frank's side. Wherever Frank went, Jez went.

'Are you serious, Jez? Sheffield's not our patch pal; as close as Chesterfield is to us, it's Baz Watson's patch. You know that well enough. We have enough problems of our own with the Wallace brothers. You know they're trying to muscle into Nottingham. We've got to sort them out. We can't have them dealing in Nottingham without our say-so, period. Now that's your fucking job. That's what I pay you for, so get over there tonight and make sure none of their kind is dealing any sort of drugs in my club, especially those happy pills or whatever the young uns take these days. If anyone is dealing in my towns, then we supply the drugs. That's just the way it works. I'm not having any young uns death on my conscience cos they've taken a bad pill. I take it you heard what happened in London two weeks ago? Poor lass.'

Frank was aware of the bad publicity a drug's death could have on a business, plus he was a father too and wouldn't wish a child's death on any parent. Of course, anyone who was killed was someone's child, and Frank had been witness to or was responsible for enough deaths by now, but that was different. That was a consequence of operating in their world where violence and sometimes death was an occupational hazard but dying because of a bad pill from people like the Wallaces was something he wouldn't tolerate.

'Yes, Frank, I heard, and I totally agree. Forget Chesterfield then. It was just I heard there was a big rave there a week on Friday and at a rave, there's money to be made. Big money but fair point.'

Jez knew when to back down, but that wouldn't stop him from putting suggestions forward in the future. He'd made Frank some serious money over the years, and Frank knew he would have some good ideas again. Frank always looked after him when his ideas came off. He gave him a percentage of the profits from it so he couldn't complain. The only trouble was that if anything went tits up, Frank wanted double the percentage back from him to cover the costs. Luckily for Jez, he had more good ideas than bad.

'I'll get over to Nottingham later and get into the club for nine o'clock, Frank. If I see anyone dealing that I don't know, I'll sort it.'

'If you see anyone you don't know, Jez, I want them at the lock-up in Arnold straight away. I don't care what time it is, but you call me on that brick you carry about in your pocket, and I'll meet you there. If it's any of Wallace's men, I want to know.'

'Will do, Frank. I'm popping into the Oak Tree for a quick one and then going home to shower and change. Speak to you later.'

Frank watched Jez walk through the patio doors and onto the very well-kept lawn and out through the bottom gate. Frank could just about hear the roar of the Cosworth as it sped off down Black Scotch Lane towards Berry Hill Lane. He swore he could still hear it as it drove into the Oak Tree car park. A quick one to Jez meant five minutes, so he smiled to himself as he thought of staying put for five minutes and listening out for Jez as he roared out of the car park.

chapter four

Frank was small in stature, with remarkable blue eyes. The kind of eyes that mesmerize women and put fear into men. He had a hard stare, but at the same time, his eyes revealed a softer side to him when he smiled. They lit up his face and often lit up a room too. People were drawn to him. Maybe it was the blue eyes and dark hair combination. He had short-cropped, nearly black hair that wasn't quite a crew cut but was close enough. He had his hair cut every fortnight without fail as he hated it to be much longer than it was when it was first cut. After his eyes, the next thing you noticed was his size. Yes, he was small in height at five feet seven, but his barrel chest and muscle mass more than made up for it. He'd always gone to the gym. He still did, even though he had one built in his house. Training at home just wasn't the same. No atmosphere, plus even though he loved training Frank needed to go to a gym so that subconsciously he knew why he was there. He was there to train, not to stand around chatting like many of the lads who went. He found it more of an effort to walk the twenty yards to the outbuilding he'd converted than he did to drive the three miles to the gym on Outram Street in Sutton.

Frank had a swagger and a confidence that he'd had since childhood. He can never remember being scared of anyone. As far back as he could recall, he'd always take on anyone, especially bullies. Frank hated to see anyone being bullied. His mother said he wasn't born that way and always pinpointed it to an incident when he was about five years old. Frank could remember this particular incident well and had heard it told many times over the years.

Frank was playing with a friend of the same age called Sam from the next street. They had a bit of a fall out over something, and Sam hit Frank in the face. Frank began to cry and ran into his mother, as most kids would. His mother told Frank to stand up for himself and go hit the boy back. Frank didn't want to, but his mother told him that she would hit him if he didn't. Frank went out and knocked seven bells out of poor Sam. Sam's mother came down to sort it out, but Frank's mum told her that she was proud of her son for sticking up for himself and that Sam had started it and shouldn't start what he couldn't finish. All the time, Frank was leaning into his mum's apron, and she was stroking his hair. When Frank thinks back to this moment, he now realises that he was receiving a lot of positive strokes for that act of violence from his mother. Even at five years old, Frank could feel the pride and adulation his mother felt for him. He'd made her proud. From that moment on, Frank never walked away from a fight again and used his aggression to gain favour with all around him. Frank was always known as an aggressive man.

One thing Frank never needed for aggression was drink. He was not a drinker. He'd have one or two but no more. He believed in keeping a clear head and keeping one step ahead. In his world, men would drink, often to excess, and this gave Frank an edge. He'd only ever been drunk once, and that was when his Renee died in childbirth. People said his eyes lost a little of their laughter that day. He knew if he were ever drunk again, it would be as a result of a tragedy. Frank didn't want to be drunk.

As he grew up in and around Stanton Hill and Skegby, both mining areas of Mansfield, he gained a reputation as a hard man. He knew early on he never wanted to work down the pit. Even when his dad had said to him many times, "Son, it's what we do. It's what people do round here. You leave school, and you go down the pit. That's what's happening, so get used to it. It's a job for life. Never did me any harm". Frank would just say, "Not me, Dad. Better things for me." They'd argue about it but no more than that. His dad died when Frank was fourteen of Pneumoconiosis, so when he left school at fifteen, he didn't have to worry about disappointing his dad. Pneumoconiosis is a lung disease due to the inhalation of dust. So much for not doing his dad any harm, he would often think.

Apart from the larger muscle mass he had now, Frank was the same size at fifteen as he was now. He was naturally barrel-chested, so he always looked menacing. He initially started nicking coal off the coal lorries and selling it cheaply to those houses that were not eligible for free coal. He and two others would do it and started making a few quid. The coal lorry drivers caught them eventually and gave them a good hiding, but Frank being as he was, would not be beaten and learned very early on the art of negotiation. Bold as brass, he approached the lorry drivers and negotiated a deal where he bought the coal off them for a backhander and then sold it to the same people as before for a profit. The drivers were happy as they kept their little scam going and Frank was happy as he turned a profit. Frank then "employed" his two mates

and gave them a cut. By sixteen years old, Frank was
his own boss, had two employees, and learned that
not everything needed a right-hander. This was where
he met Renee. Her dad was buying coal from Frank.
One day Frank called to collect the money, and Renee
answered the door. Frank just stood there. He'd never
seen anything like her before. Renee was beautiful.
She had long curly blonde hair, huge blue eyes, and
skin so smooth and soft it was like silk. Renee was
five foot, nine inches tall and had legs that seemed
to come up to Frank's shoulders. Frank knew as he
walked away from her house in Institute Street that he
would marry her.

By the age of eighteen, Frank was working on a couple
of the doors in Mansfield through a contact of one of
the coal drivers. The driver introduced Frank to Freddie
Smith. Frank had heard of Freddie. In Mansfield,
everyone knew Freddie. He was from Nottingham
and was black. In 1968 he was the only black guy in
Mansfield. When a couple of pubs in town had needed
someone on the doors to keep out trouble, Freddie had
obliged. Freddie's doors were trouble-free. Doormen
were not like they are today—no badges or training
courses. Just basically thugs who could fight, but he
soon realised that the places he worked were effectively
trouble-free too.

   In Mansfield town centre The Dial was one of
Freddie's pubs. Freddie had initially put Frank on
the Dial along with one of Freddie's contacts from
Nottingham, a guy called Brian. Now Brian is not a
tough name, but fuck me, could that guy fight. After
about a year of this, Freddie just disappeared. No one
knew why. He just didn't come back one day. Even

the guys in Nottingham didn't know where he'd gone. Gaps started to appear; doormen wouldn't turn up; trouble came back to Mansfield. What was missing was Freddie, or at least someone like Freddie, someone to take charge and co-ordinate things. Frank took charge. He and Brian became good mates. Brian brought his mate in on it; a guy called Jez Carrington. Within three months, Frank was running all the doors in Mansfield, making a fuck load of money.

At nineteen years old, Frank had it all and not a pit in sight. He had money, respect, and a beautiful girlfriend. The next thing was to buy a house for him and Renee. By the age of twenty, he'd lost the most important thing in his life. Renee went into labour, and Frank's world came crashing down. They didn't even know she was pregnant. He never did get to marry Renee.

chapter five

It was 10:38 pm. The phone rang. It was Jez.

'I'll be at the Arnold lock-up in twenty minutes, Frank. I've got Steven Wallace in my boot.'

Fuck thought Frank. *This ain't gonna end well.* He hung up and immediately rang Brian. Brian picked Frank up, and they headed to Arnold.

The lock-up in Arnold was only twenty minutes on a good run from Frank's House in Berry Hill, Mansfield. On the way there, Brian tried to make small talk with Frank but received very little response. Brian knew Frank was in a serious mood. The Wallace brothers were from Loughborough, a small town between Nottingham and Leicester. Frank's business interests had not yet reached Leicester. He'd had a dabble but had concentrated on Nottingham and Derby after taking control of Mansfield in his mid-twenties. Steven Wallace and his younger brother Gary were the guys who had control of Leicester. Now they were trying to muscle in on Frank's patch. Frank could not allow this. For Steven Wallace to be personally doing business in Frank's club, one of Frank's privately owned clubs was a real front and a real message to Frank. If Frank allowed this to go without serious consequences, he'd have every wannabe gangster and hard man trying his luck in the East Midlands. Steven Wallace knew the score. He knew he'd get spotted and that he'd get sorted out if caught.

'Why was he there in person, Brian? It doesn't feel right. He must have known he'd get taken to Arnold. Picking up Steven Wallace so easily just wouldn't happen. What d'ya reckon?'

Frank was looking for confirmation from Brian that this was some sort of set-up or part of a bigger plan.

'I know what you're saying, boss, but I don't think Steven and Gary Wallace have got the brains or balls for anything bigger. I know they've had some of their lackeys doing a bit in and around Nottingham lately, and I know we need to sort that out, so maybe because we haven't made any huge noise in their direction about it, they think they can make a personal appearance so to speak.'

'What do you mean we haven't made any serious noise? You saying I'm going soft? Stop the fucking car, and I'll show you whether I'm going soft or not. Who the fucking hell do you think you are?'

'Calm down, Frank. I didn't mean any disrespect by it. I was just saying that maybe we should have paid them a visit or something, that's all. Now Jez has Steven Wallace in Arnold. Do you really want me to stop the car so you can take your anger out on me?'

Frank looked at Brian and admired his front. He liked Brian. Always had ever since Freddie Smith had introduced them nearly twenty years ago. He'd been loyal and didn't deserve a kicking.

'No, do I fuck. We'll be there in five minutes. Get ya foot down.'

Brian and Frank had never come to blows in all the years they'd been working together. Frank was the boss, always had been. Brian knew that. Frank was a leader. Always looking to move forward. Brian was happy as his back-up. Frank had blown up many times over the years at Brian, mainly for the same reason he had now. He knew Brian was right. Frank knew he should have sorted the Wallace brothers sooner. They both knew that. Brian had always known how to work Frank. He knew that Frank would blow up by making that remark, and that was what Brian wanted. Steven Wallace needed to be taught a lesson, and now Frank was more worked up than ever. Tonight, was going to be an interesting one.

Frank walked into the lock-up in Arnold like a man possessed. Brian was still locking the car by the time Frank had hit Steven Wallace full in the face. Jez had him seated on a wooden chair smack bang in the middle of the floor. The lock-up was as basic and as bare as they come. There was something resembling a kitchen cupboard on one wall in the corner fixed above a small sink, a small worktop, and a settee. On the worktop was a kettle. There were a handful of mugs in the cupboard, a jar of coffee, a bowl of sugar, and two spoons. No milk: there was never any milk, so whenever they drank, it was black coffee. The rest of the unit was just a concrete floor and breeze block walls.

Two other guys from the club were there too with Jez. One was a black guy from St. Ann's called Del who had biceps like one of the breeze blocks. He was the head doorman at the club and was very trustworthy. The other guy was a white guy who Frank had not seen before called Terry. He was a new doorman from Ratcliffe–on–Trent, although he had a Yorkshire twang. Big enough, but looked average compared to Del.

Frank had knocked Steven Wallace over. Terry picked

him up and then picked the chair up and sat him back on it. Frank stared at him for a good twenty seconds. No one spoke. Steven stared back in between spitting blood out of his mouth and wiping blood from his nose.

Frank spoke first. 'Grew a pair, have you? I'll give ya this Steven, you've surprised me. I never thought you'd be making personal appearances. Always had you down as a one-horse town kind of guy. Big fish in a small pond. I'd heard you'd never left Leicestershire until you were twenty-five, so what the fuck you doing showing your face and dealing in my club? And where the fuck is that brother of yours... tweedle fuckin' dum or whatever his name is?'

Steven said nothing. Frank punched him again hard in the face. Terry picked him and the chair up for a second time but left the two teeth on the floor.

'Brian here told me I should have sorted you and your brother out ages ago as soon as you started to send your lackeys to Nottingham. Looks like he was right... again!' Steven said nothing. Frank continued. 'Did ya boyfriend Daryl not give you the message the other week? He got a few smacks off Jez here and was told very specifically to tell you that if we found any of your lot in Nottingham again, then I would take it personally, yet here you are. I assume you've come to apologise. Have you?' Frank was getting agitated now with Steven's lack of response. Then Steven spoke.

'It's not me you should be worried about Frank. Me dealing in your clubs really is the least of your worries.'

'And what do you mean by that? No one comes into Nottinghamshire or Derby. I've got no enemies. Unlike you, ya see, I deal with people with respect,' said Frank.

'Yeah well, you've got an enemy now Frank, and it's gonna bring a whole host of trouble to your door.

Maybe you should ask your lad Richie about it.'

Frank was now intrigued. What did Richie have to do with all of this? Richie was a football hooligan. He'd started to do a bit of work for Frank, but unlike his brother Daniel, Richie was a loose cannon. Not to be trusted with anything big. Plus, he was only nineteen. His world revolved around Saturday afternoons and the odd midweek game. He loved a fight, did Richie, but that was only with the footie lads. Dancing around with a few fists and boots here and there, but he'd never been involved in anything that had anything to do with Frank. Or at least that's what Frank thought.

'I'm asking you Wallace, and I ain't gonna ask twice. What has Richie got to do with anything?'

'Gerry Clark mean anything to ya?' asked Steven.

Frank knew Gerry Clark alright. Everyone who was anyone in the criminal underworld knew Gerry Clark. Gerry was a born and bred Yorkshireman originally from Harrogate. He'd had a reasonably white-collar upbringing in a very respectable family but, for some reason, decided respectability wasn't for him. He had from a relatively early age been into various elements of criminality. Mainly protection in the seventies but had moved onto drugs in the eighties and was now the undisputed king of the supply of ecstasy and any other recreational drug associated with the acid house movement in the North of England. It didn't matter who you bought these drugs off; the chances are that if you bought them in the North of England, then Gerry was at the top of the supply chain.

Gerry lived in Leeds now near Roundhay Park and had many business activities in and around Leeds other than supplying drugs to the acid house movement. Trouble was Frank bought his acid party drugs from

London. Frank always considered Mansfield and Nottingham to be East Midlands, not the North, and Frank always saw that his path to world domination was to venture south. Leicestershire, Northamptonshire, maybe even Birmingham, but he never saw himself trying to take over Manchester, Leeds, or the North East. So, if he now had any beef with Gerry, then he had no history to draw on.

'Yeah, I know of Gerry. Met him once actually in my younger days but nothing since, so my Richie has certainly never met him, so whatever you think you have, you're talking bollocks, Wallace.'

Frank grabbed Steven's face between his thumb and forefinger and squeezed his cheeks hard. Given the two slaps he'd already administered, this was rather painful for Steven Wallace. Frank's face was now millimetres from Steven's. So close that Steven could feel the heat radiating from Frank's red face. He also got a face full of spit as Frank said through gritted teeth.

'So, for the last fuckin' time Steven, what has Richie or Gerry Fucking Clark got to do with you dealing in my club.' Frank let go of his face and stepped back to allow him to answer.

'Ask him yourself, Frank. He'll be in your club about now. If you get your lap dog Brian to drive you very quickly, you might just get there before he smashes it all up.'

Jez's mobile rang. He answered it. It was Frank's son Daniel, calling from the office in the club.

Jez just said, 'Frank, we need to go... now!'

They left Steven Wallace alone in the lock-up. They could finish with him later. Right now, Frank needed all the muscle he could get. Terry took the keys to the lock-up from his right trouser pocket and locked up. The five of them left for Frank's club.

chapter six

Fifteen minutes later, Frank, Jez, Brian, Del and Terry arrived at Frank's club in Nottingham. There were no doormen. Frank knew this didn't bode well. He knew of Gerry Clark and that he was a force to be reckoned with, but Frank was a respected face in his own right, and whilst he would prefer to have no beef with Gerry Clark, he was more than prepared to go toe to toe with this guy. This was his manor at the end of the day, and in their world, if you didn't fight to protect what you had, you'd lose it a damn sight quicker than it'd taken you to acquire it. It obviously had something to do with Richie, and for all his faults, Frank would defend him to the day he died.

Frank burst through the doors into the main room. Typically, on a night like tonight, the place would be heaving, but it was deserted. A few half-empty pint pots sat on what tables were still upright, but the rest of the glasses had been smashed. The floor was littered with broken glass. Broken chairs were scattered everywhere, tables had been smashed, and the DJ stand was unrecognisable. The interesting thing was that the main bar was untouched. Five thick-set men stood at the bar arms folded, each with a baseball bat at their side. They looked like they'd been dressed specially for the outing as they all had black jeans on, a white polo shirt, and a black leather jacket. None of them was Gerry Clark, though. It had been about fifteen years since Frank had last set eyes on Gerry, but he knew he'd recognise him by the scar he had on his left cheek. Result of some knife fight in his late teens. Scars like that were always visible.

Frank stopped and surveyed the inside of his club. He looked around quite calmly. The other four stood behind him, two on either side waiting for some sort of instruction. Instantly, Frank knew this was one of those times where calmness and control were needed. It would be easy to take the five meatheads on who were stood at the bar. Frank had four guys with him, and with the exception of Terry, he knew the other three well and would go into battle with these guys anytime. Terry, though, by the very fact he was still here, had gone up in Frank's estimation. Maybe Terry was made of the same stuff. Frank knew though, that at this moment in time, he didn't know where Gerry Clark was or, more importantly, where his son Daniel was. Daniel had made the call, but all he'd said to Jez was *...there's a guy called Gerry Clark here for my dad.* The line then went dead. Frank assumed Gerry Clark had Daniel either at knifepoint or gunpoint and had made him make that call and had told him what to say. Frank needed to remain in control for Daniel's sake if nothing else.

Jez and Brian both knew Frank well enough to recognise the signs that calmness and control would be the order of things here. They'd seen it before, and to be honest, both were pleased that Frank appeared to be taking this stance. Whenever Frank was on the back foot and in a possible position of weakness, he would act in this way rather than go at things like a bull in a china shop. That was why Frank was the boss. Dealing with Steven Wallace was easy. He was no threat, so Frank could bulldoze his way into the lock-up and go in feet first without considering any consequence. This was different, though. Gerry Clark was in a different league to the Wallaces, plus he appeared to have Daniel.

Control. Frank thought to himself, *assess the situation, weigh up the odds, stay in control. Don't react, but respond... don't react, just respond... Stay in control.*

'Frank, nice of you to come so quickly.'

Frank looked across to his left. Gerry Clark. No Daniel though. Gerry Clark looked just as Frank had remembered. Tall, at just over six feet, and slender with it, although his hair had receded quite badly. The scar on his left cheek was still visible even at a distance. Gerry didn't look like a gangster. The only possible outward sign being that scar. Frank didn't take his eyes off Gerry.

'I don't know what this is all about Gerry, but at this moment in time, I can't think of a good enough reason for this. Unless you're gonna tell me, I've shagged your missus, this is only going to end one way, and there's only gonna be one winner. There's only three guarantees in life Gerry, and that's death, taxes, and the fact that if you take me on in my own backyard, you'll lose, and right now Gerry, it will appear you've taken me on, head-on with two fucking barrels.'

'Always been full of yourself Frank, haven't you? Even when our paths crossed, what was it fifteen years since... you always had little man syndrome? Now why don't you come and sit down and have a drink while your bar's still in decent nick, eh? I promise my lads won't bite.'

Frank was struggling to keep his composure. His voice was telling him to remain in control, but all he wanted to do was take the gun out from his inside pocket and blow this fucker's head off. His little voice won. Frank didn't drink. People knew that, and Frank was sure Gerry Clark would have known that, but Frank saw this as an opportunity to get nearer his targets. From where he was right now, even with Jez, Brian, Del and Terry with him, he was on the back foot. If he launched into these guys from here, they'd be ready for him before he got anywhere near them. Sitting at the bar would, in Frank's eyes, put him on the front foot.

'Yeah, okay Gerry, I'll have a scotch.' Gerry did the honours and put a scotch on the bar. Frank put some ice in it and took a sip. He sat on a barstool facing Gerry, who had come out from behind the bar. Jez, Brian, and Del took a few steps forward but remained standing about fifteen feet from Frank, but still facing the five guys Gerry had brought with him. No one had noticed Terry was no longer there.

'So, come on then Gerry, what the fuck is this all about?'

'Your Richie has been dealing ecstasy on my manor in Leeds. We both know you get your supply from the smoke Frank, so I don't take too lightly to your offspring dealing your drugs on my fucking manor. Plus, I have the added grief of two young lasses in St. James's hospital from a result of them taking your drugs. My E's have the letter 'P' on them. Everyone knows that. I insist on it, and these ones didn't, so they must have come from your Richie. Three weekends running, he's been in and around Leeds dealing at raves. He was warned two weeks ago, very seriously warned to keep out. I assume he told you, and I assume you gave him the nod to keep at it cos last weekend there he was again. So that Frank, is a very clear threat to me and my operations. Then I have these two young girls in hospital. The fucking grief I'm getting over that from all angles is grief I don't need, Frank. Seventeen years old they are. They might not make it, but I'm getting the blame.'

Frank took another swig of his whiskey. He never left the gaze of Gerry. Frank had no idea that dickhead of a son of his, Richie, was dealing in Leeds. The fucking idiot. Frank had always been a man of honour. He'd always treated his fellow compatriots with respect. He didn't tread on their toes, and he'd had that reciprocated over the years. The only times Frank had muscled in on someone else's territory was when he took over Nottingham and Derby after he'd been running Mansfield for a while. He took over Nottingham from a guy called Hughie McGann after Hughie tried to fuck Frank over and take Mansfield for himself, and he took Derby because no one was running Derby. Four or five little firms had their own areas and fought like cat and dog with each other, so Frank just 'unified' it, that's all. These firms in Derby still have their own patches, but they all in effect work for Frank. Now Frank had a dilemma. Gerry felt disrespected, and rightly so. Richie had undoubtedly shown no respect to Gerry or his operations in Leeds and had obviously thought being Frank Pearson's son gave him rights to do whatever he pleased. Frank would sort Richie out, no drama, but Frank also knew that Gerry had gone way overboard in his response to Richie's show of disrespect. All Gerry needed to have done was to have contacted Frank, come and had a drink, alerted

Frank to Richie's misdemeanour, and that would have been sorted. Gerry was testing Frank, and Frank knew it. Frank had to react in the same way. He could not let this disrespect for his club go unpunished. To his knowledge, Gerry had five guys with him. Frank had four. Four decent blokes plus himself. Gerry had never had a real reputation as a fighter, so Frank reckoned that evened things up a little. Frank looked over his left shoulder at his four men as he took a swig of his whiskey. He nearly choked on it as he said, 'Where the fuck is Terry?' His three remaining guys looked at each other in disbelief and then back at Frank.

'But he was here a minute or so, Frank. He was stood here next to me,' Del blurted out. Gerry laughed, a big hearty laugh.

'Been with me for a few years now, has Terry, Frank. How long's he been on your door Del? Two weeks? That'll be a week or so after Richie thought he could deal drugs on my patch. Hurry up and work it out, Del. I haven't got all night.' Gerry looked at his watch as he said to Frank. 'By my reckoning, and bear in mind I don't know these parts like you do Frank, I reckon Terry will be letting Steven Wallace out of your lock-up and putting Daniel in there right about now.'

Del immediately felt his pockets for the lock-up keys. *Shit,* he thought as he recalled Terry locking up as they left to come here. That's why the bastard had shouted to Del when they first arrived at the lock-up with Steven Wallace *chuck us the keys Del. I'll get it open for you.* Del felt a prickle of fear rise inside him as he realised what had happened and what Frank's reaction would be to him. He was just about to tell Frank he'd known nothing about this when he heard the gunshot. Gerry Clark was on the floor screaming in agony, holding his leg. Frank had just shot him in the kneecap and had already turned 180 degrees to point the gun at the five men who were still standing at the bar. In unison, they held their hands up. Jez was now standing at Frank's side, also pointing a gun at the five men.

Frank spoke, 'You know what to do, Brian.'

Brian and Del walked towards the five guys and picked up the five baseball bats. They threw three to one side. With one a piece, they mercilessly beat the five men whilst Frank and Jez continued to point their guns. Fifteen minutes ago, these five guys had looked as hard as nails. They now looked a pitiful sight and unrecognisable. None of them moved. They were all still alive, but only just. It had taken less than three minutes. Frank looked at Gerry, who was still screaming in agony.

'How many at the lock-up with Terry?' he asked.

'Fuck you,' shouted Gerry. 'You'll not recognise him by the time you get there.'

Del held Gerry down as Frank pressed the gun straight into Gerry's bollocks.

'How many Gerry?'

'Two plus Terry,' Gerry shouted

Frank ran into the office and came out with a gun. He gave it to Del.

'We'll discuss Terry tomorrow Del, but right now you need to impress the hell out of me. Keep this lot here until we get back. If any of them move, shoot them. If Gerry gives you any grief, shoot his other knee cap off.'

Del wanted to go to the lock-up to kick the hell out of Terry. He didn't want to remain here at the club, but he was in no position to argue. He just nodded to Frank. Frank looked at Brian and Jez.

'Come on... lock-up, now. Brian, get four of the baseball bats. Leave one with Del.' He stood over Gerry. 'If they've laid a finger on him, Gerry, I'll kill ya. If he's unhurt I'll let you live but either way, your operations are mine. I run fuckin' Leeds now.' With that, he kicked Gerry in the groin and looked at Del. He held Del's gaze for a few seconds. In that moment, Del knew Frank didn't blame him. Del knew tomorrow he'd be okay. 'We'll be back, Del. Keep 'em here cos if Daniel's hurt, then Gerry won't see morning.'

'No problem, Frank. Jez, do me a favour with that phone you've got. Ring my brother Michael and tell him to get himself down here now. I'd feel happier if there were two of us.'

'Will do, Del.' Jez walked towards the door dialling the number. Del just heard him say, 'Michael, need a favour pal...' as Jez and the others walked through the door. Michael arrived within six minutes. Del felt happier.

chapter seven

As Frank and the others drove at speed towards the lock-up, Frank told Brian to slow down. 'The last thing we need Brian, is the old bill pulling us over. I know we're in a rush, but for fuck's sake, let's get there. You got your gun, Brian?'

'Yes, boss... it's in my jacket.' Brian patted the left-hand side of his chest and felt the gun.

'Good, that's three of us then all with a gun. No shooting unless we have to. The lock-up is just over the back from the housing estate, so hopefully, we can sort these fuckers without shooting. Did you bring the baseball bats?' Frank looked at Brian in the driver's seat.

'In the boot, boss.'

'Okay, we go in calm. We don't know what they've got. If we go in all bats blazing and they've got a gun a piece, we're fucked. We walk in and assess. If Wallace has stuck around, that means there'll be four of them. Follow my lead.'

'What you going to do about Richie, Frank? He's starting to become a bit of a loose canon.' Jez was curious to see what Frank would say. He'd always treated Richie differently to Daniel. Some of it was well deserved in Jez's book as they were definitely different characters, but Frank certainly blamed Richie at times for Renee's death.

'I don't know, to be honest, Jez. Can't do anything

at the moment as he's just gone to Italy, hasn't he with his Saturday afternoon warriors for the world cup? He'll be there at least two weeks for the first stage and then maybe longer if England play well.'

'He'll be back in a fortnight then, boss,' Brian said, trying to lighten the mood. No one laughed as they were just approaching Arnold.

Frank snarled. 'This ain't no laughing matter, Brian. That goes for all of ya. This is serious fucking business. Anyway, it ain't just Richie we need to sort out from our side. Where the fuck were those bouncers we employ, eh? Where the fuck did, they run off to? I tell you something now, they better not be with fucking Terry. If they are, I'll hold Del personally responsible. If they ran off shitting themselves, I want them humiliated and scarred for life. Either way, I want them found and dealt with. Fucking bouncers, ten a fucking penny they are.'

Brian felt sorry for Del. It wasn't his fault.

'I can vouch for their loyalty, Frank. There's no way they'll be at the lock-up. Their bottle might have gone as there were only two of them on tonight. Never normally need more than that, do we? People know better than to cause trouble in your clubs, Frank, but leave them to me and Del. We'll sort them.'

They pulled into the lock-up yard. The yard was empty, but the door was ajar, and light was poking through. If Daniel was here, then whoever had brought him was long gone. Could still be three of them inside, though, including Wallace. Frank waltzed straight in, followed by Jez and Brian. In the middle of the room, Daniel was sat in the chair where they'd left Steven Wallace. No one else was in the room. Daniel's hands were tied behind the back of the chair, and he was unconscious. He'd been beaten quite badly, and his face was battered and bloody, although Frank had seen enough beatings in his time to know that once the blood had been wiped off, it wouldn't look half as bad. This beating had been administered by a bunch of amateurs who didn't have the stomach to issue a real warning. These guys didn't really want to hurt Daniel. If they had, he'd be a lot worse. On Daniel's lap was a piece of paper with the word *Surprise* written on it. Frank suspected Steven Wallace had left it.

'Looks like they've fucked off Frank,' Jez said.

'Yeah, can't have been gone long though, the bastards. I'll get 'em, Jez. I'll find out who they were, and I'll get every single one of them.'

They untied Daniel. He came round and was surprisingly alert and upbeat.

'I couldn't do 'owt, Dad,' he said as he felt his face for blood. 'I managed to get a few smacks in at the club, but they just overpowered me. The guy with the scar said he had a meeting with you about some business. That's why I rang Jez to tell him cos there was no answer at home.'

'No matter, Son. You're okay. A few bruises, but I've had worse.' They all laughed a little. Even Daniel, although it hurt like hell.

'Right, lads. Back to the club. I've got a promise I need to keep.'

Fifteen minutes later, Frank walked back into the club flanked by Jez and followed by Brian and Daniel. Del had done his job. Gerry Clark was still on the floor holding his leg, although he'd stopped screaming. He was now sat up on the floor against the bar. The five guys he'd brought as muscle were now all conscious, and Del's brother Michael had them all sat on their hands, on the floor in a line. Michael was pointing the gun that Frank had given Del at the five fellas whilst Del was standing over Gerry, baseball bat in hand.

'Good job, lads. Might have a place for you Michael, in the firm, if you fancy a trip to Leeds now and again.'

Michael smiled, aware Frank was saying this for the benefit of his guests, although also aware there may be a hidden message in there somewhere. He'd quite like to be on Frank's payroll. Frank stood over Gerry. He beckoned Daniel with his hand to come and stand next to him.

'Take a good look, Gerry. I want Daniel's face to be the last thing you fucking see. You took a gamble, I'll pay tribute to that, but you fucking lost.'

Gerry knew he was done for. He knew Frank would do exactly what he said he'd do. In this line of work, when at some point or another your lifestyle catches up with you, then you have two choices. You can either go out begging for mercy and leave a lasting legacy as a coward, or you can swallow it and go out with at least the little bit of the dignity you have left. Gerry was no coward. He kept Frank's gaze, refusing to look at Daniel. This was the only bit of control he had left. He'd depart this world on his own terms. Frank shot Gerry Clark three times in the chest.

He turned to face the five guys sat on their hands.

'You have a choice, fellas. You either work for me in Leeds, or I shoot you now. Have we got enough bullets left, Jez?'

'More than enough, boss. You could make teabags out of this lot.'

'If you want to live, tell me now, but make no mistake, you will all work for me, and you will start at the bottom. I don't know what you did for Gerry, but I do know that tonight you were just doing your job, following orders, and luckily for you, none of you were sent to the lock-up cos those guys when I find 'em won't be offered the same terms of employment.'

They all made their decisions instantly. They now worked for Frank Pearson.

chapter eight

Friday 8th June 1990 – Manchester Airport

Richie arrived at Manchester airport mid-morning along with six of his mates for their trip to Sardinia. The plan was to fly to Rome, stay there overnight, and then catch the ferry from Civitavecchia to Cagliari in Sardinia. They would then meet up with the Mansfield lads who were already there. Mansfield should have enough of a mob to hold their own against other English firms should the need arise and enough to take on any Italians who fancied their chances. England was playing the Republic of Ireland on Monday, and Richie was due to arrive in Sardinia on Sunday. Perfect.

Whitey was just coming back from taking a leak and pointed to a bar.

'Let's get in here, Richie. Couple of quick ones before we board. Get in the mood, eh?'

'Come on then. Get 'em in.'

They walked into the bar, and it was full of Scots. The Tartan Army was in full swing and, thankfully, surprisingly welcoming.

'Bloody hell, Richie. I never thought this bar would be full of Scots. They're halfway to Italy from up there. What are they doing here?'

'You know what the Scots are like. They'll take three times as many fans as we will. Half of Scotland will be in Italy. These lot are probably like us and couldn't get flights nearer to home. We should be flying from East Mids, not having to come over to Manc land. Should never have left the flights to Percy, should we? Three months ago, he should have sorted them, and here we are at Manchester, miles from home in a bar full of Scots and two days behind Gadget and his lot.' Richie wasn't too impressed.

'How many of Gadget's lot are already over there, Goldie?'

Goldie was a grizzly bear. Ginger hair, fair skin with lots of freckles, about six feet, two inches, and around eighteen stone. A big belly due to his poor diet and large consumption of beer. Good as gold, though, do anything for anyone, hence the name Goldie. If he were a lot smaller in height and half the weight, he'd have been a target for people to take advantage of due to his good nature, but at his weight and height, along with his love of a ruck, no one had dared to try.

'No idea Richie, a few though. Two lots have gone separately, but we're meeting up in Cagliari at the train station tonight. I wonder how many rucks they've had by the time we get there?' Goldie glared at Percy. 'Two days late, we are Percy. Fucking useless you are at times.'

'Hey, I've had problems ya know, knobhead. What with my dad dying, I haven't exactly put plane tickets at the top of my priority list recently.' Percy hit back and was pissed off with all the snide comments regarding the flights. His dad had died two months earlier of a sudden heart attack, and it had hit Percy for six.

'Yeah, sorry mate. We're only having you on. Anyway, come on, there's beer to be drunk in here. Stick with me, Percy lad. With my ginger hair and freckles, these lot will think I'm one of them.'

Goldie grabbed Percy round the head in a playful headlock and rubbed his knuckles into the top of his head. Richie looked at Whitey.

'Get me to Italy, Paul. For fuck's sake!'

chapter nine

Frank had left Jez to organise the clean-up at the club. They had contacts who could clear up a mess like this before dawn broke. By the time, the dawn chorus was in full swing, the club would be as clean as a whistle. Jez would also need to sort out the new furniture, glasses, carpets, etc. They'd be open within forty-eight hours as if nothing had happened. No one asked any questions, not even the old bill. As long as everyone kept their mouths shut, things would go back to normal, and Gerry Clark would go down within the underworld circles as just another piece of criminal history. His long-standing, long-suffering wife would be paid off and probably fuck off abroad and get some sun on her back. By all accounts, she was only with him for his money. He had a great pad in Roundhay, not far from the park, which was apparently in her name anyway and was all paid for, so as long as the payoff was decent enough, she'd be happy. It was, and so was she.

Daniel woke up the following morning with a fair old spring in his step for someone who'd just taken the beating he had. He was sat having breakfast alone as Frank had already left to sort a few things out. Once he'd eaten his scrambled eggs, he rang Phoebe, his girlfriend. He'd met Phoebe in The John Cockle pub in Mansfield three months prior. She was twenty years old, around five feet, six inches tall, and slender with her dark hair styled in a bob and shaved at the back. She'd been introduced to Daniel by a mutual friend. Initially, she wasn't interested. She didn't like what she'd heard about the Pearsons, but Daniel persisted and a couple of weeks later had seen her in Brunels, the only pub in Mansfield with a late licence. He'd taken her out to Matlock for a couple of drinks on the Monday, and so far, things were going well. Daniel liked Phoebe as she wasn't impressed by Frank or any of the Pearson's control of things. The fact it didn't impress her was what he'd liked most about her. Phoebe came straight round. She didn't work Saturdays, so now planned to spend the whole day with Daniel. She'd initially been meeting some girlfriends for lunch but had cancelled that arrangement.

'You can still go, you know Phoebe. I don't mind. I'll be fine here. I'll just take it easy and chill out most of the day. I can watch Grandstand cos they'll have loads of stuff on about the world cup.'

Daniel was into football just as much as Richie, but the difference was that Daniel didn't feel the need to run around on Saturday afternoons knocking seven bells out of folk. He just saw football hooliganism as an extension of being in the gang at school. He saw it as kids' stuff, an arena for lads who couldn't grow up. Daniel wanted better than that - to follow in his dad's footsteps. He had the ability, and everyone knew that. Richie had found his level. Daniel had set his sights much higher. He was the fixer out of the two of them. Give him a job, and he'd do it—a natural leader who had that rare quality of holding court without having to try too hard. People were respectful towards Daniel, not only because he was Frank's son but because he owned any room he was in, even at nineteen years old. People were respectful towards Richie, but only because he was Frank's son and would disrespect him behind his back. No one did that to Daniel.

Phoebe gazed at Daniel and stroked his hair. She smiled at him and pecked him on the lips.

'Are you sure you don't mind?'

'One hundred percent sure. You go and enjoy yourself but make me a cuppa first.'

She smiled again and stood up to walk towards the kitchen. Daniel smacked her arse playfully.

'It's only my face that's bruised, ya know. The rest o' me is okay,' he said laughing.

'Well, I promise to come back after lunch then, and you can show me it's all still working.'

Daniel winked at her. Flung himself back and opened a copy of the Radio Times. *Russia V. Romania,* he thought to himself. *Not the best game I'll see this summer, but better than nowt.*

chapter ten

Frank was at the lock-up in Arnold with Jez, Brian, Del, and Michael, Del's brother. Frank had summoned his main men in Derby and Nottingham to the meeting. He needed to plan for the take over of Leeds now that Gerry Clark had been disposed of. He would then get straight onto the Wallace brothers in Leicester. Leeds needed sorting quickly before any local upstart decided to muscle in, and the Wallace brothers just needed sorting, period. Frank had been busy on the phone all morning. He needed to make a few calls and quickly to ensure that his presence was felt in Leeds. The right people needed informing pretty sharpish so that they knew the score. He needed to establish himself before any firms from Manchester or Sheffield and the like got wind of what had happened. Frank wasn't concerned about these guys flexing their muscles once they knew the full story.

Frank had always treated his opposite numbers with respect as long as it was reciprocated. Youngsters nowadays want to be gangsters and jump on the drug scene with no respect. They didn't know how to conduct themselves. His Richie was a classic example. Frank thought for a moment at the mess Richie's disrespect had caused. Frank was old school in that respect, and luckily for Frank, the main men he could have trouble with were all old school. Frank had been challenged in his own backyard, and he'd had the right to retaliate. That would be noted and respected, and therefore Frank had earned the first refusal on Gerry Clark's manor and business interests. That's just how it worked. For all the criminality Frank had been involved with over the years, it often amazed him that strict codes and rules were followed at times like this. Frank had taken Gerry Clark out legitimately, and that had earned him first dibs. Leicester could be trickier. Frank knew if he just waltzed in and took the Wallace brothers out, he could have trouble, especially from Birmingham. That would be a chance he may have to take as come what may he was taking them out. He was taking over Leicester, and that was it. If it brought trouble, he'd have to deal with it.

Pat Steadman walked into the lock-up. Six feet of solid muscle. Pat was Frank's guy in Nottingham. Born and bred in St. Ann's, a rough area of Nottingham, he wasn't frightened of anyone. Pat was a trusted member of Frank's team and kept Nottingham running like clockwork. He made sure the money rolled in every week from the protection and ensured the pimps in Nottingham all paid their dues to Frank. There wasn't a prostitute in Nottingham who wasn't grateful for Pat's presence. He made sure their pimps treated them well and that the drugs they took were all from Frank's supply chain. The best thing Frank liked about Pat was the trust. Every penny Pat collected on Frank's behalf was handed over. No creaming off the top. For that, Frank was grateful as it was one less thing to have to sort out.

'Alright, Pat?' asked Jez as he walked in.

'Ah, not bad Jez, thank you. I wish you'd have called me last night, though.'

'Didn't have time, mate. To be honest, by the time

we had to think, it was all over. Everything happened that fast. We had to use what muscle we had.'

Frank looked at Pat.

'Don't worry, Pat, you'll be in on plenty of the action from now on. I want you to be my man in Leeds. Take over Gerry Clark's businesses and replicate the work you've done here in Nottingham.'

'Fucking hell Frank, why me? I like it here running things in Nottingham,' said Pat.

Frank kept the gaze, a hard stare that sent a message.

'I need someone I can trust Pat and someone who ain't scared of no one. Things won't just fall into place up there. I need someone with your presence and your ability to sort things out. I can't trust Gerry's men yet. It'll probably only be for twelve months, or so then you'll be back down here. As long as you have a trusted man to take your position up there, that is.'

'Fuck me, Frank. Got no choice then, have I?'

'Nope. This is the life, Pat. You work for me. I tell you where I need you. It's only because I hold you in such high regard.'

'Okay, Frank. When do I start?'

'Today.'

'So, who's taking over running Nottingham for you?' Pat asked.

'None of your business, Pat. It will be well looked after, though, and I'll make you a promise now. Once Leeds is running like clockwork, I'll bring you back. If you want to, of course.'

Frank wanted to bring Daniel into things with regards to Nottingham. Pat had it running so smoothly that it was ripe for anyone with some decent ability and the muscle, of course, to take it on. Daniel had that presence, and people respected him in his own right. He wasn't a loose cannon like Richie. Frank thought that Daniel could take Nottingham over as a chance to establish himself in the business and use it as a good learning curve for bigger things later on in life. Frank saw Daniel as his natural successor. He needed to start to get his hands dirty. He'd need some help, and Frank saw Del as that help. Even Del's brother Michael, who seemed a decent fella, could assist too. It could be a good team. At that moment, Frank realised what a good bloke Pat was. It seemed it needed three men to replace him. Pat wanted to sigh but thought better of it.

'I want some decent digs though, Frank.'

'You'll stop in The Queen's Hotel for a bit near the station. Find ya'self some digs asap. I don't mind paying decent money, Pat. That's the least I can do.'

Pat felt slightly better knowing that he'd at least have a decent place to live. As he thought about it, he was quite excited. New City, new shags, could be a good twelve months ahead, he thought.

'Where the fuck's Bob?'

Frank was becoming impatient waiting for Robert Davis, his guy in Derby. Bob, like Pat, was a big fella. More beefy, than muscle. It looked like he should be working as a lumberjack, felling trees. He could probably pick one up if he tried hard enough. Strong as an ox was Bob. He was in his early fifties but still, as fit as anyone half his age.

'Said he was on his way Frank when I spoke to him fifteen minutes ago. Was on the A38, so shouldn't be long,' said Del.

'Right, well, when he gets here, we need to get

moving to Leeds, so I'll fill you lot in now, and I'll relay this to Bob en route. As I've said, Pat is moving to Leeds. Only two of the five meatheads that Gerry brought with him last night worked for him. John Wright and Joe Baxter. We're meeting those two at one of Gerry's lock-ups in Harehills in a couple of hours. Fairly trustworthy they were, or so I've been informed by Arnie O'Brien in Manchester, but the interesting bit of news is that Gerry's main two men were not with him last night. According to Arnie, his main guys who ran his operations with him are Ryan Hughes and Andy Owen. Now I don't know these two. I've heard the name Ryan Hughes before but can't recall when. These two will know his operations from top to bottom. I have no idea if they will be at Harehills today. I assume they will. The other three from last night weren't on Gerry's payroll, but they're on mine now. I have no idea what reception we're gonna get today, especially if Ryan Hughes and Andy Owen are there, but we go in hard. Leeds is ours now. If they want to play hardball, then let 'em. We're taking no prisoners today, gents. You up for this, Michael?'

Michael was relatively unknown to Frank. He'd been on the fringe, so to speak, a few times, but nothing like this. All he had in his locker at the moment was the fact he was Del's brother.

'I'm up for it, Frank. Don't worry about me.'

'Good lad. Can't afford any passengers today. Pat, I told them all last night that they were starting from the bottom with me, but in hindsight, we need John Wright and Joe Baxter on side, especially if we have this Ryan and Andy to contend with, so bear that in mind. They saw what we are capable of when we blew their boss away, so I'm expecting them to keep to their word in that they work for me now. They've seen first-hand what will happen if they fuck me about. They will tell you all you need to know. The first thing I want to know though Pat, is who took my Daniel to the lock-up in Arnold and where the fuck is Terry whatshisname?' Frank looked at Del. 'You brought him in, Del. What was his surname?'

'Cooke, Frank, Terry Cooke. I only knew that he lived in Ratcliffe-on-Trent.'

'You hear that, Pat? That is your first job. Find out where *Terry Fucking Cooke* is. I want him found, and no one touches him except me. That clear?' They all nodded. Pat looked puzzled.

'You'll have to excuse me Frank, but who is Terry Cooke?'

'He's the fucker that was on the door at the club with Del last night. He tagged along. It turns out he worked for Gerry Clark. He slipped out of the club and let the guys who had Daniel into this place, and then let Steven Wallace go.'

'I see,' Pat replied. 'Number one priority, Frank. I'll find him.'

'Good. I know you will. Then we need to sort out those Wallace brothers. We'll go there on Monday. We know their regular haunts in Loughborough and Leicester. Failing that, we know where they live. Either way, we sort them Monday. By Tuesday, I want those bastards working for me. Every fucking penny they earn from Tuesday I want. In return, they'll get pocket money. I want every fucker in Leicestershire to know they now play to my tune. They all answer to me. The irony of all this is that I'm gonna take Leicestershire off them in broad fucking daylight and smile while I do it, and then they're gonna do exactly what they have been doing all these years but for me. They'll never be able to hold their heads up in Leicester again.'

'Unless you say they can, Frank.' Del quipped.

They all laughed. Robert Davis burst through the door, phone in hand.

'Frank, Frank, speak to Kevin. Steven Wallace is sat in a cafe in Mansfield right now munching on a bacon sarnie.' He passed the phone to Frank.

Frank put the phone down on the worktop after speaking to Kevin. Steven Wallace was indeed in Mansfield. Bold as brass. He was either not up to speed on last night's events, or he had a bigger front than Frank gave him credit for. The interesting thing was his brother Gary was with him.

Frank was silent, thinking for a moment.

'Fuck, wasn't planning on sorting those two today. Today was Leeds. They were for Monday.'

Brian could see Frank was torn.

'What's the plan then, Frank. Either way, we need to move quickly.'

He picked up Bob's mobile and rang home.

'Son, it's your dad. How ya feeling?'

Daniel was still supping the tea that Phoebe had made him.

'Not too bad, to be honest. Face a bit sore ya know, but I'm okay.'

'Steven and Gary Wallace are in Mansfield. Not sure why but they're in Westgate cafe. Are you up for getting involved in this if I get Kevin to keep tabs on them and I get Bonnie involved?'

Bonnie was an enforcer. Worked freelance around the Midlands and Yorkshire. He'd probably worked for Gerry Clark at some point. If someone wanted a good seeing to with no questions asked, then Bonnie was your man. No one knew why they called him Bonnie. No one had dared to ask.

'Too fucking right, Dad. I'm only a bit bruised. I'll have those bastards.'

'Hang on Son, you're only doing this if I can get Bonnie involved. No Bonnie, then forget it. Get ya'self ready. I'll ring you back.'

He looked at Jez. 'You got Bonnie's number, Jez?'

'Yep. Already dialling.'

chapter eleven

Bonnie was not overly impressed as it was a Saturday morning, and he had a very nice twenty-five-year-old blonde riding him when his phone rang, but business was business, and short notice like this would cost. He'd make enough dough from Frank today to keep his blonde companion at his house in West Bridgford until he returned. She could ride all day, could this one.

Bonnie quickly got dressed and collected the tools of his trade from his garage. He would have preferred to have spent the morning with the blonde on top of him, but in his line of work, you took the job when it was offered. He'd worked for Frank a few times and liked him. Normally a beating would suffice, but this time Frank wanted real pain, a kind of torture. Unusual for Frank was that, but Bonnie was never one to ask the reasons why. He just named his price, did the job, and made sure he got paid. He knew Frank well enough so as not to request fifty percent upfront. Frank always paid. He knew he'd get his money. Bonnie didn't even know who he was to torture. All he had been told was to be at Frank's lock-up in Arnold within the hour and to make the fuckers scream. Bonnie had just twigged...*fuckers.* That was plural. More than one, he now presumed. Frank had got himself a bargain *cheeky fucker,* Bonnie thought. Always one step ahead was Frank.

chapter twelve

Frank stroked his chin. Who the fuck could he send out of this lot to be with Daniel? Frank needed them all with him for Leeds, especially as he was unaware of the welcome he'd get. *Fucking Wallace brothers,* he thought. He couldn't risk Daniel getting done over again.

'Right Jez, I need you to go to Mansfield, pick up Daniel on the way and then pick up Darren from the Oak Tree Estate. He'll be in the Cuckoo Birch. You three, plus Kevin, should be able to pick up those two. Bring them here and leave them in Bonnie's capable hands. You tell Daniel to watch it all, Jez. I want photos. I want them to suffer. I want them alive though cos those two are gonna work for me. The shame will be better than having them dead. Serious pain, Jez. You know what I'm after. Then once you've dropped them at the lock-up in Arnold, get your arse straight up to Leeds. I need you in Leeds, Jez. For fuck's sake, I could do without this today. You okay with that?'

Jez rubbed his hands with glee. He could have been an enforcer had he not followed Frank. At times he envied people like Bonnie, working for themselves instead of being at someone's beck and call. *Maybe in the next life,* he thought.

'Leave it to me, Frank. You lot fuck off to Leeds and leave the proper work to me, eh lads?' They all chuckled.

Frank grabbed Jez's arm. 'Watch out for Daniel, Jez.'

'I will Boss, don't worry.'

'Then get yourself straight up to Leeds. Don't hang about.'

Jez set off for Mansfield, and the rest waited for Bonnie to arrive. Bonnie was there within forty minutes of receiving the call.

'I take it there's more than one, Frank,' Bonnie commented as he put his bag of tricks down. Frank laughed a hearty laugh.

'How long did it take you to work it out, Bonnie?'

'Before I got to my car, ya cheeky twat.'

Again, Frank laughed. 'Don't worry; I'll see you get a bonus on top. Once I've seen the photos, though!'

'So, who are they Frank? Makes no difference to me as you know, but you can tell me if you like.'

'The Wallace brothers from Loughborough,' Frank said, looking serious again. Bonnie raised his eyebrows and nodded his head at the same time.

'You know what Frank; I somehow knew I'd be torturing them two one day. Cocky fuckers, aren't they? Ah well, leave it to Uncle Bonnie. Payment by the end of next week, okay?'

'You'll have it by Monday, Bonnie me old pal.'

With that, Frank and the others left for Leeds. Frank thought about sitting at home tonight with a nice cup of tea watching Gladiators knowing that his presence had been felt in Leeds and that Steven and Gary Wallace worked for him. He couldn't have planned it any better. Now that the Wallaces had taken it upon themselves to turn up in Frank's own backyard the very day after being involved with Gerry Clark's escapades, he should have no grief from any Midlands firms when taking over their business. The front they had shown today would be viewed as a major disrespect to Frank and would be seen as a direct challenge to Frank's authority. That, he thought, was just the swerve he'd needed. He felt that he might even invite Gloria round tonight. He needed a shag. He then thought that by the time Gladiators was on tonight, that poor old Pat would be on his own in Leeds. *Ah well. Tough at the top,* he thought.

Jez had picked up Darren and Daniel. The three of them headed into Mansfield. Darren was in his late twenties and was an ex-druggie. He'd started to collect money for Frank in his late teens to pay for his habit. Frank had taken a shine to him and had paid for rehabilitation, mainly because even when he was at his lowest on drugs, he'd never stole a penny off Frank. Others doing a similar job would always be trying to cream some money off the top or get a free hit, but not Darren. For this, Frank re-paid him by getting him the help he needed. He now had his own little patch in Mansfield, the Oak Tree Estate, and Forest Town. He dealt all the drugs on these estates and, in return, got a wage from Frank. He was also a handy lad who could be relied upon and would die for Frank.

Daniel was on the phone to Kevin. 'They still there, Kevin?'

'Yeah, but they're just finishing their mugs of tea, Daniel. Looks like they're ready to leave.'

'Okay, stay with them. Hopefully, they'll move out of the town centre. Keep your phone handy. I'll ring you in five.'

Kevin, like Darren, looked after a couple of areas for Frank. He'd never done drugs. Just liked to be a criminal.

As the two cars headed up the M1 for Leeds, Frank was in a confident mood. He was fired up and ready for this. He'd never considered moving his operations north. He'd always planned to move south whenever the opportunities arose. Wanted to be nearer London. That's where the real criminal underworld operated in Frank's eyes. He often wished he'd been born in London, as he was sure he'd have always been a criminal no matter where life took him. Frank was a big believer in destiny, and what you were meant to have would find itself to you in some way or another. He believed that your upbringing played a big part in who you were, and his parents had instilled in him good sound morals and an excellent work ethic.

Frank just channelled that in different ways to a lot of other people. Frank had good morals, such as always to treat others as you would expect others to treat you. For most people, that meant saying good morning on their way to the local shop for a paper or opening the door for someone going into the office. For Frank, it meant not ripping anyone off during a drugs deal or only dishing out a beating that befitted the misdemeanour. Same morals just acted out differently. He would often think of the notoriety he would have had to be the gangster he was here up north, in London with twin boys. Daniel and Richie, had Richie not been such a fucker at times, could have been the modern-day Kray Twins. Now that would have been something Frank would have been proud of, but Frank knew Richie didn't have it in him the way he was behaving lately. But Frank was on his way to Leeds to further expand his criminal empire. He knew today was a day he had to show what he was about. Leeds was a decent city with a decent reputation within the criminal fraternity of the north, and now that he knew he had the blessing of the crime gangs in Manchester, he would really flex his muscles up there. Leeds wouldn't know what had hit it.

Daniel was sat in the back of Jez's car; all fired up. Just like his dad Frank, he knew today would define him as a potential successor to his dad's empire. He knew he was expected to take over the family businesses one day. Daniel had been well aware from an early age that he was the blue-eyed boy. He'd often felt sorry for Richie but was all too aware that Richie brought it on himself. Daniel had wanted to be like his dad from a very early age. He'd seen the respect Frank received from all around him and wanted the same. Frank had taught both his sons right from the outset that if people were scared of you, you could do whatever you wanted. Many people feared Frank Pearson. Daniel had worked it out when he was about seven or eight years old that the only difference between his dad and lots of other supposed criminals was that his dad was prepared to carry out the threats. He had watched many local hard men over the years threaten to do this and that but had done fuck all, whereas Frank had always done exactly what he'd promised to do. Just like last night when he got back to the club and killed Gerry Clark. He'd told Gerry that if Daniel was hurt that he'd kill him. Simple. Daniel was hurt, and Frank killed Gerry. That's what set Frank apart. There was probably only Jez, the guy sat in front of him in the front seat, who had the balls to do things like that. Only difference was Jez was not a natural leader, whereas Frank was, always had been. Daniel thought of himself as a natural leader, but did he have the balls? He thought today might be the day, but if he was totally honest, he didn't want it to be the day where he had to prove that he was a killer. He was going to show his worth though, that was for sure. He had an opportunity to show Jez Carrington what he was made of and that he could lead, and he wasn't going to waste it. He needed to get those Wallace brothers out of Mansfield and to Bonnie in the lock-up, but he needed to do it swiftly and with no messing. They needed to see who Daniel Pearson was.

He rang Kevin. 'What's the crack, Kev?'

'They've just turned left near the bus station and are walking up towards the Midland Hotel and Brunels. I'll keep following them. Stay on the phone, and I'll see where they go.'

Daniel kept the phone to his ear. Daniel was currently parked about 300 yards away near Mansfield Town stadium.

'They've turned into the Midland Hotel car park, Daniel. Gary has gone to get something from his car, but Steven has walked into the hotel. Here we go, Gary's walking into the hotel too. They're both in there, mate.'

'Excellent Kev, wait outside. We'll be there in two to three minutes.'

He disconnected the phone and placed it on the seat next to him. Jez and Darren were in the front.

'So, what's the plan, Daniel?' asked Jez as he turned and looked at Daniel over his left shoulder.

'How many baseball bats we got in the boot?' Daniel replied.

'Five, mate. All from last night. Didn't want to take 'em out as I'm taking them to Leeds with me.'

Daniel rang Kevin back. 'Kev, go inside for a piss and see who they are with. Need to know how many there are and if they are with anyone else.'

'Okay, ring you back.'

Daniel was bursting with pride as he sat in the back of the Cosworth. Jez had asked him what the plan was. That meant Daniel was running this little show, and Jez, the great Jez Carrington who was scared of no-one, was on this job working for Daniel. He had to try hard to stop himself from grinning from ear to ear. Today really was the day he'd come into his own. His phone rang. It was Kevin.

'They're with another bloke, Daniel. I don't know him, though. Never seen him before. A big fucker!'

'What's he look like?'

'Blonde hair, bit of a mullet at the back. Ya know, like they had in the mid-eighties. Bit like what you used to have, remember?' Kevin Laughed. Daniel didn't.

'Mid-thirties, Kevin? Squashed nose like a boxer?' Daniel asked.

'Yeah, that's him. You know him, like?'

'Yeah, Terry Cooke. I could fuckin' kiss you, Kevin. In fact, I will when I see ya. Stay there and make sure they don't leave. See you in a mo.'

Jez looked over his shoulder at Daniel. 'Fucking hell Daniel, this could be your lucky day. Ring ya dad and tell him.'

'Not yet Jez. I'm not saying owt until those three are in Arnold. I hope Bonnie has brought enough tools with him. Fuck me; this is a good day. All of a sudden, my bruises don't hurt me one bit.'

Jez screeched his wheels and sped off towards the Midland Hotel.

chapter thirteen

Steven Wallace looked at his brother Gary. 'Fuck me Gary, I can't fucking believe it. It was not supposed to happen like THIS.' He turned and looked at Terry. 'What the fuck are you gonna do?'

'Fuck knows Steven, but I can't stay around these parts. I'm not sure I can go to Leeds either. I'm pretty fucked really.'

'Well, don't think you're showing ya face around Leicester either. We'll have enough aggro on without you adding to it.'

'Thanks very much, mate. All different last night, wasn't it? What was it you said? *We'll be running Frank's show this time next week, Terry.*'

'Yeah, well I thought Gerry Clark would sort it, didn't I. Fucking wanker.'

'Hello Terry, Steven, and Gary. Nice to see you all together.'

They all looked up and saw Daniel Pearson standing square on, baseball bat in hand, flanked by Jez Carrington and two others they didn't recognise.

Terry moved first and picked up a chair. He fronted Daniel.

'Come on then, ya piece of shit. I was sorting upstarts like you out when you were still wiping snot from ya nose.'

Daniel swung his baseball bat and caught Terry right on the knuckle. He dropped the chair. Daniel swung his bat again and whacked him right on the side of his face. Terry dropped to the floor, holding his face. Daniel hit him again with the baseball bat to the side of his stomach. Terry was going nowhere.

Jez had, by this time, dragged Steven Wallace from his seat with both hands by the scruff of the neck. He headbutted him full in the face. Gary Wallace punched Jez to the left temple. Jez kept his grip on Steven. Darren and Kevin both jumped onto Gary and grappled him to the floor, but he wasn't going down easily. He punched Kevin so hard he nearly knocked him out. Gary was on one knee trying to get up, but before he could put any weight on his knee, Daniel kicked him full in the face that nearly took his head off his shoulders. Two down. He looked over at Jez, who was repeatedly punching Steven, who had never really recovered from the beating he'd received off Frank yesterday. Daniel had to drag Jez off him to prevent him from being totally mauled. Daniel wanted them in a good enough condition so that Bonnie could still earn his money. Jez straightened his clothes, wiped his face with the back of his hand, and then found the keys to Gary's car in his jacket pocket. In the glove box, they found a gun.

They took the three of them in the two cars to Arnold. Daniel was hoping that Bonnie would be okay with the three of them. Jez had already tipped Daniel off that Frank had got two for the price of one. Daniel decided to ring his dad to tell him the good news. They were not far from Arnold, and these three were going nowhere.

'Dad, it's me, Daniel.'

'Hello Son, how's things? You got hold of those two tossers?'

'Yep, and there's a bonus on top, Dad. You'll never guess who they met in the Midland?'

'Who?'

'Terry Cooke.'

'Ya fuckin' joking me son. Seriously?'

'Yep, and to make things even better, the three of them are with us on their way to Bonnie. You think Bonnie will be okay with the three of them?'

'Too fucking right, he will, Daniel. I'll make sure of that. If I know old Bonnie, as long as the price is right, he'll torture any number of people. I can't believe it. You done me proud today, Son. I knew you could do it. Chip off the old block. I better watch my step, eh?'

Before Daniel could reply, Frank was relaying the morning's events to the lads in the car.

'Hey, lads, Daniel and Jez have only gone and located Terry fuckin' Cooke. He was meeting with the Wallace brothers. No match for our lot, though. Daniel and Jez just waltzed in and fuckin battered em... that's what ya did Son, didn't you?'

'That just about sums it up, Dad. Terry went for me first, but I caught him a purler with my bat. After that, once Jez, Kev, and Darren jumped in it was all over pretty quickly.'

'Ya one in a million. That brother of yours is no match for you. When he gets back from Italy, he'll be working for you. I've got plans for you Son, big plans. We'll talk tomorrow, but when you get to the lock-up ring me BEFORE Bonnie does anything. I want him to know what my needs are for that Terry. Understand?'

'Crystal clear, Dad. We'll be there in ten minutes, so I'll ring you back.'

With that, Daniel ended the call and placed the phone in his lap.

Ten minutes later, they pulled into the yard. Bonnie's car was still there. The door into the lock-up was open. Daniel went inside alone. The others kept an eye on their victims.

'Alright, Bonnie?'

'Daniel, long time no see. You've grown a bit since last time I saw you. It is Daniel, isn't it?'

'Yes Bonnie, I'm Daniel. Richie is in Italy. World Cup, ya know what he's like?'

'Oh yes, I recall, spends his time causing aggro on the terraces doesn't he. I assumed it was you as I..., well ya know. I didn't think your dad would have trusted something like this to Richie. Doesn't tend to speak very highly of him.' Bonnie tried to be as diplomatic as he could. He wasn't sure how Daniel would take to someone speaking in a derogative way about his brother.

'I know, Bonnie. Brings it on himself, though. I can never understand why he feels the need to act such a dickhead at times. All his fault this is, you know. Richie's caused this little lot. Mind you, with my dad on his way to Leeds today to do the business; he might even thank him when he gets back. If it all turns out okay, that is.'

Bonnie pondered for a second. 'Mmm..., if I know your dad Daniel, and I do know him pretty well, he won't dream of letting Richie off the hook if he's brought major trouble to his door. Old school is your dad. He's a big believer in taking responsibility for your actions. I think Richie will get what's due to him when he gets back.'

'Yeah, I think ya right, Bonnie. Anyway, now the chit-chat's over, things have changed a little. There's three of them, not two. That okay?'

'Okay by me, Daniel, but it'll cost. Apart from the extra fee for the extra body, I've got a twenty-five-year-old blonde waiting patiently for me at home, and one more to deal with is going to delay my enjoyment. Who am I talking numbers to, you or your dad? Always better to get the figures agreed beforehand.'

Daniel dialled Frank's number. 'My dad wanted me to ring him anyway, as he wants to speak to you about victim number three. Wants something special for him, I think, so you can speak to him about the money.'

'Dad, it's me. I'm at the lock-up. Bonnie's here. He knows about Terry, but he wants to agree the money with you, so I'll pass him on.'

'Aright Frank. You like to keep me fucking busy, don't you?'

'Listen up, Bonnie. This extra bod. I want him killed. I want him fucking tortured to death. The other two just the usual cos I want them alive and able to work, but the scars must be visible. This other fucker kill him and do him first. That way, tweedle dumb and tweedle dee will think that's what's coming to them. No harm in making them think they're gonna die, is there? As you know, money's no issue but don't take the fucking piss. What we talking?'

'Are you wanting me to dispose of the body Frank, 'cos that'll be extra?'

'I don't know how you sleep at night, Bonnie. Yes, the body disposed of too, please. How much?'

'Five grand for the extra body Frank, all in, no comebacks.'

'A bargain that is Bonnie, you undersell ya self, pal. No fucking comebacks or I want my five-grand back.'

'There won't be Frank; you know that. Payment

Monday still?'

'Yep... Daniel watches the whole thing, though. Put him back on.'

Bonnie was happy with the five grand. With that and the fifteen hundred quid for the other two was a decent wedge for today, even if he was doing two for one on the Wallaces. It would only take him a couple of hours. He'd be getting his dick sucked by mid-afternoon, no drama.'

Frank told Daniel to make sure he took photos of the main events. Frank always liked to see what had been done to the victims. That way, he was sure he was getting value for money. It cost him a pretty penny to get them developed, but again in Frank's eyes was worth the money.

chapter fourteen

On the M1, Frank was just driving past Meadowhall, near junction 34. It was nearly completed. Frank looked at the size of it and thought what a good place that would have been to bury a body. No-one would ever find it under that lot. It was due to open soon. Frank liked his clothes and thought that he'd pay Meadowhall a visit once open. He'd bring Gloria. She'd love it. She could shop all day, every day, could that one. He then thought of his Renee and how beautiful she had always looked. Even though she didn't have two pennies to rub together when he met her, she always looked immaculate. She'd have looked beautiful in a coal bag, would Renee. Frank was sure Renee would have liked Meadowhall too. If only she was here to share it with him. *'Why did she have to die so young?'* Frank thought, once again. He'd tortured himself with that thought many times over the years. He was so angry. He felt as if it was a punishment for his chosen lifestyle. Maybe, if he'd gone down the pit, she'd still be here. These were all maybes though, for Frank. All 'ifs' and 'buts'. One thing he did know for sure was that if Richie hadn't been born, she'd still be here. If only she'd been only carrying one child, Daniel, everything would be different. Daniel would have been enough, Frank thought. Richie had brought him nothing but trouble. Even now, he was still causing Frank grief.

'I'll fucking kill that Richie when I get my hands on

him for this. Who does he think he is going behind my back, thinking he's the big shot fucking dealer? I'll fucking show him when he gets back. He'll wish he'd never heard of fucking Leeds.'

Brian and Pat looked at each other in bewilderment. Where the fuck had that little outburst come from? Two minutes ago, Frank was in a great mood after hearing how well Daniel had done. He couldn't believe Daniel had managed to get Terry Cooke too.

'You alright?' Pat asked as he looked over his right shoulder at Frank.

'Am I alright? How the fuck can I be alright Pat, when I've got such a fucking wanker for a son? All his life he's been a loser, brought nothing but trouble, from the day he was born. I should be looking forward to going shopping to that Meadow place, or whatever it's gonna be called with my Renee, but instead, I'm on my way to Leeds to face more fucking aggro over that wanker son of mine, so no, I'm not fucking alright. Alright?'

Pat turned back and looked forwards at the long stretch of Motorway ahead. He looked at Brian, who was driving. Brian just kept his eyes on the road. Pat glanced in his side-view mirror and saw Bob sat in the car's passenger seat behind them and wished he were there with Del and Michael. No one spoke. Frank just glared out of the side rear window. Pat and Brian sat silently in the front. It was going to be a long stretch up to Leeds. Brian was praying for no hold-ups.

chapter fifteen

Bonnie looked at Daniel and raised his eyebrows.

'We've only got two chairs but three victims.'

'I was just thinking the same thing, Bonnie. My dad wants Terry done first, so we'll tie Terry and Steven Wallace to the chairs, and I'll just put Gary over there on the sofa while I point a gun at him.'

'I don't mean to be disrespectful, Daniel, but if you do that, you've got to be prepared to use it... if he tries anything silly, that is.'

'I'm not scared to fire a gun, Bonnie. I'm no fuckin' wannabe ya know.'

'Fair enough, I'm only saying.'

Daniel walked out to the two cars parked in the yard. Jez was stood five yards from them with his gun in his hand. Kevin and Darren were each stood next to one of the car boots.

Daniel turned to Jez. 'Where's the gun we found in Gary's car?'

Jez patted the inside of his jacket three times, indicating it was there.

'Okay, slight issue in that there's only two chairs to tie them to, so Kevin and Darren, both of you get Terry out and get him inside tied to one chair.

Kevin opened the car door and punched Terry hard in the face. He then dragged him out, and Darren helped get him inside. They nodded to Bonnie, who returned the acknowledgement and then tied him to one of the chairs. When they returned to the yard, Daniel had taken Gary Wallace's gun off Jez and was already marching him inside. He told Darren and Kevin to get Steven Wallace in and tied to the other chair.

When Daniel walked into the lock-up, Terry was mouthing off, telling Bonnie he'd kill him and that no matter what Bonnie did to him, he could take it and that one day he'd come back and kill him. Bonnie was unresponsive. He was a professional and took none of what he did personally. He was merely providing a service.

Daniel recognised Terry's act of bravado as fear. He'd seen it many times growing up. Daniel knew that fear was an emotion, and aggression would often mask the fear. He'd seen his dad put real fear into grown men purely by remaining calm when faced with aggressive acts of bravado. Steven, on the other hand, was very calm when tied to the chair next to him. His eyes were transfixed on Bonnie, in some kind of trance. Either Steven thought he was just going to get a few slaps, or he'd resigned himself to what was coming and had accepted the punishment he was about to receive.

Once Steven and Terry were securely tied to their chairs and Gary was seemingly quiet in the corner on the sofa, Jez gave Kevin the camera. As it was one of the new fancy digital cameras, Jez had to show Kevin how to use it. He then left for Leeds. Bonnie wasn't used to having such an audience. He usually worked alone, so he felt a little bit of pressure to put on a good show, especially as Daniel was there. He turned to Daniel.

'This one first then?' Bonnie then turned and pointed to Terry Cooke. Terry spat at Bonnie, although it didn't reach him.

'That's the one Bonnie and make it special like Frank said.'

Terry felt fear like he'd never felt it before. Two days ago, he thought he was going to be part of Gerry Clark's takeover of Frank's businesses. Now here he was about to be tortured. He was out of his league. He so wanted to turn back the clock. He was only a bouncer. How the fuck had he ended up here. He wanted to cry. Part of him thought that if he showed real emotion, they'd take pity on him and go easy. Then he saw the pliers.

'What the fuck are they for?' he shouted. No one answered.

Bonnie set up what looked like a little camping stove. On it, he placed two knives. He then picked up the pliers and casually walked around the back of the chair, and one by one, he tore the fingernails from Terry's fingers. He took great care to ensure Terry had stopped screaming before he proceeded to take the next one and so on. Once he'd finished, he broke every one of Terry's fingers.

Daniel looked at Steven. His face was ghostly white. He looked scared. He then looked at Bonnie, who just smiled. 'I love my work Daniel,' he said. Terry was now crying. Steven and Gary both sat silently still.

Bonnie picked up one of the knives. He then cut both of Terry's cheeks wide open. You could see straight into the side of his mouth. Terry screamed. You could smell burning flesh from the hot knife. Blood poured out. Bonnie then told Darren to take off both of Terry's shoes, including his socks. He then took out a small axe from his bag of tools and chopped off every one of Terry's toes. Terry, by this time had passed out with the pain. His body was sat slumped in his chair, lifeless but still breathing. Bonnie then took the remaining knife off the camp stove and slit Terry's throat from one side to the other. Terry was dead.

Kevin was struggling to steady his hand to take the photos. Daniel had never before witnessed anything like this. It was the first real insight into his dad's world. The world into which he was eventually expected to rule. The world where real gangsters operated. The world where people like Terry died in circumstances like this. The world that Daniel had just realised he was made for. He'd enjoyed watching every minute of that.

'Fucking good job Bonnie, who's next?'

With that, Gary leapt from the sofa and knocked Daniel over. He had his hands tied behind his back and nearly fell over but steadied himself and ran towards the door. It was locked. There was no way out for him. He turned round and faced the room. Daniel brushed the dirt off his jeans, put his hand through his hair, and calmly walked up to Gary. He looked him straight in the eye and then tilted his head slightly to one side. He then raised his hand and shot Gary at point-blank range straight through the forehead. Gary slumped to the floor. Daniel turned round, walked towards the sofa, and placed the gun on the worktop. He then washed his face, sat down, and looked at Bonnie.

'Crack on then, Bonnie.'

Daniel Pearson had arrived.

chapter sixteen

Frank rang Jez. 'Where are you, Jez?'

'Just got onto the A1, Frank.'

'A1?'

'Yeah, I came up the A614. Easiest way from Arnold. Just approaching the Bawtry turn off. Why, is everything okay?'

'Not sure, Jez. Just got a feeling all of a sudden that something's not right. You know that sixth sense thing. Mother's intuition my mum called it, but don't suppose that's relevant here.' Frank forced a laugh. 'We've stopped at Woolley Edge services just past the Barnsley turn off on the M1. We're all having a bacon sarnie. How long will you be before you get here, cos I think we'll wait for you and go together? Just got a feeling we might need you. You know what I mean?'

Jez thought, *fucking hell. That's a bit of a detour.* 'About 30-35 minutes Frank. I'll have to come off at the M18 turn off and join the M1 that way, but won't that make you quite a bit late for the meet?'

'Fuck 'em, Jez. They can wait. I've learnt to listen to this feeling, so I'm going with it. Quick as you can. We'll sit here and wait.'

Just over half an hour later, Jez walked into Woolley Edge services and spotted the six of them in the corner supping mugs of tea.

'Have I got time for a coffee Frank? I'm parched.'

'Yeah, but make it a quick one, though. I want five minutes anyway before we shoot off.'

Jez got a coffee and sat down with the rest of them in a seat near the window. He looked at the blue sky and for a moment watched a family sat on the grass having a picnic. Mum, Dad, and three kids, all under ten, by the looks of it. Not a care in the world. He had to smile to himself as he thought how strange that at Motorway services on a Saturday morning just outside Barnsley was a family of five eating potted dog sandwiches and Victoria sponge. Twenty yards away, the other side of the glass were seven criminals, all probably carrying guns on their way to Leeds to take over someone's criminal empire. *What a strange world we live in,* Jez thought.

Frank knocked on the table three times with his knuckles. 'HELLO, anyone in today.'

Jez was snapped out of his trance-like state rather quickly.

'Sorry Frank, miles away.'

'Well, come on then. What happened this morning?'

Frank widened his eyes and stretched both arms out to his sides. Jez filled them all in on the morning's events up to and including the point where he left for Leeds. Jez was unaware of the level of torture inflicted on Terry Cooke, which he could tell frustrated Frank as he was itching to know. No one yet knew of Gary Wallace's murder by Daniel. Jez was by this time halfway down his coffee, and Frank turned their attention to the matters in hand. Before he spoke, he looked over both shoulders and behind himself out of habit more than anything else. He was free to talk.

'Right gents, not sure why but I've got a feeling things in Leeds may not go as smoothly as we'd like. Didn't feel it earlier, but as we got nearer, it just wouldn't go away. So...' Again, Frank looked over his shoulders and behind him. He continued, 'so... I assume we are all carrying?'

They all nodded except Michael. 'Erm, I assume you mean are we carrying a piece, Frank?' Michael asked.

'Well, I don't mean are you carrying ya shopping, lad.' Frank stared at Michael.

Michael felt nervous.

'Erm, no, I'm not Frank. Should I be?'

'Yes, you should, but I suppose you weren't to know. No drama, but you'll be a little exposed. That's your fault, not mine. Anyway, we digress. If we are to receive any unwarranted resistance, it will likely be by those two who, for some reason, was not with Gerry last night, Ryan Hughes and Andy Owen. John Wright and Joe Baxter, the two guys from last night who were on Gerry's payroll, will be there. That's who I've arranged this with. You know them by site Jez, don't you?' Jez nodded. Frank continued.

'So, I only want to be talking to four people today. That's Ryan Hughes, Andy Owen, John Wright, and Joe Baxter. Once we know who Ryan and Andy are Jez, I want anyone else who is there that isn't one of these four people taken out. Preferably knocked out, not literally taken out by...' Frank hesitated, leaned forward, and then whispered, 'not by being shot.' He sat back up straight and continued, 'but if that's what's required, then it has to be done.'

Jez interrupted. 'So, once I know who the four guys are that matter, I'll make a point of addressing them by name, checking so to speak, nothing too suspicious. Once they've confirmed their identities, then...' Jez looked at the rest of the crew one by one, 'then we take the rest out, BUT... you must all be aware that if you are to take any of them down, you only take the person out on your left. Is that clear? On your left. I don't want a free for all where we end up all going for the same guy. You hit the guy to your left unless that's me, of course!' Jez laughed. They all raised a chuckle—even Frank. Frank looked at Jez with admiration. He was the best number two in the game.

Jez looked at Frank. 'You okay with that, Frank?'

'Spot on Jez. If there's more than six guys to take down, we'll have to just deal with it, but come what may, we do not leave Leeds until we own the fucking place. That clear?'

They all nodded. With that, Jez supped the last mouthful of his coffee, stood up to tuck his T-Shirt into his jeans, and looked out of the window. *Wow, that Victoria sponge looks nice,* he thought.

Jez left his car at the Services. He planned to pick it up later, on the way back. If they stopped on the southbound side, he could just walk over the bridge and pick it up. Jez wanted to be on his own on the drive back as he was planning to stop off at Sheffield at a lap dancing club he liked. He liked a stripper did Jez, and this particular club did great extras, especially for Jez, seeing as he knew the owners. He just hoped he was in a fit state to enjoy the dance. Anything could happen in Leeds today. He got into the same car as Frank, Brian, and Pat.

chapter seventeen

Harehills, Leeds

Thirty minutes after leaving the Services, they pulled into the car park of Gerry's gambling club. It was surprisingly upmarket in appearance given that Harehills was a very working-class area of Leeds with rows and rows of terraced streets, populated by an array of different cultures. Frank had never seen as many different nationalities living together on the drive up to the club. One thing he'd noticed though, was that he'd not seen one empty shop. Either Harehills was punching above it's weight, or the cultures that had ended up living there all supported their local shops. Either way, Harehills appeared to be thriving. *Good start,* he thought. John Wright, one of the guys from last night, came out to meet them.

'Morning Frank,' he said.

'Never mind morning, let's just get inside.' Frank was aggressive from the start. *'Stay in control, Frank,'* thought Jez.

John took them through the doors and walked them through the club. It looked dingy inside, very dark, very 1970's and very different from the outside appearance. John took them up some stairs onto a mezzanine floor where there were three fairly large offices, with glass from floor to ceiling. Frank counted eight guys in one of the offices. One of the guys was Joe Baxter from last night. One guy was sat in a chair. All the rest were standing. One of them was standing behind the guy in the chair. He was stood slightly to the right with his hand on the back of the chair. These two wore suits. The rest of the guys wore the trademark uniform, same as the five guys Gerry had brought with him last night. Frank knew the two guys in the suits must be Ryan Hughes and Andy Owen.

Frank glanced over at Jez. Jez nodded. That's all Frank needed to see. Frank grabbed John Wright's arm and stopped him.

'I think it will be a bit of a squeeze in that office John, don't you, what with nine of you and what, eight of us. We'll not be able to turn round. Let's have this meeting downstairs on the shop floor. Lots more room down there.'

'I don't think Ryan and Andy will like that, Frank.'

Frank squeezed his arm harder. 'I'm not fucking asking Ryan and Andy, am I you fucking numpty. I'm fucking telling YOU, so get those twats out of that office and downstairs. Fucking NOW!'

John realised what he'd just said and felt a brick in his stomach. He turned to go. Frank pulled him back.

'I assume Ryan Hughes and Andy Owen are the ones in the suits, are they?'

'Yes Frank, that's them.'

Frank pulled him close. 'You've got thirty seconds to have them all downstairs. One, two, three...' Frank let go of his arm and watched as he walked towards the door. Frank turned to walk back downstairs. The rest of his firm followed. Frank noticed an area at the other side of the room with three snooker tables. He made his way there and stood with his arse, slightly sitting on the side of one of the tables and arms folded. His men flanked him either side. Frank looked at Jez.

'No messing Jez, straight in,' Jez nodded.

'Follow my lead lads,' he instructed the others. 'Mirror their stance. Take the one directly in front of you. You know who the four are to avoid but take the others out.'

Ryan Hughes walked down the stairs. Followed by the others. He was the one sat in the chair. Now, he was the only one Frank was interested in. He was obviously the leader of this little lot now that Gerry was out of the picture. Frank didn't take his eyes off him. He continued to stand there, arms folded, looking straight ahead at Ryan. 'Follow my lead, Jez,' Frank said as he took the first step forward.

Once Ryan was about fifteen feet away, Frank stuck out his hand as you would when you are ready to shake someone's hand. This was all a mind game but would put Frank in control.

'Ryan, I presume, how very good to meet you.'

Ryan was quite taken aback. He was quite stocky in build and only slightly taller than Frank, maybe an inch or so but had a rather big belly for his frame. He had presence though, Frank noticed. Ryan kept his hands by his side, just as Frank had anticipated. They were now only two or three feet apart. Andy Owen was to his right. Both sides stopped, and for a moment, there was silence; then Jez punched one of the guys full in the face. Brian, Del, Pat immediately followed this, Bob and Michael simultaneously punching one of their opposite numbers, including Joe Baxter. This act of violence caught all of them off guard. Frank's guys gave their foes no chance as they continued to punch the living daylights out of the six victims. They had not noticed Frank pull a gun from his pocket and point it at Ryan and Andy. They didn't move. Frank's men were still kicking Ryan's men on the floor in the groin or the head when Frank shouted 'STOP.' They all stood back, panting and wiping their brows. Frank had not taken his eyes off Ryan Hughes.

'Now then, Ryan. I didn't think you were going to extend the hand of friendship to me just now, so you've made it very clear where you stand. I assume you have heard of the demise of your great leader Gerry Clark last night and how he came to meet such a swift end. I also assume you do not wish to follow in the same vein and that you now regret not offering your hand to me and trying to meet me with aggression. Am I correct?'

Ryan said nothing. Frank moved a step closer and put the gun to his forehead.

'I will ask you once more, Ryan. If you continue to ignore me and show me disrespect, I will kill you where you stand. Am I correct?'

Ryan let his eyes meet the floor. 'Yes Frank, I apologise for my show of disrespect just now. Please accept my apologies.'

'Apology accepted Ryan. But it cannot go unpunished. With that, Frank pistol-whipped Ryan three times until he fell to the floor. He looked at Andy Owen. 'Hello Andy, nice to meet you.'

Andy, without hesitation said, 'Hello Frank, nice to meet you too, would you like a drink?'

'No, thank you Andy, I rarely drink, but thank you for the courtesy. I'll have a cup of tea in a minute though, if you could arrange it. Once I give you the nod, that is.' Andy nodded; Frank looked on the floor at Joe Baxter. 'I'm sorry you got a pasting just now Joe, you were not supposed to get caught up in that. Looks like just a mix-up on our part, but no harm done, eh?'

Joe, through two black eyes, just managed to make Frank out and only managed to shake his head. Frank looked back at Andy.

'Right Andy, a cup of tea for me, then I'll tell you lot exactly how things are going to be round here from now on.'

Jez thought of the family having a picnic and smiled inwardly to himself.

chapter eighteen

9th June 1990, Berry Hill, Mansfield

Frank sat in his favourite armchair, supping his favourite drink – a nice cup of strong tea. It was nine-thirty at night. It had been a long day, a very long day, and a funny sort of day, too. Two days ago, there was no way he would have believed anyone if they'd said he'd be running Leeds and Leicestershire's criminal activities within forty-eight hours. How life can change in such a short space of time, and for Frank, life had changed. It had changed a lot. He thought about how easy it had all been. Those lot up in Leeds were no match for his firm once Gerry had been removed. Ryan Hughes had thought he could swagger down those fucking stairs and show disrespect. Frank laughed out loud as he recalled Ryan apologising to him. *Soft twat,* he thought. He then thought of Daniel. Frank stared into space as he thought of Daniel and what Bonnie had told him earlier that day on the way back down from Leeds. Frank recalled Bonnie informing him of how Daniel had shot Gary Wallace in cold blood, and then more concerning, for Bonnie was the way he'd just sat down and told Bonnie to "crack on."

Now Bonnie was an old hand at administering violence, he'd seen it all and more, but the way Daniel dispatched of Gary Wallace had unnerved even Bonnie. Daniel, on the other hand, was buzzing when he told Frank. He was like a lad who had just taken more speed than was advisable. He'd "fuckin' loved it" was the way he'd expressed it to his dad and was food for thought for Frank. On the one hand, he was as proud as punch that his son Daniel had displayed the abilities that everyone had always known were there at such a young age. From around eight years old, Daniel had made it very clear that he wanted in on the firm and wanted to replicate his father. It was why people showed him respect. Respect of his own, not only on the back of Frank, and it had been why Bonnie had shown him courtesy earlier in the day when he was speaking about his brother Richie. That had not been out of respect for Richie but out of respect for Daniel. On the other hand, this may cause Frank a problem. Daniel needed to be controlled and nurtured. He could not be allowed to get above his station. Frank knew he needed to channel Daniel's aggression and lust for power correctly and not allow him to think he could go around shooting people.

Frank ran a tight ship. People knew that. People knew that the punishment always fits the crime with Frank. He was a little concerned that Daniel's killing of Gary was unnecessary. However, he had to agree that if nothing else, it would send a fucking strong message to the criminal underworld that Daniel Pearson, son of Frank, was on the radar and not to be messed with. Frank decided to put his concerns to one side and concentrate more on the positives of today's events. Pat Steadman was now up in Leeds, and he'd make his mark very early. Frank knew that. He had no worries on that score, and he now had a perfect replacement for Pat in Nottinghamshire, Daniel. The only gap in his management team was Leicestershire. Frank had planned for Steven and Gary Wallace to carry on running Leicestershire, albeit for him now, but with Gary out of the picture and Steven minus one eye and both thumbs, he was not all that confident in Steven's ability to rule with an iron fist. Frank chuckled and nearly choked on his tea as he thought how Steven Wallace couldn't even make a fist now, never mind rule with one.

'Five minutes Frank, and your steak will be ready.'

'Lovely Gloria, pink but no blood, remember!'

'Yes, I know Frank, I have cooked you steak before.'

Gloria was best described as a bit of a dolly bird but with a heart of gold. Frank had met her a few years ago, back in the mid-eighties, and she was the first woman he'd ever let share his bed since his Renee had died. Prior to Gloria, Frank had had numerous women in his life, but they had all been no more than a regular shag. Someone in Frank's position attracted women like bees round a honey pot, so a shag was never far away, but Frank had never really been one for putting it about. He was never short of female attention, and there had not been many gaps in his love life since the late seventies, but whenever he dipped his dick, it was always with someone he liked and was prepared to spend a bit of time with. Gloria was different from the others. She liked the art of conversation and never interfered with his business. Most of the others would, after a few weeks, be wanting to stick their noses in and think they could pass comment on his business activities. Frank always told them at that point to fuck off as it was, "Nowt to do with them." Gloria, on the other hand, had never thought to poke her nose in. She was the first to say, "It's got nowt to do with me, Frank." For that reason, Frank had come to confide in

Gloria and would often court her opinion. Gloria had learned to offer it when asked as she knew Frank had no one else outside of his business to talk to.

'He just killed him stone dead, Gloria. Never flinched and loved it. I tell ya he's going places Luv.'

'Don't talk with your mouth full, Frank. It's not very appealing. How many times do I have to tell you?'

'Sorry Luv, it's when I get excited, I think. I just forget.'

Gloria smiled and put another chip in her mouth. She went to speak, but Frank pointed his knife at her and shook his head.

'Not with ya mouth full, Gloria. It's not very appealing, you know!' They both laughed. Gloria took a sip of her wine.

'Are you sure you don't want a small whiskey, Frank? After the day you've had a small nip won't do you any harm.'

'No, I'm all right with me, cuppa. I'll make another one. Do you want one?'

'I'll have one later once I've finished my glass of wine.'

Frank walked through into the kitchen and put the kettle on. He was just putting his teabag in his mug when Daniel and Phoebe walked in.

'Film any good?' Frank asked.
'Yeah, really funny Dad. You should go,' Daniel replied.

'I might do, Son. You two wanna brew?'

'Yeah, I'll have one Dad. You want a cuppa Phoebe?'

'Two sugars, please Frank.'

'Coming right up. Phoebe, Gloria's in the lounge. I just need a few minutes with Daniel.

'Actually Frank, forget the cuppa. I'll have a glass of that wine. I assume Gloria's got one?'

'Of course, she has. It's Saturday innit!'

'Like that makes a difference!' Phoebe chuckled. 'I'll take the bottle in Frank. Your "chats" with Daniel always last more than a few minutes. If we need a second bottle, we'll shout up!'

Phoebe kissed Daniel on the cheek and stroked his hair. She cupped his face in both hands and gently kissed his two black eyes too.

'See you in a bit.' She picked up the bottle, got a glass from the cabinet, and walked through to the lounge.

Frank looked at Daniel. 'Come on Son. Let's go through to the office.'

Daniel looked bemused. 'Office? Is this an official chat then?'

As Frank picked up the two mugs of tea and walked towards the door into the hallway, he said, 'yep, cos as of now you are officially running Nottingham and Leicestershire for me, lock stock and barrel.'

'Eh!... what about Pat?'

Frank stopped and turned round. Both mugs still in his hand.

'He's now in Leeds. You're his replacement.'

'So why Leicester, too?'

'Cos YOU killed Gary Wallace. Your mess, you clean it up. That's how it works Son.'

Frank sat down in his office. 'Shut the door. We've got a bit to go through.'

Daniel sat down. Frank stared intently. 'You up for it, then?'

'Too fucking right Dad, I tell ya, that feeling I got today when I pulled that trigger was immense. Better than sex!'

Frank smiled. 'Keep ya voice down. I don't think Phoebe would appreciate that. Anyway, one little thing to clear up before we start. Who the FUCK gave you clearance to kill Gary Wallace?'

Daniel stayed silent. He was unsure what to say. He could see the change in his Dad's face. The atmosphere in the room had changed.

'Let me make it easy for you. You do not kill ANYONE unless I say so. You're my son, so I'll give you a chance. That was your chance. No fuckin' more. I give the orders to kill. Me alone. I run this firm, and now you're officially part of it that applies to you too. Understand?'

'Yes Dad.'

'Good. Right lets get down to business. Oh, and don't call me Dad in business. You call me Frank, like everyone else. Out of work Dad will do fine, but at work it's Frank... or Boss!'

The atmosphere lightened, and Daniel Pearson realised at that moment that he was now part of the firm. Part of Frank's firm. His dad didn't run the firm; Frank did. His dad was someone he saw at home after work. He now worked for Frank, and he couldn't fucking wait.

chapter nineteen

16th June 1990 – Sardinia

Richie stood outside the train station in Cagliari with the lads from Mansfield and a few Forest fans. The sun was beating down, and he was gagging for a drink. No one knew before they came here that there was an alcohol ban on match days. He turned to Gadget.

'Fuckin' shit this Gadget, innit?... no booze until tomorrow. Who's idea was that?'

'Fuck knows, Richie mate. It's gonna be a long day. How did you sleep last night anyway?'

Richie stuck two fingers up at Gadget. 'I didn't.'

None of the lads had booked any digs for the initial two-week stay for the group stages. They had all just assumed they'd get some rooms when they got here. Richie wasn't impressed that he'd had to sleep in the train station on a hard floor most of the time since he'd arrived six days ago. Even when they'd jumped the train up to Alghero the day after the Republic of Ireland match for a couple of days, they'd only managed a room for one night. The lads who had arrived a couple of days before Richie had got there had not slept in a bed since they left England, and the word was that there were no rooms available. Well, not to groups of England supporters anyway.

Percy asked Richie, 'What times the meet mate?'

'Four o'clock, Percy. Goldie was speaking to some

Man City lads last night, and it's on for four o'clock. Every England lad here will be outside here this afternoon. Those Dutch lads are up for it, ya know. Could go off big time later if we're lucky.'

'If we beat the Dutch today, Richie, we'll be through to the knock-out stages. You staying on a bit longer for the first knock-out game?'

Richie sat down and leant his back against the wall next to Goldie in the shade. Even though he had olive skin, he couldn't stand too much sun, and like every other English hooligan in Sardinia, he'd not thought to bring any sun cream with him. Goldie, being ginger, couldn't stand any sun. He'd spent the last six days in the shade. Richie looked up at Percy.

'Well, I'm definitely going if we get through, but I reckon after the Egypt game, I'm gonna fly home and take a trip back up to Leeds to get some dough together and then catch a flight back.'

Without even opening his eyes or turning his head Goldie spoke. 'You want to be careful up in Leeds. You've already been warned, haven't you?'

'Ah fuck 'em, Goldie. I told 'em when they tried to warn me off. I told 'em they could go and fuck themselves. They know who I am, so if they've got a problem, they can talk to my dad, can't they? Anyway, that Terry Cooke fella told me not to worry, and he knows them all up there apparently, so I ain't worried.'

Goldie continued. 'That could turn nasty, Richie. Old Frank won't like that. Don't know who this Terry Cooke fella is, but I can't see him taking Frank on if it all goes pear-shaped.'

'Fuck me, Dad too, Goldie. I'm my own man, and I'll do what I fucking like. He'll have a go at me whether I'm dealing in Leeds or not, so I may as well make a few quid, hadn't I?'

Goldie opened his eyes this time and turned his head to look at Richie. He took a draw on his cigarette and blew the smoke out slowly.

'Well, all I'm saying is that if ya dad gets the hump, don't expect me to help you out. I've seen him when he's angry. He doesn't exactly turn green, but he's not far off. Ya must be making a few quid though if you're risking ya dad coming down on you.'

Richie took the fag from Goldie's hand and took a long draw. 'More dough than you can imagine Goldie pal, more than you can imagine.'

Goldie took the fag back off Richie. 'So, who's this Terry fella anyway. You known him long?'

'Works the doors with Del, the big black fella at my dad's club. I was talking to him a few weeks ago, and he said that Leeds was ripe for dealing ecstasy. Said no one was capitalising on the potential up there. Gave me a few contacts he did, so I went up with some of my dad's gear and made a right wedge. Some local guys got the hump, as you know, but like I said, I told 'em to fuck off.'

Percy was puzzled. 'So, if you're making that much, how come you need to fly back and do some more dealing to get some more dough for the knock-out stages?'

'Keep ya fucking nose out, Percy. Got fuck all to do with you.' Richie was angered by Percy's comments. He was angry because he had no answer for it. Richie was doing what Richie did best, and that was keeping up the front and the bravado. Not letting on that when he was warned off, he'd been "taxed" by Gerry Clark's men. When they'd caught up with him, they gave him a stern warning and had taken the money off him that he'd made that day. This was known by the criminal underworld as "taxing," whereby one criminal taxed another criminal of his gains. The warning he'd received was received loud and clear by Richie, but because he'd kept up the front of supposedly telling them to "fuck off," he couldn't stop now. He had to keep going to keep face with his hooligan mates. Any show of weakness like this and his mask would slip. The mask being that all he was at the end of the day was a football hooligan, just like the rest of them and that he wasn't up to being a hardened criminal. Richie had created a persona for himself whereby his footballing activities were just a side-line for his lust for violence. He led others in the hooligan world to make them believe that he was a player in the real world of criminality, just like his dad and brother. Richie knew though that he was a long way off being the calibre of villain that Daniel was and could be. He still longed to be recognised by his father and his father's world. If only he could be given a real chance, maybe he could step up to the mark given a chance.

'Come on; I'm starving. Time for a slice of Pizza and a wander,' Richie stood up and started to walk off. His firm of hooligans followed him all waiting for four o'clock and the chance to show other firms who the front line was.

Over 2000 English lads gathered at the train station at around four. By four-thirty, they were on the move for the long walk to the ground. Various running battles ensued with the Italian police after the English charged down a long hill towards a sea of Orange shirts. Richie enjoyed his day. He was loving life. That was about to change.

chapter twenty

Friday 22nd June 1990

Richie jumped into the taxi at East Midlands airport with Goldie and Whitey still buzzing from their two weeks in Sardinia. It was just gone two in the afternoon, and the sun was shining. England had made it through to the last 16 and was due to play Belgium on the 26th in Bologna. Richie had a good feeling about the Belgium game and was confident England could go all the way. He grabbed Whitey around the neck and playfully dug his knuckles into his skull.

'I'm telling ya Whitey; we'll do it this time. I just know. Don't ask me why but I just know England will go all the way.'

Whitey managed to wrestle himself free and wound down his window. He stuck his head out and felt the wind on his face as the taxi turned out of the airport.

'ENGERRLAND, ENGERRLAND, ENGERRLAND.'

Whitey shouted at the top of his voice. The taxi driver smiled and shook his head. He looked in his rear-view mirror at Richie and Whitey in the back and asked, 'I take it you enjoyed the trip then, lads?'

Richie quipped instantly. 'Fuckin' brilliant mate. Only got a bed for two nights though, in all the time we were there. Rest of the time, we slept in the train station or on the beach. Loads of lads did, so we had a mental time.'

'So, you going back out then?' the driver continued.

'Too right, mate. Just need to get some funds together, and we'll be straight back out.'

Richie rubbed his hands at the thought of going back out to Italy. He loved the feeling of being on tour with England. Mansfield had done themselves proud out in Sardinia. They had a decent crew and had made some good connections for the coming season. They'd been in the thick of it against Holland when it kicked off with the police and had also seen action against some Italian firms that had come across to have a go at the English. It was well known that the authorities had put England on Sardinia for the whole two weeks of the group stages to contain any violence, but that had just meant that in between the games, some English firms had fought against each other. All in all, it had been a great first two weeks, and he couldn't wait for some more of the same.

Frank was at home trying hard to remain as calm as he could, given the circumstances. Richie had rung from the airport when he'd landed back to make sure someone would be at home as he'd lost his key over in Italy. That was thirty-five minutes ago. Phoebe had taken the call. Daniel had called Frank, and Frank had come straight home. He was sat on a stool at the island in the middle of his luxurious kitchen, just staring into space, not saying a word. Phoebe was making him a cup of tea. Daniel was stood at one of the worktops, arms folded, looking at Frank. He knew what was coming. Frank looked calm on the outside. An outsider would be able to tell that Frank had something on his mind and would be able to feel the tension, but only Daniel knew what was going on inside his dad's mind. Richie had fucked up big style. Not only had he brought a whole host of hassle to Frank's door, that whilst it had had all turned out well, it was also still seen as an affront to Frank's authority.

Frank had to deal with it and deal with it publicly. People had to see what Frank had done to punish Richie. Frank's firm and associates needed to see it as well as other prominent faces within the criminal underworld. The leading players throughout the UK now knew of Frank's disposal of Gerry Clark and, more importantly, the reason behind the altercations. The reason was Richie. Frank wasn't looking forward to this. In all the years as a father, he'd never so much as raised a hand to his boys. Even through all the insults and accusations made towards Richie for Renee's death, Frank had never hit his son. He blamed him for Renee's death; everyone knew that Richie better than most, and Frank had said some cruel things to Richie over the years, but this was going to be different. Frank knew that in his world, at times, you had to do things you'd rather not. This was one of those times.

Phoebe put his tea on the worktop on the island. 'There you go Frank. Listen, I don't think I should be here, so I'm gonna just get going. Leave you two to it.'

Frank looked up at her. She was a good 'un was Phoebe. Daniel had done well there.

'Thanks, Phoebe.' Phoebe kissed Frank on his cheek. She then walked over to Daniel and kissed him full on the lips.

'Be careful,' she whispered. Daniel nodded. She picked up her handbag and quietly walked out of the door.

'You okay, Dad?' Daniel asked. 'Yes Son, needs must and all that. Don't get involved, though. It's my beef, but I want you here. Once he's taken a beating, he needs to understand where you are in the firm now, and more importantly, if he still wants to be part of this family that he now works for you.'

The door opened and instantly slammed shut. Richie came bouncing into the kitchen.

'Alright you two? Fucking brilliant it was over there. Fucking brilliant.'

Richie opened the fridge and took out a pint of milk. He didn't see the fist coming. As he closed the fridge door and turned, Frank hit him full in the face. Richie dropped the milk bottle that smashed as it hit the floor. Richie fell back against the fridge. Frank hit him three more times before standing back. Blood was pouring from Richie's nose and mouth. His left eye was already starting to swell. Richie put his right hand out to protect himself from any more blows. Frank allowed him to steady himself.

Richie shouted, 'What the fuck...?' just as Frank punched him hard four times to the stomach. Richie was now doubled up and down on one knee, still holding his right hand out in front of him. He was spitting blood and coughing. He was wheezing as he struggled to breathe.

'Get up ya piece of shit,' Frank bellowed at him. Richie stuttered, 'What the fuck... what... what?'

'Stop fucking stuttering and stand up like a man. I thought you were supposed to be a hard man. I bet you've been strutting ya stuff over in Italy with ya mates acting all fucking hard. Well, stand up.'

Richie struggled to get to his feet. Frank grabbed him by the scruff of the neck and put his face into his. 'Been up to Leeds lately, have ya?'

Richie felt a prickle of real fear rise up. He felt a

brick in his stomach.

'Leeds, what you on about Leeds?'

Frank let him go, stood back, and punched him once more in the face.

'What am I fuckin' on about?... What am I fuckin' on about? I'll fucking tell ya what I'm on about, shall I? I'm on about you dealing my fucking gear on Gerry Clark's manor up in Leeds and bringing a whole host of shit to my door. That's what I'm on about. You think you're the fucking big shot now, do you? Eh? You think you can swanny off up to Leeds without my say-so and deal my gear up there? Who the fuck do you think you are?'

Richie just stood there wiping his mouth and nose and still struggling to breathe.

'If you weren't my son, I'd fucking kill ya where you stand, you piece of shit. Come on, answer me, who the fuck do you think you are? Come on, big bollocks, answer me.'

Richie staggered over to the island in the middle of the room, pulled a stool out, and sat down. He just sat there for a few seconds composing himself, holding his head in his hands. After a while, he looked up at Frank, who had also sat back down. He then looked over at Daniel and then back at Frank.

'I gather someone's been in touch then, have they?'

Frank laughed out loud. 'Been in touch? That's an understatement if ever I heard one. You have no fucking idea, do you lad?'

Frank looked at Daniel. 'No idea, has he?' Daniel just stared back and said nothing.

'Because of you and your fucking lunacy, we had a visit from Gerry Clark two weeks ago. You heard of him?

'No Dad, no idea who he is. Do I need to go and see him?'

Frank laughed out loud again. 'Ha, no Son, definitely not.'

Frank continued to fill Richie in on the last two weeks' events from start to finish, including the fact that Daniel had shot Gary Wallace in cold blood and had presided over Bonnie torturing Terry Cooke and Steven Wallace. At the mention of Terry Cooke's name Richie hung his head and shook it slowly.

'Something you want to tell me?' Frank asked.

'Terry was the guy who told me about the "opportunities" in Leeds. He gave me some contacts and told me it was ripe for making some serious money.'

Frank looked at Daniel. 'It's a good job Bonnie disposed of him, the wanker.' He looked back at Richie. 'So, who were these contacts then?'

'Some guys called Joe Baxter and John Wright. I met them on two occasions. Don't know really who they are, but they pointed me in the right direction as to where to sell the gear. I just gave them a cut. I got warned though, as you already know, and they taxed me when they warned me.'

'For fuck's sake Richie, why the fuck didn't you tell me? We'd have sorted the fuckers out.'

'Yeah, righto Dad, like you'd have understood. Look I know I fucked up, and I assume this kicking is the end of it, so if you don't mind, I'm going for a shower to clean myself up.'

Frank stood up. 'You'll go when I say you can go. I ain't finished with you yet boy. You're right on one thing that you fucked up … you fucked up big style. Because of you, three guys are dead, one has one eye and two thumbs missing and your brother here is now a cold-blooded killer, so sit the fuck back down and listen up.'

Richie sat down, regretting his little outburst. His head was pounding, and he wanted a shower, but he also wanted to prevent any further beating.

Frank stared sternly at Richie. 'You, my son, now have a choice. As of now, you work for your brother Daniel. Daniel is now running Nottinghamshire and Leicestershire for me. He's joined the big time. He stepped up to the mark and is reaping his rewards. Steven Wallace works for him too. Pat is running Leeds. So, as you can see, my empire has grown somewhat in the past fortnight. All thanks to you, Son.' With that, Frank raised his mug of tea. Richie managed a sarcastic smile. Frank continued. 'So, thanks to your stupidity I now run two new cities, and your brother is a serious player. You, on the other hand, are still a tosser who can either accept your new position as Daniel's gofer and remain part of this family, or you can go upstairs, get your things, and fuck off. If you go upstairs and get your things, be sure to understand Richie that you will never be part of this family again. You'll be on your own, and I will disown you. You will never have my protection. Do I make myself clear?'

'Crystal,' Richie replied.

'So, what's it to be?'

Richie looked at Daniel and said, 'So what would you like me to do first, Boss?'

Daniel finally unfolded his arms. 'Go and have a shower Richie and then tell ya mates that you're not going to the knock-out stages next week. We've got work to do,'

Richie sighed and hung his head. He had royally fucked up, and now he was going to miss what was going to be the best two weeks of his life. He got up and walked upstairs for a shower. Daniel opened a tall cupboard door and got the mop and bucket out and started to mop up the milk and broken glass. He then stopped, rested his chin on the top of the mop handle, and looked at his dad. 'So, what you gonna do about John Wright and Joe Baxter?'

'That my old son is down to Pat. But if I know Pat, they'll pay dearly for this. I can't work out though, whether Gerry Clark put them up to it to get Richie involved to give him a reason to challenge me, or whether John and Joe were moonlighting behind Gerry's back hoping for some sort of nuclear fall out from the ensuing battle between me and Gerry. Either way, we have them on our payroll, and we can't trust them. I'll ring Pat now.'

Richie stood in the walk-in shower in his bedroom and savoured the hot water. It stung his face, but that was the least of his worries. He now worked for his twin brother. He was a fucking dogsbody. He'd never be able to hold his head up again in the hooligan world. How was he going to explain this away to the lads? King fucking Daniel had come up smelling of roses again. Richie didn't know how he did it. It just sort of came naturally to him. This was it; he was finished, he thought. Daniel would have him doing errands, for fuck's sake. He'd be Daniel's lackey. Maybe he'd be better grabbing his things and going on his own. At least he'd be his own man. He'd always been in Daniel's shadow, and now he would be following him around, literally in his shadow. Well, on sunny days, he would be anyway. He laughed out loud. He had to laugh. What else could he do? He stepped out of the shower and looked at himself long and hard in the mirror. His face was a mess. His dad had really gone to town on him.

'Come on Richie, for once in your life, sort yourself out,' he said to himself out loud.

'Something good can come out of this, you know bruv.'

Richie looked round and saw Daniel standing in the doorway. Had he heard what Richie had just said?

'You can sort yourself out. I'll help ya. I ain't looking to make you look a twat, Richie. We can be good together. If you work with me and not against me, we can clean up. So, you've fucked up, big time, but that will all be forgotten soon enough. Dad's got two new cities. He's buzzing, but as you well know, what happened downstairs just now had to happen. You know the score. He had to sort you out for this, and if you ask me, you got off lightly. You should have seen Steven Wallace when Bonnie had finished with him!'

They both laughed. Daniel had heard Richie talk to himself in the mirror. Richie felt a wave of shame come over him. He was a twat; he knew that. He'd always been a twat. That was just Richie's way of dealing with being second best to Daniel. He'd never be as good as Daniel, so he was just a twat instead. May as well be good at something, even if that something was being a twat.

'You reckon bruv?' Richie replied. 'You reckon we could make this work?'

'One hundred percent Richie, but only if you want it too. If you don't, then you'll be running errands for me forever. If you do want it to work though, then you'll be my number two. Just between you and me, though. To everyone else, we'll be one and the same. Only we will know that at the end of the day, I call the shots. If we are smart about it, no one will give it a second thought. Take this as an opportunity, Richie. Leave the football world behind, or else you'll be approaching thirty still running errands for me and still running amok on a Saturday afternoon.'

Daniel stuck out his hand as if to shake Richie's. 'What you say Richie? Deal?'

Richie stuck out his hand and shook Daniel's. His towel dropped to the floor, and he stood there stark bollock naked.

'Deal bruv, sorry I meant deal, Boss.'

With that, they both looked at Richie's flaccid penis and laughed.

'I'll put the kettle on Richie, but it's the last brew I make you; that's your job from now on.'

'Ya can get fucked an' all,' Richie shouted.

Daniel made the brew and hoped he'd not just made the biggest mistake of his life.

six years later ...

chapter twenty-one

1996 – Papplewick, Near Nottingham

Daniel held his son in his arms outside the church. It was a great day for a christening, and Archie Franklin Pearson was just about the best thing that had happened to Daniel. He could not believe that he now had his own son. He was so precious. Phoebe stood next to him and waved at Pat Steadman. She beckoned Pat to come over. Pat was not a baby type of guy. He never felt comfortable holding them, but he just knew that's what would happen once he'd reached Phoebe.

'Do you want a hold, Pat?' Phoebe asked.

'Err, if you don't mind, I'll leave that bit to the likes of you. I'm no good with babies. I'm all fingers and thumbs. Always think I'll drop them.'

'What with those arms, Pat? You could hold this church up.'

Daniel chipped in, 'Hey, if you two have finished. I am here, ya know.' He winked at Phoebe.

'He's a cracker, Daniel. He's got your dark hair, I see.'

'He certainly has Pat. He's so delicate. I think I'm going to crush him.'

Pat laughed. 'The only thing you need to be crushing is those Asian lads I've been hearing about down in Leicester. Causing you any grief?'

'Right, I'll take Archie over to Gloria, Daniel. Leave

you to it with Pat.' Phoebe took hold of Archie from Daniel's arms.

'Okay Luv, see you in a bit.'

'She's a cracking lass is your Phoebe, Daniel. Good as gold, ain't she?'

'She is that Pat, anyway back to business. What you been hearing?'

'Just heard off Brian last week that some Asian gang is trying to muscle in down in Leicester. Opened a couple of brothels or Something like that, Brian said.'

Daniel turned to walk away from any eavesdropping. Pat followed. They walked slowly.

'Yeah, it's all under control, Pat. I'm just keeping tabs on them. Thing is, they are getting their girls to offer the services so cheaply. Fifteen pounds for a fuck, bareback too. Girls brought in from India, Pakistan, or some other hell hole, but all I know is that at the moment, they are on my radar as they are taking my custom. I'm on it though.'

'What's Frank's take on it?' Pat asked.

'He's just happy to leave it with me, as long as I keep Richie under control. You know what he's like. Richie still thinks it's Saturday afternoons at times. I have to keep him on a leash. You know what I mean don't you. You've known what he's like for long enough now.'

'I do mate, unfortunately. I'm still in fucking Leeds 'cos of him, don't forget. Six years ago, that was and I'm still there. Has my accent changed?'

'No, but you're flat cap, and that whippet you take with you everywhere you go is a bit of a giveaway.'

'Funny fucker. Anyway, what's your plan with the Asians?'

'Nowt yet Pat, I play the long game you know me. That's where I differ from my brother. Raquel is onto them too. She's a savvy bird. She fucking hates what they are doing. She may be a hooker, but Raquel likes a higher class, more expensive service offering if you get my drift. She can speak five languages, you know. Italian, Spanish as well as English, plus a couple more I can't remember. She's very intelligent and just loves sex. Anyway, they've just opened their second gentlemen's club, so I ain't gonna wait much longer before I make my presence felt.'

Pat stopped and looked at Daniel. 'Listen, I've had dealings with Asians before, up in Leeds. They're not to be taken lightly. All stick together, ya know. You take on one of them, and you take them all on. I had some serious shit in Roundhay to deal with up there. Took me a while, but they got the message in the end. Just don't underestimate them, Daniel.'

'Understood, Pat. Listen, if you've got history with 'em, why don't you come with me when the time's right?'

'It'd be a pleasure. Just keep that brother of yours out of my way.'

Daniel smiled. 'He's okay now. You need to cut him some slack and let the past stay in the past. Even my dad's warming to him. He hasn't blamed him for my mum's death in; ooh let me see, at least three days!' They both laughed.

Pat lowered his voice. 'Listen don't take this the wrong way, no disrespect intended, but I also heard that you were having a piece of that Raquel. Tell me to fuck off and all that, but there's no way I'd risk what you have with Phoebe for a bit of extra with a hooker. High class or not.'

Daniel stopped in his tracks and looked at Pat. 'How many fucks you had Patrick, off whores in your time?'

His voice was stern and low. He was trying to keep his voice down.

Pat took a step back and raised both his hands as an act of surrender.

'Fair point Daniel, well made. You're right I can't speak on that score. I assume that was a polite way of telling me to fuck off and mind my own business?'

'It was as polite as I could be Pat, given that we are at my son's christening. But you're right; mind your own fucking business.'

Pat could tell he'd upset Daniel with that remark. He wished he'd kept his mouth shut. He definitely wasn't going to be the one to tell him that Raquel was shagging Richie too.

chapter twenty-two

1996 Enderby, Leicestershire

Akrad Malik was twenty-eight-years-old. He was a businessman, like his father in the rag trade. Unlike his father, Akrad was also a drug dealer and a pimp. The rag trade to Akrad was a smokescreen to legitimise his income. Nothing more. He had no intention of sweating day after day like his father to make a pretty meagre living out of making clothes. He'd seen his father work seven days a week for years. His father had made enough money to buy a nice house in Enderby, a village about three miles outside of Leicester, but that was pretty much it as the result of years of toil and sweat. That was not for Akrad. His family had no idea of his extracurricular activities even though he and a friend had recently opened their second brothel just outside Leicester city centre.

To his family, Akrad was a devout Muslim, always going to the mosque, always accompanying his father, and praying five times a day. Akrad just played the game, though. He knew that if outwardly he looked and acted like a Muslim, he was a Muslim, which was good enough for him. He finished the lunch his mother had made for him. He loved popping into his parent's house for his mum to make him lunch. All part of the good Muslim boy act. He shouted bye to his mum and got into his BMW Five Series to go and meet his best friend and business partner Barraq Syed. Barraq was also twenty-eight. He and Akrad had been at school together and shared the same vision. Barraq was about as Muslim on the inside as Akrad was, but like Akrad, he also played the game of the good Muslim boy. Together they were a force to be reckoned with, and they were making a fortune from their two gentlemen's clubs. At *front of house,* it was very above board with scantily dressed waitresses serving expensive cocktails to their clients, but behind the facade upstairs were a selection of five rooms where basically anything went, and clients were allowed to pay for exactly what they wanted. Front of house was very plush and respectable, whereas upstairs, behind closed doors, it was dingy and seedy. The difference between what the everyday punters saw, and upstairs was so stark in contrast that anyone who ventured up there had to leave through the back entrance. They were not allowed back into the respectability of the front of house. Certainly not until they'd scrubbed themselves clean anyway.

Akrad met Barraq at the club, and they took a seat on one of the plush sofas. They were interviewing for the position of manager for their second venue. Manager was a term that in Akrad and Barraq's world had quite a different meaning. The manager was expected to recruit new girls to keep the punters interested in the fresh meat and make sure that the girls maximised their potential. Recruitment was not an issue. Akrad had a contact in London called Tariq, who could supply as many girls as was needed. The new venue had eight rooms, so this one was expected to be far more lucrative than their first one. The manager would go to London once a fortnight to view the girls that Tariq had for hire. If any girls were of interest, Tariq would arrange for them to be delivered forty-eight hours later, and he would take back the same number of girls that were no longer required. So, in essence, Akrad and Barraq never actually owned the girls. They were always Tariq's property and were basically rented out to you until you returned them. Tariq would then hire out the same girls that were returned to other clubs, so the 'meat' just got recycled. The only issue Akrad and Barraq had was making sure none of the girls ran off. That was also the manager's responsibility. If you lost one of Tariq's girls, it was time to disappear. Tariq would hunt you down and chop you into little pieces. One of the club's barmaids walked into the room.

'She's downstairs, Mr. Malik. Shall I show her up?'

'Yes please, Cathy. What does she look like?'

'She looks very respectable, Mr. Malik. Very high class if you ask me.'

Akrad smiled at Barraq. 'Sounds perfect Barraq.'

Raquel walked into the room. She was tall and extremely attractive. Long hair that was naturally brown and curly. She was slender and had high cheekbones and a flawless complexion.

'Hi, my name's Rachel, such a pleasure to meet you both.'

Akrad took her hand and kissed it softly on the top.

'The pleasure is all mine, Rachel. What a lovely name. Please take a seat. What accent is that?'

Raquel worked for Daniel at a gentlemen's club Frank owned in Nottingham. She had been assured by Frank and Daniel that Akrad and Barraq would not recognise her and that they wouldn't know her. She was nervous but hid it well. She had, after all, made a particularly good living out of being someone she was not. Her real name was Rachel, but she had learned early on in her career as a whore the importance of marketing. As Rachel, she had struggled to make any serious money, but after teaching herself all about marketing, she had called herself Raquel and was suddenly able to earn twice as much as she could as Rachel and had clients queuing at her door. It's all in the name she would tell her girls back at the club. She wasn't comfortable calling herself Raquel to these two guys sat opposite her. She would stick to Rachel. Only her mother called her Rachel. To everyone else, she was Raquel. As she sat in this rather plush front of house seating area, she'd decided to be Rachel again for these two.

Raquel was surprised at how young the men who sat opposite her looked. She'd expected them to be older for some reason.

'Spanish. My mother was Spanish, so I have lived in Spain quite a lot. That's where I first got into this kind of industry if you know what I mean.'

Barraq quipped in. 'And what kind of industry is that, Rachel? We run a very respectable establishment here.'

'Oh, come on, Mr...?'

'Mr. Syed,' Barraq interjected.

'Oh, come on, Mr. Syed. I think we both know what type of job and establishment I am being interviewed for. Sonny didn't pull any punches when he told me about the vacancy. I am a big girl, you know, and I am under no illusions what is on offer here.'

Barraq leaned forward out of his chair. He was trying to appear aggressive, but Raquel had seen it all before. Her nerves had left her, and she was in full control.

'Sonny?' Barraq asked.

'Yes, you must know Sonny Johnson, from London. Everyone in the... well, everyone in our industry knows of Sonny. I worked for him a little in Soho, and he told me about this job.'

Akrad sat forward and mirrored Barraq.

'Yes, we know of Sonny. Of course, we know of Sonny. Like you say, everyone in our industry knows Sonny.' They both sat back, looking more relaxed. 'So, Rachel, I would imagine having worked for Sonny, you have seen it all, and dare we say it more besides. Sonny isn't exactly full of scruples, is he?'

'There's nothing here that I won't have seen before, Mr. Malik. I'm good at what I do, and I make sure all who work for me are just as good. People pay good money for our services, and I make sure they get value for their money. Repeat business is key in this game.'

Akrad liked what he saw and, more importantly, liked what he heard.

'Well, you sound just ideal for us, and our establishment, and coming recommended from Sonny Johnson can only add to your appeal. Where are you living now, Ms...?'

Shit thought Raquel. She hadn't bargained on being asked where she lived. She assumed they'd be wanking themselves silly once they heard Sonny Johnson's name mentioned, and that would be that. She didn't want to give her real address, and she didn't really know anywhere in Leicester.

'It's Ms. Carter, Rachel Carter. I'm still living in the smoke, Mr. Malik. I've travelled up here especially for this meeting. Going straight back to London. If I were lucky enough to get the role, I'd just look for some rented digs locally, unless you can suggest anywhere, that is?'

'Mmm,' said Akrad as he stroked his beard. 'We were looking for someone to start straight away.'

'That wouldn't be a problem. My digs are a shit hole down there, so expensive you see, and I believe in spending money on my appearance, not my living quarters, so if I can get somewhere locally, I'd just stay up here.'

'We have accommodation up here Rachel, for our girls, so the choice is yours. If you want the job, you have to start tonight and share with them. Otherwise, we'll look elsewhere.'

Raquel sensed Akrad was testing her. She couldn't turn the job down. Frank and Daniel had forked a few quid out to allow her to use Sonny Johnson's name. She knew Akrad and Barraq would certainly check out her story with Sonny, and he had been paid handsomely to play along with it. She had to accept it.

'Of course, Mr. Malik, that would be fine. I can keep a closer eye on the girls that way, can't I? When would I start?'

'Well, let me tell you a little more about the "manager's" role.'

The fact that Akrad had used both hands to indicate speech marks around the word "manager" told Raquel all she needed to know, but she listened intently and nodded in the right places as Akrad, and Barraq told her what would be required, including the trips to London to see Tariq. Once they'd finished, and Raquel had confirmed that the role was right up her street, Akrad continued.

'Well, there is just one more part of the interview process to complete, and I think we'll be done.'

With that Akrad unzipped his flies and stroked

himself until he was hard.

'We need to ensure that you can give a good service Ms. Carter. We have special clients that pay more than the going rate for a special kind of service. That's where you will come in. Get your hands dirty, so to speak, and we can't expect our clients to be serviced by someone whom we have not experienced ourselves and gave or approval to, can we?'

Raquel was not expecting this, but she was a hooker at the end of the day, and she'd had more cock in her mouth over the years than she could recall, *so buckle up and put ya big girl's pants on,* she thought to herself as she crouched down and took Akrad's cock in her mouth. She made sure she gave a good account of herself. Once she'd swallowed, she wiped her mouth and looked directly at Akrad, who was still zipping his flies back up.

'Approved?' she asked.

'Approved,' said Akrad, with a smile.

'So, when do I start?' Raquel asked.

'Come back here at 6 pm, Rachel. We'll show you around upstairs and introduce you to the girls who are on tonight. Then we will show you your digs and then bring you back here for your first night. How does that sound?'

'Great. See you later then.'

Raquel stood up, shook both their hands, and left. As she walked to her car, she replayed what had just happened and felt physically sick. Daniel and Richie had told her some pretty bad things about these two. They were starting to get a real reputation for themselves in and around Leicestershire. The word was that they treat their girls like shit. Raquel didn't like that one bit. She'd first encountered Daniel Pearson about eighteen months ago when she'd legged it from London running away from her pimp. She'd landed in Nottingham for no other reason than she'd woke up just as the train was pulling into Nottingham Station, and she saw that as a sign. Raquel was a big believer in fate. She just knew that Nottingham was the place for her. She'd slept most of the way once the train had pulled out of St. Pancreas station and was sure Something in her subconscious mind had woken her up just before the train pulled into the station.

On her first night in Nottingham, she'd checked into what looked like a posh hotel and had decided to see what the next day brought her. She didn't have to wait that long. She was having a drink in the bar that same first night when she spotted a very handsome guy shaking hands and saying goodbye to two guys in suits. This guy had presence. He owned the room. *Maybe he owns the hotel too?* Raquel had pondered to herself as she'd sat sipping her Gin and Tonic. The guy had sat back down to finish his drink. She waited. No lady came to him. He looked rich. He looked powerful. Raquel liked powerful men. She liked the finer things in life. She'd had a very conservative, middle-class upbringing. Her parents had run their own business and were quite wealthy, but Raquel wanted some excitement. She couldn't wait to get away, so once she was old enough, she made her way to London, and through a series of wrong choices, ended up sleeping with very wealthy men for money. She soon found that she actually liked it. She liked the sex, and she liked the money. She liked the fact that the men she slept with smelt nice, looked nice, and dressed nice. Plus, they paid well, and because Raquel enjoyed the sex, she rarely had to fake the orgasms. This made her very popular as she gave them real sex. This is what had upset her pimp as she had got to the stage where she could command her own clients. She didn't need a pimp. That didn't go down too well, hence the train journey north.

As Raquel continued to sip her G' n T that first night she'd caught this handsome, powerful guy checking her out. She decided to make her move, walked over, and tried her best to pull him. She failed. This guy was not one for sleeping with whores. His name was Daniel Pearson. Daniel had been intrigued by her though, especially as he was just about to open a new gentlemen's club in Nottingham for the wealthier clientele. They spoke that first night for over three hours, and Daniel never so much as laid a finger on her. This had impressed Raquel. Daniel offered her a job there and then, at his new club, looking after the girls, making sure they were well provided for, and this too had impressed Raquel. She knew there and then why she'd gotten off the train at Nottingham. It was to meet Daniel Pearson.

Akrad made himself a coffee at the bar. Barraq was unusually quiet.

'What's up? You're quiet for a change.'

Barraq stood up. 'I'll have one of those, please,' he said as he walked over to Akrad. 'Something doesn't feel right, with her I mean. Spanish accent, from London and called Rachel. Doesn't sound very Spanish to me. Plus, all that with Sonny Johnson. I mean, why the fuck would Sonny Johnson know we are looking for someone to run this operation for us, eh? We know of him; of course, we do. He's a fucking legend in the sex world, but how the fuck does he know us, eh?'

Akrad turned round and put one hand on Barraq's shoulder, and with the other, he waved a teaspoon in his face.

'Because we're on the up, mate. We're faces now, around here. People don't fuck with us. Word spreads, doesn't it? Maybe not as quick as that Rachel spreads her legs, but word gets around, Barraq. Look at the dealings we have with Tariq, eh? He's from London, so don't tell me he's not been singing our praises. We're his best customer up here now, with the amount of blokes we have requiring our services. I bet Tariq's put the word about. He knew we were looking for someone for this job didn't he 'cos we asked him if he knew anyone suitable. Calm down. You're getting too paranoid; that's your trouble.'

Barraq smiled. 'Yeah, you're probably right. I'll be watching her, though. One wrong step and I'll fuck her up big style. Sonny Johnson, though, eh? Who'd have thought it this time last year that the great Sonny Johnson from Soho would be recommending us to people.'

They both clicked their coffee mugs together and raised them in the air.

'Leicester's our fucking town,' they shouted out loud together.

chapter twenty-three

When she got to her car, Raquel rang Daniel. 'I'm starting tonight Daniel, six o'clock.'

'Okay, good Raquel. Meet me at my house in an hour or so, and you can fill me in properly.'

Daniel was at his five-bedroom detached house in Ravenshead, a wealthy village in between Mansfield and Nottingham. Daniel and Phoebe had bought it just over a year ago. Well, Daniel had bought it, but it was in both of their names. He walked through from the lounge into the kitchen to see Richie swigging from a milk bottle.

'Use a fucking glass, Richie. This is Ravenshead, not Ravensdale ya know.'

Richie nearly choked on the milk as he heard Goldie say, 'Hey, I'm from Ravensdale, Daniel.'

'Yeah, I know ya soft twat. That's why I said it. Anyway, use a glass next time Richie, or else you'll have Phoebe to contend with. Right sit down you two, need to talk.'

Richie put the milk bottle away, closed the fridge door, and sat down at the table. Goldie was already sat with his elbows on the table. Daniel remained standing.

Daniel stared out of the kitchen window into his garden. 'Akrad Malik and Barraq Syed are becoming a problem. They've now opened another knocking shop in Leicester and are giving it the big 'un. They're selling their own drugs in there and are undercutting our prices with their girls.'

Richie interjected... 'Well, let's just go straight in and sort the fuckers out bruv, no messing, us three and a few others, all tooled up... crash, bang, wallop... sorted.'

Daniel sighed and turned to look at Richie. 'It must be great living in your world. It's not as easy as that. We can't just go straight in like that. We don't know enough about them. They've sprung up quite quickly, have those two. We don't know who, if anyone is bankrolling them, we don't know the source of their girls or anything. That's why I've got Raquel in there. She met them today, and they've offered her the job as manager for this second club they're about to open.'

Richie shouted out, 'Raquel... you've put Raquel in there? When the fuck was this decided? She'll be in fucking danger there. They're bound to know who she is. Raquel's not exactly a common fucking name, is it? That's it we go straight in and take the fuckers out, no messing.'

Daniel walked over to where Richie and Goldie were sat. Very calmly he sat down and looked at them both for about ten seconds.

'That's exactly what we are not going to do, and that's exactly why I call the shots around here. We do what I say. Is that clear?'

Daniel reminded Richie of their father Frank when Daniel reacted like this. Whenever Frank wanted to be heard loud and clear and whenever something was not up for discussion, he never shouted. Instead, he would do exactly what Daniel was doing now. Richie fucking hated this about Daniel as it reminded him too much of Frank. Richie knew that whenever Daniel was calm and in control, just like he was now that there was no way Richie could even attempt to go against him. So, Richie would react in the same old way.

'Ya getting fucking soft Daniel, you're losing it. I'd just take them out, no arguments. Fucking blitz them. You're supposed to be a fucking hard man, but here you are putting a woman in danger 'cos we need to "gather information" or whatever it is you always call it. I'm telling ya, if we don't go in hard now, they'll walk all over us. Ya going fucking soft bruv.'

Daniel kept his gaze on Richie. 'Have you finished? He asked.

'Well, you're not gonna listen, are ya, so I may as well finish.' Richie looked at Goldie for support. 'Tell him Goldie, if we'd have let other firms come into town back in the day and taken this fucking softly, softly approach, we'd have been run ragged. A fucking laughing stock Mansfield would have been. But no, as soon as we knew where the other club's firm was, we went straight in there. Caught them off guard. That's why we were respected as a hooligan firm... even if it was in the lower leagues. Come on Goldie, tell him, for fuck's sake.'

Daniel looked at Goldie and raised his eyebrows. 'Well, Goldie?'

Goldie hated it when Richie did this to him. He'd known Richie from School and had been mates with him for years. He'd do anything for him and felt he owed him for bringing him into Frank's employ with him when Richie had decided to kick the Saturday afternoon aggro into touch, but there was no way he was going to go against Daniel. Not when he was in his silent, hard stare mood.

'Well, if you want my opinion lads, I think gathering that information first could be invaluable in the long run. I'm sorry Richie, but I think Daniel is right.'

Richie looked at Goldie and shook his head. 'Wanker,' he said. He then got a glass out of a cupboard, opened the fridge, and poured himself a glass of milk. 'Any biscuits?' he asked Daniel.

'Some over there in the tin.' Daniel pointed to the corner of the room. Richie got himself two biscuits and said, 'I'm gonna go and sit in the garden. It's all too wishy-washy for me in here.' He closed the patio doors behind him.

'That's him all over Goldie, always feels the need to prove himself by going in mob-handed. He doesn't understand that we run a business here. That's how my dad always ran things, and that's how we continue. He'll get over it.'

Goldie got up to go and join Richie in the garden. He never quite felt comfortable if his best mate wasn't with him. 'I think it might also have something to do with the fact he's shagging that Raquel. I think he's quite smitten with her. Says she's a fucking good shag though.'

Daniel grabbed Goldie by the arm and swung him round. He got his face with one hand and squeezed his jaw with his thumb and forefinger. 'Don't ever let me hear you talk about Raquel like that again, Goldie. You hear me?'

Goldie was taken aback but instantly replied, 'No problem. No disrespect intended' Daniel let him go and went to put the kettle on. Goldie walked into the garden, unsure what had just happened but decided to keep it to himself. Daniel boiled the kettle. He felt a pang of jealousy inside him. Raquel was the only woman he'd slept with since he'd been with Phoebe. He didn't believe in infidelity, he wasn't impressed by it, but Raquel was something else. He'd only recently succumbed, and if he were honest, he'd done the chasing. She hadn't given him any encouragement since the first night they'd met when she'd tried to bed him. Maybe that was what had eventually attracted him to her. He now knew though that Richie was shagging her too. That didn't particularly bother him. It wasn't the fact that Richie was shagging Raquel; it was the fact that Raquel was shagging Richie that bothered him. His brother, for fuck's sake. He looked at his watch. She'd be here in twenty minutes or so. He couldn't let this bother him today. This was serious business. Raquel going to work for Akrad Malik and Barraq Syed needed his full attention. He would leave this for another day.

Ten minutes later, Richie and Goldie came in and sat back at the table. Goldie nodded at Daniel. Daniel knew this was Goldie's way of telling him that Richie had calmed down and was on board. Daniel spoke first. 'All okay, then?' he asked. Richie nodded. 'Suppose so. Got to be ain't I.'

'Yep, afraid so. Anyway, Raquel will be here soon, and she'll tell us what she knows up to now. She can't stop long as she's got to be back for six tonight for her first shift.' Richie shook his head. 'I'm still not happy about this Daniel, but I'll keep my mouth shut and go with it, but I'm telling ya... she'll come a cropper.'

Daniel knew Richie was probably looking out for Raquel and that, in itself, was something he admired, but he also knew that Richie's act of aggression and bravado was his usual style. Richie had always seen aggression as something that gained respect, whereas in most cases, Daniel knew it masked fear. With Richie, he knew it was a smokescreen to mask the fact that he didn't have the balls to deal with situations like this with control. He just hoped that Richie was never given a position of real authority within the family business. Daniel knew he'd cause mayhem and probably start a war he couldn't finish.

Raquel parked her car on Daniel's drive, walked up the gravel path, and knocked on the door. Goldie answered it and took her through to the kitchen. She took off her coat and kissed Richie on the cheek. She then sat down at the table. Daniel flushed the toilet, washed his hands, and then came through. He would normally kiss Raquel on the cheek, but today he didn't. She noticed but said nothing.

'So, Raquel, tell me what you know so far.' Daniel instructed. Raquel noted he was rather cold towards her, different in his tone to how he had been an hour or so earlier on the telephone. She didn't know why and decided not to ask.

'Well, they are two slimy fuckers, Daniel. Firstly, they think my name is Rachel, not Raquel, and secondly, they think I talk with a Spanish accent. These are the only two things I could think of to throw them off any scent they may get about me. Oh, and they think up until an hour ago I lived in London. They have a good set-up. Front of house is very plush and respectable, and upstairs by the sounds of it, is pretty dingy. I've not been upstairs yet, but when they were telling me about the role, it sounded pretty grim. My job will be to keep the girls working, not keep them happy, just to keep them working. They see them as a cash cow, nothing else. Whereas you see them as an asset to be looked after, they do not. They want them humping and sucking all day long, seven days a week. I am also to go to London every fortnight to look at new meat fresh off the delivery line. If, for example, I like the look of five girls, I will order them, and a guy called Tariq will arrange for them to be delivered within forty-eight hours. His delivery men will then take five of my girls of my choosing back with him. They will go back into the selection pool for other brothel owners to pick from. So basically, the girls get shipped around the country. Tariq owns the girls throughout. Akrad and Barraq just pay for their hire for however long they have them. They pay an upfront fee for the delivery and then a cash payment every fortnight. I'll be taking the fortnightly payments down with me. They stressed that this Tariq guy is fucking bad news, and if I did nothing else, I had to ensure that none of the girls in my control went missing. If they lost one of Tariq's girls, Tariq would kill them. They are definitely scared of this Tariq bloke. He sounds major league. That's why I'll be stopping with them in digs. I'll basically be with the whores twenty-four-seven. Oh, and before I could accept the job, I had to give Akrad a blow job, the dirty fucker!'

Richie piped up. 'See what I mean. Let's just sort the fuckers out tonight, for fuck's sake.' Daniel ignored Richie and didn't take his gaze off Raquel.

'Sound like a right couple of tossers, don't they? Keep to the script Raquel. Go tonight. Let's at least see how it all operates. You okay with that?'

Before Raquel could answer, Richie shouted, 'No she fucking ain't, alright? How the fuck can she be? This is out of order, Daniel. You're fucking losing it.'

'I'm not gonna fucking tell you again Richie, sit down and shut the fuck up, or else I'm really gonna lose it.

With you. Now keep that shut.' Daniel pointed to his mouth. He turned to Raquel. 'Are you okay with this?

'Don't worry about me. I'll be fine. I've been in worst situations in my time.'

'Have you?' Daniel asked, looking puzzled.

'No, actually I haven't, but hey, I'll be fine. Once I've done the run to London though, which apparently is at the end of the week, I want out of there. They make my skin crawl. Deal?' Raquel stuck out her hand. Daniel shook it. 'Deal,' he said.

Richie got up. 'Come on Goldie, I need a fucking drink. A good one too. Let's go into town.' Goldie got up. He turned to Raquel. 'See you Raquel, see you later Daniel. Oh, and Raquel, good luck and stay safe.'

'Thanks Goldie, I'll be okay,' she replied. Richie and Goldie left. Daniel looked at Raquel.

'How long you been shagging Richie?' he asked. Raquel was taken aback but instantly knew the reason for Daniel's coolness towards her.

'About twelve months or so, as if it's any of your business,' she quipped back. Raquel could hold her own even with the likes of Daniel Pearson.

'Of course, it's my business. Or it will be the next time you have my cock inside you.' He immediately regretted that comment. She didn't deserve that.

Raquel grabbed her coat, and before she put it on, she looked Daniel straight in the eye.

'You know what I am Daniel. I'm a whore. You knew that when you offered me that job when we first met. I might be a high-class whore, but I'm still a whore and above anything else, I'm my own person. The last person who tried to tell me who I could and couldn't sleep with I left in London. He was my pimp. I suppose whilst he owned me, he had a certain right to that. No one has owned me since, and no one ever will again. I will sleep with whom I please Daniel Pearson, including you if you still want me. You're not a pimp, so don't try and act like one.' She turned to walk away. Daniel grabbed her by the arm and pulled her to him.

'I haven't got time, Daniel. I can't be late.' He kissed her full on the lips.

'Be careful' he whispered.

'I will' she replied.

chapter twenty-four

Richie and Goldie sat in The Swan pub, in Mansfield Town centre. It was surprisingly busy for this time of the day but mainly with the people who couldn't get through the day without having a drink, plus a few office types having a sneaky glass of wine in the late afternoon before they went home for their tea.

Richie was in a drinking mood. He'd knocked back four pints within an hour. Goldie had kept up with him, but if he were honest, he'd had enough.

'Come on Richie, let's get going, eh? I can't sink another four pints. I'm seeing our lass later, and she'll be mad enough 'cos I've had these four.' Richie turned to look at Goldie.

'You go if you want, but I'm staying here. Well, not here in The Swan all night, but I'm staying in town. I'll see someone I know soon enough, so you fuck off if you want.' Goldie was in a predicament. If he left Richie in this mood, it would only lead to trouble of some sort. He'd seen it many times throughout the years. One wrong look by someone towards Richie, and all hell would break loose, but then if he were late meeting his girlfriend Sharon later, he'd have trouble on his hands there. He was punching well above his weight with Sharon; he knew that well enough. He was like a bear, and she was petite and absolutely gorgeous. He could never work out what she saw in him. She always said it was his heart of gold and his generosity. He tried to believe her, but somehow, he couldn't see why she was with him. She was by far the best-looking bird he'd ever had the fortune to have on his arm, and he didn't like to disappoint her, especially where Richie was involved. Sharon was easy-going, but she hated Richie and the life that Goldie was involved with, but he'd told her many times that he didn't know what else he could do, plus he liked being around Richie and his family.

Goldie decided that letting Sharon down was the lesser of two evils.

'I'm just going to ring Sharon. Chuck us ya phone, please.' Richie handed Goldie his mobile and watched as Goldie went outside the back door into the pub car park and dialled Sharon's number. He could just about make out from where he was sat that Goldie had to do some explaining. Goldie walked back in, looking a little red.

'You sorted it then, pal?' Richie asked.

'Yeah, just about, she's not happy though. I told her that we had a little bit of business to attend to. Didn't know what else to say. I just thought that was better than telling her I was staying with you on a bender rather than go home and bonk her all night. You better be paying for my beer all night, Richie!'

Richie laughed. 'Of course, I will—the least I could do. Come on; we'll move on up to Brigadoon or whatever that place is called these days. Changes its name every bloody week does that boozer.'

Goldie finished his pint and followed Richie out onto the street.

chapter twenty-five

Raquel was a little nervous as she walked back into the club at 5.45pm. She was nervous that she'd forget her Spanish accent.

'Why did I put the bloody accent on?' she thought to herself. It was just something else to remember, and to be honest, she knew she could do without that extra thing to think about. Akrad and Barraq were still sat upstairs. They looked like they'd not left the club all afternoon. Same clothes, same mugs still being used.

'Fancy a drink, Rachel?' Barraq asked her as she entered the room. 'Erm, yes I'll have a coffee please, Barraq, one sugar plus milk, thank you.'

Barraq did the honours and then joined Akrad and Raquel at the table. Akrad spoke first.

'So, if you're Spanish, why are you called Rachel? Doesn't sound very Spanish if you know what I mean'. Raquel had expected this.

'My dad was from London, and he insisted on an English name. Never knew why Rachel, but it's as good as any, I suppose.'

Akrad nodded. 'Mmm... okay, you'll be pleased to know we made a few calls this afternoon to contacts we have in London, and word has just come back to us half an hour ago that your story with Sonny stacks up. I must say, Barraq in particular, was a little suspicious of you, but even he now accepts that Allah has intervened once more and brought you to us. So, bring your coffee, and we'll show you upstairs. The girls for this evening will be arriving soon as their shift starts at seven.'

Akrad stood up and made his way to the door behind the bar. He stopped just as the three of them got into the hallway, the other side of the door. He pointed to another door a few metres away.

'That is the door that the clients come through. Only we use the door from the bar.' He then walked upstairs. Once Raquel reached the top of the stairs, the whole ambiance and décor changed. Gone were the plush carpets, expensive wallpaper, and fittings. Here was old wallpaper, hard wooden floors, and what looked like the original light fittings. There were eight rooms, all furnished with a double bed, a chair, a single bedside cabinet with a plant on top, some coat hooks, and all had a single washbasin and towel rail. There were two bathrooms, a kitchen area, and one more room which was the office. In the office were a chair, a desk, two filing cabinets, and a TV monitor.

'What's the TV monitor for?' Raquel asked. Akrad looked at Barraq, then at Raquel.

'Come with me,' Akrad ordered Raquel. He took her to one of the bedrooms and picked up the plant that sat on top of the bedside cabinet. He took out a little hidden device. 'This,' he said, 'Is a camera. It records everything that goes on in these rooms, everything. It's a little insurance policy we have. You must understand we get some very respectable and influential clients here that sometimes think they can fuck with us. Violence against these clients is not the best course of action on our part, so these recordings, shall we say, allow us to show them that keeping their mouths shut is an advisable course of action. We have all the evidence we need of them and their activities in this room. Understand?'

Raquel understood alright. She was glad she'd asked as she'd be on her guard whenever she was in any of the rooms.

'Are there any cameras anywhere else up here or just in the rooms?'

'Just in the rooms, that's where the action takes place,' Akrad replied. He then continued. 'The girls will be brought here for around 6:30pm by a guy called Barry. Ugly fucker and as slimy as they come but trustworthy. Well, we trust him anyway. Barry will stay here all night until the girls knock off around 4:00am. He will then take you and the girls to your digs. They are pretty grim, but if you work out for us, then we'll look to get you some digs of your own in a couple of weeks, but until then, you stay with the girls, okay?'

Raquel nodded but was thinking, *'Why did I agree to this?'*

'You'll have two bouncers upstairs with you all night, but they will probably stay in the office out of sight unless anything kicks off. Oh, and two guys called Saeed and Talal will bring the clients up from downstairs. You see what their needs are and take their money in advance. No money, no fucking shaggy shaggy, understand?' He said, laughing out loud. Raquel laughed out of courtesy and nodded. Two women then walked through the door from downstairs. One looked like she was due to draw her pension at any time, and the other looked in her early forties. Both looked like mutton dressed up as lamb.

'Ah, here they are, our two most important employees,' Akrad said, trying to be both sarcastic and charming at the same time. The sarcasm was clearly lost on these two. He kissed both of their hands, and they both looked as though they'd just met their favourite pop star.

'Good evening, Mr. Malik,' they both said as one.

'Good evening ladies, let's hope it's a good one.' Akrad then turned to Raquel. 'Ladies, this is Rachel. She is the new manager and will be in charge up here from now on. She's from London, but you wouldn't know it from her accent. Rachel, this is Brenda and Tracey. Once you have assessed the client's needs and taken their money, you will pass him over to either Brenda or Tracey, who will match them up with one of our girls and introduce them to each other. They will escort them to the room, and they will inform you who is in each room at any one time. Understand?'

Raquel was becoming frustrated with hearing the word "understand" so many times but again politely nodded.

Akrad looked pleased. 'Good, well I'll leave you all to it to get acquainted. We'll be downstairs if you need anything, but we will be back up when Barry and the girls get here. I always think the best way to learn to swim is to dive in and start swimming. You'll either make it to the edge, or you'll drown. Let's hope you're a good swimmer, Rachel.' Again, the sarcasm was lost on Brenda and Tracey, but Raquel got the humour. She looked at Akrad.

'I passed my life-saving badge and got my fifty-length badge at school, so I'm sure I'll be okay. I'll look on Brenda and Tracey as my armbands if I get stuck,' she smiled sarcastically at Akrad. He just turned and walked downstairs with Barraq. Brenda and Tracey just stood there motionless.

Raquel looked at the two women she would be

working with.

'Fancy a brew?' she asked. Brenda and Tracey looked at each other, quite surprised. Brenda, the older one nearing her pension, spoke first.

'Shall I make us one?'

'No, it's okay, I'll do the honours,' Raquel replied, walking towards the kitchen area. 'What'll it be?'

'We both have tea, two sugars, please,' Tracey said in a rather gruff voice. She sounded like she'd sandpapered her throat. 'So, what brought you up here then?' she asked Raquel. Raquel didn't want to give too much away. There was no need to furnish these two with any more info than was necessary.

'Just running away from my past, that's all. You know the kind of stuff, I'm sure.'

Brenda put an arm on her shoulder. 'It's okay, Luv. You don't need to tell us if you don't want to. None of our business.'

Raquel was quite taken aback as Brenda sounded very sincere. She thought maybe Brenda and Tracey were going to be okay. Perhaps they would give her information if she asked in the correct way. Tracey didn't seem to get the gist. 'Where's your accent from then? She asked.

'Spain Tracey. My mum was Spanish, and I lived there for quite a bit when I was younger. It's hard to lose but comes in handy as the men have always liked it. Two sugars each, was it?'

'Yes please,' Tracey replied. 'So how long you been in this game then?' She continued.

Raquel was well prepared. 'Since I left school. It's all I know how to do at the end of the day. Anyway, what are Akrad and Barraq like?'

As quick as a flash, Tracey was there. 'Fucking

monsters. Be very wary of them, Rachel. I worked for them at their other club. Viscous they are. Akrad, especially. He comes over all charming with his "hello ladies" bollocks, but we both know he'd cut you open without a second's thought. Ain't that right, Brenda?'

Brenda lowered her voice. 'Yeah, she's right. First time I've been in this game. Tracey here lives across the road from me and told me about this new club they were opening, so she got me a few shifts at the old place as a kind of trial like and I tell ya... stay well clear, girl. Just do ya job, smile, and wave, and make sure the dosh comes in. Don't even dream of creaming a bit off for yourself 'cos they'll have ya.' Brenda turned to Tracey. 'What was her name at the old place you were telling me about Tracey, her who took a few quid for herself one night?'

Tracey's eyes widened, and she held her hand to her mouth as she recalled. 'Susan, right mouthy cow she was. Anyway, she took a few quid one night. Didn't think they'd notice, but they did. Fuck knows how, but they did. She's claiming on the social now; she'll never work again bless her.'

Raquel passed them the two teas. 'Thanks, ladies. Good to know. I'll keep my wits about me. I think we'll be okay, us three.' They clinked their mugs together and smiled.

chapter twenty-six

'I think I must be getting old, Goldie. Six pints, and I've had enough.' Richie, all of a sudden, was not in the mood for drinking anymore. The period between the office workers going home and any night-time revellers coming out was always a bit of a lull, and Richie had lost his appetite for a good session. Goldie seized on the chance. It had only been forty minutes since he'd rang Sharon. He could still be on for a good night if he moved quickly.

'Come on then, that'll do me. Let's go and get a cab.'

'Nah, fuck that, Goldie. What am I gonna do with my car? I'm not leaving that in town all night. I'll be okay; I've only had six.' Richie finished the last of his pint. 'Come on, I'll drop you off 'cos I know you're still gonna shag that Sharon tonight, ya lucky bastard. Too good for you she is. Fuck knows how you managed to bag that one.'

Goldie was not going to get in a car with Richie. Not after he'd had six pints. His driving was bad enough when he was sober. 'I'll get a cab, Richie. I'm not getting in a car with you with six pints inside ya.'

'Suit ya'self. Ring me in the morning, and I'll fill you in on anything we get back from Raquel. She's working there tonight. Her first shift. I bet she sees some right wankers.'

'Will do, see ya.'

Goldie went off to the taxi rank near the bus station, and Richie walked towards his car, parked at the back of the Portland pub. Richie got to his car and sat in the driver's seat. He put his head on the seat backrest and shut his eyes for a few minutes. He'd nearly nodded off when he heard his passenger car door open, and someone got inside. 'Thought you were getting a taxi?'

Goldie sat there in his passenger seat. 'No taxis, and there was a bit of a queue. Fuck knows where all those people are going. Anyway, just drive carefully. Sharon will be chuffed to bits to see me. I'll be back in the good books.'

Richie started his car and drove off. 'Where is it, she lives again? Farnsfield?'

'Yeah, that's it. I'll show you where once we get there.'

Richie drove fairly steady up the A617 towards Rainworth, drove past the Robin Hood pub on the crossroads, straight over towards the White Post Farm roundabout. Goldie opened his window. 'Slow down, for fuck's sake. It's a bit rural round here.'

'Shut up ya wuss, no good having an XR4i if ya can't open her up a bit,' Richie looked across at Goldie and laughed.

He didn't see the car come round the bend, rather fast and crossing the white line in the centre of the road. It was too late by the time Richie had looked back onto the road. Both cars swerved. Richie almost missed the car, but it hit the rear end. This sent Richie's car into a spin. He hit a telegraph pole side-on and ended up in the ditch at the side of the road. Goldie never wore a seat belt because of the size of his stomach. He always said, *'My stomach would save me anyway. Plenty of cushioning there.'* It didn't save him. Goldie was dead.

Richie was unconscious but alive. The other car was nowhere to be seen.

chapter twenty-seven

Just after 6:30pm Raquel started to notice the women arriving at the club for work. She'd already been briefed that they worked non-stop until 4:00am in the morning, only having fifteen minutes break for refreshments and a clean up. They were not allowed to leave the premises once they arrived.

Akrad and Barraq had not taken Raquel to show her where her digs were as they'd promised. All the women were brought in by a very scruffy-looking white guy who looked like he should be a punter. He was scrawny, balding on top with a large, pointed nose. He'd brought them in a plain white van. This was Barry. Raquel learnt that Barry waited at the premises all night and took them back with him. At 3:00am he was allowed to pick one of the girls and was allowed twenty minutes with them as his perk of the job. Raquel thought how he looked surprisingly weak to have such a position of trust. There were a total of ten girls working tonight. The eight rooms would, according to Barraq, be occupied all night with two girls in the "waiting area" to entertain the guests who were waiting. Raquel was expected to rotate the girls as she saw fit to ensure they gave the punters the best experience.

Raquel noticed that three of the girls barely looked older than thirteen years old. None looked over twenty-five, but it was hard to tell as they all looked as solemn as hell. It was clear to Raquel straight away that these girls were not there to look their best. They were just there as a sex machine. Raquel imagined that the punters who came here were just after a fuck or a suck and did not care what they fucking looked like. She could understand now why Akrad and Barraq were only charging fifteen for a shag. She'd been told earlier that for fifteen pounds, they got no longer than ten minutes. Every minute after the first ten was charged at five pounds per minute. She suspected not many went over their time. It was seven pounds for a blow job where they got seven minutes max, or they could hire the room for an hour at one hundred pounds, and as far as she could make out, that was where anything went. Raquel had Brenda and Tracey keep tabs on the times for each room. Raquel was good with figures and quickly worked out that even being conservative at approximately one pound per minute for eight rooms for nine hours a day over seven days, it equated to roughly just over £1.5 million per year just for these rooms. That was without the other club they had and any other business interests they had going. Plus, she'd been told to look out for the drug dealing activities at this club, so that must be earning them a pretty penny too, she thought.

Akrad came back on his own except for two burly-looking guys who Raquel was to find out were her bouncers. Raquel was introduced to the girls as Rachel. They were all told that they now reported to her and that she would make sure they earned their money. Barry sat in the corner of the office the whole time that Akrad was explaining things to the girls and didn't take his eyes off Raquel. Initially, the ten girls all stayed in the waiting area waiting for the first punters to start to filter through the door. Two bouncers sat in the office. They barely spoke but were just there in case anything kicked off. Saeed was introduced to Raquel as the guy who would escort the clients through from downstairs. She asked where the other guy was and was told that Talal was downstairs, ready to bring the first clients up.

Akrad clapped his hands together. 'Right, that's it, time to earn ya money.' He walked over to Raquel and stuck his face into hers. 'I know what we should take tonight, so make sure it's all in the fucking till. Understand?'

'Of course, Mr. Malik. Every penny,' she replied, holding his gaze.

chapter twenty-eight

Richie wiped the tears from his face. He couldn't bear to look at Goldie. He was clearly dead. *'Fucking fat bastard,'* Richie said to himself out loud. *'Why didn't you wear a fucking seatbelt?'*

Two cars had passed him since he'd woken up. None had stopped. He was glad they hadn't. He put the phone to his ear. 'Dad, it's me. I've got a problem.'

Frank was at his club in Nottingham, sat in the office with Jez and Del. 'What the fuck's up now? Every time you ring me, it's a fucking problem. Who ya chinned this time?'

'Dad, listen to me. I need your help, and I need it pronto.'

Frank sat back in his chair. 'Go on Son, what's up?' Frank's change of tone and change of body language had got Jez and Del's attention. 'This sounds serious.'

'It is Dad, Goldie's dead.'

Frank sat back up. He swapped the phone from one hand to the other. 'Dead, what do you mean he's dead? Who killed him?'

Jez and Del both stood up. Neither knew why. It was just a habit.

'Well me, I suppose. Listen, just listen to me. We were having a drink in town. Five or six pints, we'd had. Anyway, I decided to drive and drop Goldie off at his bird's house in Farnsfield. I got just past Rainworth, and this car came round the bend. I swerved and lost it. Hit a telegraph pole, I think, and then next thing I know I wake up, cars in a ditch and Goldie's dead. He's dead, Dad. Me best fucking mate. What am I gonna do? They'll fucking hang me for this.'

'Stay there. Don't move. I'll ring you back.' Frank put the phone down and put his head in his hands. 'That fucking son of mine. He gets fucking worse.' He looked up at Jez and Del. 'It's Goldie. Richie was driving. Had a few too many. Wrapped it round a telegraph pole by the sounds of it.'

Jez sat down and rubbed his hands on his face. 'Fucking hell Frank. He was a good lad was Goldie. Only one of Richie's footballing mates that I liked.'

Del spoke, 'Well, I didn't know him, but sounds like a real fucking shame.'

Frank looked at Jez. 'Get Bishop on the phone, now!' Sean Bishop was a chief Inspector at Nottingham CID. He was one of many police officers on Frank's payroll but was ex-traffic police. He'd recently moved back into CID a few weeks ago. Jez passed the phone to Frank. 'Bish, it's Frank. I need a favour.' Frank gave Sean Bishop the details as quickly and as accurately as he could.

'Fuck me Frank, I can't do owt here. He's dead, for fuck's sake. I'm not in traffic anymore.'

Frank gripped the phone. 'Listen to me, ya bald fucker. This is what I pay you for. Thousands you've had out of me. Now it's time to earn ya fucking money. I want it sorted, and I want it sorted now, not tonight, but fucking now. If I do not hear back from you within the hour that it's sorted, I'll sort you out myself. You're in it up to your fucking neck Bishop, so do not try and fucking play me. Do I make myself clear?'

'I'll ring you back, Frank.'

Frank rang Richie to tell him to stay put and that if any passers-by tried to help, he would have to get their details and pay them a visit if necessary.

Thirty-five minutes later, Sean Bishop rang Frank to tell him it had been sorted. Luckily for Richie, the traffic police had not reached him by the time Sean Bishop intervened. The story being that Goldie was driving and was in the car alone. Richie had lent him his car. Richie had a few bruises and a couple of scratches from a fight in town. It was just a case of another drunk driver killing themselves by driving under the influence. Richie knew Goldie didn't deserve that, but he knew he had to go along with it. He'd let his best mate down in life by driving with six pints inside him, and he was letting him down in death by making out he'd been drink driving. Richie was a solemn figure as he walked into the house later that night.

'Fucking proud of ya'self are ya? He was worth ten of you, was Goldie. Heart of gold that lad had, and he'd just got together with that Sharon. Told me he loved her. He had plans, you know.'

Richie turned and looked at Daniel. 'What you doing here? Me dad's been on the blower, has he? Been slagging me off again, has he? That's all you lot do is slag me off. No matter what I do, you always put me down. It's okay for you, the blue-eyed fucking boy "Can't do anything wrong Daniel", everyone's fucking favourite. Well, what about me, eh? All my life, I've had to deal with never being good enough. Always having to listen to people telling me how good you were and how I'd never be as good as you. Well, of course, I'm not proud of myself, he was my best fucking mate, but I've never been proud of myself. Ever. So, what's fucking new, eh? What did you expect from me, eh? I've always been a disappointment to Dad. Right from being born, I was to blame for mum's death. How could I be to blame for mum's death when I was only just being born. How the fuck could it possibly be my fault? You try and live with that and see how you turn out. I'm a fucking mess, always have been a mess, my whole life's just one big fucking mess.'

Daniel walked towards Richie and put his arm around his shoulder.

'Just fuck off, will ya, just fuck off,' Richie shouted as he shrugged Daniel off. He stormed upstairs just as Frank walked through the door.

'Where is he, the fucking dickhead. The little shit. I'll kill him myself. Where is he?'

Daniel walked towards Frank and stopped him by putting both palms on his chest. 'Leave it Dad, not now. He's too fragile.'

Frank took a step back and looked Daniel up and down. 'Too what? What is this as fucking counselling session?'

Daniel took a step forward. 'Dad, I'm telling ya not now. Leave him be. He's just killed his best friend. He needs some time. Think about it.'

'I did think about it. All the way over here, all the time I was on the phone to Sean Bishop. All the time I was sorting his mess out again. Always his mess. I'm sick of it.'

Richie came down the stairs. 'Sick of it, are ya? Well, do something about it then, big man. Big fucking Frank. You've hated me all your life, so do what you want Dad, I don't fucking care.'

Frank punched Richie so hard he knocked him clean out. Luckily, he landed on the sofa and not the tiled floor. Frank stood over Richie, looking at him.

'That should've been you,' he said before walking into the kitchen to put the kettle on. Daniel followed him in.

'You might regret saying that one day Dad. It's time you let it go. Mum's death was nothing to do with Richie.' Frank slammed his mug down and turned round, fist raised. He drew it back. Daniel didn't flinch. Frank stood there looking at Daniel. Daniel looked at Frank. Frank dropped his fist. He'd never hit Daniel before.

'You know nowt Son, nowt. Anyway, enough for tonight. You get yourself off home.' Daniel turned to go but then turned back to look at Frank. 'How were Goldie's parents?' he asked.

Frank had called in on his way from the club. He wanted to pay his condolences but also to make sure they'd bought the story of Goldie driving and being alone in the car.

'Upset like you wouldn't believe. I've never seen a woman cry like that before. They believed the cops, though. His mother even asked me to apologise to Richie for the car being a write off. I tell ya something lad, it takes a lot to get me going with things like this, but I had a job to keep my emotions in check. She's a broken woman. Anyway, get ya'self off home,' Daniel turned again to go, but before he'd left the kitchen, Frank said. 'He's a fucking bad apple that brother of yours. I'd think twice before you take his side again if I were you.' Daniel just kept on walking to get his coat.

Frank walked into where Richie had been lying on the sofa. He was no longer there. Frank then heard a door slam upstairs. *Ah well, he must be okay if he's gone to bed,* Frank thought to himself. He then heard the front door go as Daniel left to go home. Frank decided he needed a drink. He walked to his bar and poured himself a scotch. He rang Gloria. 'You still up?' he asked. 'Yes Luv,' she said. 'Come round, I need a cuddle,' Gloria put her shoes on and drove to Frank's house. They fell asleep cuddled together.

chapter twenty-nine

It was just gone midnight, and the cash was coming in thick and fast. The clients coming up the stairs were constant. These girls really were earning their money. Raquel was watching everything that went off. Brenda and Tracey were decent enough women to be fair. They were hard workers and instantly took to seeing Raquel as their boss. No qualms or quibbles. They just did their job. Raquel knew it was probably to do with their fear of Akrad and Barraq, rather than a duty to her, but things seemed to be running smoothly, as far as Raquel could see. Barraq had been up twice already to take the cash downstairs. He didn't like too much money in the office upstairs out of his control.

Barry had not spoken a word since he'd arrived. Raquel had tried to make conversation a couple of times, but nothing was forthcoming. He watched Raquel like a hawk. She knew he was watching her constantly, and she tried not to let it bother her. He'd not moved from his seat except once when he went to the toilet. Brenda came over to her.

'It's time to start giving the girls their breaks, Rachel. Should have started at twelve really, but it slipped my mind. Being your first night and all that, I thought I best remind you. Akrad likes the girls to have a shower during their breaks. He says it shows him as a good employer.' She laughed mockingly.

Raquel thanked Brenda. She'd not given a second's

thought to the breaks. Time had gone so quickly. She was annoyed at herself for not thinking of the girls.

'Who goes first, Brenda?' she asked.

'Anyone really. That's up to you, but they have breaks two at a time. They must shower together and get a drink and something to eat in that time. Fifteen minutes, that's all they are allowed. It's not long enough for two of them if you ask me, but nowt to do with me. Look, I'll go down and let Saeed and Talal know that the breaks are starting if you want, and you can sort the first two girls out. Is that okay?'

Raquel smiled at Brenda. 'Thanks, Brenda. That's great.'

Raquel wanted to get talking to the three girls she suspected were definitely underage. She was sure they had only just reached their teens. She went over to two of them, who were sat together waiting.

'Hi, do you two want to take your break now?' she asked. They both nodded but did not speak. Raquel walked them out towards the bathrooms. She expected them to use one each, but they both went into the same one. Raquel put her hand on the door just before it closed.

'Do you not want to use one each?' she asked. One of the girls spoke. 'We can't just in case a client wants to use the toilet. We have to share.'

'Would you like a cup of tea?' Raquel asked them. They both looked at each other, unsure what to say.

'It's okay, I've got time. No-one is waiting at the moment. Look, I'll make two mugs of tea. If you want them, I'll leave them in the kitchen for you.' She smiled at them. They both smiled back.

Raquel went to make two mugs of tea. Tracey came into the kitchen.

'Best not to get too close Rachel, ya know. They'll probably not be here in a few weeks. Akrad likes new girls, regularly.'

Raquel turned round. 'How old would you say those two are, Tracey?'

Tracey put her hands on her hips. 'Look, I'm not getting involved. I just come here to do my job and get my money. I've got mouths to feed, you know. I can't afford to lose this job. Plus, I'd get beaten half to death. I try not to think about it.'

Raquel put the two mugs down and looked at Tracey. 'Those mouths you've got to feed... boys or girls?'

Tracey sighed and looked away sidewards towards the wall. 'I know where this is going Rachel, but trust me, keep out of things that don't concern you.'

Raquel shook her head and walked out of the kitchen and left the two mugs of tea on the side. She saw Brenda in the waiting area.

'Let me show you this,' she said whilst beckoning Raquel over. Raquel walked over to Brenda, intrigued by what she wanted to show her. Brenda got a piece of paper out of her pocket. 'Look what my grandson wrote for me,' she said as she passed the paper to Raquel. She looked at what was written on it, and it just said - *fourteen-year-olds they are.*

'Ain't that sweet, Rachel,' Brenda said quite loudly.

Raquel looked at Brenda and just said, 'Ah, that's lovely, Brenda.' She knew Brenda didn't have to do that. She gave the paper back to Brenda and whispered, 'Get rid of it. You don't want that being found on you.'

Raquel struggled to focus on dealing with the next punter as she thought about the two girls. She assumed the third one who looked underage was also just fourteen. She wanted to be sick. She'd been a prostitute from leaving home and was well aware that she was on the game at sixteen, but this filthy operation appalled her. Frank and Daniel would never allow this type of operation to happen on their manor if they knew what was going on. They'd dealt with this type of thing before and had made it clear to all concerned that any money to be made from sex on their manor was only to be made from over age women. They were not into prostituting underage girls. Frank, in particular, would be enraged. Raquel knew that she had to tell Daniel as soon as she could. She knew he wouldn't thank her for keeping hold of this information any longer than was necessary. She needed to go back to the digs tonight, as she'd been making out she had nowhere else to go up here, but tomorrow morning as soon as she woke up, she told herself she would go straight over to Daniel's house and fill him in. She looked at her watch, nearly 12:30am. Only three and a half hours to go, and hopefully, she was done with this place. She was sure that Daniel wouldn't want her to stay on until she'd been to London to see this Tariq guy after he'd been made aware of the age of some of these girls.

She looked over at Barry. He was still watching her. She'd forgotten about Barry but just remembered that at 3:00am, he could have one of the women as his perk. She hoped and prayed that he would not pick one of the young ones. She looked at him, and she just knew that he would probably do that. She was startled by a voice that brought her back into the real world.

'Have I got to stand here for much longer, or is there any chance of me getting a shag this side of Christmas?'

Raquel looked round and saw yet another punter standing there eagerly waiting to have his ten minutes of fun. 'Sorry sir,' she said. 'What can I do for you?'

'Foreign, eh? Sound sexy does that accent. I don't suppose you are on the menu, are you?'

'I'm sorry sir, but no, not tonight,' Raquel replied.

'Ah well, I'll come back another night then when you're available. I like that sexy accent. Be worth paying a bit extra to have you talking dirty to me.'

Raquel didn't see the man nod to Barry before he left. Barry now knew what he'd suspected since he'd arrived earlier on that evening. He did know this Rachel woman. Barry knew he'd seen her before in Nottingham at a lap dancing club he frequented called The Main Vault. He'd rung a friend of his earlier from the toilet, who often went to the Nottingham club. He knew his friend would be able to confirm if it was the same woman. Now he had to let Akrad and Barraq know.

chapter thirty

Daniel arrived home. Phoebe was waiting for him. She welcomed him in her usual way, giving him a cuddle and a kiss. She was okay with the lifestyle Daniel led. She understood it was something he was born into and that she would never change him. It didn't stop her worrying every time he went out though. She was always glad to see him back safe and sound. Daniel had told her about Richie and Goldie earlier, before he'd left to go to his dad's house, and Phoebe knew that Richie would be unpredictable and volatile. That was how Richie was and she was sure that he wouldn't take any responsibility for what he'd done tonight. He would just blow up and blame everyone else but himself. She couldn't help feeling sorry for Richie though. Ever since she'd come into Daniel's life, she'd seen Richie being treated like shit at times, especially by Frank. Phoebe always tried to see the best in people, and she could see, somewhere deep inside Richie a decent person trying to get out. She would notice a flicker of decency at times, but then many times that flicker would be gone and replaced by someone with a lot of hatred in them. She could see that deep down, Richie resented Daniel and all that Daniel stood for, and that worried her at times. She would often get this nagging feeling that Richie would one day be Daniel's downfall, that he would somehow be responsible for Daniel's fate. She could see it in Richie's eyes sometimes with the way he looked at Daniel. Eyes full of hatred. She understood why but could also see the irony of the situation too. Richie was in no way to blame for Renee's death, that was obvious, but he'd been blamed all his life. That was unfair, but likewise, Daniel was in no way responsible for Frank's loathing of Richie or Frank's admiration of Daniel. It was unfair that Richie blamed Daniel for somehow being responsible for the way he was treated in all this. She just knew that in all of this, nothing was fair and that where families were concerned, jealousy and loathing would often end in disaster for somebody. She just hoped and prayed that somebody was not her Daniel. She also felt for Sharon, Goldie's girlfriend.

'How's the little 'un?' Daniel asked.

'Fine, been asleep all the time you've been gone. Haven't heard a peep. Fancy a cuppa?'

'I think I need a drink Luv, to be honest. What a night.'

Phoebe gave Daniel another hug. 'How did it go? I assume you've seen Richie?'

Daniel held her tight while he spoke. 'Sure have. He poured his heart out a little. Trying to deflect the blame of course, but also off-loading. All about mum's death and that and how he's had to put up with the blame from dad. I couldn't help feeling sorry for him. I tried to comfort him, but he was too upset... or angry, or both. Anyway, me dad came home, lit the fuse, and ended up knocking Richie out. That's when I came home.'

Phoebe pulled herself away. 'Come on, sit down, and I'll pour you a drink. Do you want a beer or a whiskey?'

Daniel walked through to the lounge. 'Beer. Bring me two Luv, please.'

Phoebe watched Daniel as he savoured his beer. He was deep in thought. 'What you thinking about?' she asked. Daniel put his drink down and wiped the froth from his mouth.

'Just something me dad said earlier. After he'd hit Richie, he stood over him and said, "it should have been you". I assumed he was referring to Goldie's death, but when I said to him that he may regret saying that one day, and that Richie was not to blame for Mam's death he said to me, "you know nowt Son, you know nowt". Not sure what he meant by that, but it's just re-playing in my head. You know how things do sometimes?'

Phoebe thought for a minute. 'He was probably just angry. He wouldn't have meant it. I know he can at times seem to loathe Richie, but he would never mean anything like that, would he?'

Daniel took another good drink of his pint. 'I'm not so sure Phoebe, I think he could happily kill Richie at times. It's the bit about me not knowing anything that's bothering me. Don't you think it suggests there's something he's not telling me, or not telling anyone for that matter?'

Phoebe swapped sofas and now sat next to Daniel. She snuggled into him. 'I don't know Daniel. Who knows what goes on in ya dad's head sometimes? Anyway, we should be thinking about Goldie's parents, and his sister. They'll be absolutely distraught. Have you been in touch yet?'

'No, me dad did that bit. He's good with things like that. He called round on his way home to see them. His Mam's taken it hard. They bought it all though. I know it sounds bad, but we needed them to. I've got enough shit on what with Richie now after all this and those two down in Leicester thinking they can do as they like. Happy days, eh!'

chapter thirty-one

'I'm telling ya, Boss. It's her—one hundred percent. As soon as I saw her, I knew her from somewhere, but I couldn't think where. I kept watching her then I remembered. That's when I called Pete 'cos I knew he'd know straight away. Every time we went to The Main Vault, he would say that he wished she gave lap dances. He was a bit obsessed with her, I think, but 'cos she was some sort of manager, Pete never even got to speak to her. But it's her, I'm telling ya.'

Akrad and Barraq couldn't believe what Barry was telling them.

'What did I tell ya Akrad, I just knew something wasn't right about her. I bet she don't even speak with that Spanish accent either.' Barraq sat back in his chair.

'My mum always tells me to listen to that little voice in ya head. It's there for a reason, ya know.'

Akrad looked at Barraq. 'It's not about who's right and who's not. It's now about what she's doing here. That club you mentioned, Barry. It's owned by the Pearsons innit?'

'Couldn't tell ya, Boss. We only go because Pete lived in Nottingham for a bit, and he said they gave good dances.'

Akrad continued, 'I'm sure that's one of their own clubs. Ninety-nine percent sure I am.' He picked up the phone. 'What ya doin'?' Barraq asked.

Akrad spoke into the phone. 'Erm... The Main Vault please in Nottingham.' He looked at Barry. 'What street is it on, Barry?'

'Upper Parliament Street,' he replied.

Akrad wrote the number down from directory enquiries. 'Right, I'm gonna ring it and ask for Rachel. See if she's there.' He dialled the number. A lady answered.

'The Main Vault, how can I help you?'

'Er hello, yes is er Rachel there please?'

'Rachel? We don't have anyone called Rachel working here. Are you sure you have the right number? This is The Main Vault.'

'Yes, I know. Tall lady, attractive with long curly brown hair.'

'Ah, you mean Raquel. No, she's not in tonight. In fact, I don't think she'll be back for a week or so. Gone away somewhere. Is there anything I can do?'

'Er... no, that's fine. I'll try her next week. Thank you for your time.' Akrad replaced the receiver. 'Well, well, well,' he said. Raquel is it. The fucking whore,' he laughed out loud. 'You know what this means, don't you Barraq?' Barraq looked puzzled.

'What?'

Akrad placed both palms on Barraq's cheeks. 'This means, my friend, that the Pearsons have put her in here, and that means they are wary of us. That means...' he kissed Barraq full on the lips. 'That means we've arrived. We're in the major league now. They're fucking scared of us. If they weren't, they'd have stormed straight in here, all guns blazing. But they haven't.' He stood up and leant against the wall. 'They haven't, have they? They've sent a fucking woman in to spy on our operation. You know what she is Barraq, don't you?'

Again, Barraq looked puzzled. 'What?'

'Leverage my son... fucking leverage. We know why she's here. They don't know we know that. So, we use her as leverage to strike a deal for this city of ours.' Barraq stood up.

'They won't give two shits about her. She's no fucking leverage.' They'd both forgot Barry was there as he just sat there wondering if he should be privy to all this. Akrad continued.

'Oh, they will. She's the whore that Daniel Pearson is shagging, and by all accounts, he has a real soft spot for her. He must trust her impeccably if he's entrusted her in here with us. Plus, he's a bit old school, like his dad Frank, ain't he. Honour and all that shite. I'm telling ya Barraq they give two shits about her, and she's leverage to us.'

'So, what we gonna do?' Barraq asked.

Akrad looked at Barry. 'Forgot you were here Bazza... look, you told us you've been watching her all night. Is that right?'

'Yeah.'

'Right then, go back upstairs and do exactly the same. Don't act any different. Just behave exactly as you have done all night. When you take the girls and her to the digs, me and Barraq will be there. You can get off as normal and leave her to us two. That's all you need to know Barry. Understand?'

'No problem, Boss.' Barry got up to go. Akrad stopped him. 'Good work Barry, well done. We'll sort you a nice little bonus out for this.' Barry was elated. He'd never been praised before in his entire life. No one had ever told Barry Bray well done, ever. He felt a feeling he'd never felt before. He liked it.

Akrad was buzzing. 'This is it Barraq. This is our time, mate. We'll take those fucking Pearsons on and wipe the fucking floor with them. They've got to either react or negotiate. Either way, we'll be ready.'

Akrad had been waiting for this moment all his life. Now he had a chance to show the world what he was made of. Barraq was sure he could see the adrenalin pumping around Akrad's body. It was tangible. He could see it pumping through his veins. Barraq, on the other hand, felt a prickle of fear. He's seen Steven Wallace go from being the main man in Leicester, from someone everyone made way for, and who never had to pay for a drink or a meal in town, to someone with a false eye, no thumbs, and someone who struggled to hold his head up and look people in the eye. All because he'd try to take on Frank Pearson. Barraq was a little scared but swallowed it down and did his very best to mirror Akrad.

chapter thirty-two

Raquel had been surprised that Barry had chosen one of the older girls. She'd thought maybe she'd misjudged him, although he still gave her the creeps. He'd gone AWOL for about half an hour, but since he'd come back up, he'd continued to follow her around the room. She'd considered approaching him on it, but as it was her first night and bearing in mind, she didn't want to cause any waves, she'd let it go. Barry had had longer than his allowance, and she thought she'd best tackle him on this. She thought he was maybe testing her, and she needed to show her authority as she was supposed to be the manager of these girls after all. When he came out, she approached him.

'That was longer than you are allowed, wasn't it Barry? I think we need to establish some ground rules here. Twenty minutes you are allowed, so please ensure you only take your twenty minutes. I don't want any grief from Mr. Malik, and I'm sure you don't either, so can we stick to the twenty minutes in future?'

Barry just smiled a sarcastic smile and went and sat down in his chair. Raquel kept her composure and calmly walked over to Barry. 'Look, let's get one thing straight. These girls work for me, so what I say in here goes. I've dealt with men like you all my life Barry so please do not try and play me for a fool. I'll let this go tonight, but any repeat, and we'll have to sort it out, okay?'

Barry smiled sarcastically again and said with a hint of sarcasm.

'Whatever you say, Rachel.' He emphasised the Rachel a bit too much for Raquel's liking. She walked away and felt a tinge of trepidation in her stomach. *Did he know something?* She thought. She walked through to the office and pondered. He couldn't know something, she assured herself. *How could he?* she kept asking herself. She'd never met him before. He didn't look familiar. She quickly dismissed it as sarcasm on Barry's part and went to the kitchen to make herself a coffee. She was beginning to tire now, especially as she'd been up since seven the previous morning. She knew she would not get much sleep when she got back to the digs, mainly because she'd be waiting for morning so she could get off up to Daniel's house. She'd ring him first to make sure he'd be around. If not, she'd just go to meet him wherever he was going to be.

At just gone 4.00am the last of the night's punters had gone through the doors back downstairs. Raquel was knackered. She'd nearly been up a whole twenty-four hours, she thought to herself, and had got enough information during this first night to tell Daniel that she was sure would make him sort these two out. She needed to get some sleep first, though. She planned to get her head down wherever she could as soon as she got to the digs. She knew they wouldn't be pretty, but she was that tired she didn't really care at that moment in time. Brenda came up to her.

'So, where you laying your head tonight, Rachel?' she asked. 'Well, Akrad told me that I needed to stay with the girls in their digs for a week or two until he was sure I would work out for him. I came up from

London to see them and basically had to accept the job straight away. He said he'd look elsewhere if I didn't accept it there and then, and to be honest, Brenda I was in no hurry to go back to London, so I just said I'd take it. I don't suppose you know what these digs are like, do you? I thought about asking Barry, but he gives me the creeps.' Brenda shook her head.

'Sorry Luv, but I've no idea. I think Tracey might though.' Brenda turned her head. 'Tracey' she shouted, 'Come here a sec.' Tracey came through supping a mug of coffee. 'What's these digs like that the girls sleep in. Any idea?' Brenda asked.

'Why, who's sleeping there like?' Tracey replied puzzled. Brenda nodded towards Raquel.

'I am,' Raquel said.

'Bloody hell Rachel. I don't envy you. They're bloody minging. It's just a decrepit terraced house. Three bedrooms upstairs plus a bedroom downstairs that was the dining room I think, then a living type room and a kitchen. About twenty girls sleep in there all told. They're packed like bloody sardines. Akrad has two of his men there at all times on a sort of rota, twenty-four-seven, so they are kept an eye on at all times.'

Brenda looked at Raquel. 'You can stay at mine Rachel. I've got a spare room; well, I've got two actually since all mine left home. It's only a three-bed council house, but it's clean. I'm a stickler for my home being clean Rachel. Tell her Tracey; it's clean innit?' Tracey nodded.

'She's obsessed with cleaning. I'd stay there if I were you, definitely.'

Raquel pondered for a moment. She knew that Akrad and Barraq would not like this, plus if she stayed at the digs, she'd get a little more info, but then she thought to herself that she had enough already. Daniel just would not let them get away with this, and Frank certainly wouldn't. He would take it as a personal vendetta to sort these two out. She decided to take Brenda up on her offer as she needed a good sleep.

'Great Brenda, that'll be lovely. I'll let Barry know.' Raquel walked through into the waiting area and up to Barry. 'I'm gonna stay with Brenda tonight. She's very kindly offered me a bed, and after the long day I've had I need a comfy bed to sleep in, so I'll not be coming back with you to the digs.' Barry looked startled.

'You can't,' he said. 'I have to take you to the digs. That's my orders. I can't go off my orders from Mr. Malik.' He seemed very agitated. He stood up and just moved nervously around on the spot, not really knowing where to look or what to do.

'Look, it'll be okay,' Raquel said. 'I'll take the rap from Akrad if there is any. I'm sure he's not too fussed where I sleep tonight.'

Barry was looking even more stressed. 'I have to go' he said. 'I have to see Mr Malik.' With that Barry scuttled out of the office and beckoned all of the girls with him. They all dutifully followed. Raquel suddenly felt as though she should go with the girls. She nearly blurted out that she'd go with them but then quickly remembered that they'd all be sleeping in exactly the same place whether she was there or not. She told herself that they were not her responsibility and that she'd done enough by being here tonight. She just prayed that she was right and that the underage girls were all that Frank and Daniel would need. If it wasn't, then she'd have to take the wrath of Akrad tomorrow and be back here for a few more days. That was something she didn't want to have to do.

Barry was looking for Akrad and Barraq downstairs, but they'd already left to make their way to the digs. They wanted to be there to welcome Raquel to the accommodation. The last of the downstairs clients were just drinking up and being ushered out by the security staff. The general manager Najeeb was wanting to lock up.

'He's not here, Barry, for fuck's sake. Just get going. I need to get this place locked up.' Barry hurried out, made sure all the girls were there, and sat in his van waiting for the three women to come out.

Raquel, Brenda, and Tracey came downstairs. 'Shall I follow you then Brenda?' Raquel asked. Brenda said she'd go with Raquel as she always got a lift off Tracey, so Raquel and Brenda got in Raquel's car, and Tracey drove off in her own. Barry left the car park a minute or so later.

Brenda lit a cigarette and then said, 'It's only five- or six-minutes drive Rachel at this time of night. I'll make us an Irish coffee when we get in, and then I'll show you your room. Have you got anything to sleep in?' Raquel had brought some provisions from home.

'Yeah, I brought a few things just in case. Not much mind, but I'll just have to buy a few new things tomorrow. As soon as I get up, I'll shoot off and get a few clothes, so if I'm not there when you wake up, that's where I'll be.'

Barry arrived at the digs. He saw Akrad's car parked a few doors down. He was a little nervous. He didn't know whether Akrad would blame him or not. He got the girls out as normal and counted them in. They all scurried straight upstairs to bag the best bunks. Barry would normally have a quick coffee and then shoot off home and leave them with whoever Akrad had as the minders. Tonight, was different though. Barry walked into the kitchen. He looked at Akrad and then looked at the floor.

'She's gone to Brenda's boss.' he said. Akrad took a step forward.

'She's fucking what?'

'She's gone to Brenda's. Brenda offered her a room at her house 'cos she must have a spare room, so she took her up on it. I tried to tell her Boss, I really did, but she was adamant she needed a good rest after her long day. I couldn't force her, could I?' Akrad got hold of Barry's ear.

'That's exactly what you should have done, ya piece of shit. Do you realise who you are working for, eh? We're not a piss pot outfit here ya know. And you're telling me that you couldn't get a fucking whore over here like I asked you to.' Akrad slapped Barry hard with the back of his hand, cutting his lip. Barry staggered but stayed standing. He pointed his forefinger hard into his cheek. 'Next time you fail to carry out my instruction Barry ya fuckin' done for. Understand?' He slapped him again, hard making the cut on his lip even bigger. It was now bleeding quite fast. Barry kept his gaze to the floor.

Barraq spoke. 'Do we know where this Brenda tart lives?'

Akrad shook his head. 'Do we fuck. Tracey brought her in, didn't she? I know where Tracey lives, but not Brenda.' Barry raised his hand. 'What's up Barry? You want to say something?' Akrad barked. Barry nodded. 'Well, come on, then spit it out,' Akrad shouted.

Barry stuttered a little. 'I know that Brenda lives

a few doors down from Tracey 'cos I heard her telling Rachel, or Raquel, whatever her name is. Plus, I know what car that Raquel is driving 'cos I saw it in the car park before I left.' He took a piece of paper out of his pocket. 'This is the registration number. I wrote it down when she drove off with Brenda in the passenger seat.'

Akrad placed his hands around Barry's face and planted a kiss on the top of his head. 'I take it all back Barry. Fuckin' brilliant.' Barry managed a little smile as he wiped some blood from his mouth.

'Right then. We need to go to Tracey's. Find the car and then get that whore out of Brenda's house. We'll take her to the house on Baker's Lane, that's empty innit?' Akrad asked. Barraq nodded. Akrad and Barraq left to go to Tracey's house. Barry was left in the kitchen with the two minders. He didn't fancy a coffee. He just left and walked the mile or so to his house.

Fifteen minutes later, Akrad and Barraq were outside what they assumed was Brenda's house. Raquel's car was parked outside on the road, and it was the only house in the street other than Tracey's with any lights on. They both stood at the end of the pathway. They heard some talking and looked round. It was Tracey's babysitter leaving Tracey's house. They saw Tracey as she walked to the end of her path and wave the babysitter goodbye. She didn't see them.

Akrad turned to Barraq. 'Right, when the door is answered, we just very politely ask to see Rachel. We just say we wanted to make sure she was okay. That should get us invited in without any commotion. Once we're in leave it to me, okay?' Barraq nodded. They walked up the pathway and knocked on the door. A few seconds later, Brenda answered. She looked shocked.

'Mr. Malik, Mr. Syed. What a surprise.' Akrad took a step forward and invited himself in. Barraq followed. They stood in the hallway.

'We heard that you'd very kindly offered Rachel a room, Brenda. That was most kind. We just wanted to see how Rachel's first night had gone. You know, make sure she'd enjoyed it and all that.' Akrad said, smiling. Raquel could hear the voices from the living room where she was sat supping her Irish coffee. She instantly knew this was not good. She knew that Akrad and Barraq would not concern themselves with her welfare at this time of the night without very good reason. She knew they would not concern themselves with her welfare at any time of the day. She was unsure what to do. Her mind was racing. It was racing so much she took a gulp of her coffee and nearly burnt the roof of her mouth off. She coughed and spluttered as she spat the coffee back into the mug as it was too hot to drink all at once. Her experience had taught her that when you are unsure what to do, the best thing is to do nothing. She placed her mug on the coaster on the coffee table as she heard Brenda invite them in for a coffee.

'Hello, Rachel,' Akrad said, smiling. 'How was the night? Did you enjoy it?' He sat down on the settee next to her. Barraq sat in the armchair near the door.

'Yes, it was a good night, Mr. Malik. Very busy, busier than I'd expect for such a new club, but then again, I presume you are well known for these types of services, what with your other club.' He patted her knee and again smiled at her.

'Yes, we are a busy little club. We give good service you see. Now tell me, is it as busy as the Main Vault in Nottingham?' He squeezed her knee hard. She tried not to wince. Her mind was racing again. They knew. *Shit* she thought to herself. She tried desperately to try and remember the script she had played out in her head for this eventuality. She'd told herself that if this happened, she must remain calm, remain focused, and not let her facial expressions or body language take over her composure. Her face remained expressionless as she replied, 'The Main Vault? I don't know what you mean, Mr. Malik.'

Akrad again smiled at her as he said, 'Mmm.' She was unsure what was coming next. She didn't have time to react as Akrad slapped her across the face. It stung but did not bleed. She checked her mouth with the back of her hand. Akrad continued.

'I'll ask you once more, Raquel... it is Raquel, isn't it? Is our club as busy as The Main Vault?'

Again, Raquel replied, 'I don't know what you mean Mr. Malik.' Akrad slapped her harder across the face. This time it bled. She saw the blood on the back of her hand. She had tears in her eyes. Brenda had come through from the kitchen with two mugs of coffee and dropped them the instant she saw Akrad slap Raquel.

'What's going on?' she asked. You could hear the fear in her voice. Barraq stood up. 'Mr. Malik is just having an appraisal with his newest member of staff Brenda. As you can see it's not going too well. Have you had your appraisal yet?'

'Err, no Mr. Syed,' Brenda replied. The fear still in her voice.

'Would you like one now?' Barraq asked.

'Err, no thank you, Mr. Syed.'

'Good. Well, I suggest you sit down and keep quiet and remember, anything that's said in an appraisal between employer and employee is strictly confidential.

Do you get my drift?'

'Yes, Mr. Syed.' Brenda was shaking. She didn't want any of this. She only wanted to make a few quid cash in hand to top up her benefits. Easy money, Tracey had said to her. As she sat there trying to stop her knees from shaking, she wished she'd not offered her spare room to Rachel, but then Brenda had always been a soft touch. She'd lived in the same house since she'd just turned nineteen years old and was streetwise but would give you her last penny. That'd often been her downfall.

Akrad squeezed Raquel's cheeks hard as he put his face into hers.

'You, ya fucking whore are coming with us. Say goodbye to Brenda as it's the last time you'll ever see her.' Akrad more or less picked Raquel up by her cheeks. He continued, 'Frank Pearson will rue the day he ever thought he could mess with us Raquel.' He looked at Brenda. 'Not a word, Brenda. If you mention this to anyone, I'll slit ya throat. Understand?' Brenda nodded, crying quietly. She wanted to say goodbye to Raquel but dare not speak. She just looked at the floor as they marched her out.

chapter thirty-three

Richie could not sleep. He was lying awake in his bedroom, staring at the ceiling. It was starting to get light, and he could hear the birds singing. He liked to listen to the birds. It provided him with comfort. It made him feel good and gave him a sense of calm and security for some reason. He was thinking about Goldie. His head hurt from where his dad had punched him. He would think about all the punch-ups he'd had at the football, all the times they'd been outnumbered, and he'd just steamed straight in, without a care in the world, but he couldn't bring himself to hit his dad. He was unsure whether this was down to fear of Frank or down to respect for his father. Maybe it was a bit of both, but it bothered Richie. He often wished he had the balls to take his dad on.

Richie turned over towards the window and looked at the beam of light coming through the curtains. He thought how Goldie would never see that beam of light again. He thought about how Goldie would never hear the birds sing again. He thought about Goldie's parents and how he would have to face his mother. Richie had always got on with Goldie's mother. He always felt she understood him, that she knew how he was feeling somehow, especially with his dad Frank. She had idolised Goldie, and Richie knew she would take it really hard. Richie turned back onto his back and again stared at the ceiling. He thought about the funeral and wondered how he would cope with the guilt. Would he be able to get through it? Would he break down and confess? The weight of the guilt was preying heavily on his mind. He was not sure he could cope with this. Maybe this was what his dad always referred to when he would say, "...this kind of life's not for everyone. Some people just cannot deal with the consequences of this life. Some people just aren't cut out for it".

Richie thought that maybe he just had to accept that he wasn't cut out for this kind of life. Maybe all the violence, hatred, power, and deceit just wasn't for him. As he lay there, he thought that perhaps his mask would finally slip, but then he remembered that this life was all he knew. He'd worn a mask all his life. He'd tried to emulate Daniel and please Frank for as long as he could remember. He didn't know how to do anything else. He didn't know what he looked like without a mask. He didn't really know who the real Richie Pearson was. He knew he'd never known who the real Richie Pearson was. Unless some rival gangster gunned down Frank and Daniel, he would never be free of the mask. He thought about that eventuality and how that might free him to stop pretending and to be himself. He laughed to himself inside. *That would never happen,* he thought. He'd not met the man yet who could bring down Frank Pearson, but then he realised there were many men he'd not yet met. He sat up in bed and looked around the room. He walked to his en suite and splashed some water onto his face. He looked in the mirror at the mask. He looked hard for a good two minutes. He lent onto the washbasin and looked into the mirror, and said out loud, 'This is the only life you know Richie, swallow it down and move on. Goldie's death was an accident. Shit happens.' He knew in that moment that he'd deal with the funeral and put it to bed. He had to. It was a shit life for Richie, but it was the only one he was ever going to get. He decided as he looked in that mirror that he was going to make of it the best he could. If he had to walk over people on the way up, then so be it. He'd just make sure that they were not there if he ever met them on the way back down.

chapter thirty-four

Raquel looked at the run-down terraced houses as she arrived in Bakers Lane with Akrad and Barraq. She had no idea where she was, but Bakers Lane didn't look like the type of street where you got a warm welcome. Most of the houses looked like they were ready to fall down. The car pulled up outside number thirty-four. Akrad made a call, and thirty seconds later, a guy opened the door. He was dressed in tracksuit bottoms, trainers, and a plain white t-shirt that had seen better days. He yawned as he stood on the step with both hands down the front of his tracksuit bottoms. Akrad wound down the window. The guy nodded and said, 'Morning.'

Akrad replied, 'you alone?' The guy nodded.

'Yeah, got here five minutes ago. It's empty. Only me here.' Akrad turned to look at Barraq over his shoulder.

'Get her out and into the house.'

Raquel was manhandled out of the car and marched into the house. It was now fairly light, and there were a few lights on in various houses. She walked through the front door and was taken through into the middle room, just before the kitchen. The window into the yard was blacked out, so there was no natural light. The light bulb in the centre of the room was rather dim. It was a grim place to be. Raquel had decided to stay quiet. She was working on the theory that she was either going to be used as bait to get a reaction out of Daniel or Frank, or she was going to be used as bait for a string of clients to do with as they pleased. She preferred the first option as she was sure that if Akrad tried to take on Daniel and Frank, that he'd lose. She could see the light at the end of the tunnel with that scenario. The second option where she thought she might be used as a sex slave was far less attractive to her. She liked sex and liked the sex trade, but she much preferred to have sex with nice-looking, nice-smelling men in nice surroundings rather than the dump she was in right now. She'd also realised in the car that she'd left her handbag at Brenda's house that had her new mobile phone in it. She had no way of communicating with anyone. She felt vulnerable.

The guy in the tracksuit bottoms got hold of her from behind and held her hands behind her back. Akrad punched her. It hurt. She could feel blood trickling from her nose. He got hold of her face. 'You,' he said, 'Are going to tell me everything you know about the Pearson's operations. You're shagging old Danny boy, we all know that, so he must have confided in you in between you sucking his dick' Raquel kept his gaze. She did not want to show fear. She was scared alright, scared shitless, but she'd learnt early on in this game that if you show fear, you're finished. She'd mastered the art of holding the gaze whilst, in reality, her stomach was churning.

'I don't know anything, Mr. Malik. Why would they tell me anything? I merely work for them, nothing else.' She owed a great deal of gratitude to Daniel, and there was no way she was going to sell him down the river. If she did get out of this alive having told Akrad anything she'd never work in the industry again and would be on the run from the Pearsons for the rest of her life. Daniel and Frank looked after their own.

They'd go the extra mile to make sure their people were well looked after but go against them, and they'd come after anyone, no matter how loyal and well thought of you thought you'd been.

'Well, not Spanish after all?' Akrad commented, laughing. 'More north London, I'd say. I must say, though, it was a good effort. I really did think the accent was real. You have a talent there, Raquel.' He slapped her hard with the back of his hand. Her face now looked a mess. Her nose and lips were bleeding, and the right side of her face was bruised and swollen. The guy in the tracksuit let her go and pushed her to the floor. Akrad turned to Barraq.

'How quickly can Stubby get a photo developed?' he asked.

'Half an hour or so,' Barraq replied. Akrad took a camera out of his pocket.

'Get her up,' he ordered the guy in the tracksuit. Whilst the other guy held her upright and with her face in view, Akrad took a series of photos. He passed the camera to Barraq.

'Here, get this over to Stubby's house pronto. I want the photos back here with you within the hour.'

Barraq snatched the camera from Akrad, 'I'm not one of your lackeys ya know, talking to me like a piece of shit.' Barraq barked.

'Sorry man, point taken. Can you get it back here asap, though?' Akrad responded quite apologetically. 'Quick as I can,' Barraq replied as he shot out of the door.

chapter thirty-five

Brenda was sat in her living room. About ten minutes after Raquel had left with Akrad and Barraq she'd noticed that Raquel's handbag was down the side of the sofa where she had been sat. She'd looked in it and found her mobile phone. Brenda didn't have a mobile. She didn't want one. She just said that she'd managed to reach her sixties without one, so why would she need one now. She had no idea how to use it. She pondered for a moment, thinking about what Akrad had said about slitting her throat if she told anyone, but she knew that Tracey would know how to use it, and maybe there was a phone number in there somewhere that would mean they could notify someone of what had happened to Raquel. She got up and paced the room, holding the phone in her hand. She was scared to do anything but also knew that Raquel needed help.

Brenda had never been involved in any criminal activity in her life before and only got involved in an attempt to top up her pension. She couldn't survive on a pension alone, and who would employ her at her age. She didn't really enjoy the role she'd managed to get through Tracey, but she certainly liked the money. This wasn't about the money though, for Brenda. Brenda was a good soul who would do you a good turn rather than a wrong one, and she knew that poor old Raquel needed a good turn. She decided that she couldn't get Tracey involved. Tracey had kids to look after, dependants. Brenda's kids had all flown the nest. She thought of Ronnie. He was her youngest. Twenty-five-years-old. Worked in Dixons and was technically minded. He would know this phone inside out. She knew what she had to do. She was trembling as she put her shoes on. She struggled to tie the laces. She stopped just as she'd tied the second pair. *What are you doing?* She thought to herself. *They'll slit ya bloody throat, girl.* She looked at the phone, looked at her watch. Just gone 6:00am. Ronnie would still be asleep. He didn't get up until 7:00am. Creature of habit was Ronnie. She walked through to her kitchen, put the kettle on, and decided to have a cup of tea to calm her nerves. She needed to think.

chapter thirty-six

Akrad had made himself a coffee. He sipped it whilst all the time looking at Raquel. He took out his phone and dialled a number. Still, he stared at Raquel. He had to leave a message.

'Bonnie, it's Akrad Malik, from Leicester. I have a job for you if you're interested. Can you call me back, please? You should have my number.'

Raquel felt a shudder down her spine. Her eyes widened. Bonnie? She knew of Bonnie. She'd heard the name many times, more recently whilst working for Daniel and Frank but also previously in her former life in London. Bonnie was well-known within the criminal underworld, and as a whore, as a high-class whore as Raquel had been, you got to know a little more than you should do. Raquel's life as a hooker was not a quick shag in the back of a car or round the back of some warehousing unit. Raquel had spent most of the time on her back in a hotel room or some rich guy's house. Pillow talk was more prevalent in those situations, and men of power loved to talk about themselves. A bit too much a lot of the time. Men of power who liked high-class hookers loved to try and impress by telling tales of their criminal activities, not realising that the hooker couldn't give a shit so long as she was getting paid.

Bonnie's name would crop up now and again, especially in phone calls that these guys made or received. They would often forget that the hooker was there; they were so far up themselves. If Bonnie was to come and do a job on Raquel, then she was in trouble big time. People that Bonnie tortured didn't come out of it well. There were always pieces missing. Bonnie liked inflicting pain on people. He took pride in his work. Raquel had picked that much up. Now she was scared and was struggling to hide it. She felt sick. The only hope she had was that Bonnie was away on holiday or something and that's why he didn't answer the phone. Her mind was racing. She was desperately trying to think of what she could do here. It was fruitless. She was alone, in this shit hole of a house with two guys, one of which was waiting for a call back from an underworld torturer. She'd been in a few hairy situations before but nothing like this. She'd always prided herself on dealing with any situation she found herself in, but this was different. She could take a few punches and a few slaps and could even cope with it if Akrad used her as a sex object for his clients but faced with the prospect of Bonnie filled her with dread.

'I noticed your reaction to the name Bonnie, Raquel. Know of him, do you?' Raquel had been aware of her reaction. It was instinctive. Even the coolest cookie couldn't beat body language and natural reactions to things. That was nature, and man had not yet found a way to beat it.

'No, never heard of him, Akrad. Friend of yours, is he?' She replied, trying to be as calm and in control as she could.

'Not a friend of such, more of a business associate. Someone called upon in times of need. You know when certain jobs need doing, and only certain men can do them.' Raquel tried to remain calm. Akrad's phone rang. 'Hello,' he said. 'Ah, Bonnie, thank you for calling back.'

chapter thirty-seven

Brenda looked at her watch. Quarter to seven. Ronnie would be up soon. She knew he'd be able to find things on this phone, but Brenda didn't know what he should be looking for. She then remembered what Akrad had said to Raquel just before they'd left. Something about a Frank Pearson would rue the day he thought he could take on Akrad. Brenda had no idea who Frank Pearson was but went to the drawer to get a pen and a bit of paper. She wrote down the name. *Right,* Brenda thought to herself. *Are you going to Ronnie's or not?'* she picked up the phone and slammed the door.

chapter thirty-eight

Bonnie was surprised to hear from Akrad Malik. He'd only ever done one job for him before about six months previously. He didn't really like Akrad. Thought he was too full of himself and a good example of what was going wrong with the criminal fraternity. No morals, no standards, and just bringing the whole criminal arena into the public view. The old school villains kept it all behind closed doors, all between themselves out of the view of Joe public, whereas people like Akrad Malik thought it okay to be brazen about it all.

'So, what can I do for you, Akrad?' Bonnie asked.

'Got a job for you if you're interested—someone I need sorting out. I need to send a message to their employer, so I need them marked good and proper,' Akrad replied.

'Well, that's right up my street Akrad, as you know. Do you want him just marked for life or do you want things missing 'cos the price will be dependant on what you want me to do to him, as I'm sure you're aware?'

'Something missing would be a nice touch, Bonnie. So, how much?' All the time Akrad was watching Raquel for signs of fear. She was holding his gaze and concentrating hard on not showing any signs that she was scared.

'Fifteen hundred quid. Usual price.'

'I thought so, just wanted to make sure I'm not paying any more than the going rate,' Akrad replied.

'Oh, and it's not a he; it's a she.'

Bonnie was taken aback. He'd never tortured a female before, ever. It had just never cropped up before. He'd never even considered it would. I mean, which self-respecting criminal, high enough up the food chain to be requiring Bonnie's services on occasion, would even think of torturing a woman? This was new territory to Bonnie. He was speechless. His dislike of Akrad Malik had just intensified tenfold. He was struggling to keep his composure and professionalism, the two things he was renowned for, other than his torturing skills. He wanted to find out who this woman was before he did anything else. She could be one of his client's wives, daughters, anyone. This was something he needed to tread very carefully on. It just didn't sit right with him.

'You still there, Bonnie? Akrad asked.

'Yes, still here. A woman you say? Mmm interesting. May I ask who the lucky lady is?'

'Yeah, Raquel Carter, one of Frank Pearson's hookers. Long story which I haven't got time to go into now, but she's the one shagging his son Daniel. Why problem?'

Bonnie thought quickly. 'No problem to me, Akrad. When and where am I to bring my tools?' he asked.

'This afternoon too soon? Akrad replied.

'No, that's fine. I'm free this afternoon. As I'm sure, you are aware, it's either a feast or famine in this game.'

'Good. Three o'clock then this afternoon. Thirty-Four Bakers Lane, Thurmaston, just outside Leicester. I'm sure you'll find it. Any problems, give us a ring, and I'll direct you in.'

Look forward to it, Akrad. See you later then. Payment in advance though. You'll be there, I presume?'

'Fuck me Bonnie, you'll get ya money, don't worry.

Yes, I'll be here. I'm going home to get some kip as soon as Barraq is back. I've been up all night with this tart.'

'Good. Money can sometimes be a tricky subject, so always good to get it cleared up before I start. I remember Barraq. It would be good to see him again if he's gonna be there too?'

'We'll both be here, Bonnie. Don't you fret. I want some good photos to send to old Frank. And that son of his. They've picked on the wrong people this time. Anyway, see you later. Don't be late.'

Bonnie put the phone down and sat back in his chair. 'Well fuck me,' he said to himself out loud. 'You do have a quandary here Bonnie, me old pal.'

Bonnie had never considered torturing a woman. It just didn't happen in this game. He had never even met a criminal who had used his services who he thought would ever even contemplate torturing a woman. They'd never get away with it. Women and children were off-limits. That's just how it was. *In what world did Akrad Malik think that I would ever torture a woman,* he thought to himself as he sat shaking his head in disbelief. 'Things have changed even more than I thought,' he said to himself out loud as he dialled Frank Pearson's number. He was still shaking his head when Frank answered.

chapter thirty-nine

Barraq arrived back at the house just after 7:00am with the photos. They'd all come out fantastically well. Akrad was pleased with them. They showed Raquel's injuries rather well. In fact, they looked worse in the photos than they did in real life. Just what Akrad had wanted. Barraq had picked up a guy called Farooq en route back to the house. Farooq was an enforcer for Akrad and Barraq. Any beatings that needed carried out over and above a few slaps were entrusted to Farooq. He was a trusted member of the team and had grown up with Barraq. He lived in the gym. Pumping iron was his thing, and he had muscles on top of muscles. He was a man of few words. Quite shy but would fuck anything. Always happy to stand back from the crowd but had a lust for violence and a lust for women. He was just as happy dishing out beatings to those who owed money to his bosses as he was shagging any woman he could. Akrad shook his hand and handed him the photos.

'I know this isn't your normal line of work for us Farooq, but I need someone I can trust to deliver these. I'll pay you well for this little trip. All I need you to do is put these through Daniel Pearson's door.'

Farooq interrupted. 'Not Franks?'

'No, Daniel's. He's the one shagging her, so he's the one that will react most to these I'd say. It may have been Frank who put her up to this, but Daniel will react most. He'll involve his daddy anyway. He's such a fucking girl,' Farooq took the photos and shrugged his shoulders.

'Daniel's it is then. What's his address?' Akrad handed him a piece of paper.

'This is it; we believe. It's in a village called Ravenshead. Quite posh, so it'll be a decent place. Once you've delivered them, get in your car, and hang around. Let me know what they do, if anything. Let me know if they come out of the house. Who's there and all that. Understand?' Farooq nodded. Akrad continued. 'He's got my number, so I'll expect a call from him if I've got him right. Once I tell him Bonnie is booked for this afternoon, I reckon he'll want to talk. He'll feel responsible, feel he owes her. That's his fucking weakness. Too many scruples. Ya can't have scruples in this game, can you Raquel?' he said mockingly. 'Mind you, I bet you haven't got too many ya fucking whore' He said as he kicked her. 'Right, me and Barraq are off for a bit of shut-eye. Speak to you later, Farooq.' He turned to the guy in the tracksuit bottoms. 'Tie her up, good and proper. Any lip from her and just fucking whack her, or shag her, whichever takes ya fancy.' They all chuckled. 'Here keep this with you,' Akrad instructed as he threw him a baseball bat.

As Akrad and Barraq left the house, Akrad put his arm around the shoulder of Barraq. 'Within forty-eight hours, we'll be calling the shots in this city. He won't be able to help himself. Frank will want to talk, we'll arrange a meet, all nice and everything, and then we'll have our lads ready. They won't know what fucking hit them,' Akrad punched the air. Barraq was still a little unsure.

chapter forty

Brenda was banging on the door of her youngest son at five past seven. She could hear him coming downstairs.

'Alright, alright, I'm coming,' she heard him shout as he searched the hallway for the keys. She could see his silhouette through the frosted glass of the front door.

'Hello mum, where's the fire?' he said. 'Not like you to be round here at this time. Everything okay?'

Brenda went into her son's neat little semi-detached house. Ronnie made her a cup of tea as she told him what had happened. She told him all about Raquel the night before and all about what had occurred at her house earlier.

'Bloody hell, mum, you can't get involved in this shit. This is not about you having a word with another kid's mum when me and another kid got into an argument, you know. This is serious stuff. Heavy-duty, this is mum. If they find out you've even told me, they'll probably kill you.' Brenda sighed.

'I know that son, but they won't find out, will they, eh? How would they? You're not going to tell them, are you?'

'Too right I'm not mum.' He took her hand and placed it in between both of his. 'Why do you want to get involved? This is not your shit. Ever since I can remember you've always got involved in other people's problems. Always had to lend a hand, sort things out, rescue people. People don't always need rescuing mum. This Raquel, or whatever her name is, made her own choices. She must accept responsibility for them. You had nowt to do with that. You are not to blame for any of this, so just leave it be. She must have known what she was getting herself into. By the sounds of it, this Frank Pearson guy is the one who should be stepping in, not you. You don't know her story. You don't know what brought her to the club last night. She could have blood on her hands, for all you know. She could deserve everything she gets. All I know is mum, if you get involved, you'll regret it. If I were you, I'd leave that shit behind and never go back to that club. Tell Tracey you've done with it. You don't need it. Do it for me, mum. I need you more than this Raquel does.'

Brenda listened to her son intently. He was her youngest, but he was the one she always listened to. He was a good boy who was a hard worker. He'd bought this little semi-detached a couple of years ago. First person in her family ever to own their own home. Some had said he was getting above his station, but Brenda idolised him. She took her hand from his and cupped both her hands around his. She smiled at him.

'You're right, son; I know you're right. I'll leave it, I promise. As you say, it's not my shit.'

Ronnie smiled back. 'Leave the phone here. Bring her handbag round too. You don't want any trace of her in your house.'

'But what shall I say if they ask me for her handbag? She's bound to say she left them at mine.'

'Just say what handbag. Leave them here. I'll get rid of them for you. Trust me, no trace. Forget it ever happened. Go to Tracey's later and tell her you're not going back to the club. Please mum. Get away from this. I know you're pension ain't a fortune, but I'll help out where I can, you know I will.'

Brenda kissed her son's hand. You're a good boy Ronnie. I love you ya know.'

'Give over, mum,' Ronnie smiled. 'Just go and get that handbag.'

chapter forty-one

Frank rang Daniel. 'Get round here now. We have a problem.'

'What's up?'

'Malik and his sidekick have Raquel.'

'Fuck. I'm on my way.'

Daniel quickly got washed and dressed. Phoebe was still asleep. Archie was in his cot. Daniel could hear him gurgling to himself. He kissed him on the forehead before dashing downstairs. He left a note for Phoebe. It just said *Gone to my dad's. Got a problem that needs sorting. Love you, D.*

Daniel jumped in his car and sped off towards Papplewick. It was only about ten minutes to his dad's house in a car. Straight down the A60. He rang Raquel's phone. No answer. He tried it again, no answer. He left a message this time.

'Raquel, it's me, Daniel. Ring me as soon as you get this message. Need to know you are okay?'

He didn't want to say too much in the message. He hoped she'd return his call. When he arrived, his dad was standing on the drive awaiting his arrival. He saw Gloria's car parked in front of the double garage. His dad walked straight back into the house as Daniel got out of the driver's side. Frank was in the kitchen. Daniel spoke first.

'How do you know she's in trouble?'

'Bonnie rang me.'

'Bonnie? Why was Bonnie ringing you?'

'Akrad Malik had rung him. Needed a job doing later today. Tells Bonnie it's a woman. Now, this doesn't sit well with Bonnie. He's not into torturing women. Anyway, he asks who it is and finds out it's Raquel. Malik even tells him she works for us and wants her tortured to send a message to us. So, Bonnie rings me straight away. Now that doesn't sit well with Bonnie either. He's always prided himself on his discretion, confidentiality, and all that, but he felt he had no choice. So, this gives us a major problem, and that problem is that I had to assure Bonnie that we'd kill this Akrad and Barraq so that no one, except us, will ever know that he broke a client's confidentiality.'

Daniel stood there leaning on the worktop, shaking his head. 'Fucking hell, Dad. I didn't see this coming. How the fuck did they know so quickly who she was and that she worked for us?'

'No idea, Son. If anyone, I'd say that Steven fucking Wallace. I still don't trust that fucker. Bonnie should have killed him when you shot his brother.'

'It won't be him, dad. I'm telling ya. He's on side. I've had him watching them two for a few weeks, from a distance. He's with us believe me.'

'Well, someone must have told 'em 'cos they've never set foot in The Main Vault. I know that for a fact. Anyway, we need a plan pronto 'cos Bonnie's due there at three this afternoon, so whatever you had planned, cancel it. By teatime, them fuckers need to be sorted. Have you tried her phone?'

'Yeah, twice, no answer.'

Frank stroked his chin. He did this when he was thinking. 'Go and wake your brother up. He needs to be in on this. He's your number two now, by the looks of things these days. I'll ring Jez, Brian, Pat, and Bob and get them all here. Gloria will make us all some breakfast.'

Daniel came downstairs a minute or so later. 'He's not in his bed. Must have gone out early. Morning Gloria'

'Morning handsome. Scrambled egg alright?'

'Yeah lovely, thanks.'

Frank looked up. 'He's gone out?' When?'

'I don't know. I don't live here, do I? Maybe he's gone for a walk. Clear his head. He did have a bit of a traumatic day yesterday, remember.'

Frank sighed. 'Didn't we all. Looks like today's gonna be just as eventful.'

Three-quarters of an hour or so later, Jez and Brian had arrived. They were sat at the table waiting for Gloria to do their bacon sandwiches. Frank was upstairs having a shower. Daniel was sat mulling over in his head how they could have known. He just could not work it out. Pat and Bob had not yet arrived. Pat was coming from Leeds and Bob from Derby. The house phone rang. It was Phoebe. Gloria answered the phone. Phoebe asked for Daniel. Daniel took the phone from Gloria.

'Hi Luv, you okay?' he asked. Phoebe sounded stressed. 'Not really. I need you to come home. Someone has just posted some photographs through our door. The person in them looks like that Raquel lady. I've only seen her a couple of times but I'm sure it's her. You need to see them.'

'I'm on my way.'

Daniel grabbed his keys. 'Tell Frank I'll be straight back, but I need to pick something up from my house. Some photos of Raquel.'

Neither Jez nor Brian spoke as they were both

munching on a mouthful of bacon sandwiches, but they both nodded in unison. Gloria stood there rooted to the spot for a second or two. Daniel slammed the door just as Frank came downstairs rubbing his head with a towel.

'Where's he gone?' he said.

On his way back, he tried Raquel's phone three more times. Still no answer. Daniel arrived home to find Phoebe in the kitchen. He failed to notice the strange dark blue Escort parked about fifty feet down the road on the opposite side. Daniel's street was a very affluent street. Ford Escorts were seldom parked on that road. He put his arm around Phoebe.

'You okay, Luv?' he asked. She gripped him tight.

'Yeah, I'm okay. Just a bit shocked, that's all.' She pulled away and took the photos off the worktop. 'These are them. It's her, isn't it?'

Before she could hand them to him, he stormed outside onto the drive.

'I can't fucking believe someone has the front to post these through my house,' he raged. He ran around the back of the house, looking in the hedges, looking in the trees and bushes. 'With my wife and child inside,' he shouted as he walked. He came back inside. 'Did you see anyone?' he asked Phoebe.

'No, no one. I didn't even hear the letterbox go. I was upstairs getting Archie up. I came downstairs, and there they were on the mat. I can't have been upstairs more than two or three minutes, though.'

'I'll kill 'em, Phoebe. I'll fucking kill 'em for this.'

'Look, calm down. We're okay, and they're probably long gone now. No one would be brave enough or stupid enough to hang around our house any longer than was necessary, would they, eh?

Daniel sighed. 'No, probably not Luv, but I still can't believe they've done this. Anyway, let's have a look at them.' As Daniel looked at them, he felt a surge of rage inside. Yes, it was Raquel. His rage was partly because he felt responsible, partly because he felt his authority was being threatened, and partly because he felt a real closeness to Raquel. It wasn't love. He knew that because he loved Phoebe, and it was different, but he was still very fond of Raquel. Fond enough to do almost anything for her. He snapped out of his trance. 'Listen, Luv; I've gotta go. I need to get these back round to me dad's. Got a lot of shit to do today. This needs sorting and will be today. Do you want to come with me?'

'Look, you go, and I'll get Archie fed and ready, and I'll follow you in half an hour or so.' Daniel kissed her on the forehead. 'I'll stay, and we can go together.'

'Stop fussing. You're like an old woman,' she said playfully. 'I'm a big girl ya know. We'll be at Frank's before you know it. Is Gloria there?'

'Yeah, she is. Half an hour or I send the search party out. Deal?'

'Deal,' she said. They shook on it.

'Any noise or anything at all, and you ring me, yeah? And don't answer the door to anyone,' Daniel said loudly as he walked to the door. Phoebe picked Archie up and followed Daniel to the front door. She stood in the doorway with Archie in her arms. Daniel walked around the back of the house again and then came back about thirty seconds later.

'All clear, Luv. As you say, they'll be on their way back to Leicester now. Half an hour, don't forget.'

Phoebe blew him a kiss. Farooq watched intently through the trees and the railings. He ran back to his car as Daniel started his engine. He still failed to notice the dark blue Ford Escort parked on the opposite side of the road.

As Daniel drove away, Phoebe felt a pang of jealousy inside her for the first time in her life. She'd noticed the way Daniel had looked at the photos. She'd noticed there was real emotion in his face. A little more than she'd have expected. She'd never been jealous of the way he always seemed to put business first. He was like that when she met him. She knew from the very start that she'd always come second to the family business. Power and respect in Daniel's world would always come before her. This was just another example. She'd expected nothing less. She knew he'd shoot straight back off with the photos. That was business. Something needed to be taken care of. She understood that. Always had, but he'd been in some sort of trance as he looked at those photos. He'd looked at them longingly somehow, even lovingly. She put the thoughts to the back of her mind as she continued to feed Archie. *Come on, chop-chop, we only have half an hour, big man,'* she said to Archie as she gave him his bottle.

Farooq dialled Akrad's number. He had to leave a message. He assumed Akrad was fast asleep.

'Boss, it's me. Your man has just come back to the house, and then within five minutes has sped off again, so I assume he's now got the photos. Job done. I'm getting off. Might see you later?' Farooq was about to go when he took the keys out from underneath the steering wheel. He looked towards Daniel's house and smiled to himself as he just realised that the nice-looking totty, he'd seen through the bushes was now on her own. He opened the door, got out of the car, and walked towards the house.

chapter forty-two

Frank was at the head of the dining room table as usual. It was a big table. Very grand. Enough to seat eighteen people. Eight chairs down each side and one at each end. At the table with Frank was Daniel, Jez, Brian, and Bob. Pat was ten minutes away. Richie was still AWOL. Frank spoke.

'Right gents, as you all know we have some serious business to attend to. Pat will be here soon, but as for Richie, no one knows where he is. He's not answering his phone. According to Bonnie, he is to meet Akrad Malik and Barraq Syed at a place in Leicester at three this afternoon.' Frank put on his glasses and picked up a piece of paper. 'Thirty-Four Bakers Lane it is in some place called Thurmaston. You know Thurmaston Daniel?' Frank asked.

'Yeah. Pretty well. Don't know where Bakers Lane is but one of my men will know, so it should be easy enough to find.'

'Good. Leave that with you then. So, we know both Barraq and Akrad will be there, but we don't know who else will be. We know someone posted these photos of Raquel through Daniel's door this morning, but we've no idea who. We assume it's someone from Leicester sent by Akrad and Barraq.'

Brian interrupted... 'So, does anyone know where Richie is?'

'No, as I've said already, Brian, he wasn't in his bed

when Daniel went to wake him up.'

'Well, I've thought it, so I'm gonna say it,' Brian continued. Frank interrupted him before he could get another word out.

'If you're gonna say what I think you're gonna say, I'd think again.'

Brian pondered for a second... 'Well, you must have thought it too, Frank?'

Frank took off his glasses and pointed them at Brian. 'Let's just get one thing straight shall we, and this goes for anyone,' Frank looked around the table as he continued. 'Richie, for all his faults, is still my son and his brother.' He pointed specifically to Daniel... 'And there's no fucking way he posted those photos. If anyone wants to say differently, speak now, but let me tell you guys, I wouldn't recommend it.' No one spoke. 'Right, that's that theory put to bed. Let's continue.'

Daniel had not considered the coincidence of Richie being AWOL, and some mysterious person putting some photos of Raquel through his door, but he did now. He was not listening to Frank's delivery. It was just noise in the background as he thought this theory through. Thankfully, Pat arriving broke up proceedings. This gave Daniel a few minutes to think this through. His mind was racing. *Surely not Richie,* he thought to himself, but he remembered how Richie would not have known that Bonnie would have rung Frank and that Frank would have summoned Daniel over immediately. Maybe Richie had posted them as he thought Daniel would be at home. He tried to convince himself that he was wrong. He looked at his watch. Twenty minutes since he'd left her and Archie. His wife and child were alone in that house. *What if Richie were watching the house to see what Daniel did when he'd seen the photos?'* He thought. *What if it wasn't Richie and someone else was watching the house?* He thought. He remembered he'd only checked the house and gardens. No, he thought, *he'd only checked the gardens. He'd not checked the house, or the street, or next door.*

Frank spoke. 'Right now, that Pat's got a brew, we can continue.' Daniel stood up. 'Frank, I need to go. Phoebe's on her own in that house with Archie. I checked the garden but not the house. I need to go. I've got a bad feeling.'

Jez stood up. 'I'll come with you Daniel,' Frank told him to sit down. 'I'm coming with you, Son. You lot stay here with Gloria. Come on Daniel, get ya keys.'

Frank and Daniel went. Everyone else sat there in silence. Gloria came in.

'Here's ya bacon sarnie, Pat,' she said.

Richie had walked for miles. Thinking about Goldie mainly and about the football days. The good times they had. He thought about when Birmingham came up one cold Tuesday night and brought hundreds of lads. They were massively outnumbered that night and got run all over town. Even Goldie ran, and he couldn't run 'cos of his size. He thought about Burnley away when both teams were pushing for promotion, he thought about Italia 90 and the nights in the station trying to get some kip, and he thought about the riots on Sutton Road after Mansfield had won the freight Rover trophy in 1987. He'd walked aimlessly, not really knowing where he was going. He couldn't tell you where he'd walked, but as he came back to reality for a moment, he realised he was in Daniel's road. He stopped and paused for a moment.

How had he ended up here?' he thought. He told himself it must have been his subconscious mind leading him here. He'd been here many times before. He'd never walked it though, so he smiled to himself as he thought of how powerful the mind was. It was so powerful it knew where you were going even if you didn't. He decided he may as well pop in for a coffee whilst he was here. *I might even get a lift home,* he thought to himself. He walked up the road past a couple of BMWs, a Mazda MX5, and a Ford Escort. He stopped at the Escort. He used to have one. He had an XR3i though. This was a 1.6L. He remembered how he'd loved his XR3i. He turned into Daniel's drive and noticed Daniel's car was gone. Phoebe's was there, though. That was okay 'cos Phoebe made a better coffee anyway. The door was open. As he approached the door, he could hear Phoebe scream. 'Get off me, you bastard.' Richie ran into the house. He ran into the kitchen but realised the screams were coming from the lounge. He ran through and saw a huge guy on top of Phoebe trying to get her skirt up. Phoebe was lashing out at him. He instinctively ran towards them and tried to pull the guy off her. Farooq lashed out with his huge arm and caught Richie across the face. He staggered back. Farooq stood up and turned around. Phoebe scrambled to get from under him. Richie composed himself. Farooq was massive. His biceps were about as thick as Richie's thighs. Richie was in Football mode. His hooligan days took over. He ran straight towards the guy he'd just dragged off Phoebe, taking Farooq by surprise and kicked him straight between the legs. It took the wind out of Farooq, who bent over, and Richie punched him hard twice in the face. Farooq hardly moved. He stood up and got hold of Richie by the neck with his left hand and punched him repeatedly with his right fist. Richie's face was spouting blood. Farooq threw him to the ground. Richie struggled to try and get up. Farooq kicked him hard in the head. Richie lay motionless on the cream carpet, blood seeping from his face and head. Farooq then dropped to his knees and then fell forward, landing on top of Richie. Phoebe stood there with the kitchen knife in her hand. It was covered in blood. She dropped it on the carpet. She didn't move. She just stared at the two lifeless bodies on the floor. She heard a car pull onto the drive, and both car doors slam shut. She looked at the door and saw Daniel and Frank run in. They both stopped dead as they saw what was in front of them. Two bodies both bloodied, and Phoebe stood there with blood all over her. The knife was on the carpet at her feet. Daniel rushed over. He hugged her tight. He kissed her face multiple times. 'Are you okay?' he said. She nodded. She wiped the tears from her eyes with the back of her blood-stained hands. 'Is Richie okay? Please check if he's okay. He came from nowhere, dragged the guy off me. Please tell me he's not dead.'

Frank dragged Farooq off Richie. Richie was motionless but breathing. He looked in a bad way. His head and face were swollen quite badly. Frank then made three phone calls.

'Jez, it's me. Get yourselves over to Daniel's place now. Bring Gloria. I need her to look after little Archie. You'll see when you get here.'

'Tommy, it's Frank. I need a clean-up pronto. Daniel's house in Ravenshead. One body, carpets, the usual stuff. No trace by teatime. Okay? Good man. I'll have ya payment tomorrow.'

'Derek, it's Frank. My boy Richie needs looking

after. May need a hospital bed. No comebacks. He's at Daniel's house in a bad way. How long before someone can get here?' Frank waited on the phone for around twenty seconds. 'Great. I'll still be here when they arrive.'

He'd struggled to hear the people on the other end of the phone as Daniel rained blows down on the body of Farooq. He was venting all the anger he had inside of him. He punched and kicked the lifeless body. 'How fucking dare you come into my house,' he shouted. 'I'll kill the fucking lot of you. Every single one of you.'

Frank and Phoebe stood and watched. Phoebe rushed to pick up Archie from his moses basket who had started to cry. She held him to her, trying her best to comfort him, but she did not want to get any blood on him. She and Frank both understood Daniel's need to react like this. They both knew what he would be feeling. Phoebe wanted to comfort him but knew it was best to leave him alone. Archie needed her. Frank also understood. He understood how Daniel would feel, that he should have been here, he should have been the one to kill this intruder, but instead, his wife had to protect herself. He would take that hard. Frank knew that. In their world, this kind of feeling was hard to swallow down. A feeling that you'd failed, that you'd not protected those nearest to you. Even though Daniel had not been here, he would feel responsible and a failure. Frank let him get it out of his system.

Once Daniel had stopped beating the body, he stood up and took a step back. Breathing hard, he wiped the sweat from his brow. Frank looked at Phoebe and nodded. That was his signal that he would deal with this. He walked over to Daniel and put both of his hands on Daniel's shoulders. He stood square on. He needed to show control and composure in the absence of Daniel doing so.

'Save this anger for this afternoon, Son. Remember what I've always taught you. Remember, in times like this, you must remain calm. I know how you're feeling. You feel responsible, like you should have done something, but you can't change what's done. You weren't here; you couldn't have done anything. I know because that's how I felt when I lost your mother. I should have been in the room. I should have made the decision. I should have been there at her side, but I wasn't, and I lost her, but I had to learn that I can't change the past and look what it's done to Richie and me all these years. We can't change what's happened. Your wife and child are still here; they love you, so let it go, stay calm, stay focused. You did what you thought was right at the time. Losing the plot won't change anything. All that will do is make you make irrational, snap decisions. I need you focused. I need that anger stored for later today. That's when you let it out. When we have them where we want them. Be a leader, be the man, that's what you are Son, a leader.'

Frank hugged Daniel, and Daniel hugged him back. No words were said, there was no need. Frank had said what he needed to say, and Daniel had listened. Phoebe put Archie down and joined in the hug.

Frank bent down and again made sure Richie was breathing. He saw Daniel and Phoebe had gone into the downstairs bathroom. Phoebe was getting cleaned up. Daniel hugged her tight. Phoebe was crying uncontrollably and was quite hysterical.

'What's going to happen to me, Daniel? I've just killed someone. They'll lock me up. They'll take Archie away from me. I'll get life, won't I?' she sobbed.

Daniel held both her shoulders as he spoke. 'Phoebe, look at me.' She stayed looking at the floor. He took her chin with his right hand and brought her eyes to meet his. 'Listen to me. Nothing will happen. We will sort this out. My dad's already made the necessary calls. This will all be cleaned up within a few hours. They'll be no trace of that guy or anything in this house. These guys my dad has rung are professionals at this. It's what they do. All you have to do Sweetpea, is hold it together. What you did out there was completely justified. He was in your house. Archie was here. He was trying to rape you. You did nothing wrong. You need to be strong though Luv, but I assure you no one will ever know. I'm proud of you.' He held her tight again. She felt his warm body close to hers, and she squeezed it tight. She didn't want to let go of that feeling she got when she hugged Daniel close, the feeling of strength and security. She'd smiled inside when he'd called her Sweetpea. He always used to call her that when they first met, but it had been a while. It made her feel warm inside. She pulled away and looked at him.

'I know you're right, Daniel. It was justified. I was just protecting what was ours, especially Archie. I'm comfortable with what I did... the bastard!' They both laughed quietly, although that last comment cut deep with Daniel. He knew Phoebe had not realised what she'd just said, but she was right. She was protecting what was theirs, including Archie. That hurt Daniel, but he had to swallow it down. Phoebe had had to do the protecting this time, and that made Daniel feel like shit. Phoebe felt Daniel's strong arms again as they hugged once more.

'Come on, let's get you properly cleaned up, eh?' Daniel said as he gave her a loving kiss.

Frank looked at Farooq. He turned him over and took a mobile and a set of car keys out of his pocket. He put the keys in his pocket and looked at the call history on the phone. The last call made was seventeen minutes ago to Akrad. Frank now knew that this was the guy who had delivered the photos. In a way, he was pleased, as at least that meant there was no one else they had to worry about. At least Phoebe's attacker and the guy who had delivered the photos of Raquel were one and the same. This was now all-out war, though. It was now personal. Frank seethed as he stood at Daniel's doorway, waiting for Jez and the others to arrive. How dare they bring it to his son and heir's house. How dare they involve his daughter-in-law Phoebe. How dare they think they can take on Frank Pearson on his own doorstep. Frank was seething, just like Daniel, but no one would have known. He was in control. Frank had dealt with many situations over the years, dealing with many men who thought they could take his mantle, but this was something else. Previously these matters had been dealt with between themselves. Man-to-man. That was the way it was. That was how it always had been, but now it seemed the new wave of wannabe gangsters were bringing it into people's homes, involving women and children. This was a new breed. A new breed that needed stamping out. Frank knew what he had to do. If Akrad Malik and Barraq Syed wanted things to get personal, then so be it. Frank would personally inflict as much pain on them as he could. Three o'clock couldn't come quick enough. He made another call just as he saw Jez's car pull into the drive.

'Bonnie, it's Frank. Listen, I don't need you there this afternoon. I just need you to say you're gonna be there if they contact you today to confirm, which they probably will. I'll tell you the reasons why when I see you 'cos I'll still pay you your whack for today. You won't be out of pocket. Just make sure they think you're going and just make sure they are gonna be at that house for three this afternoon, cheers Bonnie, I owe you.' Frank turned and walked back into the house. Jez and the others followed him in. Gloria followed behind. Jez stopped in his tracks.

'Fucking hell Frank, a good start to the day,' Frank walked through to the kitchen. Come through, lads. Board meeting continues in here. He kissed Gloria on the forehead. 'Archie's in his moses basket, Luv.'

Phoebe came out of the bathroom looking a little better. She hugged Gloria. 'You can tell me about it later, don't worry about Archie. I've come in my own car. I'll take him back with me to Frank's. He'll be fine.'

Phoebe thanked Gloria and then sat on the carpet next to Richie and stroked his head. He opened his eyes. He looked at Phoebe and managed to say, 'Where is the fucker? Has he gone?'

Phoebe just said, 'He's gone for good Richie. We did him,' Richie smiled. He tried to get up. 'Fuckin' hell me head hurts.'

'Just stay lying down,' she said to him. 'Frank's rung someone to take care of you. They'll be here soon. I heard him say something about you may need a hospital bed or something. Best thing for you. Get some rest.'

Richie sat back down. 'I take it you did that?' He looked over at Farooq. Phoebe nodded.

'He'd have raped me if you hadn't have got here when you did. Where did you come from?'

'I don't know to be honest, Phoebe. I couldn't sleep,

so I just got up and went for a walk. I was just thinking about Goldie, ya know, after what happened yesterday. I just walked and walked, and when I sort of came back to earth, I was in your road. Must have just been subconsciously walking here. Fuck knows how I ended up in your road 'cos I've never walked it before. I tell ya what, though, I've had a shit couple of days, what with Goldie dying yesterday. Then when me dad got home last night, he hit me and knocked me out, then I come here today, and that big fucker knocks me out too. I bet I look a right state. I must have bruises on top of bruises. I tell ya something; I'm sick of being knocked about. Who is that guy anyway, and what's going on in the kitchen? Have I missed something?'

Phoebe told him about the photos and Raquel. She didn't know the full tale about Raquel but knew enough to give Richie the gist of things. Richie tried again to get up.

'I fucking told him this would happen. They never fucking listen to me.' He managed to get to his feet. He held his face. Phoebe stood up to assist him.

'Told them what? She asked.

'Not to send Raquel down to Leicester. I knew she'd be in danger. She didn't deserve that. Where are the photos?'

'Daniel's got them I think, or maybe Frank?'

Richie opened the kitchen door. Everyone looked at him. He looked like he'd been ten rounds with Frank Bruno.

He looked at Daniel. 'I fucking knew this would happen. I told ya, didn't I. Ya never listen to me. Where are the photos?'

'Get back in the living room, Richie. You're in no fit state to contribute to this meeting.' Frank barked.

'In no fit state?... no fit state?... that's 'cos I was getting that fucker in there off his wife cos he...' Richie pointed to Daniel, 'because he insisted on sending Raquel down there. If he'd have listened to me, none of this would have happened. He was only sent up here with them photos of Raquel 'cos she was there in the first place 'cos ...' he walked up to Daniel... ' He fuckin' sent her in there. Thinks he knows it all. The mighty Daniel.' Richie half turned his body towards the door into the living room and pointed with his right hand. 'He was gonna fucking rape her ya know. Good job I was here.'

Daniel stepped forward. 'And what were you doing here, eh?... bit of a coincidence, don't ya think? The very morning, we get a mystery package delivered, and then once I've left the house, the incredible hulk in there gets in. Funny that ain't it, and at the same time you're fucking AWOL!'

Frank stepped in between them. He faced Richie. 'Causing trouble again, aren't you? Just go back in there and wait for Derek.' Frank looked at his watch. 'He'll be here any minute. You need looking after. We've got business to attend to.'

Richie shook his head. 'Always the fucking same. Well, go and do ya fucking business then. I'm done with it, done with the lot of ya. I don't need this shit. I get beaten half to death trying to save Phoebe, and that tosser thinks I'm part of it. And you must think so too 'cos you ain't corrected him. Well, you can all fuck off,' Richie staggered back into the lounge and sat down on the floor. Two minutes later, Derek arrived with a medical crew. They took Richie with them to sort him out. He struggled to hold back the tears. Phoebe stood and watched, tears trickling down her face. She knew Richie had nothing to do with it. The way he'd tackled the guy she'd murdered and the way he was genuinely surprised when she told him of the photos and Raquel convinced her of that. Daniel's accusations had angered her. He would normally have accepted responsibility for his actions and decisions. He always did. He never shirked responsibility, but here he was acting out of character. Phoebe felt the pang of jealousy once more.

The atmosphere in the kitchen was tense. Frank needed to bring it back to some order. 'Right gentleman,' he continued, 'back to business. Daniel will make a few calls and get a couple of his men on watch at Bakers Lane. Jez, I want you, Brian, Pat, Bob, Del, and Michael, to be waiting around 2:00pm at Leicester Forest East services. Daniel reckons it's about twenty minutes to Thurmaston. Akrad and Barraq will be there. They'll be expecting Bonnie. They'll possibly have some other men there too. You can take shooters plus the usual bats, and so on. I want this to be swift. No fucking about. You get Akrad and Barraq plus whoever else they have there back to Arnold, back to the lock-up, on our turf. Me and Daniel will be waiting there for you. We're gonna torture the fucking life out of them and smile whilst we do it.' Frank then looked at Daniel. 'I then want both of their clubs torched and any other venture they are involved in. I want every aspect of their criminal empire wiped off the face of the earth. Like they never existed, and Jez, make sure Raquel is okay. Make sure you designate someone to look after her and bring her to my house. You can use the car that Daniel's two men will be in. They'll have to make their own way back to wherever they live.'

Jez chipped in, 'What about their homes, their families?'

'That's not our style Jez, you know that. They are not involved in this, so we leave them alone.'

Jez nodded. 'Just thought 'cos of what happened here you might want to repay them in the same way.'

'No, that's not how we operate, never has been and never will be. We deal with the people we need to. The innocents are left alone. They'll have the grief to deal with but that's not our problem. You can all go in a white van. Brian, ring Del and tell him to sort out a plain white van pronto, pick up Michael, and bring him to my house within the hour. Everything clear, gents?' They all nodded. Frank could hear some voices coming from the lounge. He walked through to see Tommy and the clean-up team making a start.

'Morning Tommy.'

'Morning Frank. Busy night, was it?' Tommy asked with the usual sarcasm. 'Busy morning Tommy, busy morning. Busy day too. I might need you again before teatime so keep ya phone on.' Tommy laughed.

Frank's phone rang. It was Sean Bishop. Frank answered. 'What's up, Bish?' Bishop sounded anxious. 'What's up? What the fuck's going on at your Daniel's house. We've had three phone calls about a major disturbance. Do I need to be concerned?'

'Only if you poke y' fucking nose in. Keep your boys away from Ravenshead for the next few hours. If I as much as think I've seen a police car on this road today, I'll put ya knackers in a vice. Everything's sorted. No need to worry your little arses about anything. Okay?'

'You'll get me fucking strung up one of these days,' Bishop replied.

'No Sean, one day you'll do that all by yourself,'

Frank disconnected the call.

Daniel put his arm around Phoebe. 'You did well today. I'm sorry I left you. I shouldn't have done. I'll never do that again. I should have taken you with me.' Phoebe lent into him.

'Look, I was the one who insisted you went. I'm okay. I was a bit shook up earlier, I mean, killing someone does that to you, but I'm fine. Surprisingly fine. He deserved it. The scumbag.'

Daniel smiled. That was as aggressive as Phoebe ever usually got. Calling someone a scumbag. He didn't think she had it in her to kill anyone. She turned to face him and took his chin in her hand. She looked him squarely in the eye. 'Richie was not part of this. You've got that wrong—massively wrong Daniel Pearson. I will fall out with you if you continue to say such things. He saved me from a possible rape today Daniel. You should remember that.'

Daniel dropped his head. He knew she was right. Trying to blame Richie in some way was him just trying to make himself feel better. He knew deep down he'd left his own wife and child alone in a house minutes after someone had posted those photos through the door, and he knew the reason he'd done that was because he already felt he'd let Raquel down by putting her in danger. He felt responsible for that, and as a consequence, he'd not taken responsibility for his own wife and child. He'd now let them all down, and he felt like shit. Blaming Richie was just Daniel trying to heal himself. He knew that and that made him feel like shit too. He just hoped that by tonight he'd feel better with himself after he'd taken care of Akrad and Barraq. He looked up at Phoebe.

'I know, I've been a first-class wanker today. Come on, let's leave Tommy and his lads to it.' They walked out the door and drove to Frank's house. Still, no one noticed the blue Ford Escort parked on the street. When they got there, Daniel picked up Archie and told him never to be a wanker. Phoebe playfully slapped him on the top of the head and told him not to swear when holding the baby.

Thirty-five minutes later, a white plain transit van arrived with Del and Michael in the front. Five minutes after that, the van drove out of Frank's long, impressive drive. Frank and Daniel watched it as it turned left. Their men were on their way to Leicester Forest East services.

chapter forty-three

Akrad woke up and listened to the message from Farooq. He smiled and punched the air *Fucking brilliant; now the fun will begin,* he said to himself out loud. He fully expected a call from either Frank or Daniel Pearson today. He looked at his watch. Nearly midday. *Mmm,* he thought. *I'd have expected a call before now.* He said to himself as he turned on the shower and then took the top off the tube of toothpaste. As he brushed his teeth, he thought of what to do if there was no call. He hadn't thought of a plan B. He'd been one-hundred percent sure that his actions would have initiated a phone call. Even if he'd misjudged the Pearsons' affections for Raquel, and they didn't care about her, he was sure that the very fact that one of his men had managed to drop off some photos to Daniel's house would invoke a reaction of some sort. A threatening phone call at least, but as of yet nothing. He placed his toothbrush back into the holder and stared at himself in the mirror. No reaction was not a good thing, he told himself. That meant he had no idea what they had thought to it all or what they were planning if anything. This would put them on the front foot and him and Barraq squarely on the back foot. That was not the plan. He took a deep breath and said to himself in the mirror, *"So, come on Akrad, what's the plan for no reaction?"* He looked silently at himself, and he realised that he had no plan for this. He took his shower, got dressed, and went downstairs to make himself something to eat. He couldn't go to his parents' house today for some lunch as he often did. He needed to be at the house for 2.00pm to ensure he was there in plenty of time for Bonnie. *Bonnie,* he thought to himself. *Yes, ring Bonnie.* He dialled Bonnie's number and waited for an answer. Bonnie answered after four rings.

'Bonnie, it's Akrad. How are you, all set for this afternoon?' Akrad tried to sound authoritative.

'Sure am, Akrad. I'll be leaving shortly and will aim to be at the property at 3:00pm as arranged. Everything still as we discussed?' he asked.

Akrad replied, 'Yes, all still the same as far as we are concerned. I assume you've not heard anything then, ya know from the Pearsons or anyone?'

Bonnie was surprised at this remark, but he thought he knew why it was being asked. 'Not a thing. Why would I?'

'No reason, just wondered that's all.'

'Okay, see you later then,' Bonnie replied and then disconnected the call.

Akrad put his phone down and put the kettle on. He was sure that Bonnie had not heard anything from them. Like Bonnie said, why would he? They had no idea that Bonnie was going to be involved. They had no idea where Raquel was. She didn't have a phone. They'd checked her. He was sure they had. He was only 99% sure, though. He began to doubt himself. He rang Jay, the guy at the house in the tracksuit bottoms.

'Jay, it's me. Everything okay?'

Jay sounded like he'd just woken up. 'Yeah, no bother. She's still here. Been asleep most of the time. She tried to stay awake and stare me out, but she gave in after a bit and has been nodding on and off for a while.'

'Check to see if she's got a phone?' Akrad ordered. 'She ain't got one, Boss. Well, I ain't seen one anyway.

Akrad was now annoyed, 'I didn't ask if she'd got one. I asked you to check. Now go and fucking check. Frisk her all over. I want to know if she's got a phone.'

Jay knew he'd overstepped the mark there. He knew it was always best to do as you were asked. Akrad stayed on the line. He could hear Raquel shouting at Jay 'To keep his dirty hands to himself' and Jay telling her to 'keep her fucking mouth shut.' Jay came back to the phone. 'No phone, Boss. She's got nothing, no money, no phone, no handbag, or anything. Just the clothes she's wearing.'

'Okay, see you later,' Akrad put the phone down. It had been five in the morning to be fair, but he was annoyed as he should have realised. He pondered for a while as he stirred his coffee. He then thought of Brenda. He sat down at the table and took a sip. He knew that Raquel would have taken her handbag to Brenda's as that's where she was staying. He wanted to get the phone. He rang Farooq. It went to voicemail.

'Farooq, it's Akrad. Listen, I assume you'll be back in Leicester by now after your little trip north this morning. Ring me back when you get this message as I need you to get that Raquel's handbag and phone from a house where she left them last night. I'll give you details when I speak to you.' He replaced his phone on the table. He sat back in the chair. He still could not work out why there had been no phone call. This worried him slightly. For the first time in the whole affair, he felt a tinge of fear. He didn't like the fact that Frank or Daniel Pearson had not been in touch. He didn't feel in control. He rang Barraq. Barraq had been woken up by the call. He answered it to hear Akrad's voice. It sounded a little deflated.

'It's me, listen we've had no phone call, and I know they've had the photos 'cos Farooq confirmed it all to me in a message on my phone. What d'ya think?'

Barraq didn't like this. He'd been nervous about it all from the start.

'I'll come round. Quarter of an hour. Stick the kettle on,' Barraq put the phone on his bedside table and thought, *fuck!*

Frank and Daniel were sat having a brew at Frank's kitchen Island. He listened to Akrad's message on Farooq's phone. He smiled to himself when he thought that they still thought Farooq was alive and well. At least they now knew for sure that Raquel didn't have her phone with her, and that's why no one had answered any of Daniel's attempts.

Barraq arrived at Akrad's house. There were two mugs of coffee on the table. Barraq sat down. This was one of those occasions where even though they were equal partners in their business, it was clear when shit happened that Akrad was the real boss.

'So, what's the plan?' Barraq asked whilst supping his coffee. Akrad took a deep breath and sat back, quite relaxed.

'I've thought about it more since we spoke mate, and at the end of the day, we don't know anything, so let's just stick with the plan. We're in control here. Fuck 'em. They can't know anything. If they don't respond today before we meet Bonnie, then we crack on regardless. Maybe that will get them talking to us. They are the ones who need to react, so until they do, let's stick to what we were planning. We're overthinking this Barraq. Trust me. Anyway, have you heard from Farooq?

Barraq was still unsure about all this. He was nervous about the fact that the Pearsons hadn't reacted to the photos. He was concerned that maybe they had, but him and Akrad just didn't know it yet. 'No, nothing, I thought you had.'

'Yeah, he left me a message to say he'd delivered the photos and that he was sure that Daniel had seen them, but I rang him earlier as I want him to call round to Brenda's to pick up Raquel's handbag. She must have left it there 'cos she ain't got it now, and it's not in my car. He's not rung me back.'

Barraq smiled and took another swig of his coffee. 'He'll be either at the gym or shagging a bird. You know what he's like.'

Akrad stood up and put his mug in the sink. 'Right come on then, we'll go to Brenda's en route to the house. It's not much of a detour.' he noted that Barraq seemed sluggish in his movements. He didn't spring up like he was excited at this afternoon's events. He thought he should be like a coiled spring. This alarmed Akrad a little. 'What's up? You don't seem too enthused about today?'

Barraq stopped and looked at Akrad. 'These are heavy-duty these Pearsons ya know Akrad. Don't underestimate them, that's all I'm saying.'

Akrad looked at Barraq and saw that his best pal was scared. Was he scared of taking the Pearsons on or scared of sorting them out and being catapulted into the big time? He was unsure which. He'd never seen Barraq scared before. He wasn't worried about Barraq's pedigree. He knew he'd take a bullet for Akrad. He decided that maybe Barraq's cautious approach was a good thing. It would keep him in check.

'Look mate, I know this is new territory for us, but I'm telling ya, no news is good news. It means they are cautious of us. If they thought we were small fry, they'd have been on the blower threatening all sorts. They'd be on their way down to sort it out. But where are they, eh? Nowhere. If you ask me, they'll be sat in Frank's house trying to think of a way to come to some sort of agreement. They know now that we can't be walked over. They tried to get one up on us with that hooker we have locked up, but we were smarter than them. Raquel will be tortured this afternoon by Bonnie, and then we'll drop her off right outside their club in Nottingham, where she worked. That Main Vault place. That will show 'em that we mean business. Agreed?'

Barraq nodded. Akrad put his arms around his shoulders. 'We're the fucking top boys now in Leicester. Make no mistake. Sorted?' Again, Barraq nodded like a puppy, but he still couldn't shake the awful feeling he had in his stomach.

At 1:10pm Akrad and Barraq pulled up outside Brenda's house. The front bedroom curtains were closed. They assumed she'd be asleep. Raquel's car was still parked outside. They looked inside the car. No handbag or phone. They knocked loudly on the front door for a good three minutes before Brenda opened it. She was stood there in her nightie and dressing gown. She looked rough. Akrad walked straight in and sat down in the living room. Barraq did likewise. They both waited for Brenda to speak. She looked nervous.

'I wasn't expecting you Mr. Malik,' she said as she nervously looked for a lighter to light her fag with.

'Ah, well, full of surprises Brenda, you know me.

Anyway, we have just called round to pick up Raquel's handbag. She says she left them here earlier. Left in a rush didn't we. Where is it, do you know?'

Brenda lit her fag, just. Her hands were shaking so much it was a wonder she lit it at all.

'Are you okay Brenda, you seem nervous?' Barraq asked. He took a step forward towards her as he did so. She felt intimidated by his movement.

'Err, yes, thank you. Just a bit shocked to see you that's all. Err, handbag you say. I can't remember her having one. Let me look upstairs in the room she was going to use,' Brenda was failing to make any eye contact with either of them, and Akrad saw this as a sign she was lying.

'I'll come upstairs with you,' he said as he got up from the settee. He followed her upstairs. Barraq took the opportunity to search downstairs for it. Brenda tried to look convincing as she searched the bedroom and upstairs bathroom for any sign of the handbag that she knew were at her son Ronnie's. She'd just caught him before he'd left for work. She was so glad she had. She was also pleased she'd listened to him and wished he were with her now.

'There's no handbag here, Mr. Malik, she must have taken it with her, or maybe she left it at the club?' Akrad got hold of Brenda by her hair and dragged her downstairs. She was screaming all the way down. He kept a tight grip right into the living room.

'She's fucking lying Barraq. I know it. I can just tell with her body language' Akrad threw her onto the floor and kicked her hard in her stomach. Brenda was doubled up in pain. The scars from her hysterectomy ten years ago had never healed properly, and the pain from that kick was excruciating. Akrad picked her up.

She was struggling to stand up straight.

'I'll ask you one more time Brenda, where is it?'

Brenda was fighting back the tears. She was determined not to let them see her cry. She'd never let a man see her cry in her life, so she was not going to give these two bastards the satisfaction.

'I don't know Mr. Malik. I didn't see her with one.'

Akrad punched Brenda three times. Her lips and nose were bleeding. She fell to the floor and instinctively curled up in a ball. Barraq kicked her in her back. She squealed in pain. Akrad got on his knees and put his face close to hers.

'Don't bother coming back to our club, Brenda. If I ever see your ugly face again, I'll cut it open. If I ever find out you've hidden that handbag, I'll kill you. Understand?' Brenda nodded, still fighting back the tears. She heard the front door slam as they left her house. She then burst into tears. A mixture of fear, pain, and terror at the thought of what they'd do to her and her son if they ever found out about the handbag and phone. She managed to get up off the floor with the help of the arm of the sofa chair and looked in the mirror. She didn't look good with the blood and tears. She looked like something out of a horror movie. She needed to alert her son of the visit she'd just had. She needed to make sure he'd got rid of the items. She decided to go upstairs, get ready and go to see her son in the shop where he worked. She just hoped he'd been sensible in getting rid of them.

Jez and the others were sat in the services at Leicester Forest East near Junction 21 of the M1 motorway. Jez hated Motorway services. Shit food and crap surroundings, but today he would again endure one as he needed to be able to react quickly and get on the road if needs be. He was in charge of this little operation, and he wanted to make sure it went like clockwork. They'd all had a mug of tea and a sarnie but were now sat back in the van waiting for a call. It was 1:55pm. Daniel had arranged for two of his guys to be parked up on Bakers Lane watching the house. They were to ring Jez as soon as Akrad and Barraq arrived.

Brian looked around the van. A lot of nervous tension was evident. Everyone sat silently with their own thoughts. Even though they were all confident of taking these fuckers out swiftly, it was still a nervous time. Pre-match tension, Richie would say. Although today there was no match, it was a similar situation. Richie wasn't here today. Brian thought of how he would at least lighten the atmosphere. Brian kicked Jez with his foot. Jez looked across.

'Richie would be in his element today, wouldn't he? Pre-match tension and all that bollocks. He'd be like a hot potato.' Jez laughed at Brian's comments.

'Yeah, he'd treat it like an away day. Sat here waiting for the other firm to arrive. Bit different though, when you're going into battle with two of Leicester's gangsters. Mind you, those two aren't gangsters. Just two mouthy upstarts who think they can cut the mustard. We'll show em what real gangsters do, the wankers.'

Jez's phone rang. He answered it. It was Oliver, one of Daniel's men. 'They've just arrived. Just Akrad and Barraq. They've gone in the house. A guy in tracksuit bottoms answered the door.'

Jez looked at everyone one by one. 'Right, we go now,' he said. 'Del, let's go' He put the phone back to his mouth. 'Oliver, wait there and let me know if you see anyone else come or go. We'll be what, twenty minutes or so?' Del started the van and moved off. Jez continued speaking to Oliver. 'Stay in the car when we get there. Do not get out and come in the house. You'll only get in the way. We all know our jobs. Your job is to stay in the car until we tell you differently. Got it?' Oliver told Jez that they would stay put. 'We'll ring you back Oliver, once we get to Thurmaston, and you can guide us in.' With that, Jez disconnected the call. He turned sideways so that he could look into the back of the van.

'Right, gents. We all know what to do. Me and Pat will go straight for Akrad and Barraq. Michael, you see to Raquel. Del, Bob, you two sort the other fucker out who is there. If there's more than the three of them, then we'll have to deal with it as we see fit. We only know there's one other guy with them. Straight in lads, no messing. Don't give them an inch. We take 'em back to the lock-up in Arnold as Frank has asked. Is everyone okay with that?' Everyone nodded.
Raquel heard Akrad and Barraq's voice before they'd walked into the room where she was. She was trying to hold it together. She'd managed to nod off throughout the morning. She looked at her watch. It was just gone 2:00pm. Raquel recalled Akrad's conversation with Bonnie earlier that morning. Three o'clock, Akrad had told Bonnie. Raquel was starting to panic. She thought she might even start to hyperventilate, she was so anxious. Bonnie could do torturous things, and she knew that. He would do whatever was asked of him, and she knew from the conversation that he'd been told to mark her good and proper. Akrad had even mentioned something about, *things missing.* She'd assumed this to mean fingers, toes, eyes, etc. She started to take

deep breaths as Akrad walked in.

'Ah, the star of the show,' he said as he bent down and took her chin in his hands. 'Such a shame for such a beautiful face but, you made your bed Raquel, and the guy who'll be tucking you in will be here very soon.' He looked at his watch. 'Not long now. Just time for me to have a nice brew and to pull up my seat.' He looked into Raquel's eyes, 'you know, that nose of yours is far too perfect. It needs a more natural look to it. You know, bent somehow. Mmm... I think I'll be able to sort that out for you.' He smiled. Raquel felt sick. She wanted to spit in his face, but even though she knew it would make no difference at all, she decided not to out of the faint hope that if she didn't make things worse, they might get a little better for her. She just stayed silent. Akrad got up and walked into the kitchen. He picked up his mug of tea. All three of them were stood huddled in the galley kitchen. Her hands were still tied in front of her. She wondered if Frank or Daniel knew of her situation. She knew some photos had been delivered but had they seen them yet. She looked at her watch - 2:20pm.

Jez rang Oliver, one of the guys in the car. They were about two minutes away. Oliver guided them in. As they pulled into Bakers Lane, Jez noticed that there was shared access to the back of the houses. *Perfect,* he thought. He told Del to pull up outside number twenty-six, four doors away from number thirty-four.

'Right gents, this alleyway here will lead to shared access at the back for number thirty-four. It's just like the terraced houses where I was brought up, so I know the design. It's perfect. We can go in the back door and the front door at the same time. The kitchen is at the back, so Me, Del, and Brian are going round there.

That's where they will be. Pat, you, Bob, and Michael go to the front. Give us ten seconds, and no more mind, and then kick the door in. We'll do the same. Needs to be quick this, as it's a residential street. We beat the fuckers up, then get ya guns out but don't use 'em for fuck's sake. We need 'em in the back of that van pronto. It has got false plates on it Del, hasn't it?'

'Of course, Jez, untraceable.'

Pat piped up. 'How come you think they'll be at the back of the house, Jez?'

"Cos they're waiting for Bonnie, and people wait in the kitchen. That's just what people do. At parties, people congregate in the kitchen. When people are waiting for someone, they wait in the kitchen. It's where the kettle is. Just human nature. Trust me.'

Pat shrugged. 'You should have been a Psychiatrist Jez.'

'I might do once I'm done with all this. Right gents. Let's get these fuckers, and let's get Raquel out of there.'

They all picked up a baseball bat and got out of the van.

Akrad looked at his watch. 2:25pm. 'Bonnie should be here soon lads.' By the time, the sound of the front door being kicked in had registered, the back door had done the same. The three men in the kitchen instinctively reacted by retreating in different directions. They bumped into each other as blows came raining down on them. There was nowhere to go and no room in which to get their hands up. There were now eight bodies crammed into the kitchen. Michael went straight to Raquel as instructed and untied her. He immediately got her out of the house and into the van. He told her to stay there as he went back into the house. Daniel's two lookouts in the Vauxhall Cavalier just sat and watched, mouths wide open. Jez and Bob retreated a couple of steps into the middle room to create some space. Barraq immediately filled the space created. Michael joined in, and the three of them battered him senseless. Pat had hold of Akrad and was biting his nose off. Akrad was screaming in agony. He dragged him outside. He'd dropped his bat in the melee and was slugging it out. Akrad was a handful. Del came out and hit Akrad with his baseball bat so hard he broke his jaw. Akrad staggered. His feet were like jelly.

Del caught him clean on his jaw that was now more or less hanging from his face. Akrad dropped to his knees and passed out with the pain. Pat kicked him three times whilst he was on the floor. Pat and Del chucked him in the van. Del stayed with him. By the time Pat had returned to the house, it was all over. Bob was still banging Barraq's head on the worktop. Jay was done for. Jez got out his gun and marched Barraq and Jay to the van with Michael and Bob. When they'd all got inside the van Jez, put the gun to Akrad's head and told him to look at him. Akrad looked up. Jez looked at his watch. It was 2:31pm.

'You think you're the real deal? Six minutes it's took to take you out, Akrad. Six fucking minutes. You're pathetic. For getting your guy, who's now dead by the way, to go to Daniel's house we're going to torture you for longer than the six minutes it's taken us to deal with you here. Then we're gonna kill you. What you see standing before you is the real deal. What I see kneeling before me is a piece of shit.' He whacked him across the face with the gun.

Raquel and Michael left in the Cavalier. Michael

was instructed to take Raquel to Frank's house to get cleaned up. Then he was told to go to Arnold, where the rest of them would be. Michael was glad he was in the car. He couldn't tell Oliver and his mate to walk home, so he dropped them off on his way back to the motorway. He just hoped that Frank would be okay with that as that would make him late. He hoped with all that Frank had on that he wouldn't notice.

Jez rang Frank. 'All sorted, Frank. Took six minutes in all. Raquel's fine. She's in Oliver's car with Michael. They'll be coming to your house. We'll go straight to the lock-up.' Jez turned around to look into the back of the van. Pat, Brian, and Bob had them under armed guard. He laughed. 'They look fucking terrified, Frank. And to think this shower thought they were gangsters. You'd have pissed yourself mate. Anyway, see you in an hour or so.'

'Fucking brilliant, Jez. We'll see you at the lock-up. Drive carefully now; we don't want anyone pulling you over.'

'Will do, Boss,' Jez looked at Del. 'Frank says to drive carefully.' Del smiled and shook his head. He drove carefully, especially as he had three men in the back with guns.

Akrad could barely bring himself to look at Barraq. He knew they were done for. He knew there was no way out of this. He was so cocky he'd not even took a gun with him to Bakers Lane. He'd not taken any protection with him at all, other than Barraq. He'd been so convinced that no one in Frank's employ could possibly know where Raquel was. The only other person he'd told was Bonnie. *Fucking Bonnie,* he thought to himself. *The fucking grass.* He just stared at the floor as he realised that he'd never get the chance to tell him to his face unless he was going to be wherever they were heading. *Unless he was the torturer,* he thought to himself. Akrad had thought they were the real deal, the top dogs of Leicester, but he knew they'd just received a lesson in planning and cunning from the master himself.

On the way to the lock-up, Frank's phone rang. It was Derek. 'Look Frank, I know you've got a lot on today. I could see that at the house, but I couldn't wait any longer to let you know. Richie had some sort of fit in the ambulance. Probably the result of the beating he took. He's okay now, but I've had to admit him into that private hospital off the ring road for observation. Don't worry. People have been paid. No one will speak a word of it. You owe me the money though.'

'Okay Derek, cheers. I'll see you right.'

Frank put the phone on his lap and thought of Richie. Maybe the punch Frank had given him last night hadn't helped. He looked at Daniel. He was on the phone to Phoebe telling her that he'd make the two guys who put the bastard up to it earlier pay for what they did. He didn't normally involve Phoebe in tales of his criminal activities. She knew the score but had never really shown any interest in knowing the gritty details. That way, she could pretend it wasn't happening. Today though, was different. She was involved. She was deeply involved. She'd done the killing, albeit justified in her book, and everyone else's, but she'd still joined the ranks of Britain's murderers. Frank decided to say nothing until they'd sorted Akrad and his men. He and Daniel would then go and see Richie at the hospital. Daniel finished his call.

'Phoebe thinks that twat from this morning came

in a dark blue Escort. It's been parked on our street all day.' Frank put his hand in his jean's pocket and pulled out a set of keys. 'These will be the keys then,' he said chuckling. 'I forgot about these. I took them off that bloke this morning at your house with his phone. Had them in my pocket all day.'

Daniel took them off his dad. 'Yep, Ford keys these are. We'll need to crush that car asap. Police may be looking for it once that bastard is reported missing.'

Frank agreed.

chapter forty-four

The van arrived at the Arnold lock-up just after 4pm. Frank and Daniel were waiting. Frank shook Jez's hand.

'Great job Jez, great job, all of you, now let's get these three inside quickly.'

'Frank, can I have a word first, please?' said Jez.

'Yes mate, what's up?'

Jez nodded towards the van. 'Let's sit in the van. More private in there.'

Frank was intrigued. They sat in the front of the van—Jez in the driver's seat and Frank in the passenger seat near the window.

'This sounds serious Jez, what's up?'

'Nowt to worry about Frank. I just wanted a word about torching their premises. I just think that would bring heat, excuse the pun, onto us unnecessarily.'

Frank frowned and looked puzzled. 'Not sure I get your drift?' he replied.

Jez continued... 'Well, if you torch their premises, that will involve the old bill, fire brigade, possibly those health and safety people, what they called - HSE or something, aren't they? A whole host of government officials we do not want sniffing around. The old bill knows we are rivals, so they are bound to look in our direction, especially if those three wankers in there are reported missing. You know what the old bill are like with arson. It'll be all over the news, and they will need to conduct thorough investigations. They'll need to give answers, especially with three bodies, plus that guy at Daniel's house. It'll be a nightmare. If it wasn't for the missing bodies, then no problem. I'd agree with you to just torch them, but with that, on top, I think it'll bring them sniffing around big time. You don't need to torch 'em, Frank.'

Frank interrupted...' so what's the alternative?'

'Just dispose of the bodies as usual, so there's no trace. That way, these will just be missing persons. The old bill won't give a flying fuck about them. They'll be glad they're off their patch. Even when the families make a fuss, the old bill will just play it down. They'll know what's happened, but to them, they are just missing persons. No paperwork, no HSE, no fire brigade, no press coverage. It'll go away very quickly. Plus, with them out of the picture, it will leave a void for you to legitimately move in and take over their clubs. No one would blame you for that, not even the old bill. You're a businessman Frank at the end of the day, and if you see a gap...well, you'll fill it. Nice and clean.'

Frank stared out of the front windscreen. He couldn't argue with anything Jez had just said. It made perfect sense. Frank had reacted in a fit of anger when he said he wanted the places torched. Of course, it made sense to take over their businesses. Frank was just annoyed he'd not thought it up himself. He turned to Jez.

'You know what Jez, I'm glad you're on my side. You've got a mind as sharp as a razor. Makes sense, doesn't it?' He put his hand out to shake Jez's once again. 'You're a good man Jez. I only ask one thing of you.'

'What's that, Frank?'

'Don't ever give me cause to kill you.'

They laughed, but Jez knew there was a cryptic message in there somewhere.

Michael was still driving Raquel back to Frank's house. Raquel had not said a word since he'd got in the car. Michael was not very good at making small talk in these situations. He was okay in a crowd when he had an audience to play up to, but these types of situations he found awkward. He tried to think of something to say, but nothing sounded right in his head, given what Raquel had gone through. He'd looked over at her and smiled a couple of times, and she'd smiled back, but it was clear she was happy in her own silence. Michael decided that was best and that he'd just respond if she spoke to him. He drove carefully up the M1, mindful not to draw any attention to himself, especially as Raquel looked like she'd been in the wars. She did look as though she'd been through the mill. He knew that the guys who did this to her would pay dearly, probably with their lives. He thought on the way back up north how he'd gotten into this world. He remembered the night he'd had to go to the club to help his brother Del. The night Frank had received a visit from Gerry Clark from Leeds. Prior to that, he'd done a little bit of work here and there for Frank, through Del, but he'd not been on the payroll. Since that night, though, he'd been a constant figure in Frank's employ. He did enjoy it, but he could not help but ponder as to where it would all end. He thought about whether he would one day be the one being tortured, beaten, or killed. He knew Frank would not reign forever, either old age or the life would get him, although he told himself that either eventuality would be a long way off yet. He indicated to pull off the Motorway into Trowell services, just near

Junction 25. He needed to take a leak. He turned to Raquel. He'd have to speak now.

'I just need to visit the men's room, Raquel. Do you need to go?' Raquel shook her head. 'No, I'm okay, thanks. Could do with a drink, though. If you could get me a can of pop or something? I haven't had anything to drink since first thing this morning.' Michael told her he'd get her something. Raquel sat in the car and watched the people coming and going. People who were working but, on the road, stopping for a leak. Couples sat having a sandwich, everyone oblivious to her and what she'd been through. No one even knew she was there. She was invisible in this car park. She thought about how busy people were with their own lives, ordinary lives, people with ordinary jobs, and ordinary relationships. Something she'd never had. She'd always had a strained relationship with her parents, and since she'd left home, she'd never really had any meaningful relationships. Her only relationships were with the pimps from her time in London and with Daniel and Richie now. She couldn't really call those relationships as such. At the end of the day, she was just sleeping with them both. No relationship there, just sex, but that's how she liked things. She knew this was down to her own choices, decisions she'd made, and roads she'd taken in her life. She thought about all those roads leading to here, sat in a Vauxhall Cavalier in the car park of a motorway service station having been a whisker away from being tortured. She watched the normal people once more go about their normal lives and was glad she wasn't one of them. *How fucking boring,* she thought.

'There you go, can of pop, is that okay?' Michael said as he sat back in the car. I brought you a pasty too, thought you might be hungry. That's all they had left, really.'

Raquel smiled at Michael. 'Thank you,' she said. 'That's really kind of you. I am a little peckish come to think of it.'

Michael drove off and could see Raquel in the corner of his eye munching on the pasty. He felt good inside. Just a little thoughtful thing like that could make all the difference to how someone felt, and he knew he'd just made Raquel feel good.

'What's your name?' Raquel asked. Michael looked over towards her. It had not registered with him that she didn't even know his name.

'Michael,' he said.

'Well, thank you for that pasty, Michael. It was delicious, even for a service station pasty. Just the job.'

Michael felt awkward once more. He was out of his comfort zone again. He just said, 'you're welcome,' and fixed his eyes back on the road.

Frank walked into the lock-up with Jez. Akrad, Barraq, and Jay were each tied to a chair. As much as he wanted to torture the life out of these three, he was also conscious that Richie lay in a hospital bed, and for all the resenting and blaming that Frank did towards Richie when push came to shove, he was his son, and Frank wanted to go and see him. He wouldn't let the others know that, but he knew deep down that he should be at his son's side. He wanted to get this done quicker than he'd initially anticipated. He looked at the three of them. Only Akrad held his gaze. Frank stared at Akrad for a good few seconds. Akrad never dropped his eyes. This impressed Frank. This told Frank that Akrad was the leader, the one with the balls, but also, unfortunately for Akrad, the one who had instigated all of this, especially the visit to Daniel's house. That could not go unpunished. As much as Frank felt a bit of respect for Akrad as he stood there staring at him, he knew that he would have to suffer the most. That's just how this world worked. Frank walked over to Jay, the one who'd kept an eye on Raquel. He sat there trying to look at Frank in the face but could manage no more than a second or two before he would again drop his stare to the floor. He was dressed in grubby trainers, tracksuit bottoms, and a T-shirt that looked like he'd slept in it. He was just a gofer, hired help, someone who wanted to be involved but just on the fringes so that he could muster up some street cred with his mates. Frank knew he'd just been following orders, probably out of fear more than anything else.

Frank wished at that point that he could speak to Raquel to see how this guy had treated her, but that was obviously impossible, so Frank decided there and then that he'd cut the guy some slack and assume he'd not sexually assaulted Raquel in any way. Frank decided to do him quickly. Firstly, because Frank wanted to speed things up and secondly because this guy was just a gofer, doing his job. Frank raised his hand and shot Jay at close range through the forehead. Jay fell backwards on his chair and landed on the ground on his back, still sat in the seat. Barraq nearly jumped out of his seat. If he hadn't been tied to it, he probably would have. Akrad never flinched and stared straight ahead. Frank turned to Daniel.

'That one,' he said, whilst pointing to Akrad, 'is the one you want Daniel. He's the one who most probably sent that fucker to your house. He's yours.' Frank then looked at Del. 'You need to move up in the firm. It's your turn to show us what you can do to people who think they can mess with us.' Frank pointed to Barraq. 'He's yours Del. So, gents, make it painful and make it slow.' He walked over to Akrad and stood in front of him. 'You, my son, will die a painful death. You should never have even thought you could take me on. You've got some front; I'll give you that. Even as you sit there, you're fronting it out. I like that but sending someone to my son's home, my grandson's home?' Frank waved his finger from side to side and shook his head. 'That was a big mistake. For that, you'll suffer some pain.'

Frank went and sat down on the sofa and watched as for the next thirty minutes or so whilst Del and Daniel tortured Akrad and Barraq to death. Akrad, to be fair to him, took it like a man. He hardly squealed up until the moment Daniel poured acid down his throat. Barraq, on the other hand, pleaded for mercy and screamed like a baby. Even Akrad felt embarrassed as he listened to his best friend.

After it was all done, everyone jumped in the van and drove to Frank's house. Michael was still there. He decided to tell Frank that he'd dropped the two lads off on his way out. Frank just patted him on the back and told him it was no problem. Brian immediately went back to the lock-up. Pat followed in his car. They were given the task of disposing of the bodies along with the white Transit van. Bob was handed the keys to the blue Ford Escort still parked on Daniel's street and told to crush it. It had been a long day. Daniel saw to Phoebe and made sure she was still okay. They all sat around the large dining room table as Gloria made them mugs of tea. Raquel came down from upstairs, having been for a shower and a clean-up. Frank hugged her, as did Daniel. Phoebe studied Daniel and

Raquel hard as they embraced. She decided it was nothing more than a friendly hug. Much the same as the hug Frank had given her. She felt happier with no feeling of jealousy. Raquel asked where Richie was, and Frank told her briefly what had happened. Raquel spent the next hour telling everyone there of what she had discovered at Akrad and Barraq's club and what had happened to her when they'd picked her up from Brenda's. The men listened hard, and the women showed affection to Raquel at all the right places. This was a classic example of the differences between men and women even in this game. The men just replied with things like, *the bastards, we should have sorted them fuckers sooner,* whereas the women fussed over Raquel like mother hens saying things such as, *ooh you poor thing,* whilst hugging her for the umpteenth time. Frank looked at his watch. It was 6:50pm. Frank had wanted to be at the hospital at seven. He looked at Daniel and motioned with his head.

'Come on Daniel, we need to go.' Daniel got up. Frank continued. 'We're off to see Richie. We won't be long.' Phoebe got up from her chair.

'Shall I come with you?' she asked as she looked at Daniel.

Before Daniel could speak, Frank said, 'No, just me and Daniel tonight. Not sure what state he'll be in. We won't be long, and hopefully, he'll be up for more visitors tomorrow.'

Phoebe got the message, as did everyone else, and she sat back down. As Frank walked to the car with Daniel, he said, 'We need to talk about those two clubs they ran so we can chat on the way. We need a plan.'

Frank loved his Jaguar X300. He'd not had it long but

just loved the drive. He couldn't remember the last car he'd polished himself, but with this one, he'd happily spend his Sunday mornings with a cloth and a bit of polish. It just oozed class and stature. As he drove it down the A60 towards Nottingham with Daniel, he felt a sense of pride. He loved moments like this where it was just him and Daniel, his firstborn, albeit by a mere fifteen minutes. He didn't get to spend many moments like this with Daniel these days. Frank was so busy keeping his empire going and juggling the balls in the air, and Daniel was so busy running Nottinghamshire and Leicestershire. He wanted to savour the moment but knew he had to move it onto business.

'Me and Jez had a chat earlier before I came into the lock-up. He made a valid point that us torching their two clubs would only bring aggro to our door, so change of plan. We're gonna take 'em over. We can't do that tomorrow as it'll be too quick. Have you still got Chief Inspector Marriott on your payroll?'

'Yeah, still pay him a weekly pension. Not needed him for a while, so he's due to start earning it again.'

'Good. Well, I assume as soon as those two have been reported missing, which will probably be tomorrow at some point, he'll be in touch with you, won't he?'

'I'd expect him to be yes.'

'As soon as he does, let me know. That's when we can move in. Once we are advised by the authorities that they are missing, we can move in. That's what we'd do anyway if they were genuinely missing, so we do exactly what we would normally. We need to move into these clubs quickly though, Son 'cos the last thing we need is another firm trying to move in and having to deal with them as well. We can take 'em over and run them our way. Ya know, treat the women well, treat them as an asset but keep 'em for the lower ends of society. No good changing them too much and competing with ourselves. We can keep our clubs as they are, higher prices, better clientele, and have these two clubs for the cheaper end of the sex market, but we keep the girls happy.'

Daniel agreed. 'We might get some hassle with that Tarriq bloke though that Raquel was on about earlier. Sounds a bit of a face.'

'Leave that to me. I'll speak with Sonny in London. He'll keep this Tarriq bloke in check. If he's dealing in sex workers, then Sonny Johnson will have him in his pocket.'

'What do you think of Raquel, Dad?'

'In what regard?' Frank asked, rather confused by Daniel's question.

'Well, just what do you think of her credentials and abilities? I'm just thinking we'll want our own guys in these clubs, and Raquel could maybe run one of them for us. Maybe make her a partner in it, ya know, as a reward for her keeping her mouth shut and for what she'd been through on our behalf?'

Frank looked at Daniel. 'Are you shagging her or something, lad? I know she's been through it a bit over the last couple of days, but that's the job Daniel. That's just part of the life we all lead. I don't mind her running it if that's what you think, but a partner? No way, Son. This business is ours, a family business. We're the stakeholders, no one else. Don't ever think you're gonna bring other people into our business. Not while I'm alive. Fuck me.'

Daniel knew he'd hit a raw nerve. He decided to leave it. Frank's reaction had told him that was best. Maybe he was thinking with his dick and not his head. Frank had no idea how right he was about Daniel shagging her. Daniel didn't want to carry that conversation on. Frank didn't like extramarital activity. He'd be okay with Richie and Raquel. Richie was single, but if Frank knew about Daniel and Raquel, it would be the end for her. Frank would turf her out onto the street.

'Yeah, you're right Dad, just a suggestion. A daft one all the same. I just feel for her, that's all.'

'Nowt wrong with that, look after those who look after you but don't ever give away any portion of what we have. Not to anyone. That clear?'

'Crystal,' came Daniel's reply.

'Once that Chief Inspector of yours has confirmed things, just let me know. Then we can speak with Raquel.'

About ten minutes later, they walked into Richie's private room. He was asleep. He had a drip in his arm, and his face still looked swollen, but other than that, he looked peaceful. Frank and Daniel sat down and just looked at him. Daniel thought about what he'd said to him earlier that morning about being part of what had happened and felt guilty. For all his faults, he knew Richie wouldn't do that. Daniel knew he'd just been angry at himself. Frank looked at his son and thought about how he'd hit him last night and how he'd intervened earlier that day and again took Daniel's side. No matter how hard Frank tried, he just couldn't bring himself to feel the same for Richie as he did for Daniel. He sat there and thought back to the night Renee died. Daniel went to get two coffees. He brought them back a few minutes later and sat down next to Frank. Richie was still asleep.

Daniel looked at Frank. 'What did you mean earlier today when you said to me that you knew how I felt 'cos you felt the same when mum had died. Ya know, you said that you should have made the decision and that you should have been in the room. What did you mean?'

Frank lowered his head and cupped his hands around the coffee mug. He looked at Daniel, then at Richie, and then again at the floor.

'When your mum died, it was a different era. When women were in labour the men were outside in the corridor. Some would be at the pub, but I was in the corridor. Pacing up and down. We hadn't even known your mum was pregnant until she went into labour. She'd put on a little weight, but nothing like you'd think for someone who was pregnant. She was pleased as she was too thin really. Then suddenly, we're at the hospital. I'm in the corridor thinking I'm gonna be a dad and your mum's in the labour ward having twins. I didn't know it was twins until they came and got me. They just took me into a room and told me that they'd not been able to save your mum, but I was now the proud dad of twins. Fucking twins. Six hours previously, we didn't even know she was having a baby. I was in bits. I'd just lost the most important thing in my life but was expected to be happy 'cos I had twins. I went ballistic. I wanted to know who'd made the decision, why they'd not asked me.' Frank looked at Daniel. 'They told me that you'd come out fine, but they knew at this stage that it was twins, so they were waiting for the next one to come. Fifteen minutes it took. Some complication or something they said, which is why it took him so long to come. I still don't really know what happened other than they said 'he just wasn't coming out, and we had to make a quick decision. We thought you'd want to save your son.' He looked at Richie. 'I'd have saved your mum son; I'd have let Richie die. From that moment on, I didn't want him. He was to blame. There have been moments over the years where I've wobbled and nearly let him get close to me. Times I've nearly forgotten what he did. I don't want to forget. I just want him gone and your mum back. I'd sacrifice him now for one day with your mum. I'll never forget.' Frank got up to leave and put his cup on the trolley. Daniel followed. Richie lay there with a tear rolling down his cheek.

In the corridor, Daniel stopped his dad and turned to face him. 'It wasn't his fault, dad. He was just being born. How could he be at fault? Like you said to me earlier. You weren't there. You weren't in the room. There was nothing you could have done. Do you really think mum would have wanted this? You hating her son? Mum would want you to love him like you love me. Maybe mum sacrificed herself for her two boys. To give you two healthy boys. Time to let it go, dad.'

Daniel turned and walked away. Frank thought about going back into Richie. He took a step towards his room but then hesitated and turned back the other way. He followed Daniel outside and to the car.

Richie wiped the tears from his cheek. He wiped his nose with the back of his left hand. He lay there in silence and fell back to sleep.

chapter forty-five

Chief Inspector Wayne Marriott was forty-five years old. He was around five foot, eight inches tall with a black moustache and pock marked face from acne in his youth. He also had a rather large bulbous nose which all in all made his face rather unappealing. He was quite tubby and looked nothing like a copper. He didn't look like he could run fifty yards, but he was well respected within the force as a catcher of criminals but had one Achilles heal... women. He knew he was not God's gift and would seldom get his leg over unless he paid for it due to his rather large paunch and pockmarked face, but he loved getting his cock wet and seeing as Mrs Marriott was none too active in that department, he loved to frequent Daniel's establishments. This was where Daniel first met him and where Daniel first came to an arrangement. He'd been on the Pearson's payroll for just over two years now and was well and truly in their pocket. He kept the old bill out of Daniel's affairs and in return Daniel allowed him access to the women at the club for free plus a weekly pension. The tide well and truly turned when Daniel showed him photos of himself in an uncompromising position with a few of the ladies and a video of him taking his weekly bribe. As much as Chief Inspector Marriott liked to think he was calling the shots he knew deep down that if Daniel wanted to, he could have him whisked off for a spell at Her Majesty's pleasure at the drop of a hat. He knew he might be able to take Daniel down with him but also knew that Daniel would fair far better inside than he would, and he didn't ever want to find out if that was the case or not. He'd just been made aware of Akrad and Barraq's families making a joint claim that their sons had been kidnapped, probably by some far-right activists they'd suggested. He didn't know if this had anything to do with Daniel or his dad Frank, but he did know that Daniel would expect to hear about this from him. Anything that Chief Inspector Marriott heard that had anything to do with any of Daniel's criminal rivals he was expected to pass on. Akrad Malik and Barraq Syed going missing was big news on this front and Wayne Marriott wanted to make sure he got news of this over to Daniel pronto, before he heard it from anyone else. He rang Daniel's number. Daniel answered it straight away. 'Mr. Marriott, long time no speak. I thought you'd been moved on?' Daniel said with a certain hint of sarcasm.

Wayne Marriott rolled his eyes at the comment. 'Ha, ha, that was funny the first time you said it, Daniel. Now it struggles to raise a smile.'

Daniel chuckled. He liked Chief Inspector Marriott. He was the kind of guy that given different circumstances Daniel would happily have a drink with. He knew where the line was, but he was always happy to have a bit of banter with Daniel. This was where Wayne Marriott differed from other coppers on the payroll. Other coppers would have their tongue permanently up Daniel's arse whereas Wayne was happy to give a bit back. Daniel knew exactly why he was ringing but played the game.

'So, with what do I owe this pleasure?' he asked.

'Your two mates, Akrad Malik and Barraq Syed,

have gone missing. Their families have been down at the station citing kidnapping by far-right activists or something like that. I'm sure that this is anything to do with you Daniel, but thought you'd want to know.'

Daniel sounded surprised. 'I see. Well, please tell their families that our thoughts are with them and that we hope they turn up safe and sound. In the meantime, I'll drop in on their two clubs and make sure all is well. I'm sure their families will appreciate us keeping a keen eye on the places.'

Chief Inspector Marriott laughed. 'I think I'll keep that information to myself Daniel if it's all the same. I don't think their families are aware of their business interests. Good Muslim boys, they called them. Listen, if they turn up, I'll let you know, but we in uniform are not interested, and CID are throwing a party, I think to celebrate their disappearance. No one expects them to turn up. Guys like them seldom do when they go missing. Anyway, if you are involved, make sure your tracks are covered just in case anyone starts sniffing around. I'll keep you posted.'

Wayne Marriott hung up and sat back in his chair. He knew from Daniel's reaction and comments that he already knew about them, and he also suspected that he was involved. He knew he'd need to keep his eye on developments but also knew he had the authority to play their disappearance down. If anyone were to instigate a serious investigation it was him and knowing how deep he was in it with Daniel Pearson, he was not about to do anything like that.

chapter forty-six

Daniel was at their club in Nottingham with Frank and Jez. They'd recently taken over another club in Mapperley and were sorting out the personnel who could sell drugs in there on their behalf. Frank always liked to get these things sorted very quickly. Every drug dealer in Nottingham knew that unless they were authorised to do so, they could not be seen to be selling anything.

'Well, two days it's took 'em to report them missing. I expected that call to come yesterday, Frank.' Daniel said, beaming. 'Now we can get in there and take over. I can't wait to sort that fucker Barry out that Raquel mentioned. Sounds like a right smarmy fucker.'

Frank looked at his watch. It was one-twenty in the afternoon. He wanted to go and fetch Richie from the hospital at three o'clock. He was fit to come out, and Frank had been doing a lot of thinking and soul searching since he and Daniel had been to visit the other night. Daniel had hit a nerve with him when he'd said to him, *do you think mum would want this, you hating her son?* No one had ever said anything like that to Frank before. No one had ever involved Renee. Whether that was down to fear of bringing her name into it with Frank or just that no one had ever thought about it like that before Frank was unsure, but Daniels words ran deep. Frank would never let Renee down, not even now, twenty-five years or so later. She was still the love of his life, and the more he'd thought about what Daniel had said, the more he knew that Renee would want nothing more than to look down on them all and see them all getting on, her Frank with their two sons. He looked up at Daniel.

'We could go later tonight, but I'm fetching ya brother at three o'clock. As long as he's okay, we can go together, with Jez here, of course.'

Daniel was aware Frank was fetching Richie and was pleased. He'd not made much comment on it as he knew the best way to handle it was not to make a big thing of it. Frank would want to do this thing with Richie quietly. He wouldn't appreciate people making big of it.

'Yeah, okay, I'm gonna get off home now, but if I don't hear from you to say otherwise, I'll pick you both up at your house Frank at seven. That okay?'

'Sound, be careful. See you later.'

Jez was surprised to hear that Frank was picking up Richie. 'Shall I come with you Frank, to the hospital?' he asked.

'No, mate, I'm going on my own. Just something I need to do.' Frank was staring into space, chucking his car keys up in the air and catching them with the same hand. 'I'll just see you at mine around six-thirty.'

'Okay, I'm just gonna make a brew. You want one?'

'Yeah, go on then. I'll have a quick one.'

Jez opened the office door and walked out into the main bar area. He then popped his head straight back in. 'When's Goldie's funeral?'

Frank snapped out of his trance and put his car keys on the table. 'Friday, 11:30am at the crem. I want everyone there.'

He picked up the phone and rang Daniel. 'Forgot to

tell you Son, pick up Raquel on your way to mine later. She can come with us. I'm sure she'll be up for that. We can also ask her about running the place on the way down.'

Frank walked into the hospital room at a quarter to four. Richie was ready and sat on his bed facing the window. 'Alright, Son?' Frank asked.

Richie got up and turned round. 'Goldie's funeral Friday 11:30am... did you know?

'Yeah, his mum rang me to tell me. I'll make sure everyone's there. He needs a good send-off.'

'I assume we're covering the cost?' Richie asked Frank in a rather forthright way. Frank sensed the tone but swallowed down any feeling of anger. He wanted to do his best to mend this situation with Richie. He'd now promised Renee, and he wasn't prepared to break that promise before he'd tried his best.

'Yes Son, of course. It's all sorted. The wake afterwards is at my house. The least we could do.'

Richie was taken back and suddenly felt an appreciation towards his father he'd not felt for many a while. After hearing what Frank had said to Daniel in this very room two nights ago, he was struggling to feel any sort of affection towards him. Frank walked over and got his bag and picked it up.

'Come on Son, let's go for a drive. I'll take you home, but we'll go the long way. It'll be good to have some time together.' Richie looked at his father. Was this really Frank Pearson stood in front of him.

'I thought it was me that'd taken some knocks to the head, not you. How long have I been in this place?'

Frank stopped at the door. 'No knocks to the head Richie, just a few home truths. Anyway, come on, let's go.'

They walked to Frank's car and drove out onto the main road. Frank took the A614 up towards Doncaster and turned left down towards the Burnt Stump Country Park. It took him past Nottinghamshire police headquarters, which always gave him a smile whenever he drove past it. He would think of all the coppers based there, thinking that they were fighting crime, whilst many of the coppers at the coal face were on the take. Whilst ever there were criminals, there would be bent coppers, and whilst ever there were bent coppers, there would be criminals. It was like a merry-go-round at the fun fair. He pulled into The Burnt Stump pub car park.

'Come on, let's go for a walk round here. Some fresh air will do us both good,' he said as he opened the car door. Richie was a little unsure of this. His dad had never, ever done anything like this before. He didn't know what to say. As he opened the passenger side door and got out, he could not help but think that this felt and looked like a perfect scene for a murder. Frank picking him up on his own, taking him to a relatively secluded woodland and country park and wanting to go for a walk. He stood up and looked around him. It was reasonably quiet—just a few cars in the car park. Frank beckoned him.

'Come on Son, look lively.'

Richie followed Frank rather suspiciously and tried to put thoughts of Frank bumping him off out of his head. 'What are we doing here, dad?'

'Just want to get some air, a walk will do us good. When was the last time we did something like this?'

'Never Dad. Never. We've never gone for a walk together, and we've never even been here together. I've been here quite a few times with the lads for a drink and to watch the cricket, but we haven't been here together. It feels weird.'

Frank put his arm around Richie's shoulder. Richie instinctively broke free. Frank understood the reaction.

'Would you rather we go for a pint in the pub instead?' he asked, knowing that Richie would feel more at ease in there, a familiar surrounding. Richie thought for a second and felt more at ease now that Frank had offered to go into the pub.

'No, come on, walk it is.'

Frank smiled. He'd not smiled at Richie for a long time. They walked for around forty-five minutes. Frank brought Richie up to speed with Raquel and the events with Akrad and Barraq. Richie thought Frank was telling him of the events of the past two days because he wanted to. He felt as though he was part of the business for a change. The way Frank told him the details felt like the way a Managing Director would tell a board member. He felt included. It felt good, and it felt strange but more good than strange. They were both just enjoying the peace, the fresh air, and the company. When they got back to the car, Frank spoke.

'Listen, we are going to Leicester tonight to take over their two clubs. You wanna come?' Richie looked at his dad.

'That'd be great, Dad. Ease me back in gently.' They both laughed.

'So, you wanna come then?' Frank asked. 'Definitely,' Richie replied.

chapter forty-seven

Daniel had called to pick up Raquel an hour earlier than he needed to. They were both lying in bed. Daniel loved shagging Raquel. It was different from Phoebe. With Phoebe, he made love. With Raquel, he just fucked her hard. It suited him. He needed the hard fucks. He didn't do it too regularly, probably twice a month or so. Raquel took a draw on her cigarette and passed it to Daniel. As she exhaled, she said, 'I think it's good that Frank has gone to pick up Richie, don't you?'

Daniel passed her the cigarette back. 'Yeah, hopefully, they've made progress. Richie needs a bit of love at the moment. Losing Goldie like he did hit him hard, then with hearing about you, and... well, finding that guy in my house, he's had a tough few days. He doesn't cope with things like that as well as me and me dad. I just hope they've not started arguing and had a pop at each other. We'll see how it goes, eh?'

'He's not a bad lad, you know, Daniel. He just gets the rough end of the stick all the time. He plays up because that's his only way of getting attention. We all need attention, and that's just his way of getting it. I don't think that's the real him, though. Maybe if your dad starts to pay him attention for the good things he does, he will respond to that.'

Daniel marvelled at Raquel when she spoke like this. Half the time, he didn't really know what she was on about, but it always sounded impressive. He kind of understood this talk though, on personality traits or whatever Raquel called it. He saw Raquel herself in that little speech of hers. He often wondered how the hell Raquel got into the life she led. She was very intelligent but didn't like to talk about her education. Daniel could never really understand if that were because somewhere deep inside her, she had regrets about not following her education and being successful in an academic way or whether it was because she hated what all that stood for. In the past, she had told him that the circle in which her parents mixed was one where everyone was striving to be the best and where everyone's children were expected to have a degree and a job in a suit. Anything less was seen as a failure. Raquel hated that and had sort of rebelled against the status quo by becoming a hooker. That had been her way of getting the attention she had craved. He could see that.

'I think I know what you mean.' Daniel said as he pulled back the covers to get dressed. 'Richie gets the attention by being an arsehole. It's like *look at me, please notice me,* and his behaviour is the only way he can get that attention.' Raquel pulled back the covers. She wanted an extra few moments in bed.

'You're learning, Daniel. That's exactly why he behaves like he does. Now you understand it, you should be able to stop yourself from ever reacting to one of his outbursts. Next time he is shouting and balling and threatening this, and that just ask him calmly, 'What is it that you are angry at?' I bet he won't even know. He'll probably be angry at himself.'

Daniel smiled. 'Yeah, I'll try that next time. It'll be a laugh if nowt else.'

Raquel got up and walked into the bathroom to turn

on the shower. When she came out, Daniel was sat on the bed putting on his socks.

'Just remember this,' she said. 'Whenever someone reverts to childlike behaviour, which is what Richie does in those situations, you must remain the adult. That way, you will control the conversation and the situation. Remember, Richie can't make you feel anything. Only you can control how you feel.' She shut the ensuite door and left Daniel tucking in his shirt.

Frank and Richie were waiting in Frank's kitchen with Jez when Daniel and Raquel turned up. Daniel was pleased to see that his brother and his dad seemed okay with each other and that they'd not fallen out. He shook Richie's hand and hugged him.

'Good to see you back, Richie,' he said whilst still hugging him close. He felt Richie hug him back. He pulled away, and whilst still shaking his hand, he said.

'Thank you for doing what you did and saving Phoebe and that. I owe you one. I didn't mean what I said in here the other day. I was just being a twat.' Richie pulled him close again.

'Makes a change from me, bruv, but yeah, you were a twat.' They nodded at each other, and that was enough. Richie let go of Daniel's hand and opened his arms as he looked at Raquel. She walked up to him and hugged him tightly. No words were exchanged. Raquel kissed him on the cheek and then pulled away.

'Right have we done now with all this hugging lark. We have some serious business to attend to tonight so have we all got it out of our systems?' Frank asked in a tone that had a very serious point to it.

'As you all know, we are going to take over the two clubs that Akrad and Barraq ran. Bob's meeting us just off Junction 25 on the way down. I don't expect any trouble tonight as they're not expecting us, so I assume that the usual personnel will be there running the place in their absence.' he looked at Raquel. 'We'll go to the one you worked at first. Who do we need to know about?'

The general manager is called Najeeb, Frank. I only saw him briefly, but he didn't look like anything to concern you. There are two guys named Saeed and Talal who bring the punters upstairs, but again they just looked like two fairly ordinary blokes. Then there's Barry who gets the girls from their digs for their shift and stays until they finish.'

'What's he like?'

'A slimy horrible guy. Looks like what he is... a dirty old man. Well, he's not that old actually, more middle age, but you know what I mean.'

'Anyone else?' Frank asked.

'Not that I saw.'

'Okay, so we know little about the personnel...' Frank was then interrupted by Raquel.

'Then there's the two bouncers that were upstairs. I forgot about them. They never spoke to me. Just sat in the office in case anything kicked off. Big guys, though. Definitely look like they could handle themselves.'

'Right then, so I assume they will have bouncers on the doors. We take them out straight away. Then Raquel, I want you to point out this Najeem guy.' He then looked at Jez. 'Jez, I want you and Bob to sort out the two burly fuckers upstairs straight away. When bob gets in your car later, make sure he knows the drill. Daniel, Richie, you two stick with me. Has everyone got a shooter?'

Everyone nodded except Richie. 'Not me, dad.'

Frank went to the safe and came back a few minutes

later and handed Richie the gun. 'You okay with that?'
Richie nodded. 'Good, right then, gents... and ladies.'
Frank said whilst looking at Raquel. 'We've done this
more than enough times, but as always, stick to the
drill and keep ya wits about you. Jez, you take your
car, and Bob can go with you from where we meet him.
He then chucked Richie his keys to the Jaguar. 'Your
turn to drive, Son.'

As they walked to the car, Frank grabbed Richie's
arm and pulled him aside. 'When we're discussing
work, it's Frank, not dad. It's Dad off duty, but when
you're at work, it's Frank, okay.'

Richie nodded. 'Okay, Dad... I mean okay, Frank.'
They'd just got onto the M1 when Frank turned to look
at Raquel in the back seat, who was sat with Daniel.

'How ya feeling now then, Raquel?' he asked. 'I bet
you're looking forward to seeing those fuckers down
there, aren't you?'

Raquel paused. 'I'll enjoy seeing Tracey and Brenda
again. I liked those two. Salt of the earth they were. If
I were you, I'd keep them on. They do a good job, and
from what I could see, they are trustworthy. The rest
of them though that I came into contact with, Barry, in
particular, I'd give a wide berth.'

'Well look. Got a proposition for you. How would you
like to run this place for me, you know the one you
worked at? Under Daniel's supervision. You'd report to
him, but the day-to-day running would be all down to
you. Full control. What do you say?'

Raquel was quite taken a back by Frank's
comments. This was unexpected. She'd just assumed
that once she'd been on this little outing tonight that
she'd go back to being the hostess at The Main Vault in
Nottingham. She was unsure what to say. She'd love to

run a club. She knew she'd be good at it. She was well respected within the trade and knew it inside out. She knew how to make money too. The main selling point of this to her though, was that she trusted Daniel and Frank. She was obviously held in quite high esteem for Frank to make her this offer. He didn't do things like this lightly. Maybe she could keep on Tracey and Brenda, she thought.

'Can I pick my own staff?' she asked.

'As I said Raquel, you would run it. Top to bottom. As long as you bring the money in and don't cream off the top, you can hire and fire who you like.'

'What about their other club?'

Frank frowned. 'Well, I'm not sure yet. Why?'

'I'd like to run them both. I know I can do it. I can look to put my own staff in, and I could run them both for you.'

'Both of them. Fucking hell Raquel, you aren't slow in coming forward, are you? What's our thoughts, Daniel?' Daniel thought for a moment.

'It's a big ask, Raquel. Running one will be hard enough, but two? How can you be in two places at once?'

'I wouldn't need to be. You run your businesses by putting the right people in the right places—square pegs, square holes. I would do the same. If I have a trustworthy manager in each place, I can oversee them both. I know I can do it. I thought I was minutes away from an hour or so with Bonnie, and I kept my mouth shut, Frank. I would have died with my mouth shut for you. Surely you can give me this chance?'

Frank sighed and turned around to look out of the front windscreen. He thought for a minute. He then turned around to look at Daniel. Daniel raised his

The two cars pulled up outside the club at 8:45pm.
There were two bouncers on the door. Frank and the
others got out of their cars and just stood in a line
and looked at the two guys standing side-by-side. The
two bouncers looked at each other in bewilderment
and then looked back at the five men, and one woman
stood in front of them. Frank walked up to them with
Jez and Bob on one side of him and Daniel and Richie
on the other side. Raquel was a step or two behind.
'Who runs this place?' Frank asked the two bouncers.
They again looked at each other. Frank could see they
were scared. They were two big lumps, but Frank
thought they were probably more used to dealing with
some dirty old man who'd got his cock out. 'I said who
runs this place?'

The slightly taller of the two said, 'Er, Mr. Malik
and Mr. Sayed, but they're not in.' Frank punched the
slightly taller guy hard and knocked him backwards.
Jez immediately stepped forward and punched the
other one. Frank held out his right hand. Bob placed

a baseball bat into his palm. Frank hit both men twice with the bat. Neither of them retaliated.

'Wrong.' Frank said. 'I do. My name is Frank Pearson. I now run this place. You two pieces of shit just need to decide whether you work for me now or whether you've just joined John Major's dole queue. I'll give you a few minutes to make up your mind. Now take me to Najeeb.' Frank handed the bat back to Bob.

The two bouncers, without saying a word, turned around and escorted Frank and his entourage into the club. Richie closed the entrance door behind him. Frank was taken to a very plush office where a guy was sat with his feet on the desk smoking a fat cigar. Frank walked into the office on his own. Raquel escorted Jez and Bob through the door that led upstairs. Richie and Daniel waited outside the office. Frank closed the office door behind him. The guy took his feet off the desk and stood up.

'Who the fuck are you?' he said.

'Who runs this place?' he asked.

'I do,' the guy shouted. He put his cigar in the ashtray on the desk. Frank walked around the desk, grabbed the guy by this hair, and smashed his face into the desk. He picked up the cigar and burnt it into his cheek. The guy screamed in agony as the cigar burned his skin. Frank lent forward and put his mouth next to the guy's ear.

'Wrong,' he whispered. 'I do. My name is Frank Pearson. From this moment forth, I run this place. Now. What's your name?'

'Najeeb... it's Najeeb,' he said, stuttering as he spoke.

'So, Najeeb, who runs this place?'

'You do.'

'You do, Mr. Pearson, Najeeb. Now try again.'

'You do, Mr. Pearson.'

Frank kept Najeeb's face pinned firmly to the desk. He continued to whisper in his ear. 'Now then, Najeeb. Have you ever worked at the other club that your previous bosses owned?'

'Yes, Mr. Pearson. I worked there for about six months up until three months ago.'

Frank burnt the cigar into Najeeb's cheek once more. He stood him up.

'If I ever see your feet on that desk again, Najeeb, I'll burn this cigar into your eyes. Now come with me.' Frank opened the door and told Richie to keep an eye on things downstairs and to make sure no one left. He told Daniel to bring the two bouncers upstairs.

Frank then followed Najeeb upstairs to find Jez and Bob stood over two lumps of lard whom he assumed were the bouncers Raquel was on about. Three other guys sat on the floor with their legs crossed, and Raquel stood talking to a lady who looked in her forties. There were also three young girls with next to nothing on sat on some chairs. Frank told Najeeb to sit on the floor with the other three guys.

'So, who do we have here, Raquel? Frank asked.

'This is Tracey,' she said as she pointed to the lady stood next to her. Those three next to Najeeb are Barry, Talal, and Saeed. Barry is the one who brings the girls to and from their digs, and Talal and Saeed bring the punters upstairs. Those two that Jez and Bob are stood over are the bouncers I was telling you about.' Frank looked at Najeeb.

'Who runs this place?'

'You do, Mr. Pearson,' Najeeb replied whilst looking at the floor. His face was hurting like hell, and he was struggling to hold back the tears. He wanted to wipe them from his face, but he was sat on his hands.

'That's right,' Frank said, looking at everyone in the room. He looked at Barry. 'Stand up,' he ordered. Barry stood up and failed to look at Frank. He kept his gaze to the floor. 'Look at me,' he said. Barry lifted his head.

Frank was then interrupted by a punter coming out of one of the rooms with a young girl.

'You,' he said to the girl, 'stay out here.' He then pointed to the punter. 'You, fuck off back in that room and stay there until you're told to come out.' Frank then looked back at Barry, who had again dropped his gaze. 'Look at me, you slimy fucker.' Barry looked at Frank. Frank took out his gun and pistol-whipped Barry four times. Barry's face was pouring with blood. Frank then ordered Barry to look at him again. 'If I see you again, Barry, I'll kill you. Now fuck off and don't ever let me see your ugly mug again.' Barry never knew how close he'd come that day to being brutally murdered. If Frank had known that Barry was the one who'd grassed Raquel up to Akrad, he'd have tortured the life out of him. Frank looked at those who remained. He walked up to Najeeb. 'You, my friend, had a very lucky escape tonight. The last person who asked me, *who the fuck are you?* got a bullet in his head. You are lucky you worked at their other club. That, you sad fuck, saved your life. Now get up.' He walked over to Raquel. 'This,' he said whilst putting an arm around her, '... is your new boss. You all know her from her very brief time here last week. Her name is Raquel, and she is running this place for my son and me from now on. We are now going over to the other club to have the same conversations there. I expect you all here when we return. It will take us about twenty minutes to get there. If there is any suspicion that anyone from here has tipped them off about our arrival, I will return here and burn this place to the ground with everyone in it.' He looked at Tracey. 'Tracey, Raquel spoke highly of you. You are in charge up here until we return. Make sure the punters pay their money. My two sons will be downstairs. Any shit from any of these lot, just go get them.'

Tracey was petrified. She didn't want that responsibility. She didn't want to be in charge. She didn't want to have to make people pay their money. Even though she kind of did that anyway, no one like Frank had told her it was now her responsibility. Suddenly, it sounded like a different job. She didn't want to be the one in the firing line if anyone didn't pay. She wanted to be at home. She wished she were at Brenda's house. She nodded to Frank and preyed they would be back quickly. Frank got hold of Najeem and motioned to Jez, Bob, and Raquel. He looked at the group of terrified people before him. 'Right then, people, up you get, we have money to be made here tonight.' He then looked at Daniel. 'We won't be long.'

Frank was walking towards the door when he saw a familiar face drinking in the corner of the room. Frank stopped in his tracks. Chief Inspector Marriott walked over with a glass of scotch in his hand. Frank thought how he still looked as ugly as ever.

'I thought you'd show up tonight, Frank. I knew as soon as I spoke to Daniel earlier that you wouldn't be able to wait. They'll still be warm.'

Frank stared the Chief Inspector down. The initial bravado and swagger in his walk had soon evaporated. Wayne Marriott was known as a hard bastard in the force and out on the street, but Frank could see through the uniform so well it may have been transparent. Frank looked like an awesome figure whenever he stood there motionless and stared someone down. Frank's stare with those piercing eyes could drain the confidence out of any man. For someone who stood at five feet, seven, he had enormous presence. The fact that Wayne Marriott was only an inch or so taller was neither here nor there. Frank had cut many guys down to size with his stare, who was much taller.

'What will still be warm, Wayne? The roll of fifties that you received recently, you piece of shit.'

Frank was in no mood for joviality, and Wayne Marriott could sense it. Frank had business to attend to, plus he was looking at someone who was trying to mug him off in his new club in front of his newest employees.

'Just cover ya tracks, Frank, that's all I'm saying.'

Frank got hold of Wayne Marriott and virtually lifted him off the floor. He more or less threw him through the doors and onto the pavement. Frank picked him up by his collar, and in a very controlled fashion, he said, 'Don't you fucking tell me what to do, Marriott. I know what I am. I can look myself in the mirror. You, ya slimy piece of shit, pretending to be a fuckin' do-gooder, playing the fuckin' game when all the time you're taking backhanders off the likes of me, and you try and tell me what to do in there in front of my workforce. If I didn't have serious business to attend to, I'd cut you open ya bent fucker. Don't ever try and act the big I am in front of me again. Supposed to be a hard man? You're fuck all Chief Inspector Marriott, fuck all,' Frank let go and straightened his clothes. 'And another thing. If I hear that you've been making any noise that me or any of my firm had anything to do with the disappearance of the two upstarts that used to run this club, I'll hunt you down like a fucking dog.'

Wayne Marriott was wishing he'd remained observant from a distance. That did not go according to plan. He'd just wanted Frank to know he was well up on the situation and, if he was honest, to let Frank know he was still a copper at the end of the day. All he'd done is make himself look like a fool in front of all and sundry. He had nothing more to say, so just skulked off back to his car. He just really wanted the ground to swallow him up.

Frank returned to the club around an hour and a half later. He'd dropped Najeem off at the hospital A & E department. Told him to get cleaned up and then get back to the club to finish his shift. He found the same two bouncers on the doors as he got out of the car. They made way for him to enter the premises with a *good evening, Mr. Pearson.* Frank returned the pleasantries. He walked in and was surprised to find it running as normal. You'd never know there'd been a bit of a fracas earlier. He surveyed the bar area and watched the punters and staff just going about their business as usual. Everyone could sense his presence, even those punters who had not been here earlier. Frank could see the nudges and nods going on. Frank knew people were saying, *that's him over there,* and such like. He walked up to the bar and ordered himself, Jez, and Bob a large scotch a piece. He thought he deserved a drink tonight. It was no surprise when the barman didn't ask for any money. Raquel walked straight upstairs to see Tracey.

'Am I glad to see you, Raquel. I've been a fucking

bag o' nerves here. Can we have Brenda back? I know she'd love to come back and work for you.' Tracey had just managed to briefly tell Raquel about Brenda earlier, just before Frank had come upstairs. 'I hope so, Tracey. I'd like to see Brenda back. We can pop and see her when we've finished.'

'Yeah, that'd be great. She'll be in bed, though. Shall I ring her to tell her?'

'That'd be a good idea. Tell her we'll be over around 4:30ish. Tell her to make that spare room up!'

Tracey smiled and went into the office to make the call. Raquel knew that she could mould Tracey and possibly Brenda to a degree into a good couple of number twos. People she could rely on, especially early doors in this job. Raquel was looking forward to this challenge and just knew she could make these two clubs into real gold mines. She knew she could not compete with Daniel and Frank's existing club of the same ilk, but she knew that even having to target the lower end of the sex market, she could make these clubs two classy outlets. She thought back for a moment, back to when she first got off the train that night at Nottingham. She believed in fate and that things happened for a reason, and as she looked around her and thought of what she could achieve, she knew there and then that this was the reason.

'She'll make up the bed, Raquel, and she'll have the kettle on. She's so excited to see you again.' Tracey shouted as she came out of the office.

Frank sat in the office downstairs where a couple of hours earlier, he'd burnt Najeem's face. He couldn't help but put his feet on the desk. He'd ordered a scotch each for Daniel and Richie and told them what had happened at the other club. 'Well, the take over of the other club was easier than this one, gents. There was no resistance, was there Jez?'

Jez shook his head. 'No, piece of cake, the General Manger there didn't need to have a cigar burnt into his cheek. In fact, he even said to Frank that he was hoping that we would make an appearance. It seems he didn't like Akrad and Barraq much at all.'

Frank interrupted him. 'So, Daniel, I've left him to run things up until Raquel decides what she wants to do. You won't receive any grief from that one. I reckon we could have taken that club over when they were still alive.'

He raised his glass. 'Well, here's to… what's the name of this place?' he said laughing. 'Fuck me, gents, I've taken over two clubs, and I don't even know what they're called.'

Daniel interjected. 'This one is Sabora's' and the other one is 'Razanaa's.'

'Sa' what?'

'Sabora's.'

'Fuck that I can't own a club that I can't pronounce. You'll have to change that.' Frank said, sounding quite frustrated just as Raquel walked in. 'Hey Raquel, we need to change the name of this club. Can you think of anything?' he asked.

Raquel thought for a second and said, 'Rachel's … I want to call it Rachel's.' There was silence for a few seconds, and then Frank said. 'Sounds good to me, Rachel's it is. What about the other one?' Silence engulfed the room until Richie piped up.

'What about Goldie's?'

Frank raised his glass again. 'Here's to Rachel's and Goldie's.'

Eight years later...

chapter forty-eight

July 2004

Daniel was throwing a party to celebrate his son Archie's eighth birthday. He and Phoebe had moved from their property in Ravenshead a couple of years previously to a six-bedroom huge pile on the edges of Southwell, a village in between Mansfield and Newark in Nottinghamshire. This house was something special. As well as the six bedrooms, it had a swimming pool in a separate detached building, three garages, a paddock, and a huge garden. Daniel watched from the marquee that he'd had erected for the occasion as Richie dived to his left and saved yet another shot from Archie. He could see that Archie loved his football and was, in fact, quite good at it. He loved to dribble with the ball and show off his trickery. Even at eight-years-old, Archie could do things with the ball that Daniel had never been able to master. This was all down to Archie's Uncle Richie though. Richie had always been a good footballer. As a child, he was always the better player, by quite a distance, really, but that talent had never been harnessed as Frank had never spent any quality time with Richie as a child. Richie had played in boys' teams and a bit of Sunday league when he got older, but he'd just played for the fun of it. He had always been far better than the teams he'd played for, and Daniel had often wondered if Richie could have been a professional if he'd had the proper training. As he watched them play, he thought of all the times as a child his brother had begged their father Frank to go and watch him play, but Frank had always either been too busy or wouldn't go because of how he'd always felt about Richie. As he continued to watch and supped his cold beer, he felt an arm on his shoulder. It was Phoebe.

'Why don't you go and join in? You know Archie would love you to play too,' she said as she rested her head on his shoulder. Daniel knew she was right, and he would love to join in, but resentment stopped him. He was aware that history was repeating itself. He knew that he was behaving in a similar way to how his father had done all those years ago with Richie, but he just couldn't help himself. He couldn't help how he felt. He was jealous of Richie's relationship with Archie and was envious of how Archie looked up to his uncle. They would spend hours together playing football, riding their bikes, and generally just fooling around. Richie had even started taking him to watch Mansfield Town, and Archie loved it. Richie was unrecognisable from the man he used to be. Ever since Frank had decided to put the past to bed that night back in '96 when Richie lay in hospital, he could do no wrong. The thing that was really eating away at Daniel was the fact that it was his idea for Frank to bury the hatchet. If he'd not had that talk with his dad in the hospital corridor, he doubted that Frank would ever have gotten close to Richie, such was his hatred for his twin. Daniel had often wished over the years that he'd just left well alone. He much preferred it when he was the number one son and Richie was the outcast. He didn't realise it at the time and always had down the years wanted nothing more than Frank and Richie to become close, but now they had he fucking hated it. Richie had been running Nottinghamshire and Leicestershire with Daniel as a partnership for nearly five years now. Frank's idea. In fact, it was non-negotiable. Frank thought that the two of them running those two areas side by side was a show of strength. Brothers united, so to speak. Initially, Daniel was all for it, but as time went on, he'd come to hate it. He wished his brother would just fuck off and leave him to it. He felt pushed out, he felt jealous, envious, and resentful, and he also knew that a combination like that, in their world especially, would one day have consequences. Bob was soon to 'retire' to the Costa Del Sun now that he was in his mid-sixties, and Daniel was hoping that Frank would give Derby to Richie to look after and leave him well alone with his patch. He put his arm around Phoebe.

'They're better playing on their own Luv, look at them; they love it together.' No one knew how Daniel felt. He'd managed to mask it for the last three years or so. He was very careful to keep his thoughts and feelings to himself, and whenever he was in other people's company, he would, like everyone else, marvel at how Richie had changed and how great it was to see him and Frank so close. In reality, though, it made him want to puke. He hated the fact that Richie was now the blue-eyed boy. He hated the fact that Frank treated Richie the same as him. He hated that Richie was his equal in the family business, but more than anything, he fucking hated the fact that Richie seemed to be a very honourable, warm, fair, and generous person. *No one can change that much;* Daniel would often remind himself. That was his job, not Richie's. It was as if Richie had taken his place in the world as if he'd moulded himself on Daniel. The Richie pre-1996 was just someone who was rebelling against his situation and his life at that time. Richie had historically been dealt a poor hand and had constantly been mistreated by everyone in his life, so he'd reacted accordingly. *Just looking for those positive strokes,* Raquel would always say. Richie the arsehole, Richie the twat had just acted like that to get a reaction because that was all he knew, now though Richie the fucking saint was just being himself, and Daniel despised him.

'I'm bloody knackered. He wears me out does that son of ours, Daniel. Get me a beer. I'm as dry as a bone.'

Daniel had been so immersed in his own thoughts he'd not noticed that they'd finished playing. He looked round and saw Richie slumped on a chair, beads of sweat on his brow and small patches of sweat under his arms. *Should never wear a royal blue t-shirt on a hot day,* Daniel thought to himself as he picked up a beer out of the ice bucket and passed it to Richie.

'You should have come and had a play, mate. He's a cracking player ya know. He could make it if he's nurtured well enough. Megabucks in the game now. He'd be able to buy a place like this with his first month's pay by the time he's gracing the premier league.'

Daniel tried hard to swallow down his anger and frustration. *Why the fuck did everyone have to tell me that I should be on the lawn playing with them,* he thought to himself. He knew that if one more person suggested this, that he'd erupt. He needed to mingle, to take his mind off Richie and his son Archie. He didn't want to talk to his dad Frank as he annoyed him as much as Richie. All he ever heard from Frank these

days was Richie this and Richie that, it was all he'd
heard for most of the past eight years. Archie had run
to his mum, as he always did, and was now sucking
an iced lolly. He seldom came running to his dad. That
was saved for when his mum Phoebe was not there.
He'd even run to his uncle Richie before he'd run to
Daniel, and as much as Daniel tried to tell himself
otherwise, it fucking hurt. The more that things like
that happened and the more people marvelled at how
good Richie was with Archie, the more resentful Daniel
became of the situation and the more distance there
was between Daniel and his son. At times like this, all
he wanted was to get in his car with Raquel and fuck
her brains out down some country lane somewhere,
but even their times together were becoming less and
less. Daniel knew Richie was still shagging Raquel,
and he struggled to share her with his brother, so
he had purposely let it drop off to nothing more than
an occasional shag. He'd expected Raquel to do some
chasing when he first let it drop off, but she'd not even
mentioned it. She was just there when he wanted to.
She was still a hooker in his eyes, so he'd just shag
her when he felt like it. He felt like it today, just to get
away from all these people if nothing else, but as he
looked over to her, she was having a ball. She'd done
a great job with the two clubs she'd taken on for them.
So well, in fact, that she was now running their other
club in Leicester, the one they'd already had when all
that had kicked off with Akrad and Barraq. She was a
smart businesswoman, certainly one of Daniel's better
business decisions. She made them a mint out of those
three clubs and ran them all like well-oiled machines.
He smiled as he looked at Brenda. She looked like
she was approaching one hundred years old she was

so wrinkly but was actually only about seventy. Her new set of dentures made her look better, though. He couldn't risk whisking Raquel off for a fuck today. It would be too noticeable here. They'd be missed, and the one person he still loved like always was Phoebe, so he wasn't about to do anything to jeopardise that relationship today, not for a shag with Raquel anyway. Phoebe was the one person who kept him sane, who brought normality into his life. Even she didn't know how he felt about Richie and all that. At times he wondered if she suspected, but if she did, she never mentioned anything. Even with all the money they had, the house, cars, and everything else, if you saw her in the supermarket, you'd never know. She was always smartly dressed and always had her hair and make-up done, but so did a lot of women. She drove a nice convertible car, but so did many women, but she never flaunted their wealth. A lot of women whose husbands were wealthy would flaunt it and flash the cash. They would dress provocatively, whereas Phoebe dressed very conservatively. She even insisted that Archie attended the local primary school and insisted that he was to attend the local senior school when the time came. Daniel wanted him to go to private school, but Phoebe was having none of it. He saw her walking towards him with their daughter Alice skipping along beside her. Alice was six and a half years old and was a cracker. She was her mother's double, whereas Archie looked more like his dad. Archie had dark hair like both his parents, but his features were all of his Dad, whereas Alice was all Phoebe. In fact, Daniel would often tease Phoebe and ask if she was really his. The only tell-tale sign was Alice's second toe on her feet. It was bigger than her big toe, the same as Daniel's. People would often comment that she had Daniel's eyes, but he couldn't see it. He took Alice off Phoebe when she approached him and put her on his shoulders.

'I can see the church from here, Daddy,' she said excitedly, as he jumped up and down on the spot. 'It's the Minster sweetheart, not a church, similar, but it's a Minster.'

Alice couldn't care less. She was happy because she was on her daddy's shoulders. Daniel was happy because Alice didn't like football. She was all her daddy. She liked her Uncle Richie, but unlike Archie, she much preferred her daddy's company.

chapter forty-nine

Frank sat down with his morning cuppa at his large dining room table to chair the weekly Monday morning meeting of his empire. Every Monday morning for a good while now, he had summoned his Generals to a weekly meeting to discuss any topics that needed addressing. It had been Daniel's idea just before the new Millennium. He had persuaded Frank that if he wanted to run a proper business, he needed to put structures in place like a good business would. Frank had legitimised a lot of his business interests, again after discussions with Daniel and his accountant. The bigger Frank's empire had got, the more he needed to show legitimate areas of income to account for his wealth. He'd always paid off the old bill for as long as he could remember to stop them sniffing around, but the taxman had started to show a bit too much interest in Frank's affairs a few years ago. So, he now had more legitimate sources of income than he did illegal sources. He still ran protection and security rackets in all the towns and cities he controlled and still got a cut of every drug deal going, but the nightclubs, pubs and gentlemen's clubs and the sex trades within them were all to the outside world legitimate. Frank still controlled the drug trade in all of his outlets plus the drug activity out on the street, but these legitimate businesses gave him a perfect opportunity to clean up the dirty money he made from the drugs, sex, and more recently from the influx of migrant workers flooding the country.

Since the turn of the new century, Eastern European gangs had been coming over from all the old Eastern block countries such as Poland, Latvia, Romania, and Albania to try their hand at drugs. Frank had seen them all off one by one in his areas of activity, but he was aware of some of the old firms were finding it difficult to retain the power they once had. Even Frank had to cut a few deals with some of them to keep the control he'd always had. He now bought some of the drugs he supplied from these gangs, which was seen as a way to broker a peace deal. They got their supplies into certain areas of the UK, and in return, Frank didn't get any grief off them. Frank saw this as good business sense, a way of moving with the times. The old firms around the country who were struggling to remain in power were the ones that were not prepared to negotiate with these new firms. At the end of the day, Frank had to get his drugs from somewhere. He always had sourced from abroad, well ever since he'd become a serious face anyway. It had been over twenty years since he'd sourced his drugs in the UK. Frank had always been smart like that. He'd seen early on that cutting out a part of the supply chain only increased profits. Okay, it could cause aggravation, but Frank had realised back in the early eighties that he was big enough and powerful enough to deal with any of that sort of aggravation. Since he'd switched supply on some of the product to these Eastern European gangs, he'd made more money and kept things sweet his end. It was supply and demand at the end of the day, and as Daniel had made him see, businesses switched suppliers all the time. Frank was no different. They'd tried to get in on the supply of sex workers too, but

Frank was having none of that. He'd made that very clear. He knew that their supply of girls was often too young for Frank's liking. Frank was never into making money from underage girls. He'd die rather, and these new gangs knew that, so they canvassed their services elsewhere. Migrant workers of working-age, however, were a different ball game. He had built up some good relationships with some serious players over the past few years from places like Latvia and Poland from his drug deals. Now they were wanting to talk people and, in particular, migrant workers. Frank had never previously considered this area as a way of making money, but recent discussions had made him see otherwise. Migrant workers were wanted for labour out on the farms, factories, and construction, and Frank wanted to make sure he got his cut. These workers were going to come anyway as there was a shortage of British labour willing to get off their fat arses, so Frank thought he might as well make money from it. Frank opened the meeting.

'Right, gents, just a few items on the agenda this morning. Firstly Pat, have you sorted out that tin pot firm from Whitby who were seen dealing in Castleford yet?' This had annoyed Frank when he'd heard. Firstly, because who the fuck has ever heard of a firm from Whitby causing anyone any problems, and secondly, if you can't keep trouble out of a place like Castleford, then it's time to call it a day.

'Sorted Frank. I sent Simon and Tyrone over last week. We won't hear from them again, I assure you.'

'I should think not, for fuck's sake. We're a premier league firm, and we had fucking Whitby causing us grief. Any repeat, and I'll send Gloria up to sort it out for you.'

Pat knew he'd embarrassed himself with that one. He'd been too busy shagging a bird from Carlisle recently and had taken his eye off the ball. Frank knew nothing of the Carlisle lass, and Pat wanted to keep it that way. He'd managed to sort it, and that was the end of it, he hoped.

Frank continued, 'Richie have you sorted out the payments yet from that fat piece of shit who reckoned he wasn't paying us in West Bridgford?'

Richie laughed. 'Yeah, I got a month's pay up front from him. He was all mouthy and the like until I pulled this thing out of my pocket.' Richie pulled out a brand new 9mm pistol. Got it off Peteris, the Latvian. I don't want to use it. It's so shiny and new.'

He passed it to Jez, who stroked it like he was stroking a woman's pussy. 'Fucking hell Jez if you need to knock one out, go to the toilet.' Richie said, laughing.

'It's a beauty Richie,' Jez replied whilst rubbing it mockingly against his cheek.

Frank laughed and then moved things on. 'Well, that brings us very nicely onto our next item. As you know, we have been in discussions with two guys we know from Latvia, Peteris, who Richie has just mentioned, and his partner in crime, Maris. We've had good dealings with them, so we have no reason to doubt them. They've been involved on the fringes with the outfit that has given us a good supply of class A drugs for a couple of years now, but they want to start their own business and make their own money and to bring serious numbers of migrant workers into the country is the way for them to do it. I've told them that nowt happens on my patch of any criminal nature without me knowing about it and taking my cut, so they know the score. Now, this is an area we've not really been involved in. I know we've dealt in the sex trade for years now, but this is a different ball game. They are talking big numbers of people. Labourers, farmhands and such and there is a big demand. Peteris tells me he's been bringing people back for a while now, but on a small scale. He's seen the gap in the market and wants to fill it. Fair play, but not on my patch without me making money from it too. But times are changing gents, and we need to be at the forefront. Someone is soon gonna start to flood the UK with these Eastern European workers, so why not us? Peteris and Maris have the supply, and we have the UK contacts. These are workers who will be under the radar, you know, to do the jobs that the lazy fucking Brits don't want to do, so it's all cash in hand, no papers, no National Insurance numbers, etc. Many of these will be criminals in their own countries, so they will need a firm hand. That's where we and our criminal contacts come in. They will work for us, via our two Latvian friends, so if they don't play ball, they'll get a beating. No messing. If we get in quick, we can sew the market up, or at least have a good share by the time others try and follow suit. I have a meeting arranged with them for Friday this week. Me, Richie, Daniel, and Jez are going. We'll see what they have to say and update the meeting next Monday. If it goes well and we can do some business, then Richie will head it up. He will deal with the Latvians and run the distribution to our criminal contacts.' Daniel piped up.

'How come it's Richie's gig? Who decided that?'

Frank looked pissed off. 'It's Richie's gig because I fuckin' say it is. Does that answer both your fuckin' questions?'

Daniel stared into the garden through the window. He was fuming inside. This would be an interesting and lucrative arm of the business, and he wanted it. Years ago, he'd have had this gig without any thought. Richie wouldn't have even been considered.

'Well, does it?' Frank barked.

'Yes Frank,' Daniel replied.

Frank continued. 'Richie was the first to get wind of this potentially lucrative income stream from Peteris, so he's running it. Simple as that. We'll have more to tell you all next Monday. Anyway, let's carry on with the meeting, shall we?'

Daniel heard very little of the rest of the meeting. He was so annoyed at what he saw as the latest snub by Frank. Of course, Frank was just making decisions as he saw fit, but Daniel couldn't see that. Anything that involved Richie doing anything within the firm annoyed him. His annoyance was getting worse, and he couldn't see how he could stop it.

Daniel pulled into his driveway, got out of the car, and slammed the front door behind him. He poured himself a whiskey. It was eleven-thirty in the morning. Phoebe walked in from the garden. 'Was that you slamming the door?' she asked. Daniel felt the warmth of the scotch slip down his throat. He poured himself a second. Phoebe knew he was drinking too much. She'd seen it come on gradually, but over the past six months or so, it had become a daily occurrence. It was a touchy subject, one that Daniel didn't seem too fond of discussing.

'Yes, it was me. Why is that not allowed or something?' He barked. He downed the second glass of whiskey as quickly as the first and wiped his mouth with the back of his hand. 'I can't believe he's been given that job. No discussion, no thought, or fuck all. Just handed it on a fuckin' plate. I'm pig sick of it, Phoebe. It's like I don't bloody exist anymore. I may as well be invisible in that firm. And then, to make matters worse, I get told I'm taking on Derby too. Bob's cast-offs now that's all I'm good for. Taking over someone else's patch, someone else's problems. More bloody grief. That's all I get, but him... him, he gets a brand-new venture to get his teeth into. Mr. Blue-Eyed Fuckin Boy.'

Phoebe had no idea what he was going on about, but she guessed it involved Richie. She wasn't blind or stupid. She knew her Daniel better than he knew himself, and she could see with one eye that he was jealous of Richie. It was blatantly obvious to her, but no one else seemed to be aware of it. She'd known for a good couple of years now and had tried to get Daniel to talk about it without sounding obvious, but he never took the bait.

'What are you going on about?' She asked, trying her best to sound genuinely unawares.

'Fuckin' Richie, always fuckin' Richie. I tell ya this Phoebe, I wish him and me dad had never patched things up. You know, I used to wish that more than anything, but if I could turn back the clock, I'd do it in a heartbeat. Worse thing I ever did was persuade me dad to sort it out. I should have left well alone. Things were a lot better then.'

Phoebe realised this was the first time he'd given her an opening. She had to take it.

'Better for who?' she asked.

Daniel paused and looked at Phoebe. 'Forget it. I'm just ranting on, just ignore me.' He knew he didn't want to discuss it. Phoebe wasn't letting go.

'No, come on, you said it. Better for who?'

'Look Phoebe, just leave it. I don't want to discuss it. I'm going out.'

'That's your answer to everything these days, Daniel, going out. What's happening to you, eh?' She desperately wanted Daniel to open up to her. He was bottling everything up, and she knew that wasn't good for him or anyone in that house. 'I don't know what's going on between you and Richie, but it's not good. It's destroying you, and if you're not careful, it will destroy everything you have. Jealousy and envy are two dangerous things, Daniel. They are not nice traits to have. You need to talk about it, get things off your chest, share them with me. You always used to. Whenever something was bothering you, we'd talk about it together, but now you won't talk to me.' She watched as he put his jacket on and slammed the door behind him. She stood there looking at the back of the front door and then heard his car roar off down the road. A tear rolled down her cheek as she pondered where this could end up. The thought terrified her.

Richie rubbed a sample of the drugs on his top gum. 'Yep, it's all good, Frank. Top drawer.'

'Good lad. Right Chris, get this out to your guys and get it ready for the street pronto. We need to shift this lot quick. It's late, and we have people waiting for it.'

Chris worked for Richie and Daniel in Nottingham. He was a lanky fella. Six feet, three inches tall, and about ten stone wet through but was an ex-boxer so knew how to look after himself. He was in charge of getting the product cut and out to the dealership for Daniel and Richie. He was very loyal with a broad Scottish accent. He'd come down from Edinburgh in the late eighties with a girl he'd met on holiday from Nottingham. They'd split up not long after, but he'd got involved with the Forest hooligan element, met Richie through Saturday afternoon aggro, and to cut a long story short, Richie had brought him into the firm about five years ago. He now lived in Daybrook, just outside Nottingham, and had proven to be a good reliable member of Richie's team.

'Will do, Frank. It'll be on the streets tonight.'

Frank, Jez, and Richie got back into Frank's car and drove to Frank's club in Nottingham. This was where they always retreated to when they had no other pressing matters to attend to. Once at the club, Frank made himself a brew whilst Jez and Richie poured themselves a drink.

'What was up with Daniel earlier with you, any ideas?' Frank asked Richie.

Richie passed his dad the packet of ginger nuts before sitting down on one of the plush sofas in the main office.

'I don't know Frank; he's been distant with me for a while now. I can often sense him looking at me, ya know, for no good reason. Bit weird sometimes. I sometimes think he resents me these days.'

'Resents ya, what for?'

'I don't know, maybe because I'm a face now in the firm and kind of recognised within our world. I think he preferred it when we were always at loggerheads.'

Frank dipped his biscuit. 'Nah, that can't be right. It was his idea that we patched things up. Remember I told ya ages ago that if he hadn't have collared me in the hospital corridor that night, we may never have sorted things out. He must have other troubles. I'll talk to him, but if you're right then that's his problem.

Best thing I did was put the past behind me. It just eats away at ya, Son. Don't ever bear grudges. Sort ya differences out and move on. You can't ever change the past, but you can influence the future... or something like that anyway.'

'Yeah, someone once told me that ten percent of your life is what happens to you. The other ninety is about how you respond, or something like that,' Richie said, laughing as he ate another ginger nut.

Jez shook his head. 'Here, chuck us a biscuit, Frank. I may as well have one; it's like being at a tea party for old women sat in here with you two.'

chapter fifty

Peteris Balodis stood at just over five feet and ten inches tall with short-cropped blonde hair. He was well built with a reputation in Latvia as a local hard man. He'd come over to England in 2001 to work but soon realised that the work was hard, the days were long, and the weather was shit. He wanted more. He'd got involved with a gang of Latvian criminals who were supplying drugs into the UK. It had mainly started as a way to earn some extra cash, but Peteris was not stupid. He knew the repercussions if he ever got caught with a decent quantity of class A drugs on him. That was time, serious time, and Peteris didn't want to continue running that risk for some other fucker who didn't get his hands dirty. If he was going to take the risks, he wanted a share of the huge profits. This was when he saw a gap in the market for migrant labour. He began to bring friends back with him every time he returned to England from Latvia. This had somehow grown into him supplying labour on a small scale. He didn't plan it that way but jumped on the opportunity. At first it was just a few friends and acquaintances, but it had grown quickly into friends of friends and then onto people he didn't know at all. Before he knew it, he was in over his head and was supplying migrant labour for two Latvian guys called Andris and Valdis. They were violent men who were basically into slave labour. Peteris was being forced to take the risks all over again, but for different men who didn't get their hands dirty. He was soon supplying most of the Latvian workforce in Lincolnshire and Cambridgeshire, some legal; most were not. He could see the huge profits to be made from supplying migrant labour and again found himself caught up in a criminal network for very little reward. He got peanuts for taking the risks bringing these people in. He wanted to do it for himself. He'd take the risks then, happily if the rewards were there. He knew with the right back up and contacts he could create a network that supplied the whole of the UK, not just with his own countryman but by supplying migrant workers from all over the old Eastern block countries. This is where Frank came in. He'd dealt with Frank a little on the drug side and had got to know his son Richie fairly well. Football had been their common ground, but he found Richie to be a decent bloke, and there seemed to be trust on both sides. Peteris had approached Richie about the possibility of Frank getting involved in the supply of migrant workers. He'd told Richie only half a story, though, and had made out that he was still doing it by himself on a small scale. He'd not mentioned Andris or Valdis. He was hoping he wouldn't have to as Richie had told Peteris that if it meant any supply into Frank's patch, he was involved whether you liked it or not, and it was better to like it than not! Peteris was hoping that Frank would be fully onboard and that Andris and Valdis would be outmuscled. That was his plan anyway. His best friend from Latvia, Maris Peterson was in it with him. Maris was another guy with a temper. He was an inch or so taller than Maris, bald, and was full of tattoos. He looked hard, probably because he was bald with tattoos, whereas Perteris looked like someone who you would take home to meet your mum. He could handle himself no danger, but he was a fairly good-looking bloke.

Richie met them both on the A46 coming into Nottingham. Their car pulled behind Richie's, and they both got out. Richie got out of his Range Rover and shook both their hands. Richie noticed that Peteris looked nervous, anxious almost.

'Nice car Richie, how long you had?' Peteris asked in his best English.

'Just under a year, guzzles the diesel but looks the part. You like it, yeah?'

Peteris nodded. 'One day Richie, I have car like this. When we make lots of money I buy. Cash.'

'I hope you do pal, 'cos that means you're earning some serious money. And if you are, we are. Anyway, let's get going. Are you leaving your car here?'

'Er, no we follow Richie.' Again, Richie thought how nervous he seemed. He then looked at Maris. He had not spoken a word. 'You okay, Maris? You're a bit quiet.'

Maris nodded his head.

'I drink too much last night. I have headache, but I am okay.'

Richie turned to walk towards his car. 'Right, let's go,' he said. He then heard a car door shut behind him. He stopped and turned round expecting to see Peteris or Maris getting something from their car but was surprised to see two guys stood at the side of the car, both dressed in a dark suit, one of them wearing dark sunglasses, but both looking decidedly menacing. Richie was quite taken aback as he'd not noticed any others sat in the car, but then again, he'd not been looking for anyone. He didn't like the atmosphere all of a sudden. It had changed. Even stood outside on a side road off the A46, he could feel the tension. He felt under pressure but swallowed it down. He was conscious not to show emotion. 'Who are these then?' he asked Peteris without taking his stare off the two mystery men. 'I had arranged to meet you and Maris, no one else.'

Peteris looked ashamed as he looked to the floor. 'These two men are Andris and Valdis. They will supply peoples to me, and I will supply peoples to you. They make rules. They want to see who I work with in England. If you want many peoples, we have to deal with them.'

Richie now knew the reason for Peteris's nervousness. He stared at him. He felt let down. He'd trusted Peteris, and now he felt as though he'd tried to shaft him. Peteris couldn't look him in the eye. Richie processed this and studied his body language for a moment. Something that Raquel had taught him to do recently. Richie was unsure if Peteris had tried to shaft him or if he was doing this under duress from the two twats in suits. He decided that if Peteris was trying to shaft him, he'd be arrogant and confident. He looked again at his demeanour which suggested he was embarrassed by the situation. These two guys must have forced him to bring them. Maybe they were the boss men behind Peteris. Richie didn't know for sure, but he'd knew Peteris long enough to give him the benefit of the doubt. Frank would be a different story, though. This had disaster written all over it, but as he was outnumbered four to one, he had no choice but to take them back with him to meet Frank. He needed to warn his dad before they arrived. He spoke to Peteris. 'Right then, we best get going. You lot follow me.' Richie had purposely not spoken to the two men in suits. He didn't want to acknowledge them or give them any status in all this. If they were some kind of hard men, then they'd need to show their mettle once they got to the club. Richie knew he could at least ring Frank from his car. That wasn't a call he was looking forward to, but he reckoned he could reason with Frank and get him to play along for a while.

'Shall I go in Ranger Rover?' Peteris asked, looking as though he really wanted to get away from Andris and Valdis. Richie had already opened his door and was getting inside. He needed to speak to Frank alone. He would have appreciated a few minutes with Peteris and Maris on their own, but there wasn't time for that. He glanced at the two men standing next to Peteris's car. They'd not moved an inch. They looked like statues. He looked up at Peteris.

'No Peteris. You go in that.' He nodded his head towards the old rust bucket of a car that was Peteris's. 'I need to speak to Frank, alone.'

Peteris turned and said something to Maris in Latvian. Richie had no idea what they'd said, but he just hoped it wasn't anything bad.

Frank was drinking a large mug of tea and dunking his sixth ginger nut when the phone rang. It was Richie.

'They've brought two other guys with 'em, Frank. Two serious-looking fuckers an' all. Both dressed in the trademark black suits. No idea who they are. Peteris did tell me their names, but I can't remember.' Frank interrupted before Richie could finish. 'Well, tell them the meet's off. We don't meet with anyone who turns up unannounced.'

'I can't really as I'm in my car and the four of

them are in Peteris's car behind me. I couldn't say no could I seeing as there were four of 'em.' Again, Frank interjected. 'Course ya could. Just tell 'em the meetings off and to go fuck themselves. We decide who we meet, not them fuckers.'

'Look, we'll be with you in ten minutes. I can't pull over now and tell 'em it's off. Listen, I think Peteris and Maris have had to bring these two along under duress.'

'What do you mean under duress?' Talk English, for fuck's sake.'

'I mean, I think these two guys might be who Peteris works for and that Peteris and Maris had no choice in the matter about these two guys tagging along. It was clear they were the top guys in that little foursome. Peteris looked well embarrassed, couldn't look at me, so I don't think he had much choice. He said that if we want to deal in large numbers of people, we had to go through them, so I think we need to meet these guys. Up to you, but I'd keep an open mind if I were you.'

Frank thought for a moment. He sat back in his chair. 'You still there, Frank?' Richie asked as Frank continued to think.

'Yes, I'm here. Okay, we proceed as normal but one wrong move, and they'll wish they'd never tagged along or however you want to put it.' Frank replaced the receiver. Richie took a deep breath and blew out loudly in his car. He just had a feeling this wasn't going to go smoothly.

Frank looked at Jez and Daniel. 'You get the gist of that?' he asked.

Daniel put his arms behind his head and sat back on the sofa. 'I assume Peteris and Maris are not alone?'

'No, two guys with 'em. Trademark black suits. You know the type. I was looking forward to this meeting.

Should have been nice and easy. Peteris and Maris are two handy lads, I get that, but we'd have had them doing whatever we'd wanted with no fuss or nowt. Now we've you got these two guys tagging along.'

'So, what's the plan, Frank?' Jez asked.

'We have a meeting arranged with Peteris and Maris, so we press ahead. We talk to them. As far as we are concerned, these two guys are just there to wipe their arses. Let's see what these two guys are made of. If they're anything to be reckoned with, they'll take over things at their end straight away. If not, they'll just sit there waiting for someone to massage their ego. Richie did well, though. Sussed out the situation, he reckons Peteris and Maris had no choice on the matter. Reckons these guys are who they work for, and if we want to deal large numbers, we have to deal with them. We'll see. He had it all under control, though. I tell you something, Jez; I'm glad me and you will be out of it when these two take over properly.'

Daniel smiled through gritted teeth. He tried to look genuinely pleased with Frank's remark. Inside he was feeling angry. Daniel had always been talked of as Frank's successor. Frank's only successor. This was the first time Frank had ever mentioned them both in the same breath as taking over as a pairing. *Where the fuck had that come from?* Daniel thought to himself as he struggled to look pleased. Daniel had risen through the ranks from an early age. He'd done his time. He'd earned his stripes when the business was still growing. Richie, on the other hand, had been given it all on a plate. Once Frank had put his demons to bed, Richie had had his hand held all the way. Okay, he'd proved himself a worthy senior member of the firm, which was fair enough, but he'd not had to do it the hard way like

Daniel had. The foundations were all there for Richie. Daniel had had to help lay the bricks. Daniel had had to move up the ranks, prove himself at every step. Richie went from lackey to joint Managing Director in one fell swoop.

Frank raised his mug of tea. 'Here's to the future, eh! Richie and Daniel.'

Daniel stood up. 'Just off for a piss.' *Richie and Daniel! What the fuck had happened to Daniel and Richie. He's the firstborn now, is he?* he thought to himself as he closed the office door a little too hard. Jez watched him as he walked across the floor to the men's toilet. He'd noted the strained expression on Daniel's face to be pleased. He'd thought how it wasn't a natural response to Frank's comments, and he'd not seen this before. He looked at Frank, downed the last of his tea, and wondered if that future Frank had just toasted looked as rosy as he thought it did. He kept that thought to himself. He'd learnt that in this life, sometimes it was better to say nothing, better to hold the thought. Sometimes, it's better in this life to say nothing.

Ten minutes later, Frank saw Richie walking across the main floor with Peteris and Maris a couple of steps behind, flanked by two men in suits. He looked over at Jez. 'What's with the sunglasses, for fuck's sake? Come on, let's go upstairs into the main meeting room. Bit cosy in here for eight of us.' Frank poked his head out of the door and beckoned Richie over. 'Take 'em upstairs. We'll follow in a couple of minutes.' Richie nodded, turned around, and took the stairs with the Latvians following him. Frank, Jez, and Daniel followed a minute or so later. Frank wanted to make an entrance. He sat down at the head of the table. Daniel sat on one side of him, Jez on the other. Richie was next to Daniel. Peteris and Maris were next to Richie. Andris and Valdis were next to Jez. Andris had kept his sunglasses on. Frank was dying to comment but stuck to the plan and spoke to Peteris.

'So Peteris, you want to start to bring larger numbers of migrant workers into my areas of business, am I correct?' Peteris looked over at Andris. Andris took off his sunglasses and looked at Frank. Frank could see he had a glass eye. He reminded him of Steven Wallace, and as Frank still disliked Steven, it didn't do anything to warm him to the man who was about to speak.

'We have a big opportunity to make a lot of money— lots of food factories around here. Making meals, how you say, err,' Andris motioned with his hand as if he needed a little encouragement. 'For people who do not like to cook.'

'Convenience food?' Richie said, raising his eyebrows. Andris continued. 'Yes, that is correct—lots of peoples to fill jobs. We supply the workers. I believe you may be able to help with contacts?'

Frank glared at Andris for a second and then averted his gaze back to Peteris. 'So Peteris, you want to start to bring large numbers of migrant workers into my areas of business. Is that correct?' Frank had again asked Peteris the same question and had completely ignored Andris. He could see straight away that Richie's hunch was correct. Peteris and Maris were very junior participants in this foursome and were clearly scared of the two guys in suits who sat opposite them. Maris was just staring at the table. Peteris looked nervous and anxious. Frank was becoming more and more enraged at the liberty that was being taken here. He could see the predicament that Peteris and Maris were in. He liked them both, they'd been more than trustworthy with him in the brief dealings he'd had with them up to now via Richie with the drug handling, but again he saw very clearly that they were just fringe players who could be a liability if Frank were not careful. Andris spoke again.

'As I said, we have many...' Frank looked back at Andris. He was struggling to keep the anger from overflowing but was mindful to remain calm and in control.

'I don't know who the fuck you are, but I have a meeting arranged with those two guys over there.' He pointed to the direction that Peteris and Maris were sitting, 'so unless I ask you to speak, I suggest you keep your fucking mouth closed.' Andris kept his gaze. He didn't flinch. Neither did Frank. Jez readied himself. He needed to be ready to step in to protect his boss if this guy moved an inch. That was Jez's job at the end of the day. That's what Frank paid him for. That's why Frank had him here today sat at his side and in between him and this Latvian guy.

'My name is Andris Berzins, and this,' he pointed with his left hand without taking his gaze away, 'is Valdis Olzols. We supply all of Latvian workers in Lincolnshire, Cambridgeshire, and Norfolk. We now look to supply into Nottinghamshire, Leicestershire, and Derbyshire. Peteris say you have many contacts. We work together, yes? We supply peoples to you, and you supply peoples to factories. Peoples work for you. Factories pay you for peoples, you pay people's small wage, and you pay us monies too and keep a little bit for yourself, yes? We all make money.'

Frank smiled to himself and sat back in his chair.

This guy obviously had no idea who he was dealing with. Frank had to stop himself from laughing out loud. Did this Valdis guy really think that Frank would do all that and pay him money for the privilege? Frank now knew that these two guys in suits were division one at best. Certainly not premier league. He could not believe that they'd come into this meeting today, having done no research on Frank whatsoever. He'd been momentarily impressed with the fact that Andris had not flinched and had kept his gaze, even with his glass eye when Frank had told him to keep his mouth shut, but that was clearly because he didn't know who Frank was. They'd certainly not come into contact with anyone of Frank's calibre before in their dealings within the UK. If they had, they'd have been sent packing, of that Frank was sure. He knew they must be half decent at what they must have done to have Peteris and Maris sat there like two puppies, but this was 2004, and Frank was not only premier league but was top-four material. He was champion's league, and these two were a long way off Frank. It made him realise at that moment how big the gap was from two hard men like Peteris and Maris who could handle themselves in a bar brawl and who you'd have on your side in a ruck for someone like Frank who ruled criminal empires. It was massive. These two here today were nothing more than a couple of local gangsters who thought they were the big league. Frank leaned forward. 'Andris, you say? Mmm, well let me tell you how it's going to be Andris, should I decide to allow you to supply any migrant labour into my areas of business. If, and it's still an if, at this stage, I decide to do business with you, it will work like this. You will supply the factories, the 'peoples' as you put it will work for you, you will work for me, well my son Richie in fact, and you will pay me a hefty weekly amount for me allowing you to operate on my patch. I' Frank pointed to his chest, 'I, will do fuck all apart from count the cash you pay my son every week. You, on the other hand, will do all the work, and in return for that, I will allow you to keep a small percentage of the money you are paid from these factories. That's the deal. Now then,' Frank looked at his watch, 'you have exactly one minute to think about it.'

The tension in the room was tangible. You could almost chew on it. Peteris was sat there trying not to look anyone in the eye but felt like punching the air and dancing around the room. He didn't like Andris and Valdis. They treat people like shit, especially their workers. Nothing more than slaves. They were bullies who'd bullied their way up the criminal ladder that was leant against the slave labour wall. Peteris had banked on this. He knew they'd be out of their depth against Frank. Even though he'd much rather them not have been involved at all, he knew they'd be no match for Frank. Richie was just pleased it looked as though he would come out of this unscathed and not feel the wrath of his father.

Andris looked to his left at Valdis, who lent into his partner and whispered something in Latvian. Andris turned to Frank.

'That is not how we do business. We find another partner to work with for these factories.' He looked at Peteris. 'We go. You waste my time,' Andris then stood up. Jez sprung from his chair, sat Andris back down, grabbed Andris by the back of his head, and smashed his face into the table before anyone could react. Valdis stood up and pulled out a blade. He stepped back from the table.

'We go,' he shouted. Jez still had Andris face down on the table. Daniel stood up. 'If that's all you've got pal, you're fucked.' He walked around to Valdis's side of the table. 'My cock's bigger than that.' Frank looked at Richie. It was a big knife. Richie shrugged his shoulders but got up to accompany his brother. Valdis was cornered. Andris was struggling to try to get out of Jez's grip. He smashed his face into the table again and again. Frank raised his hand. Jez stopped. Valdis looked at Frank. Frank looked at his watch. Daniel took the opportunity to kick the knife out of Valdis's hand and punched him hard in the face. Richie picked up the knife. Daniel picked up Valdis and threw him into the wall and punched him twice. He then sat him down on one of the chairs, grabbed him around the neck from behind, and squeezed. Richie then raised his hand and thrust the knife straight into Valdis's thigh. The knife went straight through his thigh and straight through the chair. Valdis screamed in agony as blood seeped through the chair and dripped onto the floor. Richie then calmly drew the knife out of his thigh and calmly went and sat back down. Andris was shouting something in Latvian. Frank looked over at Peteris. 'What's he saying?'

'He's saying you are all crazy,' Peteris replied.

Frank motioned for Jez to let Andris sit back up. Blood was pouring from his face. Frank was surprised to see his glass eye was still in place. Valdis was still grimacing and holding his thigh. Daniel still had his arm around his throat. Frank motioned for him to sit down. As Daniel took his seat, Frank leant forward and rested both his elbows on the table and clasped his hands together.

'So, do we have a deal? Your minute is up. What is it to be gentlemen?'

'Yes, we have a deal,' Andris said.

'Good, then let's get down to business 'cos I think your friend over there will need to go to hospital soon. Who's making the tea?'

Later that night, Frank sat on his luxurious sofa with Gloria, his rock. She was the one constant person outside of the firm that he could confide in. She was involved, to a degree, of course, but more by association than anything else. Gloria knew everything that Frank got involved in. He confided in her a lot. He needed to. In this life, if you didn't offload the shit you had to deal with, you'd go crazy. Gloria was like his counsellor. She would just sit and listen. Often, she wouldn't even pass comment; she'd just listen. That was good for Frank. He didn't need someone who thought they had an opinion on everything they knew fuck all about. He had enough of them in his life outside of the huge pile he lived in with Gloria at Papplewick. Gloria had moved in a couple of years ago. It had been Frank's idea. She would never have suggested it herself. She knew how Frank still longed for his Renee, and she knew she'd never take her place in his heart, but the best thing about Gloria was that she didn't want to. She was happy with who she was, comfortable with herself, and didn't want to be anyone else, not to Frank or to anyone for that matter. Frank liked that about Gloria, always had. She was as straight as an arrow and as loyal as anyone could be. That's why Frank confided in her. He knew she'd never spill the beans about anything he told her. He'd seen that in her from the very outset. He'd never marry her, though. He always told her that. Frank had never married. He'd not managed to marry Renee, and in Frank's head, that meant there was no one else for him in that department. Renee had been the only girl he'd ever wanted to marry. He loved Gloria, loved her to bits, and would die for her, but marriage was a sacred thing for Frank, not something to be taken lightly, and he still felt, all these years later that if he ever married anyone else, including Gloria that he'd be committing adultery. In his mind whilst he stayed unmarried, he was being faithful to his Renee.

'Good day's work today, Gloria. You know my two boys are really showing their mettle. They'll take this business over soon.'

'Does that mean we can retire then?' Gloria asked, half laughing.

'Yeah, we can retire to one of those old people's places, you know the retirement villages, for the over fifties, or whatever. They have one on the way to Matlock, you know.'

Gloria hit him with one of the cushions. 'If you think I'm going into one of them places Frank Pearson, to wilt away, you can think again. I was thinking more like somewhere hot and sunny.'

Frank laughed out loud. 'Yeah, but just think of the fun you'd have. They'll have bingo twice a week, line dancing probably one afternoon, and there's bound to be a few murders happen in those places. You could be an amateur sleuth.'

'The only murder that'll be happening around here is you, Frank Pearson. Now pour me another gin,' Gloria passed Frank her glass. He laughed again as he got up.

'Are you gonna have a small one?' she asked.

'Yeah, go on then. I'll pour myself a small whiskey to celebrate the deal we did today with the Latvians. Lots of money to be had there ya know. Migrant workers are big business and will only get bigger. Richie's idea was this, though. He did well today, especially when he stabbed that Valdis or whatever he's called. Calm as ya like Gloria. Reminded me of myself back in the day.'

Frank sat back down and passed Gloria her drink. 'And what about Daniel?' she asked as she placed her Gin and Tonic on the coffee table.

'Same old Gloria, calm as fuck. Ya know Daniel, he's just like me, but younger and not as good looking,' Frank winked at her as he sipped his whiskey.

Gloria had seen what Jez had noticed many times recently. She was a shrewd cookie, was Gloria, and whilst she rarely passed comment, she would watch from afar. She knew all of Frank's men inside out, knew their traits, knew their funny habits and little ways, and knew when they were happy, pissed off, or even when they were not really listening to what was going off. She also knew that Daniel had envy in his eyes. She saw the hatred and resentment he had towards Richie. She also knew that both Richie and Frank were oblivious to it. Phoebe knew, though. She and Gloria had discussed it a few times over a mug of tea or a glass of wine. Phoebe was concerned. She'd told Gloria of Daniel's mood swings and his drinking, how it was increasing and how she and the kids never really knew which Daniel would walk through the door at night. Archie had very little to do with Daniel. He was all his uncle Richie. This only made the situation worse, but Daniel was his own worst enemy. The more time Archie spent with Richie; the more Daniel resented him. It was a vicious circle, and Daniel expected Archie, an eight-year-old, to make the first move. Phoebe had told Gloria that she couldn't get it through to Daniel that his son was eight and needed his dad. He yearned for him. Daniel couldn't see that Richie was just filling the void that Daniel had created. Archie needed a father figure to show him things that fathers did. Richie was just fulfilling that role, Daniel's role. On the other hand, Alice idolised her daddy, but even Alice was cautious around him at times, especially when he first returned home. Once Alice knew it was nice, fun daddy that had walked through the door, she was all over him, but if it were 'grumpy daddy' as she would put it, she would steer well clear.

'You should tell him sometimes, Frank. He needs to hear it.'

'What you going on about, he's fine is Daniel. He knows what I think of him, he's my number two, always will be, until they take over, that is. He doesn't need to be told. He's a big lad ya know,' Frank put his arm around Gloria, and she snuggled into him. Frank really didn't have a clue.

'Maybe he's feeling the pressure a bit, ya know, with Richie coming to the front more, he was always used to it being just you and him at the forefront.'

'Nah, you're drinking too much of that gin, girl. It's making you all soppy. Gin does that ya know. Here try this whiskey.' Frank pushed it under her nose. 'Put hairs on ya chest this will.'

'Give over ya big lump. I'll stick to me gin. Think about it though, Frank.'

Frank sighed. 'Yeah, okay if you insist. I'll have a word.'

Gloria didn't really believe what Frank had just

said. She knew he was just paying her lip service to shut her up.

Daniel lay in bed. Phoebe rested her head on his chest. She was asleep. He could tell by her breathing. He lay thinking about the events of the day. The way he'd put it on a plate for Richie to stab Valdis. It was a good move by Richie, it had really got their message across to the Latvians and everyone had commented on it. No one had mentioned the fact that Daniel had made the first move on Valdis, that Daniel had kicked the knife out of his hand, or the fact that Daniel had got Valdis onto the chair in a sort of headlock before Richie plunged the knife into his thigh. After the Latvians had left to set things in motion, all the banter had been on how Valdis had struggled to walk across the floor to the exit door. How Richie had stabbed him and how Richie was gonna run that arm of the business. Even Jez got a mention for how he'd smashed Andris's head into the table. Daniel was pissed off; in fact, the more he thought about it, the more he was raging inside.

'Don't worry about it, Daniel,' Phoebe said as she lifted her head up. She'd only momentarily drifted off as she'd been lying there thinking about what Daniel had told her earlier. She'd told Daniel to stop letting it fester within him, that Richie was not a threat but was an asset to the business, as he was. She'd told him that if he didn't stop it, it'd end up killing him. Daniel had replied by saying, *it'll kill one of us Phoebe, it'll kill one of us.* That had scared Phoebe. She didn't know what Daniel had meant. Daniel just said it was just a figure of speech, nothing more, but Phoebe felt there was more to it.

Daniel didn't answer; he just kissed her on the top

of the head and turned over. He closed his eyes and tried to put his thoughts to the back of his mind. He needed some sleep. He was tired.

Eight years later...

chapter fifty-one

May 2012 – Mansfield

Richie and Archie came out of the One Call Stadium in Mansfield with the seven thousand or so others having just seen Mansfield Town lose their second leg play-off game to York City 1-0. That meant another season in the Conference League.

'Fucking hell Archie, I can't believe it. I really thought we were gonna win today. I fucking hate it in the Conference League. It's shit. Shit grounds, shit players, just fucking shit.'

I know, I'm gutted. We played well, though.'

'No good if you don't win, Archie lad. Anyway, come on, ya Uncle Richie will buy you a pint. I need to drown my sorrows.'

Archie smiled. He knew his uncle Richie would buy him a few beers. Since he'd been fourteen, he'd been able to sneak a few pints here and there, especially if he were with his uncle. No one questioned anything if he was with Richie. No one would dare. He reckoned his uncle Richie could just walk behind any bar in the town, and he'd be able to pull his own pints if he wanted to. No one would say a word. He'd dared his uncle to do just that a couple of times, but Richie had told him that was no way to conduct yourself. It was just an abuse of power. Yeah, Richie could if he wanted to, but as he'd explained to Archie, *that would just make you a dick head.*

Archie was too young and immature to understand that. He was still star-struck by his dad and his uncle, and his Grandad Frank. They seemed to be like celebrities in Mansfield, and Nottingham for that matter. Archie had been to a few Forest games with his uncle over the past couple of seasons, and he was treated like royalty there too. He knew that Richie used to be a football hooligan back in the nineties, and he still knew most of the lads down at Forest. Mansfield and Forest had been quite close on the hooligan front, apparently for a few years, so whenever they went to Forest, it was like a premier league player had turned up. He'd never known so many people want to shake someone's hand. He loved his uncle Richie always had. Archie couldn't remember a time when he'd not been with his uncle Richie. He'd just always been a feature in his life. More so than his dad, Daniel. Archie got on with his dad but from a distance. He loved his dad, and now and again, they would do some bonding, going to the gym together or just walking in the woods, but it was quite infrequent. Whenever he thought back to his childhood, he couldn't remember his dad spending time with him. His dad was always there, always part of the family, but even though he was always a constant fixture in Archie's life and had provided well for his family, he hadn't really got many memories of time with his dad. He just remembered his dad always being there. The memories engrained in his head were that of playing football with his uncle Richie, or when Richie would take him to play football for the school team, under tens, under elevens, etc. It was always his uncle, never his dad. His dad had taught him to ride a bike, and that had been fun, but he'd only been about four or five years old, and the memories had faded.

Growing up, he wanted to be like his uncle Richie, rather than his dad Daniel. His grandad Frank was someone else he idolised. Frank worshipped his grandchildren, both of them. Archie's sister Alice was the apple of her grandad's eye. She could get Frank to do anything, and she knew it. They'd both loved staying at Grandad's house when they were younger. They could get away with murder. Archie often remembered Gloria saying one day when she thought Archie wasn't listening; *they're the only two people I know who get away with murder more than you, Frank.* They'd both laughed at the time, and Archie had wondered what she'd meant. As he got older, he began to piece it all together. He wanted to be part of this world. He loved the attention he got when he was with his grandad, dad, or Uncle Richie. He revelled in it. He wanted the house, the cars, the money, and the power. He wanted to be like them and was itching to prove himself, but his dad kept him on a tight reign. Daniel had told Archie for a number of years now that the life he led was not for everyone, and before he allowed Archie into that world, he needed to be sure he had what it took. Archie would tell him that unless he let him off the chain, he couldn't prove himself. Daniel said to him that if it were in him, it would show itself. No need to go around looking for trouble to prove something that was there anyway. Archie didn't really understand, but his uncle Richie had told him that his dad was right, so he guessed it must be the case, and he'd just have to wait.

They walked in The Vic, a pub in Mansfield that was a regular for football fans. It was heaving with grown men and young lads all singing. 'Yellows, Yellows,' at the top of their voices. It was a simple song of just two words repeated over and over again, but as a Mansfield Town fan, it got your adrenalin going. Mansfield Town play in a yellow strip, and the song is a term of reference to their colours and the fact that as well as "The Stags" it's a nickname for the club. Archie was in full song as Richie got two pints of bitter from the bar.

'Fucking love days like these Richie, great atmosphere, I just wish we'd have won.'

'Yeah, well, that's, life lad. You'll have a lot more days of disappointment following Mansfield, so get used to it.'

Richie spotted someone across the bar who owed him some money, a fair bit of money. He worked for the business a bit here and there collecting debts and had apparently collected a debt of over fifteen grand a few days ago and had yet to pass the readies over. It was a debt owed to Richie personally. Richie would often lend people money as a sort of loan shark. It was a lucrative business and one that Frank allowed both Richie and Daniel to undertake on a private scale. He only allowed his two sons to operate like this. Frank would never allow anyone else to conduct any sort of business of this nature on his patch, but he overlooked it where Richie and Daniel were concerned. He saw it as a perk for his two sons to have a little side-line of their own, but the three of them knew that this was the only side-line allowed. Anything else would not be tolerated by Frank, even for his two sons. Richie passed his pint to Archie.

'Here, hold this. I just need a word with someone.'

Jason Davidson was stood holding his pint with his mates, totally oblivious of Richie's presence in the pub. He was in full swing singing songs with everyone else.

Richie was sure he'd collected the debt as it had been confirmed by the debtor, a garage owner from Kirkby in Ashfield. And Richie had no reason to doubt the money had been repaid as he'd dealt with this garage owner a few times already, and everything had been paid on time. Unless Jason Davidson was to convince Richie otherwise, he wanted his money.

Richie tapped Jason on the shoulder. He turned round to see Richie smiling at him.

'Enjoy the game then, Jason? I thought we played well, did you?'

'Err, alright Richie, didn't see you come in.'

'No, you wouldn't, would you, bit full innit?'

'Err, yeah, yeah it is. You wanna pint?' Jason looked a little nervous. His group of mates had all stopped singing and were swigging their beer anxiously, trying to look anywhere but directly at Richie. Archie was stood watching. He had to stand on his tiptoes to be able to see what was going on. He decided to move a little closer. Richie shook his head.

'No, you fat cunt, I want fifteen grand.' Richie flashed his right hand three times to signal fifteen. 'You hear me? Fifteen grand.'

'He ain't paid me yet, Richie. I've been round three times, but he ain't paid me. Each time he says he'll have it for me for the next day, but when I go, he says it'll be tomorrow. Honest, I ain't lying.'

Richie held his gaze. He was unsure whether to believe him or not. Richie could normally tell when someone was lying, a skill Raquel had taught him, and if he was honest, he thought Jason might be telling the truth.

'Well, that don't fit with what he told me. I rung him yesterday, and he said he'd paid you last Friday, which, seeing as tonight is Wednesday is nearly a week ago.' Richie moved a step closer into Jason's face. Archie was now only a few feet away and could see that Jason was scared. He was a big lad, quite chubby really but just big all over. Jason was at least two inches taller than Richie and a good four stone heavier, but he looked like a rabbit caught in some headlights. Archie could see he was trying desperately to look unconcerned, but he could see the fear in his eyes. Richie stuck his finger into Jason's cheek. 'I'll pick you up at nine in the morning. Me and you will go and see Andy Barnes, but let me make myself clear, if you're lying to me, I'll rip your face in two. You got that?'

Archie could not hear what Richie was saying due to the noise in the pub, but he could tell by Richie's body language and Jason's face that the fat lad was getting a warning. Jason nodded.

'I ain't lying Richie, honest, I ain't lying.' Richie took his finger out of Jason's cheek.

'See you at nine.'

He got his pint from Archie and took a big drink.

'Right lad, your round, I think?' Archie was too excited to go to the bar.

'Who's that Richie, he fucking shit himself.'

'Just someone who owes me money, that's all. Keep your voice down. He's had his warning.'

'So, what you gonna do now?'

'Nothing for you to worry about, now get to the bar. That'll be your last too. I'm not taking you home pissed.'

'Can't we stay for a few more... Something might kick off,' Archie said excitedly. Richie laughed. He reminded him so much of himself at that age, all excited about a bit of a brawl at a game.

'Fuck off, ya daft sod. York will be long gone by now. Here, here's a fiver, should be enough.'

'I thought it was my round?' Archie asked, knowing that he never bought a drink when he was out with Richie.

'It is, but just with my money as usual.'

An hour or so later, Richie dropped Archie off at Daniel and Phoebe's house in Southwell and then drove the short journey back to Mansfield. He'd bought the old family home in Blackscotch Lane from his dad when his dad finally came to sell it. Frank had kept it when he'd bought his house in Papplewick but after a few years had been persuaded to sell it by Richie. He'd always liked that house and preferred to be in Mansfield. It was his hometown and where he felt safest. It was the first house he'd bought, and he never really wanted to live anywhere else. For all his bravado Richie liked to be where he felt safest and for somewhere to live, Mansfield was it for him. Even though he'd spent most of his childhood in that house and at times his childhood had been unhappy, he still had an affinity to the house in Blackscotch Lane. He knew that his girlfriend Marie would be waiting up for him. He'd never really settled on a long-term relationship. Throughout his twenties, he'd been too busy with football, beer, having a good time, and trying to cement his place in the family firm to worry about relationships. He'd just had lots of short-term flings that had suited him. He'd had a few more serious relationships in his thirties that had lasted a while but no one that he felt at home with. Marie was different, though. She was thirty-seven years old, quite shy, quite reserved almost, slim with long blonde hair, green eyes, and a lovely husky voice. He often thought of how similar the women were in the lives of the Pearson men. Frank had always said that their mum was the quiet, reserved type, Phoebe was similar, and now Marie, who Richie had been dating for over three years, were of a same make-up. Even Gloria, who was a little more confident in herself, was rather quiet and kept to herself. None of the women in their lives were loud, brassy types. None of them thought they could interfere with the business, and none of them lauded it about. Richie had not purposefully gone out looking for anyone like Marie. She'd just served him one day in the supermarket. That very night they'd gone to the cinema and had been an item ever since. He still fucked Raquel on occasion. He always felt guilty when he returned home to Marie, but Raquel was such a good shag that sometimes he couldn't help it. He just needed that bit of extras that he got from Raquel. He'd never felt guilty before with any of his other girlfriends, but with Marie, he felt a pang of guilt every time he did it.

Marie had moved in about eighteen months or so ago and had made it into a home. Cushions on the sofa, candles in the bathroom, those sorts of things, and Richie liked it. Like Phoebe, Marie knew what Richie did for a living. She knew of him and his family before that day she'd served him in the supermarket but had never in her wildest dreams ever thought she'd be living with him. She'd been married before, divorced about five years ago after she'd caught her husband for the third time having an affair. She'd lost twins in her mid-twenties whilst carrying them and could no longer have children. This suited Richie. He loved kids, loved Archie and Alice but had never really harboured after kids of his own. He always thought that was because of the childhood he'd had, maybe it was, maybe it wasn't, but at forty-one, he was happy with his life, happy that he was at the top of the firm with Frank and Daniel, happy that he lived in his ideal home and happy that he shared it all with Marie. The only two things that ever made him sad were when he thought of his childhood, all the unhappy times, the fights, the tears, the lonely nights sat in his bedroom, and the time he was in hospital after saving Phoebe from being raped. That night he'd heard Frank tell Daniel that he'd have still traded Richie for one day with Renee and that he didn't need him, and that Daniel would have been enough for him. That had hurt Richie. It still hurt him now. He still, if he was honest, had not dealt with it all, the childhood memories and what he heard that night. Even now, if he were honest with himself, he knew that it would not take much to bring all that back to the fore again. He hoped it never would, but while ever they were all still breathing, Richie knew that his dad had never wanted him. Now, his brother resented him, and if they could both turn back the clock, Frank would save his mum and let him die, and Daniel would go back to 1996 and would never tell Frank to make things good with him. Once things were said, they couldn't be unsaid. You could apologise, make amends, and try and put things right, but at the end of the day, as Richie well knew, if they had the chance, they'd put it all back to how it was, how it could have been, or in Frank's words, how it should have been. Whenever Richie thought about it, he would become angry, resentful, and hurt. He would swallow it down and put the thoughts away, but over time they would re-surface. As time went by, they would re-surface more and more often.

He walked into the house and flung his keys on the hall table. He took off his jacket and walked through into the kitchen. Marie was already pouring him a beer.

'I thought you'd need this after losing one-nil,' she said, 'Doesn't that mean they've lost?' Richie shook his head.

'Course it does, ya numpty. If they didn't score and York did, then I'd say they lost, wouldn't you?' He picked up his beer and put both his arms around her waist.

'Yes, I know that I'm not that daft. What I meant was that they've lost over the two legs, haven't they?' Richie put his cheek at the side of hers.

'Aye, it does, I'm afraid. Never mind though, par for the course with Mansfield.' He swung her round and lifted her onto the worktop and kissed her neck.

'Err, I think you need a shower first, mister,' Marie whispered into his ear. 'You've been out of the house since this morning, so shower if you want any of that,' she said as she rubbed his erection through his jeans.

'Okay, ten minutes, and I'll be ready,' he shouted as he ran upstairs.

chapter fifty-two

Jason Davidson was getting dressed. It was 8:20am, and he was expecting Richie in just over half an hour. Richie was never late, something he was known for, so Jason knew he'd have to be ready. He was nervous. Whilst he knew he wasn't lying; he was still nervous and anxious. He only had his word that Andy Barnes had not paid him, and according to Richie, Andy had said he had, and as it was all paid and received in cash, how could he prove it? Surely Richie would believe him. He'd never done him out of any money, never would, but then again, Andy Barnes had always paid up on time. He'd borrowed from Richie a few times and had always paid on the nose. The thing that was going to go against Jason was the fact that he'd not reported into Richie after each of his visits. He'd visited three times in the past week but had not kept Richie up to date. That looked bad. Jason usually did, not every time but more often than not, but on this occasion, he'd missed paying him three times running, and that stuck out like a sore thumb. He fastened his jeans and went down to make a brew and have a couple of crumpets. He needed something to settle his stomach.

Richie picked up Darren en route. Darren still dealt some drugs for the Pearsons in Forest Town and on the Oak Tree Estate but, over the years, had become a bit of an enforcer. He was a handy bloke, now in his early forties and still as trustworthy as ever.

'So, what's the crack then, Richie?' he asked as he put his seatbelt on.

'Not sure, mate, to be honest, either Andy Barnes is fucking us about, or Jason has done the fifteen grand. One of 'em's lying.'

'So how you gonna know who?'

'Well, Andy said he paid Jason last Friday. Jason says not, says he's been three times in the past week to collect.' Richie looked over at Darren. 'So, Darren, me old pal, either way, I want to know who's lying, that's why you're here.' Darren smiled. He knew that either way, he was going to dish out a beating to someone, and he liked that, he liked that very much.

Both Richie and Darren could see how nervous Jason was. Richie could understand, but Darren thought if he were telling the truth, why would he be nervous? They pulled into the garage just out of Kirkby town centre. The three of them got out. Darren and Jason followed Richie into the office where Andy Barnes was on the phone. He looked up, saw who had just walked in, and said, *I'll call you back.*

'Andy,' Richie said as he sat down in the chair that was obviously for customers. 'I rang you on Saturday, and you said you'd paid the fifteen grand to Jason here last Friday.'

Andy sat back in his seat and lit a cigarette. 'Yes, that's right, gave him fifteen bundles of a grand. Crisp new notes.'

Jason flew around the side of Richie and grabbed Andy by the neck, pulled him up, and shoved him against the wall. 'Ya fucking lying bastard. Ya gave me fuck all. Three times I've been here.'

'Let him go, Jason, if the guy says he paid you, then I need to know where the money is. Darren, stand by that door will you and make sure no one escapes. We need to sort this out gentlemen,' Richie said as he stood up. 'One of you is taking me for a prick. Now, this ain't gonna end well for one of you. I'm not bothered who gets hurt. I just want my money.'

Jason let Andy go, who brushed himself down. 'I've fucking paid, so I ain't paying another penny.'

Richie sat back down. 'Sit down, Andy. Jason, you just stand there. Now then, gents, we can have this sorted very quickly.' He then looked at Andy. 'I know Andy that you have CCTV in this garage.' He pointed to the TV monitor that was showing four separate pictures on the screen simultaneously. Two of these pictures were of the very office they were sat in. Richie could see all four of them on the TV. 'And I know how your system works, 'cos I know who fitted it. They very kindly gave me a crash course in how to operate your system at seven o'clock this morning. They're good fellas, you see, and according to them, it records for a fortnight before it starts to re-record over itself, so if you did pay Jason last Friday, it would be on your CCTV. If you didn't then, we would see Jason call three times over the past week, having collected nowt. Now then gents, pull up a chair as the film is about to begin.' Andy Barnes's colour drained from his face. He looked as though someone had just sucked all the blood out of him with a syringe. He swallowed hard. He probably didn't even realise he'd done it, but Richie knew that was a clear sign that he was under pressure. He stuttered.

'Err, I'm err, I'm not, err, not sure if it works right, Richie. I've had it a while ya know. Can't rely on that, I wouldn't have thought.'

'Well, let's try, shall we.' Richie smiled as he took control of the mouse that operated the system. Jason felt a huge wave of relief come over him. He looked up at the ceiling and sighed. He'd had a fair few shags in his life, even being a fat bastard, but he'd never experienced a feeling quite like the feeling he felt now. It was euphoric. He watched Andy Barnes's face as Richie scrolled back to Friday 2nd of May. He looked as though he wanted to cry. He'd never seen anyone look as frightened as Andy Barnes did right now. Richie had it on fast forward. He then paused it and rewound it back a little. You could see Jason come into the office. 'Ah, here we are Andy, here's Jason here look, and there's you sat in ya chair. Can't make out what you're saying, mind, but I can see Jason wagging his finger at you, and his face looks rather aggressive. I can't see any money, though.' They watched it for a further two and a half minutes until they saw Jason leave. They then saw Andy sit back in his chair and do the wanker sign to the door, obviously aimed at Jason who'd just left. Richie paused the footage, sat back in his chair, and crossed his arms. He shrugged his shoulders to Andy as if to say, *well then?*

Andy again swallowed hard. 'I thought I'd have had the money by now, honest. I was trying to buy myself a bit of time. I wasn't not going to pay you, honest. It will be here tomorrow, one hundred percent guaranteed. On my life Richie. I'll have it all tomorrow for you.' Richie shook his head.

'The biggest disappointment Andy was the lying, trying to get Jason here to take the rap. I fucking hate liars, worse than a thief a liar, never know where you are with a liar.' He stood up. 'I'll see you outside boys, but remember I need him in a fit enough state to get me my money tomorrow.' Richie walked out of the office and stood outside breathing in the morning air as Jason and Darren beat Andy Barnes black and blue. They didn't beat him to a pulp as they knew they needed to leave him able to get Richie's money. When they were finished, they walked outside. Richie walked back in. He knelt and picked Andy's beaten face off the ground.

'If you let me down tomorrow Andy, you'll never walk again.' Richie walked back outside. He shook Jason's hand and nodded to him. Jason nodded back. No words were spoken, but they both knew what was meant. 'Right lads, breakfast on me.' Richie said as he straightened his tie.

Richie got up the next morning bright and early. He was an early riser; he was making breakfast for him and Marie. Scrambled eggs and crumpets. Marie still worked at the same supermarket where she had been working when she'd met Richie. She'd worked there for over fifteen years. Richie had told her to give it up, but she liked the job. She enjoyed the banter with her colleagues, loved the customers, and above all else, it allowed her to earn her own money. That had always been important to Marie. She'd never liked to be totally dependant on anyone. It had started really because of her husband's infidelity. She knew her marriage would not last forever. She'd tried to leave him a couple of times beforehand but just didn't have the strength at the time. It took a third affair before she finally realised that she was worth more than what she had become. She'd dropped her hours to part-time but wasn't going to give it up completely. They'd been supportive when she'd lost the twins, and even though she knew she'd repaid them tenfold since it happened, she still felt a sense of loyalty. Richie understood and had stopped nagging her to leave, but he still hated it when she had to work weekends, which thankfully was only one in four.

Richie left home mid-morning for a meeting with Peteris. The business of bringing in migrant labour had gone well. Peteris was now running it for Richie. They met once a fortnight for a catch-up. He still had Maris at his side, but Andris and Valdis had fucked off after the first twelve months. It just didn't work. Valdis had been a pain in the arse and never forgave Richie for stabbing him in the leg. Andris never quite managed to get hold of the fact that he worked for Richie and that Frank overruled everything. He'd been used to calling the shots, so a fallout was inevitable. Frank had given them an ultimatum after a row over the state of the workers when they first arrived. They looked like something out of a war camp. It had happened before, so Frank being Frank, had told them if it happened again, they were out of it. It did, and they were. Last Peteris had heard, they were plying the same trade in Wales. Peteris was trustworthy and had the same ethics as Frank and Richie. The workers were assets to be looked after. They were the merchandise and like any other product, needed to be well presented and in good working order. Other people had got in on the game, so competition was aplenty. Business was good, though. Peteris had his Range Rover, something he reminded Richie about constantly. It was his pride and joy. It was always immaculate. In fact, he was on his second. After having lunch with Peteris, Richie made his way over to Kirkby to see Andy Barnes. He took

Peteris with him just in case he needed any muscle, but he wasn't expecting any aggravation after the beating Andy had received yesterday. They went in Peteris's car; they always did if they went anywhere. Peteris just loved to drive it.

'You should buy new one Richie; my car is newer than your old thing. People think I am boss. They will think you work for me,' Peteris laughed out loud as he said it. Richie laughed too. He liked Peteris, liked his sense of humour.

'In ya dreams, son, in ya fucking dreams. Anyhow, next left, and it's just halfway down that road on your right. Just pull into the yard.' Peteris did as he was asked. As they pulled into the yard, Richie sat bolt upright. The yard was empty.

'Where's all the fucking motors?' Richie shouted as he undid his seatbelt. The yard was usually full of cars waiting to be sold. Andy would have at least thirty to forty at any one time. Nothing ever too fancy. Lots of runabouts under ten grand. Richie jumped out of the Range Rover and spun round in the car park. He had a bad feeling. He just knew what was coming. He tried the door into the office. It was open. He walked in and saw a big piece of white card perched on the desk resting on the top of the back of the seat. It just said - 'GO FUCK YASELF RICHIE, 15,000 TIMES.' Richie stopped dead in his tracks. He rubbed his face with his hand and sat down. He laughed out loud and shouted. 'You fucker,' to himself as he took in what Andy Barnes had just done. He'd just signed his own death warrant. Richie sat forward and put his elbows on the desk. He looked at the CCTV monitor. It was blank. He looked at the cameras in the office. They were gone. He'd taken the CCTV out, so now Richie couldn't even see who'd taken the motors. He shook his head and looked again at the card and the chair that Andy was sat in yesterday. 'You fucker,' he said again. He looked at Peteris. 'I'll hunt that fucker down Peteris if it's the last thing I do. The sly old bastard.' Peteris didn't know what to say. He just said.

'If you need any help boss, you know where I am.' Richie patted him on the back.

'Cheers, mate.'

Richie got back to his car after being dropped off by Peteris and immediately got on the phone to Ray Parkes. Ray lived in Oxfordshire in a very nice house by a river. Ray was an ex-copper from the Met who now worked freelance as a private investigator. He'd been a bent copper most of his working life and had done a little stretch at her Majesty's pleasure when they caught him. Ray kept his mouth shut, did the time, and was very well rewarded by quite a few well-known faces when he came out. He was now quite comfortable financially, but the difference with Ray was that he did more work for criminals in his current role as a PI than he did for Joe public. Ray could find anyone you see. If the person were alive, Ray would find 'em. No one knew how he did it half the time, but then again, no one asked too many questions. He always kept his mouth shut, never told anyone who he was working for or who he was looking for. He was totally trustworthy. He'd proved that when he did his time. He was well known throughout the criminal underworld and would work anywhere at any time for a hefty fee. It was money well spent, though.

'Ray, Richie Pearson, Frank's son, how ya doing?'

'I'm okay, Richie. I hear you're no longer the

black sheep?'

'Fucking hell, Ray, how long were you inside? Things have been good this end for fifteen years or so. How long since I last saw you?'

'I dunno boy, eight years or so I think, anyway time flies and I have more important things to do than think about whether you are back in favour or not. I assume this is not a social call, I mean, you're not coming to visit for the weekend, or anything, are ya?'

Richie laughed. 'No Ray, I need someone finding. He's ran off with fifteen thousand of my new £1 coins, so I'd like to track him down if you get my drift.'

'I certainly do, now then let me pull over, and then you can give me all the details you have, and then I'll tell you how many of the new £1 coins I'll be taking off you as my commission when I find him.'

'I didn't think it was free, Ray.'

'Ah well, that's only if I don't find him, but as you well know, I've never not been paid yet, so just assume you'll be shelling out. Right, I'm parked up. I've got my pen and my notebook, so off ya go. What's his name?'

Richie gave Ray all the details he had. He then rang Jason to get him to ask around the locality and see if anyone knew who took the motors off the yard. He then sat in his car and looked out of the window. No one had ever taken a liberty like this before with him. He was so mad; he was calm. It was strange to Richie as he'd never had this emotion before. He was as calm as he could be, but inside, he was fucking raging. This was how his dad reacted when he was faced with a situation, he could do nothing about or when he was on the back foot. He now knew the control his dad felt when he was in a situation like this. At one time, Richie would have been running around smashing things up, threatening all and sundry, but now he just made a few calls, got things in motion, and would now sit back and wait for the phone call from Ray Parkes. Richie Pearson was finally the real deal. Richie Pearson had finally arrived.

Nearly two weeks had passed without any sign of Andy Barnes. It seemed that he'd just disappeared off the face of the earth. There was no sign on social media of any activity on any of his accounts, and Ray Parkes was drawing a blank. This was frustrating Ray as he'd never had this issue before. Two weeks was a long time in his game, especially when working for the criminal underworld. In that world, people didn't stay hidden for long. It was accepted that Andy Barnes was not a face of any sort, but if he wanted to disappear, he would need the help of someone in the criminal fraternity, especially if he wanted to change his identity. That sort of paperwork needed criminal help, and criminals of the kind who provided these low-level services could seldom keep their mouths shut. Someone always let something slip, mostly accidentally, but nevertheless, it didn't usually take this long for Ray to get a sniff of something. It was now the 21st of May. Richie and Peteris had gone into the garage to find the garage empty on the ninth. Nearly two full weeks had passed. Richie was getting impatient and was starting to vent his anger at Ray, who didn't like the insinuations that Richie was implying.

'So, what are you trying to imply Richie?' Ray shouted down the phone, 'Every one of my clients gets the same treatment from me. One hundred percent effort, no matter who you are. I'm not finished with this yet. He'll turn up somewhere, I guarantee it. You'll just have to be patient.'

Richie had tried to imply that Ray was not giving it his full attention because he somehow viewed Richie as inferior to Frank and Daniel. He'd suggested that if Ray were dealing with Frank that he'd have found him by now. That was not the case. It was just a resurfacing of Richie's issues of self-worth where he felt he wasn't being given due respect. Sometimes he'd get those feelings if he felt people were not taking him seriously.

'Patient, I've been fuckin' patient Ray, for nearly two weeks. You're supposed to be the best at this. I'd hate to be dealing with the worst. Fifteen grand I'm owed, it's not small fry, so get him fuckin' found for fuck's sake,' Richie put the phone down.

Ray sighed and shook his head. One thing he hated was people losing their temper and shouting at him for no reason. He could not understand why people thought he could just take on a case and find the person the very next day. He usually found them within a few days, a week at most, given the contacts he had in the criminal world and the police force, plus he only got paid when he came up with the goods, so it was in his own interest to get them found as quickly as possible as he was running up expenses in the meantime. He worked on a fixed fee, so any costs incurred were down to him. The longer it took, the more he had to shell out.

Three days later, Richie was sat at home watching the TV when the phone rang. It was just gone seven o'clock at night. Marie was washing the pots and making a pot of tea. He answered his mobile. It was Ray Parkes.

'I've found him, Richie, told ya to be patient.'

'Never mind that, where is he?'

'Venice'

'Where?'

'Venice, Italy.'

'Fucking Venice, what the fuck's he doing there?'

'I have no idea Richie, not interested in what he's doing there, but he used his credit card, silly man, in a hotel right in the centre, nice hotel, not cheap. One of my friends at the Met was keeping an eye on his cards for me and ping up it popped, about an hour ago. It would appear he's used it to secure a booking as the amount has not been taken, just reserved. You know how they do when you check in, so I would say he's staying there.'

'Fucking Venice, eh? Ah well, at least it's a nice place to go. I might take Marie with me, make it a mini-break, cheers Ray. What's the name of the hotel?'

'I'll text it ya, look it up on the old internet, nice place.'

'Yeah well, he has got my fifteen grand, plus I assume he'll have got a few quid for all those motors he got rid of.'

'Any joy on who get them?'

'No, seems they must have taken them in the middle of the night, no one seen fuck all and his CCTV was ripped out so no idea pal. All I want is my fifteen grand and him dead as a fucking Dodo... right then Ray, once I have him, I'll sort ya money out but I'm not paying until I have him.'

'No worries, if his card gets used elsewhere, I'll let you know straight away.'

Richie put the phone down and rubbed his hands. He'd never been to Venice; in fact, he'd never been to Italy since the world cup in 1990. *Good old Andy Barnes,* he thought as he fired up his laptop. Marie brought in the mugs of tea.

'Who was that on the phone?'

'Just a bit o' business, that's all.'

Marie knew not to press him when he said that. If he'd wanted Marie to know, he'd have told her. She just sat down next to him. 'What you looking at?'

'Fancy a few days in Venice?'

'Venice?' she said, sounding quite surprised.

'Yeah, supposed to be one of the most romantic places in the world, isn't it?'

'Thought we could go for a few days, go on one of those Gondola things and all that. What you think?'

'That would be lovely Richie. When are you thinking?'

'Tomorrow?'

'Tomorrow? I can't, I've got work.'

'Just ring in sick. It'll be fine. No one needs to know where we are going. Just be our little secret. I won't say owt to anyone, and if you don't then, you'll be fine.'

'Well, I'm not sure, I don't like it when people do that.'

'Look, it'll only be one day 'cos you're off for three days after tomorrow, aren't you, so you'll only be doing it for one day.'

'Why does it have to be tomorrow, so soon?'

'It just does, I need to see someone out there, and I need to go tomorrow, so just ring in sick, and we can have a few days in the sun. It'll be nice this time of year.'

Marie knew that this little trip was to do with business. The speed of which it had to be was evident of that. Her little voice in her head was telling her not to do it, but she'd never been to Venice and had always wanted to go. She'd seen lots of pictures about it and had always thought how lovely it looked. She wouldn't be involved though, in whatever business Richie had to deal with; she could go shopping or have lunch or something. She never involved herself, and this would be no different, she thought, just in a different country that's all.

'Okay,' she cooed, 'I'll ring in sick first thing.' Richie put his arm around her shoulder.

'Great' he said, 'you best get packing.'

While Marie ran upstairs to see what she should take with her, Richie proceeded to sort out the flights. No flights from East Midlands, so it would need to be Manchester or Birmingham. Manchester had better flight times, so he booked them. He then reserved a room at a hotel about fifteen minutes by bus or tram from the centre of Venice. He decided he didn't want to be staying at the same hotel as Andy Barnes and wanted to be out of Venice itself in case he needed to get away from any heat his actions may bring down on him. He rang Frank and Daniel and told them he was going away for a couple of days. He didn't say where to, and they didn't ask. If any of them just said, *I'm going away for a couple of days,* and didn't offer to say where to, it was understood that they didn't need to know. It was just one of those unwritten rules that everyone in that life understood. It was Richie's business, and no one else needed to know what he was doing.

chapter fifty-three

Venice, Italy - 25th May 2012

Richie and Marie jumped in the taxi to take them to their hotel, a sixteenth-century villa that was now a boutique hotel just outside Venice. The hotel had sent the taxi, and Richie and Marie were the only people to get in it. This had pleased Richie as he hated queues to check into a hotel. Once he arrived, he just wanted to get checked in and then get sorted. Fifteen minutes or so later, they arrived at the hotel. It was set back off the road in beautiful surroundings. The interior was like that of a sixteenth-century villa with beautiful murals painted on the walls. The check-in was swift, and they were taken to their room on the ground floor. The room was beautifully appointed, with French doors leading to a lovely garden with patio furniture. Outside there was a pool with an outside bar set in beautifully landscaped gardens with little bridges, a stream, and a peacock roaming around. The peacock looked beautiful when it showed its feathers and was a real hit with the guests. It was so peaceful and quiet. Marie wanted to unpack and sit around the pool immediately. There was an indoor pool too, on the ground floor, and a huge gym on the first floor, but Marie wanted to lounge around the outdoor pool. It was 1:20pm and twenty-eight degrees. Perfect for a quiet afternoon reading and the occasional dip.

'Well look, we'll unpack, and you can sit around the pool and read your book or whatever, and I'll go into Venice. I just want to get my bearings and all that. I have a bit of business to attend to, as you know, so I want to know where things are. That okay?'

Marie was a little disappointed. She wanted to spend the afternoon with Richie. The garden looked so romantic, but she knew the real reason they were here, so just wanted to take advantage where she could.

'Okay, but don't be too long, though, will you?'

'Quick as I can. They reckon it's only twenty minutes or so from here, so I'll be back before you know it.' Richie kissed her on the cheek and patted her bum. 'I'll just get changed into some shorts. It's bloody roasting out there.'

Richie quickly got out of his jeans and put on a pair of cream shorts, a pair of trainer socks, and his trainers. 'Right, I'm off, save me a sun lounger, won't you?' he shouted as he shut the door.

Once in the corridor, Richie quickly made his way to the reception. He wanted a taxi asap to take him straight to Venice. He was going to track down that fucker as soon as he could. He put on his sunglasses and hat to look as inconspicuous as he could, and he reckoned looking like a typical Brit abroad would help him blend in and become invisible to everyone around him. The lady at reception booked him a taxi. It took ten minutes to arrive and a further fifteen minutes to arrive in Venice. Richie had never been to Venice before, and he was rather unprepared for what was to await him when he got out of the taxi. He had not realised that it would only drop you off right on the edge of Venice city itself. That was the end of the road for road vehicles.

He stood at what was called Piazzale Roma, which was essentially the bus and tram station. The hotel was just off St. Mark's Square, which according to his city map, and the taxi driver was forty-five minutes walk away. He could have taken a water bus or water taxi, but he quite fancied a good stroll after the flight and taxi ride. He was amazed at how busy the place was. He set off over a large bridge, which he soon found out was one of the hundreds in Venice. Bridges, and tiny, narrow streets full of people; it was picturesque but busy and in thirty-degree heat was not something he overly enjoyed. He walked past what he was told was the train station and on to St. Mark's Square. After half an hour of walking, he told himself that on the way back, he would get a water taxi. *Fuck this heat;* he thought to himself as he took another stroll over another bridge. He was so hot he took his T-Shirt off and wiped his brow.

No sooner had he done so than an old Italian guy started to shout and point at him aggressively. Richie told him to do one, but an English guy told him he needed to put his T-Shirt on or face a twenty-five euro fine. He pointed to a sign on the wall outside a cafe. It was all in Italian, but Richie could make out the pictures. Men could not be bare-chested, and women could not just wear a bikini. *What the fuck's this all about?* he muttered to himself as he put his top back on and smiled at the old Italian guy who walked off talking to himself. Probably saying, *fucking tourists,* or something like that.

Richie eventually got to a huge square which according to his map was St. Mark's Square or St. Marco as the Italians would call it. He sat down outside a cafe and ordered a coffee and still water.

A few minutes later, he was downing the water and watching the masses of people walking about. He looked in amazement at the size of the queue to enter Doge's Palace Museum. It must have been half a mile long. He wondered what could be so interesting for people to queue for that length of time in this heat, but then again remembered that a few years ago he'd have stood in a queue like that to watch England play in a world cup, so he kind of got it. He finished his coffee and paid the small fortune for the privilege and remembered where he was. It was Venice, after all, and he was supping it in St. Mark's Square, so he told himself just to enjoy it, whatever the cost. He followed his map round the corner and walked over two more bridges to the hotel. Before he went in, he asked at the water bus stop what the situation was with the buses and how to get back to the main bus station. He was ready to buy a ticket until he was told he only had seventy-five minutes to use it before it expired. An hour and fifteen minutes may not be long enough, he thought, so he decided to buy one once he'd finished at the hotel. He stopped and looked around outside of the hotel for a few minutes, scanning the crowd to see if he could see Andy Barnes. He knew he couldn't kill him. He had no weapons for a start and having seemingly walked down every street en route from the bus station, he couldn't see how he could make a swift escape. He smiled to himself as he thought of him running through the narrow streets that were packed with people. The waiter had told him at the cafe that Venice at night was a lot quieter as the cruise ship tourists had gone for the day, back on their ships. He thought how maybe he should have come to sort out Andy Barnes in the evening. He didn't even know if he was still here, but as Ray Parkes had not told him his card had been used again, he assumed he'd not yet paid his room bill.

Andy Barnes was in his hotel room. He loved Venice; he'd been here quite a few times over the years with various lady friends. He wasn't sure why he'd come here this time, on his own. He just seemed to be on autopilot when he decided he needed to get away from Nottinghamshire. He was no match for Richie Pearson. He knew that Richie would have returned the next day with a bit of muscle, and he would have taken a worse beating than he had the previous day. He'd had the fifteen grand when Richie came round. In fact, he'd had it when Jason had called a few days earlier, the day they'd looked at the CCTV. He'd already planned to fuck off to Venice, though. He was bored with his lot, selling cheap cars for a living. It's all he'd ever done, and he wanted some excitement in his life. He was in his mid-forties and was having what people would refer to as a mid-life crisis. He didn't know how to do anything else other than sell cars, and he just couldn't face doing that for any longer. He now had excitement on a grand scale. He was running from one of the UK's biggest crime families. He was scared but also excited. On occasions over the years, he'd had a few conversations with a few people about selling up, and one guy in the trade had always said that if ever decided he wanted to sell up, he would buy all his motors off him for cash. After Richie had left the other day, he'd called this guy and arranged for them to go that night, all of them. Forty-two cars in total. It took them most of the night, but Andy just wanted to be out of there pronto. He'd got eighty grand for the lot, but retail they were worth at least two and a half times that all told, so it was a decent deal all round. With Richie's fifteen grand plus his bit of savings, he had just over a hundred grand. He'd hidden the eighty-grand back in England with a trusted friend who lived on the south coast. Andy had gone there as soon as he'd left Nottinghamshire. He'd shaved his hair off so that he now sported a closely cropped crew cut. It made him look quite different. Once he thought the dust had settled, he'd then decided to come to Venice and had brought the rest of the cash with him to have a good time before he slipped back undetected to pick up his eighty grand. He decided to go downstairs into the bar and have something to eat and a beer. He would probably sit outside and watch the people go by. He liked that. It still hurt him a little to eat sometimes after the beating he'd received, so he ordered the soup and some soft bread and headed outside to sit in the sun.

As he walked from the bar to the front door, he walked past reception. He heard a voice he recognised. He stopped in his tracks and looked to his right. There, talking to reception, was Richie Pearson. Richie had his back to Andy; he hadn't seen him. Andy froze. A feeling of absolute fear came over his entire body. He wished he'd stayed in England. This was no longer excitement; it was pure fear. He stayed rooted to the spot for a few seconds, but it seemed like an absolute age. He carried on and went outside. He turned right and walked towards St. Mark's Square. Then he stopped. *Think,* he thought to himself, *think.* He knew he was done for; he could not outrun Richie. He'd found him. He'd only been in Venice a couple of days. *How had he known he'd been here so quickly?* he muttered to himself. He knew that his friend back in England would not have said anything. He'd state his life on it. He decided that he needed to see what Richie did. He spotted a men's clothing shop. He walked in and bought a hat and some sunglasses. The bruises had just about all disappeared, so at least that wouldn't be a give away, plus he'd kept the closely cropped crew cut hairstyle. Even so, he was scared shitless. He headed back towards the hotel and sat outside a cafe a few doors down. He could see the entrance to the hotel. He would see if and when Richie came out. He ordered a coffee. He could not understand how Richie had found him. He'd paid for a fake passport. He was now Paul Gregory; he had booked the flights and hotel under that name. He just hoped and prayed that the hotel policy meant that Richie would not be able to get any details from the receptionist. None at all, no matter how small. The feeling of fear was still there, within him. He decided there and then that a mid-life crisis was not for him. He just wanted this to go away and go back to normality.

Richie was getting annoyed. He was in no mood for this receptionist. He'd just walked for well over an hour in the baking heat and was starting to become a little upset. He was trying to remain calm so as not to draw any attention to himself but was finding it hard not to raise his voice.

'I'm sorry sir, but it doesn't matter how many times you ask, I cannot give you any details about any of our guests. If you think you know someone who is staying here, you will have to wait for them in the bar or come back later.'

Richie sighed again. He knew he was not going to get

anywhere. He didn't really want to wait too long as he'd promised to get back to Marie. He was happy to wait for so long, but for all he knew, Andy Barnes might not still be here. He knew he might have to come back later tonight. He knew that he'd have to be smart to get any information out of the receptionist, and he thought his charm would do the trick, so he'd just walked up to her and told her that he was looking for a guy he'd met in a bar last night. He described Andy Barnes and had hoped the receptionist would recognise the description and offer some details. She didn't and by the sounds of it was never going to. He smiled at her and thanked her for her time in a sarcastic manner and then went into the bar and ordered a beer. He looked around and saw only a handful of people, all very well-dressed people. He felt out of place in his shorts and T-shirt. He felt scruffy almost. He'd opted to dress like this to avoid standing out. He smiled at the irony. Even in the searing heat, the people he was looking at were all smartly dressed as though they were about to go out for dinner. He was annoyed at the situation and himself. Annoyed that he'd just assumed, like back in England that because of who he was, he would get whatever information he wanted. He was annoyed at how stupid he'd been by thinking he could just come to Venice and find Andy Barnes at the first attempt.

This may take some time, he thought to himself, *unless he walks through the door now.* The barman poured his beer and stared at him a little too long for Richie's comfort. Richie stared back hard. The barman looked away. Richie then took a swig of his cold beer. It tasted good. In fact, in this heat, it tasted bloody fantastic. He didn't see the dark-haired guy in a single-breasted suit walk up and stand beside him at the bar.

He felt his presence, though.

'You English?' The guy asked. Richie turned his head. He knew this guy was Italian by the accent.

'Yes, why?' he replied.

'You should remember to treat the receptionist with respect,' the guy said. Richie looked at the guy with dark combed back hair who was maybe in his mid-twenties and admired his very well-fitting suit and white open-necked shirt. Richie looked him up and down. His shoes were highly polished. He brought his head up to meet his gaze. The guy oozed confidence. Richie kept his gaze.

'And who are you?' Richie asked in a calm, relaxed but assured voice.

'No matter who I am, the receptionist is the important one here. She does a good job. You should remember that.'

The guy remained motionless. Richie could feel the tension. He was intrigued. The guy had presence and reminded him of his father, Frank. Richie kept his gaze.

'My dealings with the receptionist are not your concern,' he said, again remaining calm but speaking with authority. The man standing in front of him had not yet taken his eyes off Richie. There was silence for a couple of seconds. The man turned sideways and leant on the bar and looked straight ahead at the bottles of spirits that lined the back of the bar.

'Everything in Venice is my concern.'

Richie then heard someone yell something in Italian. All he could make out was Luca. *Maybe that's the guy's name?* he thought to himself. The guy then stood up straight and looked again at Richie.

'Everything!' he said. He then straightened his suit

and walked off towards the guy who had shouted. Richie assumed the guy he had just been talking to was Luca. He looked at the guy who had shouted, and as they both walked off together out of the bar into the reception area, Richie supped his beer. He was inwardly fuming that this guy had the front to speak to him like that. Who the fuck did he think he was? If that had been in England, Richie would not have tolerated it, but as he was in Italy looking for Andy Barnes, who owed him fifteen grand, he wasn't going to jeopardise anything by causing a brawl in the hotel bar. He told himself it was probably just a local hard man trying to impress his mates, or maybe he was something more, something like Richie was in England. Either way, he was gone now, so Richie swallowed his anger and told himself that no liberty had been taken as this guy had no idea who he was; no one in the hotel did. He was just a tourist, having a beer. He didn't need to react to anything or anyone. Here, he was nobody, and for a minute or so, he liked being a nobody. He was pleased with himself that he'd remained calm. It felt better than kicking off all the time. It showed composure and control, just like his dad.

Richie was intrigued at how much he was modelling himself on his father. Frank had always had presence, always had control when things needed it. That's what had set Frank apart from the other criminals from an early age. It had taken Richie a long time to realise that the real criminals, the ones who ran the underworld, all acted this way. They didn't need to be aggressive all the time, just when it was necessary. These guys were the real deal. The ones to be wary of. The thing that had gone unnoticed by Richie was that Luca had acted in just the same way. He was the real deal. He was someone to be wary of. A fact that had gone straight over Richie's head. He ordered another drink.

The barman poured his beer and looked at him a few times as before. Richie noted it again. What was up with this guy? Again, Richie held his stare, then the barman said, 'I see your tattoo. Were you there, Italia 90?' Richie laughed, that's why he'd been staring.

'Yes, I was, great time it was too,' the barman was Spanish and turned out to be a huge football fan. He was there also in Italia 90, following Spain. Richie spent the next fifty minutes or so reliving tales of his times in Sardinia and listening to the exploits of the Spanish barman, so much so that he almost forgot why he was there. He loved reliving his youth as a football hooligan. He'd really liked those times. He was a top boy back then, in that world, and had loved it. He supped the last of his third beer and looked at his watch. Nearly an hour he'd been sat there and no sign of Andy Barnes. He re-focused, told himself the real reason he was there. He asked the barman if he knew a Mr. Barnes in the hotel and described him to him. The barman could not recall anyone of that description or name in the hotel. He confirmed to Richie that there were quite a few English staying there. Richie decided to call it a day and go back to the hotel. He couldn't leave Marie on her own much longer. Although he was disappointed not to have seen him, he was resigned to the fact that it would take a little bit more patience than he first thought. He decided he'd come back tomorrow for most of the day and bring Marie for dinner here tomorrow night if he'd not spotted him beforehand. He could kill two birds with one stone. He figured that Andy Barnes would be around and about having dinner and would come back to his room to sleep sometimes. He knew he still must be here as Ray Parkes had not rung him to say he'd used his credit card again. He rang Ray Parkes from the bar.

'Ray, it's me Richie, I'm in Venice. Any further info on the credit card?'

'No, nothing more. He can't have used it again as it would have been picked up. My contact at the Met is good at these things. He would let me know straight away.' Richie disconnected his call and looked at the barman.

'Listen mate, I have to go now, but I'll be back tomorrow. I'll see you then.' The barman shook his hand.

'I will be here. I work all day and all night. I see you tomorrow.' Richie stood up and handed the barman his credit card and settled his bill. He looked at his watch. 4:10pm. He just had time to get back, an hour or so in the sun, quick shower, and change, and then a nice meal for him and Marie. He would then come back tomorrow. He knew Marie wouldn't like it, but he needed to get his money back and sort that fucker out. She would just have to shop. She liked to shop, so he just hoped that she would understand. Just as Richie was about to leave, the barman called him back.

'We have a photo, yes?' Richie nodded.

'Yeah okay, if ya like?'

The barman called over a colleague who took the photo. Richie got one taken on his phone too. He smiled as he thought of why people do this, take photos with people they'll never see again once they go back home, but he seemed a decent bloke the barman, so he smiled his best smile. The barman pointed to the tattoo on Richie's neck and smiled too.

Andy Barnes had not taken his eyes off the hotel
entrance for the past hour or so. People had been in
and out, but no sign of Richie. He wondered what he
would do if Richie just stayed in the hotel until he saw
Andy. His money was all in his room safe. He only had
about fifty euros on him, and he'd already ordered
two coffees which, given where he was sat, would eat
into his fifty euros rather quickly. He was starting to
panic. He began to wonder if Richie was checking into
the hotel. Maybe he was staying there, which, if that
were the case, meant Andy could not go back to get
his things. He then remembered that Richie had no
luggage with him, but maybe he'd already checked in,
and Andy just hadn't been aware. His mind was racing.
He then saw Richie come out of the hotel entrance. He
watched as he stood and looked around him. He was
obviously looking for Andy. He started to walk his way,
still looking frantically right, and left, like you would if
you'd lost your child in a crowd. He then stopped. He
was only twenty yards or so away. Andy dropped his
head so as not to make eye contact. A minute or so
went by and he looked up. He saw Richie talking to a
guy in a water taxi. He was leaving by the looks of it.
He watched until Richie got into the taxi and watched
it pull away from the stop. He breathed a huge sigh
of relief. He had no idea if Richie knew he was still
staying at the hotel or not, but he did know that he
needed to get out of there quickly. He had to check
out today and get away from Venice. Venice was too
risky for him. He walked into the hotel and through
reception. The receptionist called him over.

'You left without having your soup, Mr. Gregory,'
she said smiling.

'My soup?' Andy replied, trying hard not to look too

concerned.

'Yes, you ordered soup, then you left. We will still have to charge to your room I'm afraid, sir,' Andy smiled and just said. 'Err, I'd like to check out, please. I will be down in about twenty minutes; please can you have my room bill ready.'

'So soon?'

'Yes, something has happened. I just need to go, sorry.'

Andy Barnes rushed upstairs and packed as quickly as he could. He took his wads of cash from the safe and put them safely in his suitcases, a mixture of sterling and euros. He'd brought two cases and hid the cash within his clothes. He'd been a bag of nerves coming through the airports but had not had any bother. He was surer than ever that a mid-life crisis was not for him. He checked out and paid his bill with cash. As the receptionist counted the money, she told him that the card he'd used as security would not be charged. She must have heard the penny drop. *The credit card!* He thought. He patted his forehead with the palm of his right hand. *Of course, the credit card!* The receptionist looked up and smiled and gave him his change. He smiled back. He was now sure that Richie Pearson would not know that he'd checked out. His demeanour changed. He felt relief wash over him and remembered the water taxi pulling away with Richie Pearson on board. Andy Barnes did not know where he was going but headed towards the train station in a water taxi. The quicker he was on a train, the better.

Richie got back to the hotel just over fifty minutes later. It was now just gone five o'clock. He'd got a taxi from the bus station in Venice. Marie was still sitting around the pool. She was drinking a glass of Prosecco.

'Did you get your business sorted, darling?' she asked, giggling as she did so. Richie knew that wasn't her first glass of prosecco.

'How many glasses of them you had?' he asked as he leant in and kissed her forehead.

'Three, would you like one? I can't believe how cheap prosecco is over here, Richie. It's a lot cheaper than at home.'

'Is it? Probably because it's nowt special over here. We Brits have probably just made it into something expensive. We do that ya know. Same with Pizza. I mean, think about it, Pizza is just a bit of this, and that chucked on a piece of dough. It's probably Italy's version back in the day of bubble and squeak, but we make it a gourmet meal and charge a fortune for it back home. Brilliant. I mean, whoever thought of that was a genius.' He then took off his t-shirt and lay on the sun lounger next to Marie. It was still quite hot.

'So, did you get your business sorted?' She asked again. Without opening his eyes, Richie just said, 'No, I'll have to go back tomorrow. I thought we could go in after lunch, have a wander around, and then you could do a bit of shopping whilst I take care of this business. We can then stay and eat there in the evening if it all goes to plan. That sound okay?'

It wasn't what she'd had in mind for their full day in Venice, but she was too tipsy to really care. She just nodded and said.

'Yep, sounds fine. I like to shop, even if I don't buy anything,' Richie smiled. He still didn't open his eyes.

'Anyway, order me a beer and another prosecco, then we'll go and get changed for dinner. The restaurant here looks beautiful.'

Marie called over the poolside waiter and ordered the drinks. Later that evening, Richie and Marie dined in the hotel restaurant. It was like something out of the middle ages with all the paintings on the wall. It was a beautiful setting. It was a beautiful evening.

chapter fifty-four

Venice, Italy 26th - May 2012

Richie and Marie arrived in Venice just after 1:30pm in the afternoon. It was again extremely hot, approaching thirty degrees. Richie, this time had opted for something a little more conservative. He dressed in some brown brogues, dark denim jeans, and a white cotton shirt. He was hot, but he felt more like Richie in this attire. Yesterday, when in his T-shirt and shorts, he'd felt scruffy, almost like the typical Brit abroad and Richie was not a typical Brit abroad. He was a major face in the British criminal underworld here to collect a debt of fifteen grand. He was anything but typical as he wandered the streets of Venice. He'd felt out of place yesterday in the hotel bar. Clothes were just something most people wore without any thought to what they were wearing. In Richie's world, clothes meant something; they were often a statement. It was important to look the part as well as act the part, and today he felt the part. Yesterday, he'd just felt like any old member of the public. He'd almost enjoyed being inconspicuous, being a nobody, but only for a couple of minutes. He wanted to feel like who he was, someone to be reckoned with, and today he felt more like that person. Marie had a nice white cotton dress on, a large, rimmed hat, and white sandals. She looked amazing to Richie. For her age, she had a particularly good body, all the curves were in the right places, and the white dress against her tan made her look beautiful. He looked at his watch. It was approaching 1:40pm. He wanted to be back at the hotel at around 5pm. That gave him just over three hours to enjoy the beauty of Venice with Marie.

They wandered around the narrow streets arm in arm, drank coffee in the beautiful cafes overlooking the square, and went on a Gondola ride. Richie was not the overly romantic kind. He never had been, but that ride in the Gondola through the backstreets of Venice and then down the grand canal was breath-taking. Even Richie was taken aback. He now knew what romance was all about. Marie thought she'd died and gone to heaven; it was so beautiful. By the time they'd got off the Gondola it was just gone 4:15pm. Richie suggested making their way to St. Mark's Square. He wanted to be there for 5pm and would wait all night if he had to. He'd made up his mind that if Andy Barnes were still at his hotel, he was going to see him today, even if it meant he and Marie would dine there. He wasn't leaving until he'd got his fifteen-grand back, or at least taken it out on Andy Barnes's face. One way or the other, he was getting some sort of justice today.

Richie and Marie arrived at the square at just after 4:50pm. Marie knew that Richie had to go and sort some sort of business. She still didn't know what. She didn't want to know. Richie told her to keep her phone on, and he would ring her once he'd finished. He kissed her on the cheek and made his way to the hotel. As he walked across the square, he felt anger rise inside him. He'd kept calm for long enough now. He'd had enough of the likes of Andy Barnes taking the piss. He tried to keep it down, but the more he tried, the more it rose inside him. He felt different to yesterday, maybe because he'd realised that finding Andy Barnes may not be easy, and he'd wanted it to be easy. He'd wanted to just walk into that hotel yesterday, see him sat in the bar, get his money, beat the fuck out of him and come away. That had not happened, and it was annoying him.

Richie walked into the bar and took up the same seat he'd sat in yesterday. The Spanish barman shook his hand and poured him the same beer. Richie had a few little chats with the barman about football but kept a close eye on the surroundings and the people. He was scanning the place all the time, looking for Andy Barnes. It was busy today, with people in and out of the hotel. A lot more than yesterday. Richie went to the toilet and took the opportunity to walk around downstairs, through the lobby, into the restaurant, and then outside onto the terrace. He told himself that he must be out and about but was bound to be back soon, or at least at some point tonight. He went outside to the front of the hotel. Still nothing, lots of people about but no sign of Andy Barnes. It was now just gone six o'clock. He decided to go upstairs and walk the corridors. He just needed to do something to find him. He saw that there were suites on the top floor. Richie thought that if anything he'd be staying there. He knew he had fifteen grand at least to splash out so why wouldn't he. He walked up the stairs to the top floor. His phone rang. It was Ray Parkes.

'Richie, it's Ray; got some news for you. He apparently paid for a fake passport and other fake ID. He's now called Paul Gregory. I bet he's booked in under that name if anything.'

'Great, cheers Ray, owe you one,' Richie stopped to

think. He was now on the top floor. He rang the hotel. The receptionist answered.

'Hi, do you speak English?' he asked.

'Yes, sir, how can I help?' the receptionist replied.

'Could you put me through to Mr. Paul Gregory's room, please?' he asked in a very polite voice.

'Mr. Gregory?' she asked.

'Yes, Mr. Gregory please,' Richie confirmed.

'I'm sorry sir, but Mr. Gregory checked out late yesterday afternoon.'

Richie disconnected the call. He stood there motionless. The rage he felt inside was one like he'd never felt for a long time. He'd missed him. He was here yesterday afternoon, and he'd fucking missed him. Richie thought of his movements yesterday. He must have seen him, must have spotted him. The fucking bastard had seen him. He was within his grasp. He couldn't contain his anger. The control, the calmness had gone. He wanted to smash this fucking hotel with his bare hands. He punched the wall twice and let out a roar. *How dare he do this to me again,* he thought. *He's a fucking small-time garage owner, for fuck's sake.* Richie shouted out loud.

'You again,' he heard someone say. He looked up. Stood before him was a guy in a single-breasted suit with dark combed back hair. The same guy from the bar yesterday. Luca. He was stood a couple of metres away from Richie, square on. The door to his suite was open a few feet behind him. Richie launched himself at him and punched him hard in the face. His anger was raging. Adrenalin was racing around his body. He was a man possessed. He was angry, angry like he'd not been for such a long time. Luca reeled back from the punch. He staggered.

Richie took advantage and punched him again. The adrenalin made him feel stronger than normal. He threw Luca into the suite through the open door. As Richie followed him in, Luca grabbed him and threw him into the wall. Richie grabbed the lamp from the chest of drawers and hit Luca over the head hard. Luca staggered back, blood pouring from the wound. He sat on the bed, dazed from the force of the blow. Richie hit him again and again. He stood back, breathing hard. Luca was lying on the bed with blood pouring from his head. His lip was also split. He was motionless. Richie heard a voice. He turned round and saw a guy in his underwear stood in the hallway with his mouth open wide. He put his hand over his mouth. He looked at Richie, then looked again at Luca. He took a step back. He looked over his shoulder down the corridor. Richie came out of the room, grabbed the guy by the hair, and marched him into his suite. Richie killed him with five blows to the head with the lampshade base. He never muttered a word. He grabbed the guy's shirt off the bed and wrapped it around his hand. He closed the door to the man's room and returned to Lucas's suite. He closed the door. He was now calm. He stood and looked at Luca. He looked dead. Richie's breathing was regulating. He wrapped the other guy's shirt around the stem of the lamp. He looked at his clothes. They were spattered in blood. He needed to change. The wardrobe in the bedroom was open. In it were five suits and five shirts, all neatly hung. At the bottom of the wardrobe were four pairs of polished shoes. Richie got changed. He washed his hands and face, put on a shirt, a suit, and a pair of shoes. The shirt and suit fitted okay; trousers were a bit snug but not overly uncomfortable. The shoes were probably a size too small, but again he could live with it. He looked at himself in the mirror. He looked fine, certainly not like someone who had just murdered two people. He was still calm. He needed to go, needed to get out of here, needed to ring Marie. He walked back into the main room. Luca had not moved. He checked his watch. It was approaching 6:30pm. He saw a briefcase on the drawers. The top was slightly open. He looked inside, a gun and a few bundles of cash. He closed it and was careful not to move the combination numbers. He assumed how they were currently set would open it again. He saw a bag, looked like a gym bag. He opened it up, empty. He stuffed his old clothes and the lamp inside. He had to squash the lampshade down to make it fit. It zipped up. He looked in the mirror one more time. He looked ordinary. Just a guy in a suit with a briefcase and a gym bag. He wiped down anything he had touched. He left the room and walked down the stairs.

Richie walked along the corridor and through the bar into the lobby. It was busy. Lots of people. He started to walk quickly; his breathing increased. As he neared the front door, he broke into a jog. He knocked two guys over as he got to the main door. He turned right towards St. Mark's Square. He heard the two guys shout something at him. He couldn't understand, but it didn't sound nice. He slowed to a walk. He needed to be calm. He needed to look normal. He stopped at the square. He rang Marie.

'Hi, it's me. Where are you?'

'Err, I'm not sure. All the streets look the same to me.'

'Can you make it back to St. Mark's Square, where I left you?

'Err, yes think so. Are you okay?' She thought Richie

sounded anxious, out of breath almost.

'Yeah fine, meet me at the square near the two statues of the lions. Quick as you can.'

Marie was nervous. She didn't like how Richie sounded. She asked someone for directions to the square and made her way to meet him.

chapter fifty-five

Tristano looked at the body of his Godson Luca on the bed, then at his watch. It was 6:45pm. Luca's face and head were badly swollen. He could not believe what he was looking at. Who would dare do such a thing? He just stood there staring at him. Filippo had told him seconds earlier that he could feel a faint pulse. Luca was alive, if only just. Tristano wanted no fuss from the outside world. This was Mafia business. He asked Filippo to take care of it. He wanted this contained in this room. He wanted his people to take care of Luca. He did not want this getting out. Filippo rang some associates to come to the hotel as quickly as possible. He explained the situation with Luca. The medical arrangements were made, the hotel staff was spoken to. No one would breathe a word. People downstairs were aware that something had happened. The local Italians knew better than to get involved. They remained silent and carried on with their evening, just keeping one eye on any developments. The tourists were a different ball game. They didn't quite understand what was happening. They were asking questions, but the hotel staff knew what to say. This kind of thing didn't happen in Venice. Mafia activity was kept low-key, but the local people knew enough to stay well out of it. The last thing Tristano wanted was for the local police to become involved.

Tristano was pacing the hotel room. He was angry,

very angry. He immediately assumed this was not
Mafia-related. It couldn't be. There was no internal
fighting going on. They had no enemies they knew of
who would dare do such a thing. He knew it had to
have been opportunistic, had to have been a tourist,
or an outsider at least. He wanted answers. He wanted
revenge. He wanted to hunt down whoever did this and
kill them with his bare hands. He would not rest until
justice had been done. Luca was his Godson. Tonight,
was supposed to have been a night of celebration.
He would see to it the Luca's attacker was found and
punished in the only way possible for something of this
nature. He first needed to make sure Luca was taken
care of. He knew that medical help was on its way and
that Luca would be in the best hands possible. Filippo
saw to that. Once he was sure that Luca was being
looked after, he would start the process of finding out
who did this, and he would begin right where he was,
at the hotel.

Marie saw Richie standing next to the two lion statues.
She ran up to him. He held her tight.
    'Come on; we need to go,' he said. 'Now.'
    'What's wrong Richie, you're scaring me?'
    'Don't ask any questions. You don't need to know,
Marie. You don't need to be involved. Let's just walk.
We need to get to the bus station, but I want to walk.
No one must know where we are going, just trust me.
Come on.' He grabbed her hand and walked all the way
briskly to the Piazzale Roma, the bus station in Venice.
They spoke very little except for Marie to ask where the
briefcase and gym bag came from, plus the suit and
shoes. Richie told her she didn't need to know. Marie
was scared, more scared than she'd ever been in her

life. She remembered the little voice in her head that had told her not to go to Venice. She remembered how she'd ignored it. She now regretted that decision. Once at the bus station, they got a taxi and got dropped off outside the entrance to their hotel. They walked straight past reception and straight to their room. Once inside, Richie put the gym bag and briefcase on the bed.

'Where did they come from then? I need to know Richie. I do not know what I am involved in here, but you owe me an explanation at least.'

'Keep your voice down, for fuck's sake,' Richie whispered. He sat her down and took her hand, and then stroked her hair.

'Look, you know what life I lead. It's no secret. You know I am involved in business that is not legal, you know all that, but that's all you know. You don't need to know any details. I choose not to tell you, and you choose, very sensibly not to ask. If you want me to tell you the truth about tonight, I will, but if I do, then you must understand something very important.' He placed her hand between both of his. And kissed them.

'What do I need to understand Richie? Tell me.'

'You need to understand that if I tell you what happened tonight, then you have crossed a line, an important line because then you will know as much as me, and that makes you a potential liability to me. If I tell you, then you must understand that if you ever breathe a word of it, I'll kill you. You are the best thing that has happened to me, Marie. The best thing in my life, but I value my own life more. I need you to understand that I am prepared to tell you 'cos I trust you. You're the only person other than myself that I trust. I love you Marie, but I would kill you if you ever betrayed me. Do you still want to know what happened tonight?'

Marie looked deep into his eyes. She knew what Richie was, knew what he did for a living, but he was right. She only knew that and nothing else. No details, nothing where she could betray him. She knew that he didn't tell her partly because he was protecting her from the very situation, she now found herself in. She loved him, though, and she knew that with love, you could conquer anything.

'Yes, I want to know Richie. I know I will cross a line, but I'm with you no matter what. I'll never betray you. You know you can trust me.'

He looked at her for a few seconds, looking for signs of regret to what she had just said. He saw nothing except devotion. They lay on the bed, and Richie told her the whole story about Andy Barnes, Paul Gregory, and the guy he thought was called Luca. Marie just lay there and listened. She didn't pass comment until he'd finished. She then turned into him and snuggled in tight. All she said was, 'what time is our flight tomorrow?'

'Nine-forty in the morning,' he replied.

Marie kissed his chest through his shirt. 'What's in the briefcase and bag?' she asked for the third time.

'Cash, a gun and the murder weapon, in the briefcase and my old clothes in the gym bag.'

'How much cash?' she asked.

'No idea, didn't have time to count it.'

Both sat up. Richie opened the briefcase, and they counted the cash. They counted 8,750 euros. Marie cleaned up the base of the lamp. The next morning, they left for the airport bright and early. Richie had gone for a walk around 5am and dumped the gun along the river walk at the back of their hotel. He knew he'd never get it through customs. He also burned the lampshade. They took the base of the lamp back to England with them along with the briefcase and gym bag. Richie packed his blood-stained clothes in his cabin bag. He always wanted them with him. They arrived in England late morning. As they walked towards passport control, Richie grabbed Marie by the arm and pulled her to one side.

'No one knows we've been to Venice, no one so as far as we are concerned, we've been to London for a few days. We stayed at The Savoy and just did a bit of shopping if anyone asks, understand?'

Marie nodded. 'Yes, no problem.'

'Don't ever mention Venice to anyone. In fact, if anyone ever asks, for any reason, just deny it. You've never set foot in the place.'

'Don't worry, I'm with you all the way,' Marie kissed him full on the lips. As they carried on walking, Marie knew her life would never be the same again. She looked behind her to see if she could see the line she'd crossed. She couldn't. It was in Venice. She smiled to herself and linked arms with Richie Pearson.

chapter fifty-six

Luca was still unconscious but was alive. He was being cared for at Tristano's home by a team of medical staff. They said they thought he would pull through, but he was still very poorly. Tristano and Filippo, plus two of their men, Lorenzo and Marco, had just arrived. It was just gone nine in the morning. Tristano had spoken to the hotel manager the previous evening and paid him handsomely to give them access to anything they needed and assurances that nothing would be spoken of this incident. When they had walked into the hotel this morning, the manager had immediately told them of the second body. This posed a real problem for Tristano. It was a member of the public, nothing to do with him, but it must have happened because of the attack on Luca, or maybe the other guy was killed first, and Luca was attacked trying to help him. That made sense. Luca was like that. He would intervene to help someone. The manager agreed to wait until Tristano, and his men had seen the CCTV. He knew what to do. He would have co-operated for free, but Tristano believed in paying people for assistance, especially in instances like this. They viewed the CCTV images of the top floor. It was not of great quality. They could see what happened, and as they watched it unfold, both Tristano and Filippo were struggling to contain their anger. Luca had been attacked first. They could see that he'd approached the man in the corridor, but the images were not good enough to make out his face. This angered Tristano.

'How the fuck can we have such shit images in 2012,' he yelled. He stood up and paced the room.

'I want him found, and quickly, I don't care what we have to do, I want him found and killed.'

Filippo hugged Tristano. 'We'll find him. Trust me, we'll find him.'

Tristano sat back down. They saw Richie come out of Luca's room and force the other guy back into his own room, and then a couple of minutes later, they saw Richie come back out. Still no good footage of his face. They then watched the empty corridor for a few minutes and then saw Richie come out of Luca's room dressed in a suit.

'Stop it,' Filippo shouted. 'Pause it there.'

'What's up?' Tristano asked.

'The guy in the suit yesterday, remember he knocked the two guys over near the exit door. He had a briefcase and a gym bag. Look, there they are. It's him. We noticed him.'

Tristano nodded. 'Yes, that's him. That's the fucking guy, and we saw him yesterday. We fucking saw him. He was there, Filippo; he was there.'

'We didn't know though, Tristano, we didn't know. He was just a guy in a suit. There were lots of guys in suits.'

Tristano stood up. 'We need access to the CCTV on the streets. We need to follow this guy wherever he went. Lorenzo, get me access to the city CCTV. Whatever it takes. Marco, get the CCTV for the rest of the hotel from yesterday. That guy must have been here before he went upstairs.'

'Wait,' said Filippo. 'Two days ago, Luca spoke to a

guy sat at the bar who'd been giving the receptionist some grief. He was English, dressed in shorts and T-shirt, around three o'clock in the afternoon, two days ago. Could be the same guy, worth a look.'

'No problem Filippo, I'll take a look at that too,' replied Marco.

Tristano went to see the hotel manager. 'Listen, that other body, no police. It's the same guy did both.' The manager looked worried.

'But I have to report it.'

'If you do, it'll be the last thing you ever do. We will get rid of the body; we will arrange the clean-up. We will do everything. All you have to do is keep your mouth shut. Luca is my godson, and no fucking police officer is gonna mess this up. We will deal with this. Who found the other body?'

'The two maids who were cleaning the room.'

'Get them here. I need to speak to them.'

Tristano spoke to the two maids, who were a bag of nerves. They agreed to keep quiet. They had no choice. Tristano then arranged for the clean-up of the other room to begin. He then spoke to his contacts in the police. He knew he'd have to make some sort of call to them. It was better coming from him. They had already heard whispers of something at the hotel and heard stories of who was involved. They had decided to wait for the call. It was a good decision. Tristano was now sure that no one would speak and that he could get on with tracking down the bastard who had nearly killed his godson.

Just under an hour later, Tristano and Filippo were talking to the Spanish Barman. Marco had seen from the CCTV that he'd spent time talking to Richie two days ago and also yesterday, just before Luca was attacked. He co-operated fully. He valued his life. He told them what he knew. He also showed them the photo he'd taken on his phone. Tristano held the phone for a good while and just looked at the face of the man he was going to kill. He memorised it. The barman sent it via text to Tristano and Filippo. They both wanted it. They now knew what he looked like. The barman never got Richie's name; he now wished he had. He could not believe that the man he'd been reminiscing with about Italia '90 was the same guy who had attacked the two guests on the top floor. He'd seemed such a nice man.

By early evening Tristano and Filippo were standing in the reception of a hotel, getting the passport details of two guests that had checked out earlier that morning. The two guests were Richie Pearson and Marie Taylor. They now had their names and address in the UK. It had taken them less than eight hours from walking into the hotel in Venice that morning to find out who the man was who had attacked Luca. Lorenzo had been able to persuade someone in the CCTV department in Venice to track the guy in the suit coming out of the hotel. He'd persuaded him by sticking a gun under his chin. Even under that pressure, the guy was able to track Richie and Marie very quickly to the taxi at the main bus station. The taxi driver had been traced within the hour and had given up the information without any hassle. Now, in the hotel they stayed in, the staff were just as accommodating. It always amazed Tristano how accommodating people were once they realised who they were dealing with. The Mafia did things like that to people, made them want to help, want to appease. Most of the time, it was under the threat of extreme violence, but nevertheless they always got what they wanted. Tristano thought how it would have taken the police days to find out this level of information, maybe even a week, but the Mafia's power had resulted in them getting all the information they needed at the same time as a normal working day.

As Tristano and Filippo got into their car outside the entrance to the hotel Tristano's phone rang. Luca had passed away. Tristano sat there for a few minutes, staring into space, not saying a word. A tear ran down his cheek. He looked over at Filippo, who returned the look. Neither spoke, but they both knew what they needed to do. Filippo rang someone he knew at the airport who was on the payroll. They sat and waited, saying nothing. Five minutes later, Filippo's phone rang. 'Manchester airport,' the voice said, 'They flew to Manchester in England, landed there this morning.'

Filippo disconnected the call. He looked at Tristano.

'They flew to Manchester this morning. They are already back in England.'

chapter fifty-seven

England 28th May 2012

Filippo, Tristano, Lorenzo, and Marco landed in Manchester just after 9am. It was two days since Luca had been attacked. It was raining, but warm and pleasant. They'd tried to get a flight to East Midlands, but that would have meant waiting another two days. Tristano was not prepared to wait.

'Apparently, it always rains in England, Tristano, all the time,' Filippo commented.

'I know, this is the fourth time I've been, and it's rained each time.'

They walked out of the airport and jumped in the Mercedes E Class car that was waiting for them outside the car hire company. Lorenzo drove. They had the address of Richie's house in Mansfield, assuming he'd given his home address to the hotel. They would make their way there. They had flights booked back to Italy the next day. They did not expect this to take too long. Tristano wanted a quick clean hit, whereas Filippo wanted to torture the guy to death slowly. Lorenzo and Marco had no opinion. They were just there as back-up if needed. Tristano wanted to shoot Richie. He felt he needed to do what was right by Luca. He wanted to blow Richie's head off. He would normally have agreed with Filippo, but this was a foreign country, and Tristano did not want to draw any undue attention to them. In and out, quickly was his way. No mess, no fuss, no comeback. Filippo was more violent than Tristano by nature and would happily chop Richie up into little pieces, but he understood Tristano's rationale.

'When we get there, leave it to me as agreed. Me and Filippo will knock on the door. If he answers, we kill him in his house, not on the doorstep. No mess, understand?'

Everyone agreed, everyone knew the score, everyone wanted the same thing, Luca's killer dead. Only then could Tristano rest.

Just over two hours later, they reached Mansfield. They'd stopped only once to go to the toilet and had grabbed a coffee on the way. *Italian Coffee,* the sign had said in the window.

'Authentic Italian Coffee.' Filippo nearly threw his cup at the Barista who served it. He spat it out over the counter and refused to pay. Tristano intervened and calmed things down. The last thing he needed was unwanted attention over a cup of coffee. Filippo loved his coffee and was very proud of the Italian roast. The Barista did not understand what he was saying, but she knew he didn't like it. She refunded the cost. Filippo was still swearing in Italian as they walked out into the car park.

As they pulled in Black Scotch Lane, they were surprised at the size of the houses. They were not huge mansions like they lived in back home in Italy but were big enough. They had expected something a lot less desirable. The road was lined with trees, and the houses were all individual and set back. They approached the house and drove past it slowly. Lorenzo parked about twenty metres down. Tristano and Filippo checked their guns. Both had silencers on. Both were fully loaded. Tristano looked at Filippo.

'Remember, I shoot him. He was my godson.' Filippo nodded.

Tristano tapped Lorenzo on the back of the shoulder. 'Keep the engine running, Lorenzo.'

'Will do,' he replied.

They both got out and walked the twenty or so metres to Richie's house. They looked up and down the street. It was very quiet. No one was about except for a dog walker on the opposite side of the road. The dog walker shouted, 'Good Morning' Tristano replied with, 'Bon Journo.' They then saw a car pull out of a drive about six or seven houses up and turn away from them. Tristano pulled the photo up on his phone of Richie. It was just as he remembered it. If he answered the door, he would know him instantly. They both had their guns in the inside pockets of their suit jackets. They walked up the drive and knocked on the door. They heard a male voice say,

'I'll get it,' and ten seconds later, the door opened. There standing at the door, was a guy who looked exactly like the man in the photo. Tristano punched the guy hard and knocked him backwards. As he steadied himself, he punched him again.

'What the fuck?' the guy said as he put his hand out to stop himself from falling. He looked up at his attacker. Tristano fired a bullet straight through the forehead. The man dropped to the floor. He'd died instantly. He stood over him and fired another shot again through the head. He then stood back and said in Italian, 'That, you fucker was for my godson Luca. He was worth ten of you.'

Tristano and Filippo walked out and closed the door

behind them. They walked calmly down the driveway and turned right towards their waiting car. They got in and Lorenzo drove away.

Richie could see the Mercedes from the upstairs window. He knew instantly who had just called at his house. He heard the Italian words Tristano had spoken as he'd stood over the body. He'd heard the word Luca. Richie calmly walked downstairs and looked at Daniel's body. There was surprisingly very little blood. He thought he must have died instantly and realised that they must have thought that Daniel was Richie. Daniel had just saved his life, and he thought of how he was finally free of the brother he'd despised all his life. Richie thought of how he would now rule the family business. He smiled, then he laughed, then he jumped for fucking joy.

chapter fifty-eight

Richie finished his coffee and washed his mug before replacing it in the cupboard. He rang Marie.

'Hi sweetheart, where are you?'

'I'm still in Nottingham with Phoebe and Alice, you know us girls, we can shop for England.'

Richie smiled. 'Yeah, I know, okay, just seeing how you were getting on, ring me when you are on your way home.'

'Yeah, will do, ooh just a minute, phoebe says, is Daniel still with you?'

'No, he left a while ago, didn't say where he was going.'

Marie repeated what Richie had said to Phoebe. 'Okay, no worries, see you later, love you lots.'

Richie again smiled, 'Love you too.' He put his phone back in his pocket and walked outside to Daniel's car, and opened the boot. He looked down at Daniel's body. He felt nothing, no remorse, no sadness, nothing. He always knew his time would come. For sixteen years, Richie had played the game, being all nice, playing out the doting brother, doting uncle, doting son. He hadn't expected it to come to him this way, though; Richie hadn't even had to do anything. Well, he knew he'd killed two people he didn't even know in Italy, but by the looks of it, Richie was free of any hassle there too. He couldn't have planned it better if he'd tried.

Richie closed the boot and walked round to the

driver's side door. He stopped and looked again for any signs of anyone. There was no one. He got into the car, adjusted the seat, and then drove the car to Daniel's house. He stopped at a garage on the way to get a drink. He didn't need a drink; he liked the fact that no one knew he had a dead body in the boot. He enjoyed the adrenalin rush, liked the feeling of power. It made him feel invincible. When he got to Daniel's house, he placed the body in the lounge. He knew that as it was a bank holiday Monday, Archie was at Matlock all day with his mates, so the house would be empty. He left it looking just as it would have done had the hit took place there. He knocked a few things over to look like a struggle but not too much. He then walked into Southwell and called a taxi. He got out at the Oak Tree Pub near his house and walked the quarter of a mile to Black Scotch Lane. While listening to the radio, Richie happily cleaned up a small patch of blood that he'd missed earlier off the recently laid real wood floor. It was barely a month old. He stood back and looked at his home. You'd never know. He then sat and waited for the phone calls.

chapter fifty-nine

28th May 2012

Richie was driving to Daniel's house. He'd taken a phone call from Marie at just after 4:30pm. She was hysterical. Richie acted shocked; he'd played this out in his head whilst waiting for the call. He knew exactly how to act. He was good at acting; he'd been doing it non-stop for sixteen years. He needed to behave exactly as any doting brother would. This was his final curtain call, the final act of the play. He needed to be a professional to the end. He screeched into Daniel's drive, just as he would have done. He ran into the house, just as he would have done. He stood over the body, just as he would have done, and he got down on his knees and cradled Daniel's body, just as he would have done. He then managed to cry, just as he would have done.

'What happened?' he asked, 'did anyone see anything?' He looked up and looked at Phoebe. She was sat on the sofa staring into space. She had been sobbing. She looked a mess. She looked like someone whose world had just come crashing down. Phoebe didn't answer. He looked at Marie. She'd been crying too. He then looked at Alice. She was fourteen years old and was sat next to her mum with her head lying on her lap. Her eyes were closed. She was still crying. He asked again. 'What happened?'

Phoebe spoke. She was on autopilot. Her eyes never moved. She just continued to stare into space.

'We came home, and there he was, dead, just as you see him now. I knew this day would come, I just knew it, but I didn't think it would be for a few years yet. I'd tried to prepare myself.' She was still on autopilot.

'Have you rung my dad and Archie?' Richie asked, still playing a good part.

'Yes, both on their way.'

Richie knew he would have to play a blinder when Frank arrived. He was aware that Daniel dying could send Frank back years, right back to before he and Richie patched things up. He knew that this could put Frank right back to when Renee died, and if it did, Richie didn't want the old feelings and resentment for him coming back to the fore. He needed to be there for his dad, right at his side. Richie got up and went to console Phoebe and Alice. They reciprocated the sentiment; after all, Richie had lost his twin brother. They were united in their grief. He then stood and cuddled Marie. She held him tight. He sobbed a little more.

Ten minutes later, Frank arrived with Jez, they both ran through the door.

'Where is he?' Frank said before stopping dead in his tracks. He looked down at the body of his first-born son. He stood motionless and then walked slowly over to where Daniel lay. Just as Richie had done, he knelt, took Daniel's head in his arms, and sobbed like a baby. This was the first time anyone in that room had seen Frank Pearson cry. He sobbed. He shouted.

'Who would do this? Why would someone do this?' Whilst looking around the room at the faces for answers. Richie comforted his dad. Frank responded.

It was a warm embrace.

'It's just you and me now, Son,' He said quietly into Richie's ear. 'We need to find out who did this, you and me together, for Daniel.' Richie smiled inwardly.

'Me and you dad, we'll avenge this, for Daniel.'

Frank patted his son on the back and pulled away from the embrace. Phoebe stood up and looked at Frank. He didn't know what to say. At that moment, Frank knew that this wasn't just about him. He realised that Daniel's death left Phoebe without a husband and Alice and Archie without a father. He walked over to Phoebe and Alice and hugged them tightly. He hugged them for nearly two minutes. They both needed Frank. Phoebe needed his strength, and Alice needed her grandad. Phoebe eventually pulled away and took Frank's chin in her hands. She looked deep into his eyes.

'Get whoever is responsible, Frank,' she said, 'and when you do I want to personally remove them from this earth.' He wiped his face and nodded.

'I will, Phoebe, I will, I promise.' He then hugged her again. 'Listen, I think it's best that you, Marie, and Alice go over to my place for a few days. Me and Richie need to make some phone calls. Things need to be put in place quickly. You don't need to be here.'

Phoebe nodded and looked at Marie. 'I'll go and get some things.' She took Alice by the hand and led her upstairs. Frank looked at Marie.

'Gloria will be back soon. I told her to go straight to ours.'

'Okay, that'll be good. I'll put the kettle on, make us all a brew.'

Marie walked into the kitchen and filled the kettle. Frank, Richie, and Jez followed and sat at the table.

Frank composed himself.

'This gents looks like a professional hit, not some opportunistic murder. Whoever did this was a professional. It's like the Mafia came to town or something. We didn't have any enemies that would do this, did we? Did Daniel?' he asked.

Richie hoped and prayed that at the mention of the Mafia, he had not changed his expression. His stomach had turned over when he'd heard Frank mention them but tried desperately to remain motionless. Richie didn't know for sure that it was the Mafia but given the swift and professional way they had despatched Daniel, he was sure it was.

Jez and Richie both confirmed that, to their knowledge, they had no known enemies who were capable of doing this type of hit. Frank shook his head.

'We need to know who did this, gents. We need to speak to everyone we know. We need to find who was responsible.'

Jez agreed that he would speak to Brian and Pat and that he would personally speak to the firms in London, Manchester, and Newcastle. Richie would make enquiries on his and Daniel's own patches and talk to the undertaker. Frank would speak to his contacts in the local police. He wanted this kept low-key; he knew they'd need to be some sort of police involvement, but he knew he could ensure that any "investigation" was minimum and that it was wrapped up quickly.

Marie put the mugs of tea on the table and kissed Richie on the forehead. Just as she was leaving the room, she heard Frank say, 'Had he been dealing with anyone abroad, any firms you know of that he'd upset overseas?'

She didn't hear the responses, but a shudder ran

down her spine. She closed the door and stood there for a few seconds mulling over what had happened. *The Mafia,* she thought, *overseas, upset anyone?* She felt sick. She'd not realised the coincidence until now. *Had the Mafia come over here and shot Daniel?* she thought to herself. She could hear Phoebe and Alice upstairs getting their things ready. She looked at Daniel's body. She wanted to throw up. She ran to the downstairs bathroom and was sick. She cleaned herself up and looked in the mirror. She thought of what Richie had told her. She thought of how that was only two days ago. She tried to convince herself that there was no way that what Richie did had any bearing on what had happened to Daniel. How could it? The guys Richie murdered were not Mafia, were they? Richie had said they were just two guys who were in the wrong place at the wrong time. Her mind was racing. It was a coincidence; she knew that but then again, why would they come to Daniel's house? They wouldn't know Daniel. They wouldn't even know where Richie lived, never mind Daniel. She told herself she was being paranoid, and that Daniel must have some enemies. He had to, living the life he led. She straightened her clothes and turned round to go back into the lounge. Then she stopped and took her hand off the handle. She thought of the gun, the cash, the briefcase. Why would a guy in the wrong place at the wrong time have a briefcase with a gun and over eight grand in used notes in it? *It is the Mafia,* she thought, *it has to be, that would explain the gun and the cash.* She was scared; her heart was pounding; her mind was racing. She wanted to go back over the line. She wish she hadn't crossed it. She didn't want these thoughts. She wanted her old life back. She wanted to be oblivious to all this again. She wanted to run but knew she couldn't. She heard a voice. It was Phoebe. She opened the door and walked into the lounge. She pushed the thoughts away. She needed to be there for Phoebe.

It was nearly 10:00pm when Richie got back home. Gloria had dropped Marie off, who was sat on the settee in total darkness. Richie switched on the light and sat beside her. He didn't say anything. He just held her hand. No words were spoken for a good two minutes as they both sat with their own thoughts. Marie was torn between sympathy for Richie, who'd lost a brother, and the thoughts of whether Venice had had any bearing on today's events.

'I can't believe what has happened,' Richie said, hoping he would get some sympathy from Marie. She held his hand.

'How are you feeling?' Marie asked.

'Numb, just numb, who would do such a thing? We've all made a few calls, and no one can believe it. No one knows anything, nothing. He was my twin brother, always there for me. My life will never be the same.'

She snuggled into him, still trying hard to suppress her thoughts, but as hard as she tried, they would not go away. She, like many other people, didn't believe in coincidences. Things like that just did not happen. There was always a reason behind it. She just hoped that the reason did not lie in Venice.

Richie spent the next three days permanently at Frank's side. He wanted to be there for his father, as any son would in times such as these. Frank appreciated the company. He needed family support, and Richie was the only family he had left. Any spare time he had, he would be with Phoebe, Alice, and Archie. Archie still idolised his uncle Richie and Richie knew it was a good place to be. Archie gave him the platform on which he could play out the role of the doting uncle perfectly. He took him with him sometimes to Frank's house, saying that he needed to be around his uncle and grandad. Everyone agreed that it would do him good. He was fairing up well, and Richie was helping him along the way.

Marie was left at home with her thoughts. She could not suppress them. Round and round, they would go in her head. She would go from thinking that she was being silly and convince herself it was nothing to do with Venice to then being unable to explain why someone who was a nobody would have a gun and eight grand on them. Plus, she thought they were in one of the top suites. Richie had said he was on the top floor, and according to the hotel website, the top floor was reserved for the best suites. This guy must have been a somebody, must have had friends in high places, the sort of friends who could get information and who could get over to England so quickly. At times like this, she did two things. She would clean, and she would walk. This morning she was cleaning. She decided to scrub the floors, all of them. It would take her mind off things. Usually, she would use a mop and bucket, but today she was on her hands and knees with a bucket and a cloth. She'd scrubbed it like this only a couple of days before they went to Venice and knew it didn't need doing, but she wanted to keep herself active. Richie used to have a cleaner, but Marie liked to clean, so the cleaner had not been for a few months. She stopped scrubbing and sat up on her knees. She rubbed her forehead and saw on the back of her hand there were beads of sweat. She put down the cloth and went through to make a coffee. As the kettle boiled, she scrubbed a little more. She scrubbed between the cracks of the real wood floor planks as that's where the dirt would sit, and there it was, a little streak of pinkish reddish water. She stopped and wiped it clean with the dry cloth. Then she looked closer. In the crack, it was a deep red, almost brown colour. She scrubbed a little more. The same thing, a watery reddish colour. *Blood!* she thought. *How odd.* She sat up again on her knees. She again wiped her brow. She stood up and went through to pour the water into her coffee mug. Her mind was racing again. *How did that get there?* She opened the cupboard and grabbed a biscuit. She dunked it and ate it all in one go, all the time thinking. *The floor is only a month old. It's brand new. I scrubbed it before we went to Venice, just over a week ago.* She did not like one bit what she was thinking, 'fuck me,' she said out loud. She finished her coffee and put on her jacket. She needed a walk.

chapter sixty

Marie had walked for over an hour, her mind still racing. She had mulled things over again and again, trying to explain to herself where the blood could have come from. She was convinced it was not there when she scrubbed the floors before they went to Venice, totally convinced. When she cleaned things properly, she was very thorough, and she knew that she would have noticed it plus in any case, it could not be more than a month old as the floor was only laid just over a month previously and even taking that into consideration, she could not explain how any blood would have got there. She tried desperately for an explanation but could not think of one other than it had to be Daniel's, and that would mean only one thing, Richie was lying, and more importantly, could have been involved in Daniel's death. Her blood ran cold, but the strange thing was she was no longer scared, only determined. She knew she could not divulge this to Richie. She had to keep it to herself. She had to think about what to do next. She needed a longer walk. She snapped out of her trance and realised she was back in Black Scotch Lane. She'd been on autopilot. She decided to go back, clear up the cleaning stuff and have a bite to eat. She crossed the road and saw Mrs. Bowler walking towards her with her two bulldogs, Walter and Ronnie. She walked them twice a day, every day, the same route, and more or less at the same time.

'Morning,' she shouted as she approached.

'Morning,' Marie replied, 'Nice day for a walk.' '

'Every day is a nice day for a walk,' Mrs. Bowler replied, 'You can't beat fresh air. It's the ingredient to a long life.'

Marie bent down and stroked the two dogs, both vying for more affection than the other.

'Did you catch up with your Italian visitors the other day?' Mrs. Bowler asked. Marie stopped stroking the dogs but stayed crouched down. Her heart missed a beat.

'Italian visitors?' she replied, trying desperately to keep her voice calm.

'Yes, I spoke to them whilst I was out walking these two. I didn't know which house they were going to, but Walter here decided he needed to do his business, and I watched the two gentlemen walk up your drive. I'm sure they were Italian, they said *buongiorno* anyway, which is good morning in Italian, plus they had the accent.'

Marie felt like her legs were going to give way. She was still crouched down. She felt like the whole world was going to come crashing down on her.

'Probably someone my husband knows,' she said as she stood up and steadied herself. 'Anyway, I must dash, have a nice day.'

Marie walked quickly to her house, opened the door, and just stood in the hallway in silence, unsure what to do. She finally took off her shoes and walked through into the kitchen. She replayed what Mrs. Bowler had said to her. She tried to piece it all together. She thought how they must have come over from Italy, that they must have been looking for Richie. She knew Daniel was at the house, Phoebe had told her, plus

Richie had rung her to check where she was, and he'd told her to tell Phoebe that Daniel had just left. She was now sure that Richie was involved in Daniel's death in some way, and she was just as certain that he'd been there when it happened. Someone had tried to clean the blood up but had not gotten into the grooves where the wood planks connected. That had to be Richie. She had no idea what she was going to do, if anything but decided as she stood in the kitchen looking into the garden that she would not do anything at all until after Daniel's funeral. He needed to be put to rest, and Phoebe and the kids needed to be able to do that. She had three days to think, three days to decide if she were going to tell anyone or do anything that could put her at odds with one of Britain's fiercest crime families. There was no way back over that line now. She already knew that she could not keep this secret to herself, but who could she tell, who would share this burden with her? She felt alone, alone as she stood there recalling the little voice in her head that told her not to go to Venice.

Richie and Frank were at Frank's club in Nottingham. Frank had been somewhat subdued since Daniel's murder. He'd taken it hard. He knew that in this life, things like this could happen, he'd heard of this type of thing before happening to other people in other firms, but he never thought it would happen to him or one of his own. He always felt that he was a cut above a lot of the others, especially in the way he conducted his business. Yes, he was ruthless, yes, he was violent, but only when needed. He was honourable, everyone said that, always had been, and he'd brought Daniel and Richie up to be the same. Daniel had always been a model of Frank in his dealings with any associates outside of the firm, and Richie once they'd sorted out their issues, had been moulded the same way. Respect was dished out when earned and was always reciprocated. Murders like this always occurred when disrespect had been shown or serious liberties had been taken, and to Frank's knowledge, Daniel had neither shown disrespect to anyone nor taken any liberties. Frank had spoken to all the main faces around the UK, and they were all as shocked as Frank. No one could understand it. There was nothing Frank could unearth that would explain Daniel's death happening in the way it had occurred. This was eating away at Frank. This was why he was subdued. He just could not fathom it out. Something did not fit; he was missing something. Someone must know something. He was sure of it. Daniel's murder was professional. Someone must have ordered it, but no one was saying anything. Frank could only assume that was because no one knew anything, or Daniel had seriously pissed someone off, and they were keeping quiet. He wished he knew who. He looked up at Richie.

'We need to sort out who is gonna run Daniel's patch with you. We're vulnerable otherwise,' Richie nodded.

'I know, dad. I know, but Daniel's death has just knocked me for six. He was my only brother, my big brother, if only by fifteen minutes. I just can't seem to bring myself to replace him. He was everything to me, dad, everything.' He dropped his head.

'I know, Son, mine too, but we can't change the past. We can only influence the future, and Daniel would not rest if he thought we were losing our edge out there. We must be strong Richie, for Daniel if nothing else.'

Richie stood up. 'I know, look once the funeral's out

of the way, I'll make it a priority. We've got a strong network; some good blokes, so don't worry about that. We are stronger than ever. One thing me and Daniel did well together was build up a strong team. We didn't really have to do anything. You know the score, dad. We talked about this at length ya know. We needed to have that sorted 'cos you ain't gonna rule forever, ya know. I'll have to divide the patch up. No one can replace Daniel's presence in that large area. I need to break it down. Straight after the funeral. I just can't deal with it before then, dad, too upsetting.'

Frank stood up and hugged Richie.

'He'd be proud of you, as I am.' Richie hugged him back. *I'm fucking good at this,* he thought to himself. Frank broke free.

'Remember, it's Frank in 'ere. What's with all the dad shit, ya soppy fucker,' Richie smiled. Frank smiled back. He was only glad that he still had his Richie and was just thankful that he'd healed the rift all those years ago. He wouldn't have coped if he'd lost Daniel while he was still angry at Richie.

chapter sixty-one

Three days later, Daniel's funeral took place. It was a big affair; criminal faces from all over the UK came to pay their respects at Mansfield Crematorium. Mansfield had seen nothing like it. It was similar to something you only saw on the TV. The mourners were from the UK's biggest criminal networks. Daniel had made his mark in that world, and Frank, although hugely upset, was also tremendously proud to see so many known faces there. He really was Frank Pearson's son. The police were also there in large numbers, which annoyed Frank. He'd personally requested that the police stay away or if they had to be there to only have a minor presence, but you'd think world war three was about to break out; there were so many. Frank made his feelings known but was careful not to spoil the occasion. There was still no information on who had done this, and Frank was starting to think that he may never know who had killed his son. People were careful not to labour the point too much at the funeral, but one or two major faces were still relaying their dismay to Frank.

Frank had the wake at his house in Papplewick. He had a huge place, but it was full to bursting with all the mourners that came back. It was not a dull affair; Frank had made sure that everyone knew that once they got to his house, they were to leave their miserable faces at the door. Daniel would not have wanted to see a house full of mourners. He'd have wanted everyone to have a good time and to celebrate his life.

Frank was courting as many known faces as possible, both national faces and a few local ones that worked for him in one capacity or another. He was desperate to find something that may be of help in identifying Daniel's killer. Jez was stood with him chatting to a local guy called Ben, who was the firm's local head bouncer.

'I still can't believe it, Jez. I just said to the missus earlier that sometimes you just know that someone's gonna one day come a cropper, but I never saw that day coming for Daniel. He was so well respected, so well thought of. I just can't believe it.'

Jez sighed and took a swig of his beer. 'I know Ben, me neither. I'll miss him; he was a good bloke.'

Ben nodded his head slowly. 'They don't make 'em like that anymore. My missus saw him that day too coming out of that petrol station off the Southwell Road, the other side of Rainworth. She wished she'd had a chance to speak to him now. She waved to him, but he never clocked her.'

Jez took another swig of his beer. 'That must have been when he was on his way home from Richie's. She was probably the last person to see him alive.'

Ben looked at Jez. 'I won't mention that to her. It'll send her over the edge.'

Marie spent the whole day watching Richie. This was the first opportunity she'd had to see him in this kind of situation since the murder. She was purposely not drinking any alcohol, saying she had an upset stomach, but really she'd wanted to keep her mind clear. She wanted to see how Richie acted. She'd noted he'd been outwardly upset since the murder, as you would expect, but today would be a different ball game. She wanted to see if he slipped up, if his mask slipped or if she could see any signs of an act. If he were acting, he was doing a cracking job, but she knew with all these people here today, plus the alcohol could result in a slip-up or two. She was watching his body language closely, watching his facial expressions, seeing how natural the grief was. She was particularly interested in all of this when he was in earshot of people talking about Daniel. How would he react when constantly hearing how good a bloke Daniel was, how he was one of a kind, how there would never be another like him, how his dad was so proud of him? She needed something. She didn't have to wait long.

Ray Parkes was watching Richie. He needed to catch a word with him about the payment for finding Andy Barnes. He'd located him and wanted paying. Richie had not yet come up with the goods. Ray had cut him some slack because of what had happened to Daniel, but knew he had to tackle the issue sooner rather than later. He was a little uneasy about raising the subject in any way, shape, or form today, but he also knew that Richie would be aware that he'd not yet paid him. He had hoped that Richie would take the opportunity today to have a quiet word with him and even apologise for not yet paying up. He picked up a sandwich from the beautiful spread that had been laid on and watched Richie go upstairs. He decided to follow him and take his chance. He moved quickly across the room and took the stairs two at a time. It was a winding staircase that was the centrepiece of the downstairs. He managed to call Richie's name just before he went into one of the upstairs bathrooms.

'Hi, Ray, how ya doing?' Richie asked as he held out his hand to shake Ray's. 'I'm okay, Richie, I'm okay. How are you, though?'

'Yeah, I'm doing okay, mate. It's been a tough few days, ya know, but we'll get through it.'

Ray rubbed his chin with his right hand. He felt a little uneasy and was wishing he'd just stayed downstairs. He'd paused a little too long. 'Did you want me for anything Ray, 'cos I'm bursting for a piss?'

Ray took his hand away from his chin and put it into his trouser pocket. 'Well, I just wanted to remind you that I've still not had my money for locating Andy Barnes. I know it's a little awkward today, and I know you've had a lot on, but I just thought I'd mention it, ya know. There's no issue. I know you're good for it, but didn't want it to slip your mind mate, that's all.'

Richie looked at the floor and shook his head. He then brought his gaze up to meet Ray's 'Ya think I'm paying ya do ya? I still ain't got my fifteen-grand back, so until I do, you can go fuck ya'self.'

Ray was startled, and now he really wished he'd stayed downstairs. He thought this reaction must be down to the emotions of the day.

'Look, I know this was a bad time. I shouldn't have said anything today. I'll ring you in a few days, and we can sort it out then, eh?' Ray smiled as he said it hoping it would defuse what was feeling like a pretty tense situation. He didn't want any aggro here in Frank Pearson's house on the day of his son's funeral.

'You can ring me whenever you like, but I ain't paying ya until you find that little cunt and I get my money back, so save ya phone credit until you've found him. That clear?'

Ray was starting to become annoyed. He knew he

was in an awkward spot here. He knew this could turn into a really bad situation for him, but he'd had to deal with non-payment before in his line of work, and experience told him to be firm. He had respect for the service he offered and wasn't about to let that go for Richie Pearson. If it went pear-shaped, he'd have to face it.

'I found him. I told you he was in Venice; that was my end of the bargain. I did what I said I would do. I can't be held responsible if you didn't find him when you went there. That's not part of my deal.'

'Yeah, well, that's tough shit, Ray. He must have seen me 'cos he'd checked out the day before you rang me to tell me he was now Paul fucking Gregory, or whatever that name was you told me. When I get my money, you'll get paid, but until then, you can get fucked.'

Ray shook his head. 'I'm surprised at you Richie. You know he was there, so I did my job. I can't help the fact he may have seen you. I want my money, and I really hope we can sort that without any unpleasantness. Your father and brother were good payers.'

Before Ray could finish his sentence, Richie grabbed him by the throat and forced him up against the wall. He had him pinned tightly with his forearm across Ray's throat. Richie looked left and right to check no one was coming.

'My father and brother were good what? I don't give a fuck what my brother was. He ain't here, I am, and I'll be heading this firm before long, so you, Ray Parkes, better be careful what you say. You ain't dealt with me before, have ya? Well, let me tell you something. I call the fucking shots when I'm dealing with someone. I'm nothing like my brother, and I ain't nothing like that fucking has-been downstairs, so what you see before you now is the fucking future.' Richie pressed his forearm harder. Ray was struggling to breathe. 'So, get fucking used to it. Find that bastard Andy Barnes and find him quick. I want my fifteen grand. Then you may get your money.' Richie let him go. Ray tried to regain his composure and to get his breath back. Richie pressed his arm hard again against Ray's throat. 'And another thing. No one knows I've been to Venice. If I ever hear you mention my name in the same breath as that fucking city, I'll kill ya. I'll fucking murder ya.' He let Ray go again, straightened his suit jacket, and went into the bathroom. Ray coughed a little and eventually managed to regain his composure. He straightened his clothes and calmly walked downstairs. He walked straight out into the street and got into his car. He didn't say goodbye to anyone.

Raquel stood motionless in the bedroom behind the door right next to the bathroom. She could not believe what she had just heard. *Richie was in Venice,* she thought to herself repeatedly. She stayed where she was until she heard Richie come out of the bathroom. Only then did she allow herself to breathe properly. She sat on the bed and rested her hand on the small suitcase she'd brought with her. She was staying the night, courtesy of Frank's invitation. She sat there in silence for a few minutes, recalling what Richie had told Ray Parkes. *No one knows I was in Venice.* Then she thought of what else he'd told him. *I'm nothing like my brother, or that fucking has been downstairs.* She felt sick. She thought of all the times she'd slept with Richie, as recently as three weeks ago. She'd not suspected a thing. Raquel, like everyone else, had thought that Richie Pearson had come good, really believed the image he portrayed, really believed that he had a good heart deep down. Now she knew that had all been a sham, all been an act. The real Richie Pearson was nothing like Daniel or Frank. The real Richie Pearson was the man they all knew before 1996, before Frank had put his demons to bed, and now, by the looks of it, he was back. *Why would he keep Venice a secret?* she asked herself over and over again. *What happened in Venice?* All she knew was that he never caught up with this Andy Barnes guy. She tried to recall the other name Richie had mentioned, Paul something, but she could not remember the surname.

Raquel walked downstairs and made sure that Richie didn't see her. She didn't want him to know she'd been upstairs. She grabbed a glass of wine off the tray that the waitress was walking round with. She watched Richie. He was in full conversation with a face from down south. Raquel had seen this guy before but did not know his name. She then scanned the room for Marie. She watched as Marie watched Richie. She watched some more. She watched for a good while as Marie watched Richie. She was intrigued. It was as if Marie was watching Richie for a reason. Raquel's mind was racing. She was coming up with all kinds of scenarios, but none of them made any sense. Venice was something she wanted to know more about, though. She took her phone out of her pocket and walked over towards Richie. She began to talk into her phone.

'Hello, can you hear me? Hello, hello.' She then tutted and said, 'bloody phone.' She then looked at Richie, who had heard the latter part of her conversation. 'Can I borrow your phone Richie, can't get a bloody signal with this thing for some reason?'

Richie took his phone out of his pocket and passed it to Raquel. 'Here you go.'

'Thank you.'

'No worries,' he then continued speaking to the guy from down south. He'd not given a second's thought to letting Raquel use his phone, just as she'd hoped. She walked outside. The sun was shining, and people were chatting amongst themselves, all caught up in their own conversations of crime and power. No one noticed Raquel walking towards the bottom of the massive garden on her own apparently deep in conversation. She was, of course, speaking to no one, only giving the impression she was. When she was far enough away, she took Richie's phone from her ear and began to look through his photos. She started with the most recent. There were photos of Richie and Marie in Venice. A photo of them on the Gondola, a photo of them in St. Mark's square, and a photo of Richie in a hotel with a good-looking barman. She looked around her; no one had seemingly noticed her. She then, one by one, sent herself the photos of Venice from Richie's phone. She then deleted the texts. Now she needed to speak to Marie.

chapter sixty-two

Richie sat down at the breakfast table opposite Marie. Scrambled eggs were one of his favourites, especially when Marie made them. He could never quite work out what she did, but her scrambled eggs were the best he'd ever tasted. She said it was all in the stirring when they were cooking, but he'd tried that and could still never get them as light and fluffy as Marie could. She was unusually quiet this morning. She'd hardly spoken a word since they'd woken up. She couldn't have a hangover as she wasn't drinking at the funeral yesterday. Richie felt a little worse for wear, but nothing a good plate of Marie's scrambled eggs couldn't sort. He took a swig of his tea. Marie was playing with her eggs.

'What's up, everything okay?' he asked. Marie kept her head down, looking at her eggs as she pushed them around the plate. After a few seconds, she looked up at him.

'Do you think Daniel's death had anything to do with Venice?' She noted Richie's eyes narrow. He put down his fork.

'Why would you think that?' he said in a rather blunt tone.

'Just been thinking that's all. It's just a bit coincidental that with what happened in Venice, someone bumps Daniel off two days later. You must have thought the same.'

'Why would I think that? Daniel wasn't in Venice, was he? It's nowt to do with us; it's just that someone, for some reason, caught up with Daniel. Who knows what he was up to or involved in? We'll probably never know. If anyone from Venice was coming, they'd come for me, wouldn't they, come here, not go to Daniel's house. You're putting two and two together, Marie, and making five... or even six, now put Venice out of your mind. Remember, we've never been to Venice.' His voice was sharp and a little aggressive.

'But what if they thought Daniel was you?'

Richie again put down his fork and glared at Marie. She felt a pang of fear. She didn't like the look. He stood up and slowly walked around to her side of the table. He grabbed her by the throat and squeezed, not too hard to leave a mark, but hard enough, so she knew he meant it.

'Listen to me. No one came here. No one thought Daniel was me. No one is gonna come here looking for me, not now, not ever, so put that little conspiracy out of your pretty little head. Mention Venice again, and I'll punch you so hard you'll have to pick every one of your teeth off the floor. Everyone. Remember when you crossed the line, you crossed it forever. You know too much, Marie. They say knowledge is power, but unfortunately, you have the knowledge, but you have no power. I have all the power. Remember that. You're in it for good now,' he stroked her hair. 'You'll never be rid of me, never, so be a good girl and keep ya fucking mouth shut. Is that clear?'

Marie nodded. She was scared, scared out of her wits, but as he took his hand away from her throat and walked back to his chair to finish his scrambled eggs, she realised that Richie had no idea just how much knowledge she had. He had no idea she knew as much as she did, no idea that the blood was still there between the grooves in the wood, no idea that she knew that some Italians had visited the house and no idea what she was going to do next, but then again neither did she.

It was just before lunch. Marie's neck still hurt a little from when Richie had grabbed her earlier that day at breakfast. She'd checked in the mirror a few times, and there was no mark. She was glad about that, glad that she would not have to explain anything away. She heard the doorbell ring. She opened the door. Raquel smiled.

'Hi Marie, thought I'd call in for a coffee before I shoot off back home.' Raquel had left Frank's house half an hour earlier.

'Come in, nice to see you. I'll put the kettle on. I was just about to make a drink. Sugar?'

Raquel took off her shoes and shouted, 'Just one sugar, please.' She then walked through into the kitchen. 'Anyway, I didn't get a chance to ask you yesterday, how was Venice?' Marie dropped the sugar jar. It smashed on the kitchen floor, and millions of granules of sugar spilled across the tiles. She still had her back to Raquel. Raquel walked up behind her and put her hands on both shoulders. Marie tensed up. 'It's okay Marie. I know you went to Venice. Shall we have something a little stronger?'

Marie turned round and sobbed. Raquel held her close. She didn't speak; she just held her and let her cry. Marie eventually stood back and wiped her eyes.

'I'm so glad you came, Raquel. I need to talk to someone. I feel like I'm going crazy, but I'm scared, more scared than you would know.' She then went and got a dustpan and brush from the cupboard. Raquel took it off her.

'This can wait. Richie will be hours. He's gone to Nottingham with Frank to meet with Jez, Pat, and a few others. Frank's still looking for answers, but I kind of get the impression he should have come here. I'm right, aren't I?' Marie nodded.

'I need a drink, Raquel. Come and sit in the lounge, I need to confide in someone.' She then took Raquel's arm. 'I can trust you, can't I?'

Raquel held her hand. 'That rather depends on what you tell me. That's a chance you're going to have to take.'

Marie took a deep breath. 'Take a seat then. I'll pour the wine.'

Frank was in his main office at the club in Nottingham. It was just approaching midday. He was in no mood to just sit around any longer. He'd finished with being sombre. He needed to keep active otherwise, he'd do nothing but sit and think about Daniel. Thinking like that wasn't always a good thing, especially when you didn't have the answers and Frank had nothing, still nothing to go on. He had hoped that someone yesterday would have given him something to go on, but nothing. He could not believe that all the main faces of the criminal underworld were there, and no one knew anything. He'd canvassed a lot of people yesterday. He'd courted people he would not normally give the time of day to, and he'd massaged egos that were not fit to lace his boots, but still nothing.

'Someone knows fucking something,' he shouted as he paced the office. 'Why is no one speaking? What the fuck did Daniel do?'

'Frank, you need to calm down; this ain't gonna do you any good. We may never know.'

Frank looked hard at Jez, his trusted right-hand man, the man who had been by his side since the beginning.

'You fuckin' what?'

'We may never know?' Frank walked to Jez and put his face right into his. 'We fuckin well better get to know. I won't rest until I know who killed my son. Someone knows something, and I bet they were drinking my fuckin' wine yesterday. Do you know something, eh? Well, do ya?'

Jez looked into Frank's eyes with pity and sorrow. He knew his boss didn't mean what he'd just said. He knew he was hurting and looking to anyone for answers. 'You know I don't, and I'll forget you just asked me.' Jez turned and walked away. He wanted to get some air. Richie looked at Frank and said.

'Sounds like a guilty conscience to me, Frank, does that, walking away. Can't face the truth, eh?' Jez swung round and punched Richie hard, knocking him backwards into Frank's desk. Pat immediately got hold of Jez and held him back. He looked like he was ready to kill Richie. Richie tried to pull Pat off Jez to get at him, but Pat swung his arm back and caught Richie in the mouth with his elbow. Frank got hold of his son and told him to sit down.

'I'll fuckin' kill him, Frank; he's a fuckin' has-been.'

'Sit down, Richie, just fuckin' sit down.' Frank barked. Pat had restrained Jez, who was now straightening his clothes. 'I ain't taking that from him, Frank. I'll take it from you, but not him.'

Frank pointed his finger around the room at them

all. 'We need to be stronger than ever, gents, not fighting amongst ourselves.' He looked at Jez and held out his hand. 'I take that back, Jez, what I just said. I was out of order.' Jez shook Frank's hand. Frank then turned to Richie. 'I think you ought to do the same, Son.'

'What for speaking my mind? What is this a fuckin' tea party? He cracks me one on the jaw, and I have to apologise. Fuck that.'

'We ain't having any internal fighting here, Richie. We never have, so we ain't starting now, so fucking apologise like a man, and let's get on with trying to find out who shot ya brother.'

Richie saw the opportunity. 'Yeah, ya right, Frank, I think it's just still affecting me more than I realise. I think it's got to all of us.' He stood up and held out his hand. Jez paused for a second but then shook it. He saw in Richie's eyes that it wasn't genuine. In that second, Jez Carrington saw someone he recognised from years ago. Richie Pearson, the old Richie Pearson. The Richie Pearson he thought was dead and buried. He never thought he'd see that person again, and it dawned on him that he'd come to the fore about ten days after his brother had mysteriously been murdered.

Frank continued the meeting in the main room upstairs. He was insistent that everyone on the payroll spent time looking for answers to Daniel's murder. He also wanted to discuss the new hierarchy of the firm with his best men. It was as they'd all expected. Richie was taking over on a day-to-day basis. Frank was taking more of a back seat. They would all report to Richie from now on. The only exception was Jez. He was still Frank's man. Jez was around the same age as Frank, and Frank knew he was thinking of his future and wouldn't accept reporting to Richie. Frank felt he owed Jez that much as least, so he kept him out of the new set-up. Richie needed his own right-hand man. Frank had wanted him to pick Brian, who was another original firm member. Brian was a year older than Frank and Jez but was still hungry for the fight. He had nothing else in his life and had always said he'd retire when he dropped dead. Richie wanted a younger man, though. Brian was too old for this role. He chose Pat Steadman. Pat had been in Leeds since they had disposed of Gerry Clarke back in the early nineties, but Richie knew he'd still jump at the chance to come home, back to Nottingham. Pat had a good network of people up in Leeds and had primed a guy called John Hughes to take the lead up there. John was born and bred in Yorkshire and was ripe to move up the ranks. Richie took over the meeting and told everyone how things were going to be from now on. He wanted to grow the empire; he had plans. They all listened intently and were excited about how things were going to be, all except Jez. He saw the old Richie. He'd been fooled long enough, like everyone else, but he'd seen something downstairs in Richie's eyes that he couldn't shake. He kept quiet, telling himself that he could be wrong, but he knew deep down something did not feel right.

After the meeting, Richie toasted the new era; even Frank had a tipple to the future. He'd watched in admiration as Richie took the floor, as he took control and showed himself to be a great leader. Frank was still the boss, but Richie was the man now. Frank tried to swallow down his mixed feelings, as he'd have loved nothing more than Daniel to have been there too, to share in the leadership of the family firm. He toasted

Daniel. Everyone raised their glasses in genuine admiration for Daniel Pearson. All except one and Jez made a mental note of the very fact that Richie had struggled to raise his glass.

Raquel bent down and looked at the red stain within the grooves of the wood floor planks. She'd seen enough blood in her time to know that what she was looking at was the real thing. This was no red wine stain. It was blood. She got on her knees and looked closer. She then sat back onto her bum and crossed her arms over her knees. She sighed hard. Her cheeks were like a puffer fish. She looked up at Marie.

'Fuck me, Marie. I don't swear very often, and I can't remember the last time I was speechless but what you've just told me is something else. You sure she said they were Italian?' Marie nodded.

'One hundred percent, Raquel. Well, I mean, she didn't see their passports, but they spoke Italian to her, and they ain't been back since. What are we going to do?'

Raquel sighed again and puffed her cheeks out once more. She shook her head and stared into space.

'I've no idea. I really haven't. I need to sleep on this; that's if I can sleep with this going round in my head. I'll never sleep again if we allow Richie to get away with this. Mind you, we have no proof, do we, that this blood is Daniel's or that Richie drove Daniel's car, or that he had Daniel in the car at the time, or that he put Daniel's body in his house. It's all hearsay, Marie. We have nothing concrete.'

'What other explanation is there, though?' Marie said, looking desperately for a definitive answer. For a third time, Raquel took a deep breath and puffed her cheeks out as she exhaled loudly.

'There isn't one. It's the only explanation for the blood, for the fact Daniel's body was here, and the Italians were here too, and most likely because of what happened in Venice. It does all fit, and I think our scenario is probably correct, but I have no idea what we do about it. Do we tell Phoebe? Do we tell Frank? Do we tell Richie that we know? Fuck knows, Marie. I heard Richie yesterday at the funeral talking, well shouting at that Ray Parkes guy, that was the old Richie. I'm telling you your life will be hell if you don't act on this, well if we don't act on this.' Raquel stood up. She took Marie's hand. 'You asked me earlier if you could trust me, remember?' Marie nodded. 'Well, you can—one hundred percent. I'm with you, but from what I heard yesterday up them stairs and with what you have told me today about Venice and what we think happened in this house, we can't let Richie get away with it. He needs to pay, but we are not strong enough to take him on. We need help.'

'Who from?' Marie asked.

'No idea, but I'm on it. I'm bloody well on it.'

Frank and Jez left the meeting and drove the short journey to Daniel and Phoebe's house in Southwell. Frank wanted to see how Phoebe and his grandkids were doing but also wanted Jez to drive Daniel's car over to his house. Phoebe had her own car; in fact, she had two. She found Daniel's Range Rover too big and didn't like driving it. It had not moved since Richie drove it with Daniel's body in the boot, so Frank decided he'd keep it at his house in one of his garages. He just wanted to be able to sit in it whenever he wanted to, something of Daniel's to remind him of his son. They pulled into the long drive and saw Daniel's car still sat there as it was ten days ago. It needed a wash. Frank would see to that. It would look like it had just come out of the showroom this time tomorrow. Phoebe came out to greet them and hugged Frank.

'How are you? He asked. 'So, so,' she replied. 'Come in, and I'll make a brew. Alice is upstairs. Archie is watching the TV,' Frank and Jez followed her in.

Phoebe put the kettle on and passed Jez the keys to the car. He put them in his pocket. Alice came down and hugged Frank.

'You okay, Grandad?' she asked.

'I am now I've seen you,' he said and gave her a big kiss.

Even though she was fourteen, she still loved a kiss from her grandad. Frank walked through into the lounge and sat next to Archie. Phoebe poured the tea and passed a mug to Jez, who took a sip and placed it on the worktop.

'I'll just go and make sure it starts,' he said, wanting to get out from the house more than anything. He felt awkward and didn't know what to say. He went out to the drive and pressed the key fob. He heard the door unlock. He opened the driver's door and went to sit in the seat. He was surprised to find the driver's seat too far forward. Daniel always drove as if he was lying down. It was well known to everyone that if you got into a car to drive it after Daniel had been driving it you better take your sleeping bag as you'd be more or less lying down. Jez drove his car similar. Not as far back as Daniel, but further back than the average person. The seat was too far forward. Jez had to adjust it to get in and then adjust it again for himself to drive. This was strange. Jez sat there thinking, stroking his chin. *Someone else has driven this car after Daniel,* he thought to himself. He knew the car had not been moved since Daniel had supposedly driven himself to his house that fateful day. Something caught his eye, and he glanced right to see Alice run into the house. He started the car up, revved the engine a little, and then switched it off. He went into the house and finished his tea quickly.

'Has that car been driven since Daniel drove it that day, Phoebe?' he asked.

'No, it's never moved. No one has even been in it. Why?

'No reason,' Jez replied. 'Just started straight away, been stood for ten days, hasn't it? Great these modern cars are, anyway, shall I get off then, Frank?' he shouted as Frank was still in the lounge.

'Bloody hell, Jez, what's the rush?'

'Well, I've got a few bits to do before I drop the car at yours later. I'll see you at your house later.'

'Okay, I'll then drop you back at the club for your car,' Frank said. He then looked at Archie. 'Taxi service I am these days.' Frank laughed. So did Archie.

Jez drove straight round to Richie's house. He knew that Richie would still be at the club sorting stuff out with his men. He just hoped that Marie would be in. He was surprised to see Raquel's car in the drive parked alongside Marie's and also Richie's other car, a BMW X5. He knocked on the door, Marie answered.

'Hi Jez,' she said, looking a little surprised. 'You okay?'

'Yeah, fine, Richie back yet?'

'Err no, I thought he was with you and Frank and some others at the club.'

'Yeah, he was. Maybe he's still there. I've just been to pick up Daniel's Range Rover to take it to Frank's. I was wanting to have a little look at the X5, thinking of getting one, but not one hundred percent sure. I was hoping Richie would have been in, so I could have a look.'

'Well, come in, I'll get you the keys. Are you gonna take it for a spin?'

'Err, no, don't think so. I just wanted to have a look at the interior, driving position, you know what us men are like with our cars. Hi Raquel, how are you?'

Raquel had just come out of the lounge. 'Fine, thanks, Jez, just popped in for a coffee with Marie before I shoot off back to Leicester.'

Marie passed Jez the keys. He walked outside and pressed the fob. He then opened the driver's door to get in. He had to move the seat back and then adjust it again to suit his driving position, exactly as he had to do in Daniel's car. He sat there and pondered again. He stroked his chin like he always did when he was deep in thought. He was then startled by a knock on the window. It was Raquel.

'Something on your mind, Jez?' she asked. He shook his head. 'No, just thinking about cars, that's all.'

Raquel smiled. 'You haven't run the risk of coming here uninvited to look at Richie's car Jez for no good reason any more than I've just popped in for a coffee. I know what the meeting was about earlier. Richie's the man now and plus, you've only had your car for two months. Now, I've just asked Marie to put the kettle on. If you want to share your thoughts, you are more than welcome to join us. You might be glad you did.' Raquel looked at Jez in a way that made him aware that she had something to tell him. Whatever it was, he wanted to know.

Jez got out of the car. This was a clear indication from Raquel that she was also struggling to put two and two together and come up with four. He followed her in and sat down with a mug of tea. He took a sip and looked at Marie and Raquel; both sat opposite him at the kitchen table.

'So, you a little curious too then, I assume?' He said obviously being a little reserved in what he said. He was sure he was reading this situation correctly but didn't want to show his hand just yet.

'A little curious? Ha, that's a laugh,' Raquel said, rolling her eyes. 'If you mean, do we think Richie had some hand in all this, then yes, I could say we are a little curious, more than a little, though. Richie and Marie here went to Venice a couple of weeks ago.'

Before she could continue, Jez said, 'Venice? I thought you went to London. That's what Richie's told everyone anyway.' He looked confused. Raquel took her phone out of her handbag and showed Jez the photo of Richie in the bar with the Spanish waiter. Jez nodded his head slowly. 'Yep, that's Richie, alright.'

Raquel turned to Marie. 'Tell him, Marie, tell him the whole story.' She then looked at Jez. 'You'll like this, Jez.' Raquel then sat back in the chair and crossed her arms, ready to hear this unbelievable tale again.

'He killed two guys in Venice, Jez, two unknown guys. We still do not know who they are.'

Jez put his elbows on the table and put his head in his hands.' He killed two guys. Why?'

'Well, apparently he was out there looking for a guy called Andy Barnes who owed him fifteen grand, someone called Ray Parkes had tracked him down.'

Jez interrupted, 'Who's Andy Barnes? I know Ray

Parkes, but who the fuck is Andy Barnes?'

'I have no idea,' Marie replied.

'Me neither,' Raquel confirmed.

'I've never heard of him, anyway sorry to interrupt, carry on.'

Marie continued to tell Jez the whole tale right up to the point of finding the blood and Mrs. Bowler confirming that two Italians had visited the day of Daniel's murder.

'Then there was what Raquel heard yesterday at the funeral. Wasn't there, Raquel?' Marie turned to look at Raquel, who nodded her head and sat forward.

'What I heard yesterday was Richie of old, Jez, that guy from back in the nineties, not the good old Richie of late.'

'So, what did you hear?' Jez asked.

After hearing Raquel's story of Richie and Ray Parkes's conversation, Jez again put his head in his hands. 'Where's this blood?' he asked.

Marie showed him the blood that you could just still see between the grooves.

'You reckon that's Daniel's then? He asked. Marie nodded.

'It's certainly not mine, or Richie's, that I am sure of, and no one else to my knowledge has bled in here. The floor was only laid a few weeks ago, as you know.'

He nodded, 'Yeah, you're right.'

Raquel continued, 'So what was your concern then, Jez? Does it tie up with what we just told you?'

Jez stood up. 'Well, kind of, but my suspicions are nowhere near as intriguing as yours. I just saw the old Richie appear this morning, as you saw yesterday, but then when I picked up Daniel's car, I had to adjust the seat to get in it. As I am sure you know

Daniel always had his seat almost bloody horizontal, I couldn't understand why the seat would be like that if he was the last one to drive it. Phoebe confirmed that no one had driven it or even sat in it since the day of the murder, so someone else other than Daniel must have been the last one to drive it. I knew Richie had his seat a lot closer to the wheel and more upright, so I came to see what his seat was like in the X5, and it was as I suspected. Exactly the same. I wasn't sure where I was going with this, but after listening to you, I'm convinced that Daniel was murdered here, and Richie drove his car to Southwell.'

'That's the conclusion we came to too,' Marie confirmed. Jez walked slowly back into the kitchen. He sighed heavily. 'Thing is the cops have tracked his car all the way from Mansfield to Southwell on that day. They even blew up a photo, which was pretty grainy, but it looks like Daniel driving.'

Raquel shook her head. 'Jez, come on, you know that on that sort of photo that you'd never tell the difference between Daniel and Richie. They're more or less identical. Plus, you weren't thinking of anything like this at the time, so of course, it would look like Daniel to you. Why wouldn't it even if it were actually Richie?' He stood hands on hips looking out of the window across the very neat, large lawn.

'Yeah, you're right, anyway, have you got a cotton bud?' he asked Marie.

'Err, yes, I think so, just a minute.' Marie went to get the cotton bud from the bathroom. Raquel knew what was coming. Jez wet the cotton bud with warm water and squeezed it between the crack in the wood. When he pulled it out, it had blood on it?

'I'll have this back by tomorrow, no questions asked.

Then we will know for certain if it's Daniel's blood. We have to be one hundred percent sure, agreed?'

Marie and Raquel nodded in agreement. 'Act normally until I get back to you, but it should be tomorrow. In fact, let's arrange to meet here tomorrow at lunchtime. If Richie is around Marie, you'll have to let Raquel know. Then she can let me know, okay?'

Again, they nodded. 'He goes out every day, Jez, tomorrow will be no different, I'm sure.'

Raquel went to get her coat and to put her shoes on. Jez stood and looked around the room. He saw something that made his blood run cold.

Jez and Raquel then both left at the same time. Jez told her to go straight to the Oak Tree Pub. He needed a word.

chapter sixty-three

Richie had finished the meeting and had had a separate chat with Pat, his new number two. Pat was up for the job and was chuffed to bits to be coming home finally. He'd enjoyed Leeds and had come to think of that as his home, and he was prepared to finish his days up there, but this chance to come back to Nottingham and move up the ranks was one that he was not going to miss. As Pat left the club to return to Leeds for the next few days to tie up loose ends, Richie got out his phone. He logged into the website that allowed him to access the covert cameras he'd installed the day before the funeral. He'd done this to keep an eye on Marie. Since they'd returned from Venice, she'd been tense. He was worried that she'd crack under the pressure of what she knew, so he wanted to keep an eye on her, make sure she was not doing anything stupid. The system he'd had fitted allowed him to watch things from his phone. He logged in and saw Marie sat on her own on the sofa in the lounge. He looked at the camera in the kitchen and noticed three mugs on the table. This made him curious. Who had been round? *This was why I got this fucking system,* he muttered to himself as he pressed the button that would allow him to watch the recordings from earlier. He watched as Raquel came, he watched as Raquel looked closely at the floor, he watched as Marie and Raquel sat chatting, Raquel obviously astonished at what was being said. He watched as Daniel's car pulled into the drive, he watched as Jez got out, he watched as Jez got in his car, he watched as Raquel said something to Jez, he watched as they sat chatting, he watched as Jez got the cotton bud and got something from the floor. He watched as Jez and Raquel left. He looked at his watch. That was five minutes ago. As he walked to his car, he rang the company that installed the CCTV. They answered straight away.

'Hi, is Joseph there, please? Tell him it's Richie Pearson.'

'Just one moment, sir.'

Richie sat in his car and waited on the phone.

'I'm sorry, Mr. Pearson, but Joseph is on the phone. Can I help?'

Richie tried to remain calm. 'Why can I not hear any sound on my phone when I log into the system?'

'Just a second, Mr. Pearson, while I have a look.'

Again, Richie waited.

'I can't understand that sir, but I have just reset the sound parameters on the system, so you should now be okay. Please accept our apologies.'

Richie put the phone down and started his car. He was going straight home.

Raquel waited in the pub car park as Jez finished on his phone. They then walked in together. Jez got the drinks and sat down with Raquel.

'He's got secret cameras in there,' he said.

'What, where?'

'All over the house. Had them installed two days ago, the day before the funeral. I saw the one in the hall just before we left. Very small it is, but I knew as soon as I saw it. If you didn't know what to look for,

you wouldn't know. I've just made a call as I knew who
he'd have used. They didn't want to say anything, but
I eventually persuaded them. I was hoping that he'd
had them installed before the day of the murder but no
such luck. That would have firmly nailed him. '

'Do you think they'll let Richie know?' Raquel asked.

'I doubt it. I spoke to Joseph. He knows me well
enough and knows what I'll do if they did. I made that
very clear. The thing is Richie will no doubt watch
it at some point. He's bound to. Joseph told me he
could access it from his phone at any time, so that
puts Marie and yourself in danger. I can handle Richie
Pearson, but you and Marie will be dead meat. He'll
see us all there. We ain't got time to get this DNA stuff
done. Listen, I need you to park up somewhere safe
and watch the house. I need to know when Richie
returns home.

' What you gonna do?'

'Leave that to me. Just for fuck's sake, let me know
the moment he returns.'

Raquel was scared, scared more for Marie than
herself. She was a fragile thing and would be no match
for Richie. She knew she was also in danger, but at
least she was not in the house, and at least she knew
that Richie would probably know she'd been there.
That at least put her on the front foot. She downed her
drink and walked to her car. Jez walked with her.

'Don't forget Raquel as soon as he lands, I want to
know.'

'Will do. My heart's going ten to the dozen.' Jez
laughed.

'This is the life I lead, Raquel. Mine does that all the
time.'

As Jez walked to the car, he stopped dead in his

tracks. He recalled the conversation with Ben, the head bouncer at the funeral. He jumped into Daniel's car and screeched out of the car park.

Raquel drove the short journey back to Black Scotch Lane. She drove past the house and saw that Richie was not yet back. She had no idea how long it would be until he was back. She didn't even know if he had watched the footage of her there or even if he would watch it today. She knew Jez was right, though, and that Richie probably would watch it, and soon. *Why would he install it and have it on his phone?* she thought. *To watch it at any time, anywhere, that's why* she reminded herself. She was scared, though. Richie knew her car. He would recognise it instantly. She parked quite a distance down the street, facing the way she knew he would come into the road. Her only chance of not being seen was to be far enough away that Richie wouldn't notice her. She needed to be alert, though and see every car that came into the road from the direction of Berry Hill Lane. She was parked up and sat there as nervous as hell.

Jez pulled into the garage forecourt and parked up at one of the pumps. This was a small local garage, but he could see two CCTV cameras pointing towards the pumps. He walked inside the small shop. He looked above the counter. There was a CCTV camera pointing towards the till area. Behind the counter was a middle-aged woman with dark, scraped back hair. Jez waited until the customer she was serving was out of the shop. He approached the counter.

'Does that thing record?' he asked as he looked up at the camera.

'Err, yes, why?'

'How long does it go back?'

'I'm not sure, why? Who are you?'

'Look, it don't matter who I am. I need to see the footage, and I need to see it now for 28th of May.'

'I'm sorry, but I cannot show you that. It's confidential.' Jez grabbed the woman by the throat.

'Look, the last thing I want to do is hurt you, but I will if you don't show me that fucking footage.' The woman struggled to speak. Jez glanced to his right as he saw a guy coming out of a small office. His name was Tony. He recognised Jez as a local gangster and someone not to cross. He didn't know where he knew him from, but he'd seen him before and knew not to tackle him.

'Please put her down. We don't want any trouble.' Jez released his grip on the woman who was gasping for air. The man beckoned him through to the office. He looked at his employee sympathetically and said, 'We don't want any trouble from these Lynn. Are you okay?' She nodded whilst still trying to regain her composure and get her breath. Tony joined Jez in the office. 'What do you want?' he asked.

'I need to know if your CCTV still has the 28th of May on it.'

'Yes, it will have, for another two to three days.'

'I want to see if from about midday.'

Tony got the images up for that day. He fast-forwarded to midday and then slowly forwarded the footage until Daniel's car came onto the forecourt. Jez watched as either Daniel or Richie got out of the car. It was still difficult to tell who it was from the forecourt footage. Tony then clicked onto the camera above the counter. He watched as either Daniel or Richie stood in a queue behind two others. They then got to the front of the queue. Jez was sure it was Richie. His hair was very slightly longer than Daniel's, but again he couldn't be one hundred percent sure. He asked Tony to zoom in. The person in the image turned to look out onto the forecourt as the woman Jez had just manhandled rang the drink through the till, and there it was, as clear as a bell. A tattoo on the left-hand side of the neck. It was Richie, he was sure. The image had the date and time on it, as did the image showing Richie getting out of Daniel's car. Jez took photos of the images on his phone. He looked at them. He knew what would follow would not be pleasant.

Jez drove straight to Frank's house in Papplewick. Frank was not there. Jez rang him. Frank answered.

'I'm at your house, boss. You gonna be long?'

'Just on my way, I'll be ten minutes or so. Gloria should be in, though.'

Jez had parked next to Gloria's car. He sat there for a few minutes and logged into the site that allowed him access to Richie's CCTV. Joseph had given him the log-in details. Jez didn't tell Raquel this as he didn't want to alarm her any further. He entered the password and saw five little screens on his phone. He clicked onto the lounge. It was empty. He pressed the back button and returned to the original screen of five. He then pressed the kitchen image. He could see Marie sat at the table. The three mugs were still there. He could hear the radio playing in the background. Joseph said he would have audio too. Little did he know that he only had this facility as Richie had called the CCTV company while he was on the phone to Joseph. He had a play about with it and could see that he could leave it on his phone even if he were using a different function of the handset. This was good news. Jez was okay with technology. He was by no means a tech wizard; he easily managed to get around this system but could not fathom out how to play back any pre-recorded footage. This meant he was very reliant on Raquel making contact as soon as Richie arrived back. He wanted to be able to see that Marie was safe. He still had the cotton bud but wanted to be close should Marie seem in danger. Getting the DNA tested would mean a trip into Nottingham to see one of his contacts on the force, and at the moment, that was too far away. He rang Joseph. He needed to know how to playthings back. Joseph talked him through it. He was still uneasy about all of this, but Jez reminded him of the consequences if he talked. Jez had a plan, but everything needed to fall into place for it to come off. He looked out of the window. The sun was shining. He just hoped that the wind was blowing in the right direction too. He stepped out of the car and decided to go inside and have a coffee with Gloria.

Raquel had been sat there forty minutes now. Eleven cars had driven down towards her, but none of them were Richie's. She prepared herself for a long wait. She changed radio channels to something a little more interesting. She liked a good debate, did Raquel, and would often listen to the channels that were not just full of music or adverts. She looked up. Still nothing. She had Jez's number already on her phone. All she had to do was press the button. She relaxed in her chair. She looked straight ahead. The road was empty. Just a few parked cars. She'd parked behind one of them to hide her from view about fifty yards from Richie's house.

She rested her head on the backrest and momentarily closed her eyes. She brought her head back up and looked up. There it was. Richie's Range Rover, coming into the top of the road. She instinctively crouched down even though she was sure he would not see her. Realising what she had done, she raised her head to see him turn into his drive. Her heart was racing, her breathing heavy. She pressed the button. It rang. Jez answered.

'He's just got home,' she said.

'Wait there, keep your phone on. If anything happens I need to know about, ring me straight away.'

Jez disconnected the call. He heard the front door slam shut. Frank had just returned home.

'Put the kettle on Gloria, Luv. We'll have a brew, and then I'll take Jez over for his car,' Frank shouted as he took off his shoes.

Frank was smiling when he walked in. It had been a while since Jez had seen him smile.

'Quick brew then Jez, and then we'll get over to the club for your car? I've got someone coming to clean Daniel's thoroughly in a bit, so I want to be back for then. I want that car gleaming. I want it to be a real example of what Daniel stood for. I'll never sell it ya know Jez.'

'I know Frank, I know. Listen, we need to talk.'

'What about? Anything serious?'

'You could say that, Frank.'

Frank narrowed his eyes and frowned. He pulled up a chair and sat down. He just looked at Jez, waiting for him to speak. Jez took a deep breath. He could see Gloria out of the corner of his eye making the teas. He was glad she was there.

'I think I know what happened to Daniel.'

'What, who, who the fuck was it, Jez? Come on, who the fuck was it?'

Richie took off his shoes and walked into the kitchen. He noticed the three mugs were now gone. He kissed Marie on the cheek.

'You had a good day, sweetheart?' he asked.

'Yeah, not bad, you?' she replied.

'Busy, got a few things sorted, a few bits and pieces tied up and all that. Anyone been round?'

'No, no one, I've not seen a soul all day.'

Richie swung his arm and caught Marie right on the side of the jaw. She staggered back and screamed.

'You fucking liar,' Richie shouted. 'You lying fucking bitch.' He now had Marie up against the wall in the lounge. 'What the fuck were that whore and me dad's fucking goffer doing in my house. You've got one last chance to tell me before I break your fucking jaw and watch you pick up all of your teeth off this floor, just like I told you I would.'

Marie was crying. She was petrified. Richie punched her in the stomach. She bent over and fell to the floor. She rested her head against the kitchen unit and looked up at him.

'They've worked it all out, Richie, and me too. We know Daniel was killed here, we know you were here too, and we know you drove his body to his house and set up all of this charade. I know the Italians were here the day Daniel was murdered. They came for you, didn't they? Eh, didn't they? They killed the wrong man. It should have been you. They came for you, Richie, not Daniel.' Marie sobbed and put her head in her hands. 'I told them about the killings in Venice; they know it all.' She sobbed some more.

Richie dragged her by her hair around the floor. 'You told me you wouldn't betray me, you fucking bitch. I told you I'd kill you if you did. Didn't I? I'll fucking kill ya.' He then laughed out loud. 'They know fuck all, you silly cow. I'll just deny it all. They can't prove anything. They can think what they like.' He walked over to Marie and dragged her up off the floor and slapped her hard twice. Her lip was now split. 'And you know what, you fucking piece of shit, you're gonna deny everything too.' He picked a knife out of the knife set on the worktop and put it to her throat. 'If you don't deny everything, I'll cut your fucking throat. I'm the fucking boss now. I run this firm, and no one, including you, is gonna ruin that for me. My brother was a fucking waste of space, and I'm fucking glad he's dead. I'd have done it myself in time, but in the end, I didn't have to. All my fucking life I despised that man, but I had to play the game once that fucking has-been I have as a father, decided to play happy families. He'll be fucking next, but I'll do him myself. He's lost it; he's fuckin' over the hill.' Richie spat in her face. 'I'll see to that fucking whore Raquel myself too, and that goffer who licks me dad's arse, ha! I'll do that fucker at the same time as my dad.'

Frank sat there watching the screen on Jez's phone. He then looked at the photos from the garage. He sat in silence. A tear rolled down his cheek. Jez stood there looking at the man he'd called boss for as long as he could remember and wanted to hug him. He knew that was not going to happen, though. Frank looked up at him. Tears filled his eyes. Jez tried desperately to stop them, but he could not hold back his emotions either.

A tear rolled down his cheek too. These two hard men of the criminal underworld stood in the kitchen staring at each other, neither saying a word but both knowing exactly what the other was thinking. Mutual respect was there in abundance, and the bond these two men had would never be broken. Frank nodded, as did Jez. Nothing else was needed.

Frank picked up his phone and dialled a number. 'Bonnie, it's Frank. I've got a job for you.'

'Anyone I know, Frank?'

'Yes,' Frank said. 'You know him well.'

Seven years later...

chapter sixty-four

28th May 2019
Mansfield

It was seven years to the day that Daniel was murdered at Richie's house. A case of mistaken identity, something that should never have happened. As Frank sat in the care home waiting for the family to arrive on this momentous day, he reflected on the events that lead up to the murder of his first-born son. The son that he'd worshipped right up until the day he was brutally murdered in cold blood. He watched the care nurses come and go, all busy attending to the needs of their patients. He turned and looked out of the window, trying to see if he could spot anyone. He knew that all his family would be here to share the day with him. He stretched his neck a little and saw the dark blue X6 that was Archie's pull into the car park. He looked at his watch. They were right on time. He turned to Gloria.

'Bang on time, Gloria, as always.' She smiled at him and squeezed his hand. Frank then saw Alice's car pull in two cars behind Archie's. They were all here. Now the day could begin. It was just approaching eleven o'clock in the morning. Frank caught the eye of the receptionist and nodded. She nodded back and picked up the phone. '

So, once round the block Gloria, then we can get off

and enjoy our day.' Frank said as he heard the door open. He looked round and saw one of Richie's carers wheel him through in his specially adapted wheelchair. He was dribbling as usual. Frank stood up. 'Thank you, Gaynor. We won't be long. Once around the block as usual. We'll have him back in twenty minutes or so.'

Frank took control of the wheelchair. Gaynor disappeared back through the double doors. Frank smiled at the receptionist, who smiled back. Frank wheeled Richie outside to greet his family. He then stopped the wheelchair and walked round to the front and looked Richie in the eyes.

'Come on then, Richie, you can come and spend the annual twenty minutes or so with your family, you know the family who despises you, you know the family who love to think of you rotting away year after year, in this lovely care home, shitting ya pants, and dribbling ya food down ya top.'

Richie Pearson was confined to a wheelchair for the rest of his life. He needed 24-hour care and was unable to control any part of his body other than his eyes. He held Frank's gaze. That was the only control he had. Richie had been this way from the moment Bonnie had finished with him. Frank had been specific in his instructions, and Bonnie had delivered. Richie was living a life of torture, and that made Frank Pearson an incredibly happy man. Once a year, on the anniversary of Daniel's death, Frank would collect Richie and walk him around the block. Today was a warm and pleasant day unless you were in the shade. Frank walked on ahead, with the rest of his family a few yards behind, all individually wondering what Frank was saying to him. Gloria always prayed for forgiveness. Phoebe wanted only more suffering, as did Alice. Archie had mixed emotions. He had always idolised his Uncle Richie, but even he knew that for what Richie did, there could be no allowance. They could hear Frank talking but could not make out what he was saying.

'Well, Richie, another year of hatred has gone by, but thankfully you're still alive, and I can sleep easy in my bed knowing that I will hate you for another year and that you will despise every morning you wake up. I know you fucking hate being in that wheelchair, Son, and I fucking love it. It makes me a happy man. As you know, today is the anniversary of the day your brother was murdered in your house. The day you drove his body to his home and pretended you knew nothing. You're a selfish bastard, but you're a selfish bastard that will never wipe his own arse again. It's good to be alive.'

The 28th of May was the only day Richie ever saw anyone other than the carers in his care home. The 28th of May would be etched in his memory forever. Only the care home manager knew of his other visits.

Frank pushed his wheelchair into the care home entrance and turned and looked at his family stood on the entrance steps. He smiled at Gloria. Gloria smiled back and blew him a kiss. He smiled at Phoebe, the doting Grandma who was holding Archie's daughter Mary. He smiled at Archie, the proud father, he smiled at Sarah, Archie's wife, and he smiled at Alice, who was stood resting her head on her boyfriend's shoulder. They all smiled back at Frank. It was a good day, and Frank was enjoying himself. Frank then looked at Richie, who was sat dribbling in his wheelchair. Richie's carer was now with him, wiping his mouth. Richie made a noise that indicated he was angry. He was always angry. Richie Pearson was confined to a wheelchair and was a very angry man. Frank walked towards his family.

'See you next year, Son,' he shouted behind him.

'Do we have to keep coming, Grandad?' Alice asked.

'Yes, we do. Today is a day all about remembering—a time to reflect on the past and a time to remember. I like him to be reminded of what he's done and to see what he's missing sat in that chair all day. It makes me feel good,' Frank replied. Frank kissed Mary, his great-granddaughter, on the forehead.

Archie's phone rang. It was Paul, Del's son. 'What again?' Archie said down the phone. 'Keep him there until I get back later. We're just going to Clumber Park for a walk. You know what day it is today? I'll deal with him later. Couple of hours or so,' Archie disconnected the call.

'Trouble?' Frank asked.

'Just some dealers from an estate in Nottingham dealing drugs we ain't supplied Grandad, that's all. I'll sort it. It's the second time we've caught them. I'll sort 'em good and proper this time.'

Frank looked at Archie and smiled. He reminded him so much of Daniel. Today was a good day, and Frank was enjoying himself.

the end

COMING SOON ...

THE WRONG MAN – BOOK TWO

Two Months earlier - March 2019

George Burbanks sat in his plush Manchester office, and it was plush, very plush in fact. The carpet was so thick you felt like you were walking on air whenever you walked over it. His brother Ivan was waiting with him for their three o'clock appointment. Ivan had nipped to the loo. It was now 2:53pm. George hated lateness and was surprised that the man he was waiting for had not made an effort to turn up early.

The meeting they'd arranged was going to be tricky. The brothers' conversation was not something they were used to and certainly something alien to them. It could go tits up big style. It could, if mishandled, bring trouble to their door. Trouble they did not want but would deal with if needs be. George and Ivan had discussed this issue many times and how to best deal with it. The criminal underworld in and around Manchester was becoming unstable. They could not let it continue. Ivan came back through.

'Isn't he here yet, for fuck's sake?' he asked, as he stood there wiping the last bits of water from his hands using the tops of his trouser leg. Ivan was just over six feet tall, with receding dark hair that bore very little sign of any grey. He stood proud, was always immaculately dressed, taking special care of his shoes. Both brothers mirrored one another and were always highly polished. He was a broad man with many scars that were a reflection of his lifestyle.

'Nope, not yet,' George replied. 'He best not be fucking late, though. That would not be a good start. If he's late, then the deal's off. I fucking hate lateness.'

George was slightly shorter than his brother, and like his brother, had dark hair, but he'd managed to keep a full head. Much to the annoyance of Ivan and something George reminded him of many times of late. In comparison, George had very few scars, mainly because he was the more measured one of the two. George would weigh things up more than Ivan and look at things more long-term. They were a good match, and both had characteristics of their father in equal measure but were quite different in their personalities.

The one thing both the brothers shared was that they both had nerves of steel, and neither of them had ever backed down from anyone. They were well respected, well thought of in their patch, and outside of London were probably the most discussed. They were the real deal, and alongside Fletcher O'Brien, Frank Pearson from Nottinghamshire, and Rory Hammond from the West Midlands, they were the leading players outside of the capital. They had good dealings and good relationships with Frank and Rory, who were similar types to George and Ivan. The top three players in London were Tariq Mali, Paul Dutton, and Harry West, all of whom understood the rules of the game in the same way the Burbanks, Frank Pearson, and Rory Hammond did. They would often cross paths, but they all understood the value of peace, and none of them wanted a war, so any crossovers were resolved between themselves over a stiff drink and with a firm handshake. The only problem seemed to be Fletcher, and he was getting worse. The phone rang on George's desk. He picked it up.

'Yeah?'

'He's here, boss. He's clean. Shall I show him up?' came the reply from one of George's most trusted, a man called Shaun Bonsall.

George checked his watch. 2:57pm. Three minutes early. That'll do.

'Yeah, bring him up. We'll see him in here.'

George replaced the receiver. A minute or so later, Shaun brought him in. George eyed him up and down and noticed how he tried to appear confident and unnerved. George liked that. He needed to know this guy was what he thought he was. George held out his right hand, and with a firm and solid handshake, George gestured to the chairs near the door.

'Sit down.'

The guy took a seat. He still didn't know why he was here. He'd just received a visit from three of Ivan's men and was told in no uncertain terms to be here at 3pm today. That was only just gone midday, and of course, he'd been told, again in no uncertain terms, not to tell anyone. It was clear what would happen if he did.

'Now, I'm sure you want to know what this is all about?' George said as he leant forward.

'You could say that.' The man said. George noticed he'd not addressed him as George or, more importantly, as Mr. Burbanks. That struck a nerve. George let it go, but he wouldn't let it go twice.

'We want to talk to you about Frank Pearson.'

synopsis

Archie has been thrust into his grandad Frank's world. His uncle murdered his father, so Archie is the natural heir. That's how Frank wants things, so it has to be. Archie is only twenty-two years old. Is he the man for the job? Is he ready? People are unsure, including Archie.

He has little time to find out before a leading player in the UK criminal underworld makes his move. The time is now, and only Archie knows if he is the real deal or not. He has to step up. Frank expects it, but Archie knows the day will come when he can no longer rely on his grandad. That day is coming.

acknowledgements

Writing this book has been a journey that has enriched me and made me realise that there is more to life than the daily job at the office. I would, though, like to thank quite a few people, mainly people who read "The Wrong Man" as I was writing it, or at least shortly after and who all, in their own way, gave me tremendous support and encouragement.

Firstly, my wife, Debbie. A lady who inspires me and has been my rock, best friend, and soul mate over the past thirty years and someone who without, I would not be the man I am today. Debbie helped me put the characters and plot together and has been with me from day one, offering advice and feedback as I wrote it. I love you Debbie, more than you'll ever know, and thank you for always being at my side.

My mum. A lady who has never sworn in her life, but who read my book as I was writing it and despite the swear words soldiered on. Thanks, Mum.

My mum-in-law Jean. A lady who treats me like a son and who also read it despite the swearing. Thanks, Jean.

Our very good friend Heather Brown who I think was the first person outside of the family to read the book from start to finish and who constantly badgered me for the next chapters. Thank you, Heather.

Bob Hart, a man who I have known for nearly 25 years

and who is unique. Your feedback was superb, Bob, very descriptive and very constructive. Thank you. You really are a legend.

Our next-door neighbours Nick and Mandy, who also read the book. They are great people to know and do a great G&T. Don't ever move and thank you for your encouragement.

Andy and Jayne, two people who, as well as dog walking buddies, were both so supportive in their encouragement. Andy, I would also like to thank you for your IT help too. Thank you both.

Andrea Colbert, a lady who I met last year and who read the book within three days. Thank you for being so enthusiastic about my novel.

Paul Scott, a man I have known since childhood and who I would say was a lifelong friend. We do not meet many people in our lives who we know will be there no matter what. Scotty is one of those men. Thank you, Paul.

Linda Clark, a lady who has become a very good friend in recent years and who supported me in more ways than she probably ever realised. Thank you, Linda.

Maria and Terry, our very good Australian friends who have both read the book. Two wonderful people who we very much hope to see again. Thank you

Rebecca from Phink Photography. A lady who is responsible for that photo of me in this book and also for the one on my website. As you can see, she is very good at her job. She had to work hard to make me look that good! Thank you, Rebecca.

Dr. Carla Rainbow, a very good friend and an inspiring lady who very kindly interviewed me, so that people buying the book could find out more about me and the novel. I was able to use the interview on social media and my website. Thank you, Carla.

Anne Mannion, a lady who very kindly helped me along the way with certain aspects of the content. Thank you, Anne.

...and then there's Gail from The Solopreneur Ltd. The lady who spent hours proofreading this book to make sure it was grammatically correct—a lady who conversed with me endlessly on commas. I do think we spoke more about commas than most people ever do about commerce, but she summed it up in two sentences, and then the penny dropped.

No more gin. No, more gin.

See the power of commas! Now I get them. Gail, you have been an inspiration and a joy to have on this journey. Without you, The Wrong Man would not be the book it is. Thank you for all of your hard work in helping me get this published.

about the author

For many years I worked in 9-5 jobs, leaving the house early in the morning and not getting home until ten or eleven hours later, and like many people, I just thought that was how life had to be. I'd seen from a very young age my father working hard in a factory to provide for his family and, like most other young people, just assumed there was no other way, but  my wife would often tell me that it didn't have to be that way. In 2019 I decided to do something different with my life and decided to leave a well-paid position in a company that I had shares in and do what I wanted to do. Initially, I had planned to go into buying and selling property or to become a Landlord, but of course the pandemic hit us, and lockdown came, so I put the property dream on hold.

I then decided to become a Funeral Celebrant, providing services for non-religious funerals. I do this on a part-time basis, meeting some wonderfully interesting people. I find it very rewarding. The families I meet are so appreciative of what I do in helping them in this emotional time. But I still had one other dream. I'd always wanted to write a novel. I have always been a fan of crime fiction, and thrillers so I wanted to start my writing career with a book of this genre. I suppose, never really thought I could achieve this, but my wife Debbie believed in me and knew if I put my mind to it, I could do it. So, we sat down, and between us, we put the story and characters together for my first novel – The Wrong Man.

I wished I'd done it years ago. I remember sitting in my garden, with the sun shining, writing away, listening to the water trickling down the water feature in the corner of our garden thinking, *this is how life should be. This is not work!* So, between delivering funeral services and writing, I feel very fulfilled and content.

I have been married to my wife Debbie for twenty-six years. We have two daughters, Heather and Georgina, and three grandchildren. I am fifty years old and live in Mansfield in the heart of Nottinghamshire, a short drive from Sherwood Forest, and I hope that I can make a career from writing novels to sit alongside the funeral services I do.

I have already written a second book, a psychological thriller which I hope to publish next, and am I'm now partway through writing a sequel to The Wrong Man.

M J Elliott

contact me

Email: info@mjelliottauthor.co.uk

Facebook: mjelliottauthor

Instagram: @mjelliottauthor

LinkedIn – Michael Elliott

Website: www.mjellliottauthor.co.uk